A SONG OF LOVE

Last year, before Acre on the shores of the Saracen Sea, one of King Richard's minstrels had sung of a knight who had died for his love of a woman not his own. The fool in the verses had not died from wounds in that lady's defense, but from heart sickness in her absence. Payen had laughed at the tale and asked for a better song, of war and lust and all that should matter to a man.

Now, in the gray north with winter soon to come, and the cold pain of parting weighing heavy upon his heart, Payen understood that song. He wished he had listened to the final words.

FOLLOW THE MOON

Linda Cook

Zebra Books
Kensington Publishing Corp.

http://www.zebrabooks.com

ZEBRA BOOKS are published by

Kensington Publishing Corp.
850 Third Avenue
New York, NY 10022

First Printing: September, 1999
10 9 8 7 6 5 4 3 2 1

Printed in the United States of America

For
Mary and Walker West
and Rocky, the plucky mollusk

Chapter One

Nantes, Brittany
15 October 1193

He had not thought, in his haste to reach the meeting place, that it could be bad luck to buy back his legacy in a Nantes brothel. Only now, with blood streaming from his arm and the blow to his head still throbbing with each heartbeat, did Payen begin to blame himself for not questioning the site, or the hour of parlay. For risking Mathieu's life and his own.

When Mathieu, slumped against the barred door, regained his breath, Payen would tell him so.

He looked again at the dead upon the planked floor of the common room, weapons still bright in the tangle of limbs. Two men had run when the fighting had turned against them, and might return; there would be looters as well, gathering in the darkness outside the whore's house. There was no time to waste in regrets.

The whore's fine table linen had been bloodied in the fight;

Payen cut a clean length with his dagger and began to wrap his arm. He had become careless as he had neared the end of his waiting. After a decade lost to exile, living among men of uncertain honor, he should have expected treachery in this most important, most critical time. Instead, he had granted Malebis's demand for secrecy in their first meeting and had walked into a trap with only one man to watch his back. But for Mathieu's timely sight of the armed men hidden in the whore's bedchamber, they would have been murdered and robbed; and their bodies would even now be on their way to rest upon the deep mud beneath the river's flow.

There was no movement among the fallen; six were dead, and another wounded, near death. The dying man had been the first to draw steel and the first to meet Mathieu's blade; he would make his end without waking to see that he and his six fellows had met defeat at the hands of the two men they had been set to murder.

In the struggle Payen had forgotten the whore. A slow, careful look about the chamber found her hiding beneath the trestle table, half hidden by the sprawled corpse of Walter Malebis.

"The woman—"

At his word, Mathieu heaved himself from the door and stumbled forward; he followed Payen's gaze. "She was still here? She saw it all."

Payen lowered his sword. "Come out, girl."

The whore ducked back under the table and scrabbled to the wall.

Payen wiped the blood from his hand and pulled the woman from her refuge, wincing at the pain of it. "Listen to me, girl—"

Her costly silken kirtle, woven pale and sheer, was hemmed with crimson and dust. Above the stained cloth the whore's face was livid with fear. Payen spoke again. "Listen to me. There will be others to follow these men. If they find you here, you will not survive their questions."

The woman drew a drowning breath. "My lord, I will not speak—"

"No, you must not." Payen dropped his sword and dragged his blood-smeared saddlebag from beneath a nameless corpse. With sudden violence the woman threw herself back against the overturned table and cowered from the thing Payen flung to her. She crouched in the shadows, her hands raised before her face.

At her feet, gold coins burst from the leather pouch and rang loud in the silence, then rolled unsteadily amid the dust and blood. The whore lowered her hands and stared without comprehension at the gold, shrinking from the stray denier that came to rest upon her ruined slipper.

Mathieu bent at her feet to salvage the coins. "All of this, Payen?"

It had been a small part of the gold he had promised to Malebis, enough to show the young fool that Payen was in earnest but not enough to provoke this night's carnage. Payen closed his eyes. "Let her have it all. Take her from here and buy passage for her down the river this night. The roads will not be safe."

Mathieu stood and muttered brief words to the whore; she closed her fist upon the gold and backed away.

"And for us, Payen?"

"The two who fled will have reached the crossroads by now. Soon there will be more of them, coming back to find Malebis." Payen wiped his sword upon the remaining linen and saw that Mathieu was steady upon his feet. "You may go with the woman if you choose."

Mathieu shook his head. "I'll see you through it. I said I would."

"This is the end. There is no hope now with Malebis dead at my hand."

There was a small gasp from the loft ladder. The whore had found her cloak and clutched a small bundle of cloth to her side. The pouch of gold was in her hand, and the blood still upon it.

Payen drew a long breath. ''Do you understand, girl? Leave this place, and do not return. Buy yourself another house, far from here, in another town. And never speak of what you saw, nor where you got the gold.''

When at last she found words, her voice was as thin and high as a child's.

''I won't tell. My lord, I swear—I'll not speak of this.''

''Keep silent for your own sake,'' Payen said. ''Not for mine.''

''Payen—''

''Get her out of here.''

''What will you do?''

He shook his head. ''This is the end of hope. I'll not get the land back with bribes. Not now. If I spill more blood, I'll be outlawed, and my kin will suffer.''

''What will you do?''

''Nothing. Get out of Nantes if I can.'' He pulled the mantle over his injured arm. ''If I live past spring, maybe then—'' He waved away Mathieu's arm. ''Take the woman to the harbor, and if you wish, find me when the moon is down, on the north road, where it passes the ostler's byre.''

''The north road? You would go back—''

''Who else would have us? Where else but—'' Payen broke off and lifted the bar. The narrow track before the house was dark and silent; if there were looters without, they had not yet found the courage to approach. ''Go now, and find me before dawn.''

Payen waited, sword in hand, as Mathieu and the whore made their way to the turning of the road. Before he left, he rolled the body of Walter Malebis onto its back and brought a taper to its face. He had been young—barely bearded—with a taste for finery. The fool had worn a rich tunic to betray and kill Payen. And his sword, a good blade encumbered with precious stones to ruin the grip of the hilt, lay scarce bloodied at his side.

The night was not a complete disaster. Payen had concealed the horses in the trees behind the ostler's byre, out of sight of the north road. If local thieves had found the beasts, they must have turned away at the sight of Arsuf's bared teeth and restless hooves.

The mantle he had bought in the marketplace that morning was warm and dark; it hid the mail upon his hauberk from the moonlight and kept the sharp autumn chill from his bones. There was a chance—a good chance—that he would be many miles along the road before the stiffness of injury made his sword arm useless.

He had thought Mathieu might change his mind and had considered giving up the wait. In the final hour, as the moon was setting, Mathieu had whistled from the road, then approached the hiding place with deliberate, heavy steps, to be sure that Payen would not hear treachery in his approach.

"She's gone," Mathieu said. "I roused the master of a merchant ship bound down the river, and then out to sea, and to Dinan. He sails at dawn."

"Good."

"She knows not to talk, and to keep her gold hidden until she reaches port."

"If she keeps her wits, they will never find her."

Mathieu sighed in the darkness. "She knows. She's a good whore. I liked her."

"You had her this night? Mathieu, you're a fool."

"No—I had her this morning, when you sent me to find the house. Can you ride?"

"I'll manage."

"We could sleep in the byre."

"No. When we're clear of Nantes, I'll sleep, then we'll find the road east and look for Mercadier. He told me he might move his camp toward the coast."

They walked in silence, leading their mounts from the stand of oaks. "He knew, then, that we might be back?" Mathieu asked.

There was a smothered gasp as Payen climbed into his saddle. "Only the devil knows what Mercadier knows. I told him nothing of Malebis. And nothing of Rochmarin."

Mercadier had grown careless with the boundaries of his camps. Any stranger who was bold enough to seek him might come unarmed and unscathed through his sentry lines; many such men, but not all, left again in good health. The mercenary general's reputation had grown through the years; few would wish to bait him, and none would dare attack him in the midst of his camp of well-paid, well-skilled killers.

The sentries showed no surprise to see Payen and Mathieu ride through the lines with the dust of miles upon their cloaks and week-old blood stiffening their hauberks. They waved them past and resumed their sport with a richly dressed young stripling upon a fine black riding mule, calling to the rider to make haste out of the camp, all the while frightening the mule with mock growls and a wolf's head on a pike. The lad was having a hard time of it; the harp-shaped bundle upon the crupper of his beast sounded in resonant discord with each jarring movement.

Payen drew Arsuf to a halt and raised his good arm to point to the mule and its rider. "Does Mercadier pay you to torment that beast, or does he wish you to keep your eyes upon the picket lines? I saw two dogs beyond the horses. Could have been wolves—come to seek their kin."

In the time it took for the sentries to search the shadows for beasts of prey, the mule gathered its courage and bolted past the guards, taking the lad and his harp onto the western road.

"They need a good war," growled Payen. "Or a small rebellion to keep them amused. When the Plantagenet comes home, they will be too busy to torment harpists."

"Why do you care?"

Payen shrugged. "It would have been a wasted harp and a dead singer. It is bad luck to harm a bard."

"Breton thinking. Payen, when you get your lands back, you'll settle down to grow superstitions to leaven your bread."

"I'll not have them back if you speak of them in this camp."

Mathieu sighed. "I'll remember. But get us out of here, Payen, when your arm is healed—before Mercadier takes his army upon the next campaign. It would be a bad thing, when you have passed so close to your lands, to die without seeing them again."

By evening the camp's surgeon had resewn the worst of Payen's wounds and pronounced his head close to healed. Mercadier bade Payen eat at his own fire, before the fine leather tent in which the general's servants made him more comfortable than were many a lord in drafty Breton keeps. A long trestle board, likely pillaged from a nearby manor, stood level beneath the awning flap of the tent. It was laden with ale pots and meat from the campfire. The roasted pork and wheels of cheese were gifts, Mercadier declared; Payen saw, in the richness of the bribes, the terror of the farmers who had awakened to see a small army of killers encamped upon their meadowland.

"There's no bread," continued Mercadier. "There's an abbey hereabouts, and I'll send to it in the morning to tell them to send us bread. That's the worst of moving camp," he muttered. "Finding bread."

"If you paid them," Payen said, "the farmers would bid their wives to bake all you need."

"Why should I pay? The villeins should be glad to have my men near at hand. They'll have no grief from brigands with my army camped here." Mercadier downed a cup of ale and drew the jug before him. "It's little enough for them to do in return. A few loaves of bread each day for the peace I bring them."

Payen smiled. "And have any of these villeins or their lords need of more than peace from you? Is there a rebellion to put down?"

"Not a one. But the old queen Eleanor has paid me to keep watch for her, here and in Normandy as well, until King Richard returns. She pays well, but the men are restless. If things continue so peaceful, I'll have to go in search of a war." He poured a third cup of ale and raised the jug for Payen. "I heard you had some of the queen's gold for taking her bishops abroad to treat with that cowardly prick Hohenstaufen. Did they succeed?"

Payen shrugged. "King Richard will come home when Hohenstaufen has half his ransom gold. The emperor will hold hostages for the rest."

Mercadier hurled the empty jug into the campfire. "The fancy bastard would hold my dagger in his guts if they'd let me near him."

"That's why you're here, waiting for trouble, and not dining with Hohenstaufen. You have a heavy hand with intrigue, Mercadier."

The mercenary sat back and sighed. "There are some who think I've got light-footed assassins to spare." He looked at the bindings upon Payen's arm and raised his brow. "If you've a mind to earn some gold while you're healing, there's a dirty task which you could manage with your lame arm."

Payen shook his head. "I can't stay."

"That's as well. You would refuse the task. And I am tempted to forget it. I've not killed a woman yet, but there's much gold to be had for knifing this one. The young harper who came with the message left ten gold pieces here just to consider the thing. There's fifty more, he says, for the man who does the deed."

"The lad with the harp upon his mule? That lad wants you to kill a woman for him?" Payen drank again. "I should have let the sentries steal his mule."

"It's not the lad who has hired me. He came on behalf of another, a noble lord he would not name. He left the gold and the name of the woman who needs killing—a noble lady, by the sound of her name.

Payen frowned. "Who is she?"

"Johanna Mercat, widow of the young lord Malebis. The lady of Rochmarin."

Payen lowered the cup and waited until his pulses slowed, then raised his gaze to Mercadier. "Are you speaking the truth? You are killing women now?"

"This one deserves it. The lad said so."

Payen sat back. "Why? How did she earn killing?"

"She sent assassins to kill her lord."

With effort, Payen managed to shrug. "And have you found a man to kill her?"

Mercadier shook his head. "Not yet. I've no stomach for it tonight."

He was weary and needed a fortnight's cure for his arm. There was no way he could stop the killing by turning Mercadier from the task; the scoundrel had his own peculiar honor, and would not turn from a charge once he had taken gold to do it. Payen stifled a groan and met Mercadier's gaze. "Then give the task to me," he said.

The clever eyes within the florid face moved back to Payen's injured arm. "Time was you wouldn't hire yourself for aught but clean warfare. Are you so much in need of gold? Or do you know the woman and wish her ill?"

Payen stood. "I don't know her. She is to be found at Rochmarin?"

"Yes. You know the place?"

He nodded. "I know the place."

"When you have—when it's done, the harper lad will bring the rest of the gold to Dinan and wait for you. I told him if he cheats me, he'll die next." Mercadier gestured to the untouched platter before him. "Your meat grows cold. You do not intend to leave tonight—"

Payen placed his empty cup upon the board and picked up his sword. "I'll ride tonight. With Mathieu, if he's willing. If I sleep now, your surgeon's work will stiffen."

"Did the leech bungle it?"

"No," Payen said. "But he misliked Mathieu's stitching."

Mercadier sighed. "You mean to do this woman-killing?"

"Send me."

"Then choose the men you need."

"Only Mathieu."

Mercadier nodded. "Sit down, then. There's no need for haste. The lad said the deed is to be done on the road from Rochmarin to an abbey—St. Martin's, he said—in the forest nearby. The woman will ride that way before noon on the feast of All Saints. That is when he wants it done."

Payen made himself smile. "I'm not such a fool that I would do the job when and where the lad's master demands. I've no wish to be caught and hanged for the death of a woman."

"You'll finish it before the day?"

"A little before."

Mercadier frowned. "But be sure the lad pays."

"I'll find him."

Payen went in search of Mathieu. Long after he left Mercadier's fire, he felt the mercenary's questioning gaze upon his back.

Chapter Two

It was the moon that wakened her, that touched her face in pale beckoning and moved across the chamber to the empty hearth. The shutters stood open upon the night. How, in these dark times, had she forgotten to bar them?

Moonlight would take her beauty. A woman might sicken or grow barren in the poison light of that witching star. The Breton maids had told her this, and for a time she had taken care to keep the light of the moon from her body. But her husband was now beyond looking for beauty—or heirs; Johanna Mercat, the lady of Rochmarin, no longer had reason to sleep hidden from the night sky.

The moon was still low in the heavens, and came far into the chamber, touching the well-trimmed rushes, moving past the richly carved chest that Johanna had brought mere months before to her young husband's keep. The low light reached past the bed to the far wall.

To the man who waited, cloaked in black and silence, beside the dead fire.

Wakefulness sharpened into cold alarm. For the space of a loud, painful heartbeat, Johanna considered and put aside the risk of drawing the dagger from its fold within the bolster at her cheek. The man was too close, and the chamber door, barred against the night, was too far. Johanna's gaze moved once again to the plank of wood. It was in its place. And would keep the guards from the chamber if they heard a cry. How had this man—

"You are awake."

The breath caught in her throat. She was strangling upon her own fear.

He shifted slightly but kept his distance. "If you value your life, do not cry out."

The breath rushed from her lungs in a hoarse sob.

"Look there. Look beside you."

Upon the rushes lay a sword, its moon-bright steel a barrier between Johanna and the specter across the chamber.

"My sword is there beside you. My dagger as well."

"Why?" At the sound of her own voice, the trembling began.

His face was dark, and only his eyes caught the moon's light. His unblinking gaze held her own and told her, in its stillness, that he would not move. Yet.

"Why?" she said again.

"To keep you from calling the guard. To show you I mean no harm." His voice was low and deliberate and held the rich hoarseness of silk dragged upon uncut stone.

"What do you want?"

"To speak with you. Will you listen?"

The silence grew to unbearable length.

"Will you?"

Johanna had heard, dismissed, and returned to consider the hint of desire she had heard in his voice. "If you want a woman," she said at last, "go to the village. I have the pox."

For a brief moment a smile flashed white. "You may keep your pox, Johanna Mercat. Now, listen—"

"And you will leave?"

"If you wish it."

She sat up, drew the coverlet upon her shoulders, and slipped her hand into the bolster to find the dagger. "Speak," she said. "Then go."

The face that had begun to form in the moon shadows was strong-featured and unmarked by emotion. The voice, when it came again, was a night whisper, at once low and harsh. "You have an enemy, madam, one who has bought your death."

She had thought her breath had returned. Now his words had numbed the very life within her throat. Johanna thrust her hand farther into the stuffing of the bolster and found the cold hilt of her dagger. She would not die easily. Not without scarring that dark, impassive face.

Still, he made no move to approach her. "From you?" she said at last. "You are the one he paid?"

"I took his gold, that he would not hire another. He will soon tire of waiting and look elsewhere. You must be gone before that happens."

He fell silent. In her fear, Johanna felt a desperate need to keep him talking. "How many were you to kill?"

The man straightened and took a long, slow step from the wall. "What do you mean?"

"My husband is dead at the hands of brigands. Now you have said I have the death mark as well. Does your master wish to kill all who bear the name of Malebis?"

"There is another?"

"No."

He sighed. "You need not have lied, madam. I know there is a young sister of Walter Malebis."

"She is but sixteen years old."

"And will live to be a crone, for all I care. The gold was offered for your life. Only yours."

"You took his gold—"

He made a small gesture with his hand. "Do you fault me for deceiving him?"

"No." Once again the moon found the whiteness of his smile. Johanna eased the dagger from the bolster and onto the bed linens. If she could keep him talking, he might not tire of his game and turn upon her. "Who? Who paid you?"

A sigh crossed the darkness. "For a woman who has received the gift of her life and an offer of help to continue it, you are too sharp of tongue."

"Can you not tell me?"

"I have no name for him. He sent a trouvère to speak for him; a young lad with a harp brought the gold to buy an assassin. Do you know such a lad?"

"No."

"He came on a fine black riding mule."

"I do not know him or his mule." She drew the dagger to her side, hidden beneath the coverlet.

The assassin leaned back against the wall and crossed his arms before a broad chest. "Madam, your guards are drunk in the hall, and there has been no sentry at the foot of the chamber stair these two nights past. They must know that the lady Johanna Mercat's life is forfeit."

"The garrison is loyal. Normans, all of them. Paid by my own hand."

"And willing to take a few more coins to remain far from your side while an assassin is near. What they do not know," he said, "is that I was hired to kill you on the feast of All Saints, on the road south of here, near the abbey."

Beneath the heavy coverlet she wiped the sweat from her hand and got a better grip on the dagger. "And you have come before time," Johanna said.

"To warn, not to harm you." Soft laughter sounded in the darkness. "Fear is clouding your reason. Think again—had I wished to keep the bargain, I would have slain you as you slept."

"There was no sport in that—"

"This is no sport."

"And instead, you torment me."

There was a sigh. "I do not torment the helpless. Had I wished to kill you, you would not have awakened, nor felt the knife."

He moved then, to stand three paces from her bed, within reach of his sword. "Now, listen, Johanna Mercat. Put your fear aside and listen. Two days from now is the feast of All Saints. It was to happen on that day, before noon, two miles from here, as you ride to take alms to St. Martin's, upon the abbey road. Do you understand? If I do not strike then, the one who bought your death will think of another way to end your life. Next time there may be no warning."

Johanna imagined that his gaze had softened as he spoke. "I understand."

He held out his hand. "Come with me. Now. I will take you from here and send you wherever you wish to go. I give you my oath—"

"Stay back." She winced at the sharpness of her words. "I—I thank you. But stay back."

"Find your cloak and I'll take you out of here, to the coast—"

"No—"

"You will stay here—and wait for the next killer?"

"I have your warning. I will defend myself."

There was a long silence. "Then there is nothing more to say."

"No."

He sighed. "I will take up my weapons now—not to use them but to leave. Do me the favor," he added, "of not sending your dagger into my back when I turn away."

"I have no—"

"You sleep soundly, madam. I know what you had in the

bolster. You have it now, I think. Beneath the coverlet, in your hand.''

Of all the things he had said, this last was the most frightening. ''Why did you not take—''

''It kept you from screaming, did it not?'' He paused. ''You should know—a short time ago, before you awakened, someone tried to open your chamber door.''

''It—it has happened before.''

''And still you will not leave?''

She shook her head.

''Then keep your dagger at hand. Good fortune to you, madam. You will need it.''

With a swift movement and a muffled grunt he picked up his sword and his knife and moved to the narrow embrasure—and was gone.

There was a soft, scraping sound, then silence. Johanna held her dagger before her as she crept to the open shutters. Without, a rope hung close to hand, swinging wide in the cold, still night. Beneath the embrasure, upon the moon-washed earthworks that ringed the high walls of Rochmarin, there was nothing. Not even a shadow.

Beneath her free hand there was wetness. Johanna Mercat raised her hand to her face and smelled the hot, copper scent of blood. The man had been injured scaling the walls to reach her, or wounded before he had begun to climb. He had left his blood upon her chamber sill.

It was impossible to call him back. At dawn, would the guards find the trail of his blood, and the assassin at the end of it?

The dagger slipped from Johanna's fingers. She sank to the rushes and hid her face within her hands. In the months since she had come to this place, in the dark days following her brother's death, even in the fortnight since her husband's murder, she had not felt so fearful. Johanna was alone in the darkness, in a country whose people held no love of her own, and somewhere in the night slept a soul who had paid for her death. And the man who had taken gold for her blood—the assassin who had decided, on a whim, to let her live—was gone. If she called to him, he would not hear. She had not thought to ask his name, or where he would go from Rochmarin.

For the first time since Walter Malebis had met his death, his widow began to weep.

Chapter Three

Johanna waited until she saw the faint light of dawn touch the shutter boards and listened for the early sounds of Rochmarin stirring from its sleep. Huddled in cloak and coverlet against the wall, she fixed her eyes upon the embrasure through which the man in black had disappeared. She had spent a sleepless night considering her next move, and in the hour before dawn, as the first birdsong had reached the dark walls of Rochmarin, Johanna had begun to mutter her thoughts aloud and speak back her own answers, just as old Herleva the shepherd woman had done each dawn in the long byre at Gunndale.

In Yorkshire, in Gunndale, Johanna would be safe. To return, she must traverse miles of black forest and cold ocean; if God and his saints saw her safely home, she would never leave again.

She rose to her feet and opened her dower chest. The warm crimson kirtle she had worn at her only wedded Yuletide lay close to hand; she hesitated only a moment, then pulled the rich garment over her shift. There was no reason, now, to save it for feasting times. If she left Rochmarin this day, she must do it in furtive flight and leave behind the dower chest and all it held; she would take only the small pouch of gold she had kept secret from Walter Malebis and the clothes she would wear upon the road.

The sounds from the hall had become louder, but there was no note of alarm in the voices below the bedchamber. The man in black, whoever he was, had not left evidence of intrusion to alert the folk of Rochmarin of his presence.

Johanna crossed to the shutters and opened them upon the dawn. The smooth granite walls of Rochmarin held no hint of the man's passage; there was no body, no mark or sign of tragedy beneath the embrasure. Once again Johanna felt a weak discomfiture at that sudden disappearance; in all the long hours she had sat staring at the shutters the previous night, she had fought an odd, unreasoning wish to call him back.

She had no name to put to him, and this troubled her. It was madness, of course, to wish the intruder back again, or to want his name. The time he had spent in her chamber, speaking of doom and flight to her half-waking, fright-numbed mind, had lasted only a few moments. Yet in that time Johanna had conceived a foolish, ridiculous thought that she might trust him.

He had told her in grisly detail how he might have slain her if he had wished to earn her enemy's gold. In the light of morning Johanna recognized the ploy for what it might be—the beginning of a scoundrel's plot to convince her to give him gold, or a brigand's scheme to win her trust and take a rich widow to wife.

Beneath these reasoned morning thoughts ran a darker current—strong, insistent, and unceasing: In her fear and near-madness she had begun to believe the intruder's words. Not for all the gold within York's long walls would she have left her chamber to follow the man, but she had trusted him. And she believed she must heed his warning.

Johanna drew a long breath in the cold autumn morning and began again to braid her hair.

A rapid knocking at her chamber door sent her heart hammering. She pulled herself back from the steep drop below the shutters and closed the panels above the small bloodstain upon the sill.

"Are you sleeping still?" came the voice of Agnes Malebis.

Johanna lifted the bar and opened the door to admit her sister by marriage. Young Agnes's face was clouded in concern; the steaming hot water she carried before her only imperfectly disguised the hint of recent tears in her pale eyes. She moved her long, graceful fingers from the base of the earthen jug and held it to Johanna. "You look troubled," she said. "Did you weep for Walter last night?" Agnes moved past Johanna and sat upon the dower chest. "Why did you bar the door? Do you fear to sleep alone?"

Johanna sighed. "Walter always barred it. I do the same."

"And your shutters closed tight—are you certain you are not ill?"

Johanna moved to the table beside the shutters and threw her cloak upon the sill to hide the bloodstain. She crooked one panel open upon the cold dawn air. "I thank you for the water, Agnes. You needn't have—"

Agnes's lush mouth curved in a timid smile. "You would have waited forever. The maids are distracted this morn."

"Why?"

After a slight hesitation Agnes's smile deepened. "They were late with my own washing water, and I found them distracted with their Samhain nonsense." She settled back against the wall and shrugged. "My father tried to put an end to the worst of the devil-wardings when he first took this place, but the Bretons are stubborn folk, and the abbot counseled him to leave them to their fears. It keeps them from sin and murder, he said; they fear that those they wronged will seek them out for vengeance at Samhain." Agnes shrugged again. "It's only one day and a long night. The rest of the year these folk are reasonable enough. I washed at the kitchen fire and brought you the rest of the water.''

With a folded square of linen Johanna began to bathe her face in the warm water. ''My thanks, Agnes.''

''I wanted to speak with you alone.''

Johanna's hand began to tremble. She put down the cloth and turned to look out upon Rochmarin's dense forest as she dried her face. ''Is something amiss?'' After a moment's silence she turned back to find Agnes daubing her eyes with her wide, broderie sleeve; her smile had vanished as quickly as it had come. ''What troubles you, Agnes?''

Had the man in black come to more than one chamber last night? Was he a trickster, or a madman bent upon frightening the women of Rochmarin?

Agnes tossed her head and attempted a thin smile. ''The tomb,'' she said. ''The Samhain nonsense reminded me of Walter's tomb. I would like to have his effigy set upon it.''

''We agreed that if the next harvest is good—''

''Can we not have it carved this winter? If we wait, there might be no stonemasons who would remember him—none who would carve a good likeness. It is all I will have—''

It was a monument Johanna would never see, God willing. She placed a steadying hand upon Agnes's shoulder. ''If that is what you wish, then find a mason to work in the chapel. Perhaps Mauleon will know—''

Agnes smiled. ''I will ask him. Will he come today? If not, I might ride to Mauleon tomorrow—''

Tomorrow. Tomorrow the assassin was to have waited in the forest. If Agnes rode forth— Johanna placed a second hand upon Agnes's shoulders. ''Wait for him here. Do not ride to Mauleon.''

''Why?''

Only you, the man in black had said. Yours was the only name I was given.

Johanna considered and rejected the thought that Agnes should know of the warning. If word spread, through idle rumor or malice, that the widow Malebis had been told of her danger, others would come to do the task in their own way. The intruder had brought her a warning at the risk of his life, and she would not waste it in foolish talk. Nevertheless, she would like to see Agnes away from Rochmarin tomorrow. "Agnes, shall we go together to Dinan to seek a mason? You have not stirred from Rochmarin since I came here as a bride. Do you not wish to see Dinan again? The markets—"

"Adam Mauleon brings me word of Dinan. I need not go. Let us ask Adam to bring us a mason. Could we not?"

Johanna turned from the painful simplicity of Agnes's words. The girl seemed infatuated with Adam Mauleon and would not make a move without his advice. Was Mauleon himself the source of the assassin's gold? His betrothal to Agnes would bring him control of Rochmarin. And as husband of the young heiress, Mauleon would add Rochmarin to his own lands as soon as Johanna confirmed that she did not carry a child of the dead lord.

Why, then, had Adam Mauleon brought his hints of marriage to Johanna if he willed her dead? He did not seem a woman-killer, but who else would profit from her death? Would Agnes be safe if Johanna removed herself from the dilemma, leaving Mauleon satisfied to have the heiress and the lands?

"Agnes, dear, is there something which troubles you?"

"Will you give me the gold for the effigy? May I then give it to Adam, to find a mason?"

"Soon—"

"Now, Johanna. Please. I find myself forgetting Walter's face."

"It will come back, Agnes. The dead we loved will live forever in our memories."

Tears welled up in the sea-pale eyes. "I have been cruel to speak so," Agnes whispered. "For you have lost two beloved in a short time. Your brother first—'' The girl clapped a hand over her mouth. ''You havc no cffigy for him. Is that why you hesitate? Forgive me, Johanna.''

Johanna closed her hand upon Agnes's fingers. ''There was no question of an effigy,'' she said. ''He was here such a short time, and there were few who knew him well. Walter was generous to give him a place within the Malebis crypt, and I was content to have him there, with his name upon the tomb.''

Agnes squeezed Johanna's hand. ''Forgive me, but I had not thought of Harald. But Walter was a knight, and the lord of this place, and he must be remembered. The gold, Johanna. May I have the gold?''

Johanna nodded. Gold. It was gold that had sent her there, that had given her merchant family the courage to seek a marriage bond with the noble Malebis of Rochmarin. And it was gold that had, for a time, sweetened her arrival at this place and obliged the Malebis to accept young Harald Mercat to train him as a knight and lift him from the ranks of merchant sons to aspiring nobility. And it was gold, perchance, that had inspired young Agnes's loyalty to her merchant marriage-sister.

She sighed. ''I will write to my uncle, Agnes, and ask him to help. What funds we have now will go to your dowry, sister.''

The sky-blue eyes blinked wide. ''Has Adam spoken to you?''

''He spoke to Walter,'' Johanna said. ''Did he not tell you?''

''But after Walter died, there was no—''

''It is too soon for talk of marriage,'' Johanna murmured. ''Mauleon would not wish to offend you by haste.''

''When lands are without a lord, haste is necessary. You do not understand—that is how things are done, in noble families.''

Johanna ignored the unwitting insult. ''Then he will speak to you soon. Within the month—''

''Are you with child?''

''I told you, Agnes. I believe not—''

"Then tell him. He asks me each time he comes here. That may be why he waits."

Johanna took a deep breath. How, in the face of Agnes's haste and careless, youthful infatuation, could she manage to turn the girl's thoughts to a journey to Dinan? None but Johanna was at risk, the intruder had said. Agnes must be left to the wardship of Dinan and the protection of Mauleon. For Johanna, her safety would lie in flight. Secret flight.

Agnes rose to her feet and turned the sweetness of her smile upon Johanna. "Will you come down with me?"

"Not yet."

"You should. It is not good to keep to your chamber, thinking of Walter."

"Go ahead, Agnes. I'll follow soon."

Johanna barred the door, moved back to the place from which she had watched the early dawn, and turned her mind to the thought that had, from her first days at Rochmarin, dominated her waking hours. It had begun in early winter, this uneasy longing for home, for the open fields and steep dales of Yorkshire; it had become a near obsession in the days following her husband's death. Johanna Mercat had felt shame, as she had knelt in Rochmarin's small chapel to hear Walter Malebis's funeral mass, that her thoughts of home had been so consuming, and her grief for her dead husband so small.

Wed but a scarce, swift year to a Norman knight younger in mind than in body, with the ungoverned desires of a callow lad, Johanna had felt little but relief when Walter Malebis had announced his journey to Nantes. Over the winter and the early spring Malebis had spent her Mercat dowry upon repairs to the fabric of Rochmarin but had saved the larger part to purchase the splendor to which he had believed the Malebis family must aspire once again. Johanna had watched without emotion as her family's dowry gold had bought lead to roof the keep, and had frowned when Malebis ordered a fine new hauberk and jewel-hilted sword for his own use. Two months ago Malebis spent the last of Johanna Mercat's rich dowry upon a great, fierce destrier that had proved too ill trained to remain in Rochmarin's orderly stables.

When the dowry was gone, the destrier sold cheap to Adam Mauleon's stable, and the semiprecious hilt of the new sword beginning to lose its large jewels, Walter Malebis began to mutter that he was ill matched with the daughter of a wool merchant, a woman who could not conceive his heir, nor likely carry a babe to term.

Hearing her husband's words, Johanna had begun to think of leaving Rochmarin. When Malebis told her that he would go to Nantes to collect an old debt from a blackguard returned from Palestine, Johanna took care to conceal her relief. Soon, she had hoped, Malebis would put her aside and take another woman. When that happened, she would be free to leave the dark, devil-ridden forests of Brittany and travel home.

Then the incredible word had reached her, only a day before Walter Malebis's body was carried through the gates of Rochmarin: Malebis had died in Nantes, the victim of brigands who had likely taken the gold Walter had received from his debtor.

Johanna had set aside, for the moment, her wish to leave the black forests of Rochmarin and the dark old gods of its people; she had turned, instead, to the many tasks, sad and small, that should occupy the days of a new widow.

And then, in one moonlit hour, in the words of a reluctant assassin, she had found that her wish to leave Brittany had become a necessity. Within the day she must have a plan to leave Rochmarin, and accomplish the feat before the feast of All Saints, the appointed time of her murder.

Johanna touched the carved lid of her clothing chest and thought of her old bedchamber overlooking the riverbanks at Whitby. Two days ago, when the longing for home had fallen heavy upon her, she had come close to leaving for Dinan, where she might find a ship going down the river to the sea, and then to England.

It was Agnes Malebis, younger than her years and foolish to an extreme, who had kept Johanna at Rochmarin. Young Agnes, who moved with absolute sincerity from one obsession to the next, could not be left without kin to protect her.

In Adam Mauleon, Agnes's most persistent obsession, Johanna might find the solution to her dilemma. Mauleon had offered for Agnes before Walter Malebis died, and the betrothal had been near done when Walter left for Nantes. His death had ended the slow negotiations of dowry and dower lands and bride price; indeed, Mauleon's frequent visits to Rochmarin had held subtle hints that he might better turn to Malebis's widow, now that Johanna was free. Agnes, thank the Blessed Virgin, seemed unaware of Adam Mauleon's recent turn of mind; she had spoken, when the first mourning days had passed, of little else but her desire to wed him.

Johanna sighed. If, in this day, she could persuade Mauleon to make formal his earlier offer for Agnes, the dilemma of the girl's safety would be solved and Johanna would be free to find her way back across the water to England.

The sounds from the great hall below Johanna's bedchamber were growing louder. Soon the maids would come to find her, wondering why she was still abed with her door barred. Was it a maid who had told the killer of her plan to ride to the Abbey of St. Martin on the morrow? Or had the stable lads given news of Rochmarin's lady to those who wished her ill? The garrison, the stranger had said, had neglected its sentries for these two nights past. And how had he known? The garrison—

Johanna took up her warmest cloak and moved to the embrasure to look again at her narrow view of Rochmarin's defenses.

The clear, cold sky was without color or cloud. The rope that had dangled, mere hours earlier, in the moonlight had disappeared. Had the guards upon the battlements recovered it, there would have been an alarm at first light; Johanna's intruder had lived to remove the evidence of his incursion into her chamber.

She unbarred the door and descended the stair to the long hall. If she began to avoid the eyes of those who attended her at Rochmarin, suspicion would bloom and might provoke an early attack. If she trusted the stranger's tidings of murder, she must also trust his words describing the time and place. If the intruder had spoken the truth, Johanna had two days in which to make her plans and flee Rochmarin. She crossed the great hall and went out to the stable yard to discover where her saddle was kept. When she left Rochmarin, there would be no stable lads about to fetch her mount.

Adam Mauleon found her in the stable. "They told me you were here. Is something amiss?"

Johanna stepped forward into the low autumn light and remembered to smile. "I had begun to fear my palfrey would think me a stranger," she said. "I haven't been through the gates this fortnight past."

Touched by the sunlight, Mauleon's hair was palest gold; it was the first thing Agnes had said of him when she had first confided her love of him to Johanna.

Johanna smiled. "Agnes is in the hall. Will you come with me?"

Together they made their way across the bailey yard. "Tomorrow," Mauleon said, "I will ride with you and Agnes when you give alms to the abbey."

He knew. Adam Mauleon knew of the plan. Johanna fixed her gaze upon the ground before her and drew a long breath. "There's no need," Johanna managed to say.

Mauleon's voice held both curiosity and a trace of impatience. "Agnes told me that you would take alms to St. Martin's abbey for the feast of All Saints, as your husband would have done. Or have you decided not to make the journey? There are reports that Mercadier's army is camped only three days from here; I'll ride with you, in case there is trouble."

There was nothing in Adam Mauleon's gray-blue gaze, nothing in his deliberate, slow words, that hinted of enmity. Was it possible that this lord, rich in gold and honor, had any part in the threat against her?

Johanna had eaten a small bowl of pottage and left Mauleon to share a trencher with the adoring Agnes. There were questioning looks from the serving maid who saw her walking toward the stairs. "Are you ill, my lady?" the woman asked.

"No," Johanna said. "I'm weary. The moon kept me waking last night."

"You should not let the moon shine upon—"

Johanna shook her head. "I closed the shutters," she said. "But still it shone through."

"The Samhain moon is strong this year. Take care you do not let it touch you." The Breton maid's French was heavily accented, but the woman had the goodwill to speak slowly, as she had done from the beginning for the odd, foreign wife her Norman lord had brought from England.

One could not mistrust an entire settlement, and this woman had always shown Johanna respect and a timid sort of kindness. "What do you do," Johanna asked, "when the moon is so strong at Samhain? Do your menfolk fear to stand sentry duty?"

"When Samhain approaches, all fear. Men, women, and the young. It is the moon of the dead, lady. And it brings the dead to life and out of their graves by night at Samhain."

The face of Walter Malebis in his hollowed stone coffin, though washed clean of blood, had haunted Johanna this fortnight. Above the shroud, his jaw had been rigid, as if a final anger had followed him into the next world. If the dead could walk, as the Rochmarin folk believed, would Walter Malebis mount the stair to his widow's chamber to see whether she had wept for him?

The maid's face paled in dismay. "My lady, you are sad,

now, to remember our dead lord. You have said such prayers, lady, at his tomb, that he would not wish to rebuke you."

Her prayers had been for herself as well, for her safe homecoming, her deliverance from this dark, demon-ridden place. "No," she said. "He would not wish to trouble us."

Across the great hall two more serving maids frowned in her direction and turned to place ale and cheese upon the board before Mauleon and Agnes. Johanna had tried, when she came as Walter Malebis's bride, to win their loyalty. Had she failed so completely? How many of these Rochmarin folk knew of the threat to her life?

Agnes rose from her bench and walked to the stair. She cocked her head to glance back at Mauleon and smoothed her maiden's long hair back from her brow. "I went to the chapel after we spoke."

Johanna forced herself to smile. "And did you imagine a fine effigy for Walter?"

"I prayed last night for his soul. And have set aside my mother's gold ring for the abbot at St. Martin's to pray for his peaceful repose. Until his murderers are found, that is all we can do. That and the effigy."

Johanna closed her eyes. Agnes had the notion that no common brigands had robbed and killed her brother; she was much given, of late, to speak of royal intrigues and secret enemies. Johanna had not had the heart to tell Walter's young sister that he had been found with his men in a common brothel, and the gold he had gone to Nantes to collect, an old debt made good by their father's ancient friend recently returned from Palestine, missing from his money pouch. The prosperous young whore had disappeared that night from her bloody house, killed by the same brigands or abducted following the carnage.

"Walter must have had enemies," Agnes continued. "Important ones who knew and followed his every move. Adam has agreed to ask the count's justiciars to discover the truth."

Johanna nodded and began to listen to the litany of grand

suspicions that Agnes had aired each morning since Walter had gone into his tomb. This time she listened with more interest. Naive though she was, Agnes's view of Malebis's importance in Breton affairs might hold a kernel of truth.

"And are you fearful?" Johanna asked at last. "If your brother had such enemies, do you not fear that you or I will be harmed next?"

Agnes shivered and stroked her hair back from her shoulders. "It is possible."

"Then we should travel to Dinan and seek help," Johanna said.

Agnes's eyes grew bright. "Lord Adam would help us. He has offered us his protection."

"I do not think—"

Adam Mauleon rose from the board and crossed the wide chamber to stand before Johanna. "You and Agnes may wish to come back to my lands after we return from the abbey," he said. "My sister will welcome you, and will insist, as I do, that you pass the winter with us. I'll send some of my own men back here to manage your garrison. There should be no need for more than a single sergeant, unless Mercadier begins raiding in these lands."

Agnes's pale face had turned rosy in excitement. "May we, Johanna? We would both be safer in Adam's keep."

"Of course." Johanna looked into Adam Mauleon's clear eyes. "Will you sleep here this Samhain night?"

A spark of warmth kindled and vanished within his gaze. "No," he said. "There are matters awaiting my decision. But I will return tomorrow, before noon, to ride with you to the abbey."

Johanna attempted, once again, to persuade Agnes to go with her to Dinan; and once again, the girl's infatuation with

Mauleon made her deaf to anything but her plans to ride to Mauleon's keep on the day after the feast of All Saints.

It would take more than reports of anonymous messages to budge Agnes from Mauleon's side. Short of abduction, Johanna could think of no way to turn Agnes from her purpose—to wed the man she worshipped.

Once again Johanna went over the words of the reluctant assassin who had come to her by moonlight. Only Johanna's name, he had said, had been given to Mercadier. Only Johanna's death was required.

With reluctance she decided that she must leave Rochmarin under cover of darkness that same night, trusting that the Breton watchmen's Samhain fears would keep them from following her into the forest beyond the walls.

Once she reached the safety of Dinan, she would send a small army to bring Agnes out of danger.

Chapter Four

The giant oak, a gnarled sentinel post from which an agile young boy of ten had often watched Rochmarin's distant bailey yard, had not fallen, nor lost its massive branches to the harsh winds of eighteen winters. During the short, cold daylight hours of Samhain, Payen had watched and waited in its branches, descending only to move Arsuf from one grazing spot to the next. At dusk he descended to meet Mathieu, to hear news of Rochmarin's lady.

Mathieu had managed to find a place in the garrison three days before, and had, so far, escaped the notice of any men-at-arms who might have recognized him as one of Mercadier's men. Drawing the late-night guard duty that by custom must fall to new recruits, Mathieu had taken Payen past Rochmarin's defenses and had found him a hiding place in the stable loft. There he had left Payen to sleep by day and prowl by darkness until he had managed, at last, to locate and penetrate the widow Malebis's bedchamber. Before dawn Payen had slipped through Rochmarin's gates to hide in the forest once again.

"What did you promise the lady?" Mathieu asked. "The widow turned up at the garrison yard this morning and gave each of us a good, long look. Half the men thought she had lost her mind, and the other half began to hope she was looking for more than bodyguards."

"She asked for bodyguards? I told her to trust no one—"

"She didn't. The widow gave us each a cold look and spoke to those she didn't recognize. Gave me some bad moments with her questions, but she didn't guess."

"And the abbey? Is she still taking alms to St. Martin's tomorrow?"

"Hard to say. She chose four bodyguards and told them to be ready to leave at noon, when the lord Mauleon would arrive to escort her. Spoke with the stable lads about her palfrey. The young sister, the lady Agnes, will ride with them."

Payen sent a fallen branch into the underbrush. "If riding out with one knight, a young girl, and four guards likely in the pay of her enemies is her idea of escape, the woman won't survive the day. Or will she run before time?"

"May do so," Mathieu said. "She was about the stables this morning, checking the saddle and fussing over the saddlebag. Didn't want to lose the alms pouch, she said. Stable lads were out of sorts with her—said she always trusted them before."

Payen frowned. "She may make her move this night, when the guards stay close to their fires."

"Or tomorrow, when she's on her way to the abbey. Maybe she chose bodyguards she has reason to trust and will bid them, once they're clear of Rochmarin, to take her to the coast."

"I told her they had left her unprotected these last few nights. They must have been bribed, some of them—perhaps all of them."

"Did she heed your words?"

Payen shook his head. "Hard to tell. She listened to the warning—and took it to heart, I think. She may not have heeded the advice."

"I told you, Payen. If you had sent a monk from St. Martin's abbey to speak to her, you could have saved yourself a trip down that wall and saved the woman the fright. Women will listen to priests."

"I'll leave St. Martin's and the monks out of this. Remember, Mathieu, I know this place. And I have my reasons. Now, tell me," Payen continued, "what the woman did after she left the stable yard. Did she keep to her chamber?"

"Lord Adam Mauleon came. The widow met him at the gates and took him to the hall, where the Malebis girl was waiting. Talk has it that there's a betrothal soon to come between Mauleon and the Malebis girl."

"That might explain it. It may be that Mauleon wants the widow dead to clear the girl's inheritance."

"You think he's the one?"

Payen shook his head. "It would be too simple. And too easy for Mauleon to arrange for himself, without others, if he wants her dead. No, it smells like a distant enemy, with a few of his own men in place at Rochmarin."

"Why kill her? She is young to have enemies."

"I pray we'll never know. When she runs, we'll follow her and see her safe to the coast. If my luck turns good, she'll take ship for England and never come back. And that will be the end of it."

"It would have been simpler to ride away with her last night."

Payen sighed. "With that woman, nothing would be simple. She has cunning—and keeps her wits at a hard trot even when she's speaking."

Mathieu untied his mount. "Then, she'll have no trouble leaving Rochmarin."

"It doesn't follow. She was taut as a bowstring, even in her sleep. The widow trusts no one and may trip over her suspicions when she makes her move.'' Payen held the mount as Mathieu clambered into the saddle. ''Go back and watch her,'' he said. ''When she runs, I'll be right behind.''

In the years of his childhood there had not been a Samhain night as cold as this, nor a sky so clear. The moon shone in a bright flood upon the keep of Rochmarin, and whitened the forest road in each open place where the dark canopy of the trees parted to admit the light.

The people of Rochmarin, believing that the dead would walk upon this night, had grown uneasy as the moon rose so bright in the sky, and feared that in the clear, brilliant path of that witching star, the dead would move easily to their trysts. To those who feared anger or vengeance from fallen enemies, this Samhain night was more dangerous for its clarity.

As was the custom, the younger, more daring men of Rochmarin, those with no wife or child to see through this terror-laden night, had built a great fire beyond the bailey walls, the length of an arrow's shot from the relative safety of the small chapel.

Their fire, larger than those that burned inside the bailey and upon the sentry posts at the gates, must show travelers the entrance to Rochmarin, and bring them to the safety of Rochmarin's walls should they be lost in the forest in this most terrifying night. To leave the beacon fire unlit or untended would invite the vengeance, in future Samhains, of those who had fallen prey to the ghosts who walked the night.

In all the years of Rochmarin's history, the outer fire, the travelers' beacon, had never brought a single innocent to safety; the deep-drinking men who had, in their ale-won courage, undertaken to tend the fire, would have been unnerved to see a human form come up the moon-washed path to seek shelter. It was this certainty that would give Payen the advantage he would require should the widow Malebis choose this night to flee Rochmarin.

It looked as if the widow was planning in earnest to make her move. For the first time in all the nights Payen had watched her chamber, the shutters were open upon the night, and the golden light of a hot-burning fire illuminated the distant walls of the chamber, flickering as if the lady Johanna sat safe at her chamber hearth, feeding the fine wall hearth with Rochmarin oak. The widow Malebis would appear, to all who were watching the keep, to be staying close beside her fire on this Samhain night.

Payen did not have long to wait. In the early night, soon after the false bravery of the sentinels at the fire had faded and the keepers of the flames had begun to tell long, disjointed tales of Samhains past, of ghosts come to claim vengeance upon their ancient enemies, there was a pale stirring at the great gates of Rochmarin. A gray palfrey with a cloaked burden picked its way past the Rochmarin gates and moved into the darkness beyond.

The eldest of the keepers rose and stood in the road with his back to the sparking columns of fire that warmed the cold night. It was the Englishwoman, Payen heard the keepers mutter. It was the widow, gone foolish in her grief.

In the next moment the widow vanished,turned from the road into the cover of the black trees. Into the forest, where the dead walked.

"Lady," the leader called. "Come back from the forest. Come to the fire."

Silence was their answer.

"It's not the lady," said another. "If it were the widow lady, she would not have turned from the light."

"Are you blind? I saw her. It's the widow."

"You thought it was the widow, but those who walk at Samhain are tricksters. Yon was a ghost."

"It was the widow."

"If so, she's set to deal with the devil."

"She's soft in the head, like all English. She'll come out soon enough."

The second man picked up his bow. "Aye, and when she does, if I see the ghost light around her, I'll shoot before she reaches us."

"No, put it away."

The bowman did not answer.

Payen moved closer to the fire and tied Arsuf to a young sapling near the Rochmarin track. If the beast became restless and made noise, there were none gathered around the beacon fire who would dare leave the safe loom of the flames to find the horse. The garrison might be Normans every one, but the terrors of Samhain were universal, and the strength of the Breton beliefs more than a seasoned soldier might sensibly ignore. Around the beacon fire Payen had heard only Breton voices and had sensed the fear the Normans had begun to share with the folk of Rochmarin.

Mathieu appeared at his side. "God's angry breath," he muttered. "I'll risk my neck for you willingly, but never again send me wandering about a Samhain night. She's in the forest, beyond the fire. I lost her there."

Payen caught Mathieu's bridle and quieted the horse, never taking his eyes from the beacon fire in the distance. "You have learned some Breton foolishness to leaven your own bread, Mathieu?"

"By the White Christ, if this many folks, however foolish, believe the dead walk tonight, who am I to gainsay them?"

"Keep your fears for the arrows of the living. To be taken for a ghost this night would be a fatal mistake."

"And the Rochmarin woman? You believe she will risk the same?"

"She may. She has little choice since she refused my help."

Mathieu shrugged. "She refused to dangle upon your rope

with only your arm to keep her from falling to her death. If you had offered an easier way, she might have taken it.''

With sudden violence Payen seized the reins of his mount and vaulted into the saddle. The men at the beacon fire were standing now, their weapons at the ready, watching the face of the forest. One man, bolder than the others, seized a torch, bolted into the wood, and shouted for his comrades to follow.

The widow Malebis picked that moment to spur from her hiding place beyond the beacon fire and set her horse down the Rochmarin track. Seeing the confusion around the bonfire, she urged her horse forward and hunched low upon the neck of the beast.

The men beside the fire drew back from the beast's approach, and from the edge of the woods came the whistle of an arrow in flight. In the crimson gold of the firelight a deeper red bloomed across the crupper of Johanna Mercat's mount. The archer beside the fire drew another arrow and set it to his bowstring.

If the Norman soldiers of the garrison had turned their arrows upon her, the widow would have died at the first volley. But these were farmers of Rochmarin, men with little skill at arms, hiding their fear—

Far beyond the fire, on the high walls of Rochmarin, the guards were shouting. Torchlight bloomed above the gates. The men of the garrison would soon ride out to join the confusion.

Payen drew his sword from its scabbard and took his mount onto the track, to the south of the bonfire. Beyond the flames the widow's mare was plunging and turning, pain crazed and fearful to approach the fire that burned high between the walls of Rochmarin and the narrow road to freedom.

With difficulty Payen kept his mount upon the track, advancing steadily, without the appearance of fear, upon the scene of shouting, flames, and blood.

Payen raised his sword. ''Cease,'' he bellowed. ''Does Rochmarin spill the blood of its women?''

As he had hoped, surprise gave him the advantage on this night of walking ghosts. He filled his lungs again and bellowed a Breton curse from his early memories, blasphemy his father had used when provoked.

"Christ Jesus," the man with the torch cried. "It is the old lord come from his grave."

Payen advanced, his sword upheld, slowing his mount as he drew near the fire. In the accents of his childhood tongue he sent his demands into the dumbstruck huddle before him. "Let the woman pass," he bellowed. "Stand aside, or ride with me back to hell."

Beyond the fire the widow Malebis did not hesitate. She nudged her horse forward, down the incline to the bonfire, past the shrinking, trembling men. At the turning place her mount began to toss its head and shy from the flames. Would she lose her seat?

"Send her to me," Payen called, "or I'll see you in hell this night."

From the crowd the bold one with the torch stepped forward to slap the rump of the balked palfrey, bringing his palm down upon the grazed, bleeding crupper of the beast. With an outraged bellow to match Payen's sudden cry, the beast began to plunge and turn in a tight, mad circle, seeking to bite the pain.

The woman held her own but came close to falling beneath the frantic hooves. With a bellowed threat and the flat of his sword Payen cleared his way to her side, pulled Johanna from the maddened palfrey, and retreated with her threats ringing in his ears.

In the struggle Johanna Mercat's cloak had flown into her face, muffling her cries and blinding her to the moonlit flight away from Rochmarin. The strength of her protests and the desperate violence of her efforts to free herself set Payen's wounds bleeding afresh and brought the woman's arms perilously close to the edge of his unsheathed sword.

Payen pushed her down across the saddle bows and ignored

her cries as he reined his mount to a stop and turned into the forest beside the track.

"Be silent," he growled. "You know who I am."

Her shrouded head bobbed up, and her hands, tangled in the folds of her cloak, sought to clear her face from the cloth.

"My horse—"

"Ran back to the gates." He pulled the cloak from her hair and set her before him. "The arrow had grazed the beast's hindquarters. You would not have managed her far."

The woman stiffened and shrieked a warning. "Behind us," she cried.

Payen pulled his half-sheathed sword free and wheeled Arsuf around. The woman scrambled from the saddle, landed with a soft, crackling thud amid the fallen leaves, and ran into the trees.

"Come back," Mathieu called.

Payen vaulted from the saddle and sheathed his sword. It would be hard enough finding the woman in the darkness without risking an encounter with the edge of his sword in the confusion.

He looked back over his shoulder; the bonfire was far behind them, its light only a pale aura glowing through the trees. Above them the moon had risen to its highest point and shone in uneasy brightness upon a small clearing into which the widow Malebis had disappeared. The faint sound of voices came through the night; soon the Breton watchmen might gather their courage and follow to see what the specter of their long-dead lord might have done with the troublesome Englishwoman.

Payen stopped at the edge of the clearing. Once before, he had forgotten caution and risked both Mathieu's life and his own in the disaster at Nantes. He turned back and took Arsuf's reins. "Ride on, Mathieu. If she doesn't come back before the moon sets, I'll find you outside the abbey."

"If the Bretons see her come out of the woods, they may panic and shoot."

"She must know that," Payen said. He turned back to face the trees. "If she had the sense of a she-goat or the courage of a broody hen, she would show herself now and keep us all from the watchmen's arrows."

He gestured to Mathieu to stay quiet and stood with his sword in hand as the sound of hesitant footsteps drew near. Johanna Mercat stepped into the moonlight and stopped just beyond Payen's reach.

"You did not tell me there were two of you. How many more?"

"Only Mathieu and myself."

The woman turned to Mathieu. "I know your voice," she said. "You were the new one in the garrison."

"Aye," said Mathieu. "And I haven't yet been paid."

"The garrison is paid every fortnight."

"We have no time for this," Payen said. Once again he rammed his sword into the scabbard and caught Arsuf's reins.

"And I don't pay spies."

"Spies?" Mathieu's voice rose in outrage. "It was for you I was spying, lady."

"Speak louder," Payen snarled. "And maybe the watchmen will send you your wages with their next arrows." He climbed into the saddle and nudged Arsuf to stand beside the widow Malebis. "If you're coming with us, move now."

"I will come." She held up her hand and turned her face away from the moonlight. A moment later she turned back and frowned; she stretched both arms to Payen. "I'm ready," she said.

Payen placed a hand upon Arsuf's hindquarters and turned to regard the widow Malebis. He kicked his boot free of the stirrup. "Climb up, then. I've heaved you to my saddle once too often this night, and you were not grateful—"

She lowered her arms and stepped back. "I'll thank you when I'm free of this place. There will be gold for you—and for your comrade—when I reach home. I swear it."

"We'll speak of gold later, madam. Come up on the saddle."

The woman hesitated no longer. She seized the saddle bow, placed her booted foot up in the stirrup, and did not flinch when Payen pulled her the rest of the way to sit before him. "If we meet opposition," he said, "do not move from the saddle. I'll tell you if you should go down, and when to do it."

Johanna Mercat shifted forward and drew her knees before her to rest upon the saddle bows. "Do not think me ungrateful," she said. "I know you acted as best you could, back at the watch fire—"

"As best I could? I saved your life, madam."

"I was on my way past the fire when you came forward."

"And you were about to be shot by the watchmen. Do you not understand that those who ride by night at Samhain must not appear furtive, lest they be taken for ghosts? You were within bowshot of the watchmen and lucky to survive. Your horse was lucky only to be grazed. Why did you not answer the watchmen? If you had but called your name—"

"To give my enemies a better shot?"

"Why did you ride out the main gate? You knew there would be watchmen."

"I saw no watchmen until I passed through the gates. How was I to know how the fires are tended here? Samhain fires should burn inside a bailey wall and within home hearths. That is where civilized people gather. The beacon fires should be set and left to burn untended, for none but thieves and other desperate folk would be abroad in the deep night after the flames die. That is how the fires are set at home."

Behind them in the darkness, Mathieu snorted.

Payen shrugged, and felt the woman shift again, to sit in a less rigid posture.

"I wish to go to Dinan," she said. "My uncle sells wool in that port, and I will find a merchant who knows him well enough to lend me gold for the journey home."

“Not Dinan,” Payen said. “You would not be safe. I’ll take you east into Normandy.”

“I will go directly to those who would know me in Dinan. I will be safe enough.”

“If you wish to cast your life away in Dinan, after the trouble I have taken to see you clear of Rochmarin, then you may reach it on your own,” Payen said. The sweet warmth of the woman left Payen’s chest as she sat forward, rigid once again. “Stay with me until dawn,” he said. “I’ll see you on your way by daylight.”

Chapter Five

Within the hour of her flight from Rochmarin, Johanna had lost her palfrey and gained the company of two brigands: the first, who had chosen to bring a mortal warning by night to her bedchamber and nearly stopped her heart with the terror of that first waking moment, and another, who had joined the Rochmarin garrison only days before to spy upon her. Neither, it seemed, had thought to ride through Rochmarin's gates, beg leave to speak with its widowed lady, and tell her, in the light of day, of the danger to her life. Both, she suspected, must be well acquainted with the assassin's arts they had been paid to use upon her.

To be honest, she had been grateful for their appearance at the watch fire. Ignorant of Rochmarin's Samhain customs, Johanna had not expected to find a large, armed group about the beacon flames below the main gate. When discovered, she had not expected that the sight of Walter Malebis's widow upon a familiar palfrey would inspire the watchmen to fear her approach and to attack her. The first brigand, the one who had brought his midnight warning, might have been right when he said that she might have enemies among her dead husband's people.

There had been no question of continuing her journey alone. Her horse was gone, and she had no wish to face the abbey road alone, even if she had known her way back through the forest to find it. The two brigands had saved her life, and had offered her no threat or insult as they took her deeper into the forest, farther from the small villages below Rochmarin's walls. After the first hour's passage through the darkness, Johanna had ceased to fear immediate danger but had nevertheless kept a hand upon the small dagger tucked within her broderie belt, hidden behind the stitching.

They continued through moon-silvered oaks. Riding single file among the massive trunks, their mounts' hooves cushioned by many seasons of fallen leaves, they made steady progress into the wilderness. They stopped once, and the men spoke a few words of shelter, but Johanna saw no sign of a track or settlement nearby.

Johanna had lost all sense of their direction; the moon was high above them and had not yet begun the descent that would provide a marking point in the confusion of stars. They might have been traveling in a broad circle for all she could tell, but the two men had not seemed to hesitate as they guided their mounts through the silent trees.

The assassins' haven would be a well-hidden cave, or a hovel set far from the path of honest travelers, so remote that none but murderers and their kind would frequent it. The men with whom she rode were likely as dangerous as any fugitives who had settled in this desolate place.

Johanna reminded herself that it was too late to regret trusting the man with whom she rode, and there was no profit in speculating as to his character. He had balked at killing a woman and had taken the trouble to ride to Rochmarin to warn her. Beyond that act his honor and his motives were a mystery.

The men would expect gold for their trouble; gold they would have, and her gratitude as well, but only when they had brought her to the safety of Dinan. Why had they refused to take her to the river port? Were they such notorious assassins that they feared recognition in a large town in the light of day?

She had asked a few subtle questions to bring her companions to tell her where they were heading, but her words brought no answer save silence and an inquiry as to the state of her health. They had stopped a mile past the watchfire to take a woolen cloak from Mathieu's saddlebags and place it around her shoulders. Last night's intruder, the man with whom she rode, had ceased to speak after that hasty delay. He had never spoken his name, nor had his man Mathieu used one.

At last, she nodded asleep, and awakened to find they were still moving in the failing light of a low moon. In the cold, still night, the sound of the horses' hooves upon the dry leaves of the forest seemed loud, and likely to bring predators to follow. When the moon set, there would be hours of darkness in which the beasts of the forest might stalk them unseen.

"Are we near?" she asked

"Near where?"

"Your den."

"I have no den."

"Your home, then."

"I lack that as well."

The silence began to grow. Again the need to hear her companion's voice came upon Johanna. "I'm sorry," she said.

"You're no trouble. Not now."

"I'm sorry that you have no home."

There was a sound of indrawn breath and a long hesitation. "It is my choice," he said at last.

She turned to peer back at his face in the last of the moonlight. "What is your name, sir?"

"Payen."

"You are a Breton?"

"You heard me speak to the watchmen. I am a Breton."

"Then you must know where we are going."

"Better than you, madam. And it is not Dinan."

Once again the silence grew. And once again Johanna broke it. "Do you have an enemy in Dinan? One who would harm you if you showed your face? If so, you could leave me outside the town and—"

"No."

"You won't leave me nearby? If I could find a horse and groom to ride with me, I could pay when I reach Dinan. You would not need to approach the town."

"You send your questions so fast and crowded that you cannot hear the answers, madam. I have told you that I have no enemies in Dinan. You have one—at least one—in that place; I will not take you tomorrow to meet the doom from which I saved you this night."

"How do you know they wait in Dinan?"

He reached forward to guide his horse around a low boulder and spoke softly beside Johanna's ear. "In Dinan, in a waterfront inn, there waits a harper lad with fifty gold pieces to pay the man who brings news of your death. To my mind, Johanna Mercat, that is an enemy. You must not embark for England from that port."

"I would find help there from my uncle's friend. There will be gold for you and your man, and a ship to take me home. There is no other port in Brittany where I could find a friend—"

"And where a man waits with gold to pay your murderer."

They halted beside the face of a granite outcropping and led the horses to shelter between the darkening forest and the rough gray wall of rock. With a gesture that mocked a noble lord's manner, Payen gave Johanna the support of his arm to bring her down from the saddle and steady her first benumbed steps to shelter. He bade her wait as he heaped dead leaves into a deep pile. "We will have no fire," he said. "Use the leaves to keep yourself warm, and if there should be trouble, stay where you are, with your cloak to cover your face. You will not be seen.''

Johanna sank down upon the leaves and turned her face from their dry, spicy scent. ''Where will you be?''

''Not far. Now sleep. Dawn will come soon enough.''

The yellow moon sank below the treetops, and shone, in its last moment, straight through the woods, casting the heavy, ancient trunks into brief silhouette before blackness descended. Above Johanna's bed of leaves the stars had disappeared; the damp scent of land mist came to her face, and a thin breeze touched the leaves beyond her bed. If the rains came this night, there would be no sleep for any of them. Yet, Johanna was warm beneath the heavy cloak, with the leaves to keep her from the chill of the ground.

Somewhere in the darkness Mathieu and Payen were speaking in low voices. Johanna tried to follow the words, but sleep came before she caught the drift.

He woke her in darkness, and she protested that she had slept but a moment, and that dawn would not come for hours. At Payen's second urging she rose and saw, above the jagged mass of granite, a yellow-gray smudge in the blackness. She retreated behind the outcropping for a precious moment of privacy, and attempted to wash in the dew that had collected in a fissure in the cold stone. That gesture, and a quick shake of her braid to rid her hair of leaves, was the extent of Johanna's efforts to make herself ready to face the day.

When she returned to the sleeping site, the dawn was coming fast; for the first time, Johanna looked upon Payen's face. It was as she had half seen, and half imagined in the moonlight these two nights past: vivid, deep-set eyes of azure blue, dark hair that caught the morning mist in its deep whorls, and the prominent, fine-molded features of a predator.

His mouth curved in the slow smile she had sensed in her moonlit bedchamber. "As you see," Payen said, "I am not the devil come to take you." Johanna took the waterskin he offered and accepted a large hunk of bread from Mathieu.

"Do not fret," Mathieu said. "We'll eat well as soon as we reach the abbey."

Johanna lowered the bread untasted. "The abbey? The abbey at St. Martin's shrine?"

Mathieu nodded. "That's where we're headed."

Payen cut a wedge of cheese and offered it to Johanna. She shook her head. "My late husband's sister and Adam Mauleon were to ride to St. Martin's at noon."

He frowned. "Not with you missing. We should be at the abbey soon after dawn. If we see any but monks and pilgrims when we reach the abbey, we'll ride past and none will know we were there. If it's safe, we'll buy you a horse and find food."

She looked past Payen into the dense forest. There were no landmarks, no sign of Rochmarin's stone keep upon the horizon. "Are we near the place where you were to—wait?"

He shook his head. "Your death, lady, was to happen upon the road north of here, not halfway to the abbey from Rochmarin. If there are any watching the place, they will be too far north to hear us pass." He frowned at the lightening sky and took the bread from her hand. "Come, you may eat as we ride. We must finish our dealings at the abbey before noontide."

Johanna followed Payen to his horse and accepted with mild surprise a boost into the saddle and the hunk of bread back in her hands. "The monks will recognize me," she said. "I brought them alms at Eastertide, and again at midsummer."

Across the small clearing Mathieu snorted.

Payen swung up behind her and brushed his hand past her hair. He held a small leaf before her in the palm of his hand. "I doubt that the monks will look for the widow Malebis's face upon a woman who rides in the saddle before me, looking as if she has traveled the length of the duchy."

Johanna placed the bread in a fold of her cloak and pulled her braid forward to see that she had caught more leaves in the loose strands escaping the once-splendid silken tie. "Leave them," Payen said. "They will make you seem a pilgrim woman and—they do not look ill."

"Even pilgrim women brush their hair."

He reached around her and took the heavy braid from her hand. "Your hair is the color of a young tree," he said. "And the leaves look fine upon it."

Odd words from an assassin. Johanna turned in surprise; the bread fell upon the forest floor.

Mathieu nudged his horse forward and began to clamber down to fetch the bread.

"Leave it," Johanna said. "I thank you, but I'm not hungry."

Payen lifted the reins and turned the horse away from their rock-bound shelter. "Has fear stopped your appetites?"

"I am not afraid."

Payen shrugged. "The abbey is not far. You'll have warm food there." He pulled her braid back to rest upon her cloak. "I'll not take you to the coast if you refuse sleep and food. If you fall ill before you take ship, you may perish in the crossing."

"Not if I find a good ship—a big merchant cog like the ones that sail from Dinan."

Behind her she heard Payen sigh. "Never have I heard a soul—man or woman—so eager to meet death. Find an early doom if it pleases you, lady. But find it after I see you bound for England on a ship that sails from any port but Dinan. And if you go back to Dinan, I pray I'll hear no word of your fate—I'll count myself a fool for taking you from a fast, clean death at Rochmarin and setting you free to stumble into the trap once again."

"If I could but send word to my uncle's friend—" Had she imagined that swift tug at her braid?

"Do me the kindness," Payen said, "of leaving the subject of Dinan."

They emerged from the forest a short distance from the abbey and rode along the deserted road and through the narrow gates of St. Martin's. Within moments Payen and Mathieu had drawn the saddles and bags from their mounts and tied the beasts to the stable-yard paling, among the palfreys of the abbey guests. A slight pressure upon Johanna's arm warned her not to speak to the monk at the door of the pilgrims' hall, nor to the large number of travelers who had passed the Samhain night in the safety of the abbey's sacred walls.

Johanna accepted bread and cheese from a pock-faced novice monk and found a bench against the wall. She sat as close as she dared to a group of old women and turned her attention to the food in her hands. Payen had been right. With the dust of dried leaves upon her cloak, and the hood pulled halfway over her hair, the lady of Rochmarin might pass unrecognized before the eyes of the monks who had so recently received gold from her hand.

Mathieu soon followed Johanna and stood between her and the long table of more prosperous abbey guests, who had paid for their bread and a place at the board. The old women, seeing Mathieu's scarred hauberk and the fine jewels upon his rough hands, rose as one and moved to the far side of the wooden hall. Through the rising smoke of the fire pit they regarded Johanna and her guardian and whispered among themselves.

"Come," Mathieu said. "We'll take bread out to Payen and be on our way." He stroked his flame-red beard. "Those harpies have noticed you."

"Those harpies noticed your rings," Johanna said. She rose

and followed Mathieu from the hall. "Are they prizes from your victims?"

Mathieu shrugged. "Payen will have my guts for garters if we speak within these walls. Keep silent, lady."

"Where is he? Where is Payen?"

"Buying a horse."

"I have gold. I will pay the price."

"You're to keep your head down and stay out of sight."

At the stable yard there was no sign of Payen. Between the great black gelding that had carried her to the abbey and Mathieu's bay was a dappled gray mare with a small saddle upon her. "Mount up," Mathieu said.

"Where is—"

"He will come." Mathieu led the mare to a large stone at the end of the palings and offered his hand as Johanna stepped upon it and into the saddle. When Mathieu moved from her side to saddle and mount his beast, Johanna looked over the low barrier and saw Payen at the stable door, deep in speech with an ancient, painfully stooped monk. Payen pressed a money pouch into the spidery hands and placed his palms upon the warped shoulders in a swift, gentle embrace.

The monk's hood fell back to reveal thick black hair as dark as Payen's own, and a pale, smiling visage, radiant above the twisted body of a cripple.

Johanna's breath caught in her throat.

Payen looked up and saw her. With a murmured word Johanna could not catch, he left the monk beside the stable door and walked through the stockade gate. His face had darkened in anger.

The cripple's features had resembled Payen's own, close enough that he might be kin. Johanna followed Payen through the abbey gates and did not speak for the first hour as he led them at an uncomfortable trot through the forest. Brigands—even the worst of them—must have families; by the look of the booty Mathieu wore upon his fingers, these assassins were prosperous enough to give some of their heavy gold to their kinfolk.

They rode on in silence, for Johanna lacked the courage, in the rising light of day, to speak again of her wish to travel to Dinan. Later, when they had reached a place far enough from Rochmarin to be safe but populous enough for her to buy help with the silver sewn into her hem, she would thank Payen for his trouble and find another to take her the last few miles to Dinan.

Johanna's silence did not please her companions. Payen had become suspicious and glanced back often to be sure she followed him. Behind her, Mathieu had fallen back far enough to see her path should she make a sudden break from their company. Though they crossed three narrow tracks in the forest, they ignored the paths and continued to make their way through the wilds. Johanna rode in place and ignored the uneasy prickles between her shoulder blades. She had felt safer in the darkness of night, mounted before Payen, hearing his complaints when she tried to question him.

At noonday they stopped beside a deep-flowing green river and led the horses to drink. Payen pulled a saddlebag from his mount, placed it upon the stump of a wind-fallen tree, and beckoned Johanna to his side. "Eat and sleep if you wish. Mathieu will keep watch."

The prickles became painful darts. "Are you leaving?" she said.

He was distracted, looking up the river and into the forest as if searching for a landmark.

"Are we lost?" she asked.

He turned back and shook his head. "I'll be back for you." He walked upstream and did not look back.

Mathieu did not seem surprised by Payen's disappearance. "How long will he be gone?" Johanna asked.

"An hour. Maybe more."

"He hasn't eaten since daybreak."

Mathieu sat upon the forest floor and leaned against the tree stump. "He will when he wants to."

"Who was the monk in the stable yard?"

"A monk."

"Why did Payen give him money?"

Mathieu opened a bloodshot eye and regarded Johanna with exasperation. "He paid for your horse, madam. We are not thieves."

"He gave the monk a large purse of coin. More than the price of a horse, I think."

"She's a good horse. Ladies know nothing of the cost of things." Mathieu's chin dropped onto his hauberk, and he closed his eyes against the sun.

Johanna stood and crossed the clearing to the river. The noonday sun had softened the autumn chill, and the sharp cold of the river water felt good upon her face. About the riverside clearing, the birds had ceased to sing; only the sound of the three hobbled mounts moving beneath the canopy of green relieved the silence of the forest.

Johanna moved downstream, in the opposite direction that Payen had taken. She dared not move far from the horses or leave Mathieu far from sight; for all their grudging kindness, she still did not trust Payen and Mathieu to wait for her should they decide to leave before she returned.

It was instinct rather than a sound that brought her farther downstream to a larger clearing peopled by massive, moss-covered stones that rose in a ragged circle half obscured by a stand of beeches that confused the line of sight. Johanna halted and stepped back from the place. Even in the clear light of midday she must not cross that circle.

Johanna closed her eyes in resignation. She had lived too long among the Bretons and had begun to fear the ancient spirits of which they sang.

Soon she would be back across the sea, in Yorkshire, where the old stones were not so big, nor so well hidden that the moss and vines that grew upon them seemed as green men's locks and beards, and the lichen did not form into wide, staring eyes that dared her to approach.

A sudden movement at the base of the largest stone sent Johanna skittering back into the forest to take refuge behind a hawthorn bush. Payen was there, digging with a piece of dead wood in the earth beside the pagan stone. Johanna's lips began to move in silent prayer. Had she left Rochmarin and come this far with Payen only to end her days in this remote place? Would her body sleep until the day of judgment in that unhallowed earth?

The sound of digging ceased. Payen reached into the shallow pit and drew forth a soiled leather bag; bright gold spilled from it into his hand. A different brilliance, of well-honed steel, shone of a sudden in the other. His gaze found the place where she had hidden, and the knife slid once again into its scabbard. "If you would stay unharmed until we reach the coast," he said, "do not hover about watching me when I have told you not to follow."

Johanna stepped before the hawthorn thicket and attempted to keep her voice calm. "I had no intention of taking your gold."

He shrugged, and turned his attention once again to the coins. He spilled a good number of them back into the sack and began to cover them once again with the rich Breton earth.

"How long have you kept that gold buried?"

Payen turned to regard her and placed the remaining coins in his money pouch. "A few years," he said.

Johanna walked to his side and helped Payen cover the new earth with a layer of dead leaves. "Why do you keep it here? Place this gold with a reputable smith, and you may have it whenever you need it, with no fear that you will lose it to thieves or forget the cache place."

"I have never forgotten them."

"Them? This is not the only place?"

Payen frowned. "They are far from here, each of them. If one is discovered, the others will not be obvious."

Johanna frowned back. "And if you should need the gold when you are not able to dig it up, what then? This is a foolish way to treat your riches, leaving it wantonly about the countryside, doing good to none, and likely to be lost for many reasons."

"Is it your custom, madam, to berate those who mean you nothing but good? Is this the thanks I will get for saving your skin?"

"I am telling you what any half-reasonable merchant could teach you, Payen. You should take the gold—some of it, at least—and let a goldsmith keep it for you. Or use it to buy cattle or land and let it make more gold for you."

"I am no farmer, madam."

"Then find lands with folk to work them for you."

Payen's face darkened. "And how, madam, do you imagine a mercenary soldier might convince a great lord to give lands into his keeping? You are foolish to suggest it."

"I know nothing of lords and their choice of vassals, but I do know—"

"You knew one lord very well indeed."

"I—I was wed to Walter Malebis less than a year. And I have done with landed lords—I shall not know another as well."

Payen turned to her in surprise. "What do you say?"

"I am a merchant's daughter, unused to lords and their problems. But I know gold and how to keep it safe and ready. And you, sir, do not."

"A merchant's daughter. No wonder—"

"What?"

"You did not understand why I placed the sword upon the floor, beside you as you slept."

"I would have cut my feet to ribbons had I stepped down from the bed."

"I put it there as a sign to you that I meant no harm."

"I was close to screaming and killing us both. The sword did nothing to reassure."

He sighed. "It is a miracle, is it not, that we did not manage to kill each other with our blunders. Mine, in assuming you understood the language of gesture, and yours, in attempting to ride past the watchmen."

She lowered her gaze. "I have not yet thanked you. I would not be ungrateful." Johanna pointed to the gold resting within his palm. "There will be more of that awaiting you at Dinan, should you agree to take me there."

"By Christ's eyeteeth, woman, we will speak no more of Dinan. Better I had slit your throat sleeping than let you be murdered in the streets of Dinan."

Johanna sat back and considered what she had seen. This man had no need of the fifty gold pieces offered for her death. There were fifty or more in the mud-stained pouch he had reburied at the foot of the standing stone. Yet he had crossed Brittany to reach Rochmarin and warn a woman whom he had never met. Why had he involved himself?

No lord would take a mercenary as vassal, he had said. Was this, then, her value to him? Did he mean to keep her from sight and wed her to gain the lands of Rochmarin?

The forest was silent still, and none but Mathieu would hear should Payen turn against her. Her questions must wait until they reached the next village—better still, a town with a garrison, a lord to whom she might appeal.

"Why do you not trust me in the matter of Dinan?" he asked. "You have trusted me in all else."

"Not all," she said.

"You trust me better than any in Rochmarin. I watched you, madam, for two days before I spoke. You were nervous of the Bretons and cautious with your Norman husband's sister. And you were avoiding, I think, the company of the Norman Mauleon. Each night you scarce touched the wine at your board and fled to your bedchamber earlier each day. You barred the door and did not call for your maids, nor open the door to them from evening to dawn—''

''You saw all this?''

He shrugged. ''I saw, and heard the rest from Mathieu.''

''Of course—Mathieu.''

He stood and brushed the leaves from his chausses. ''I am no warlock, Johanna Mercat. I did not pass invisible through your chamber walls.''

If she did not accept his proffered hand, he would sense the rising fear within her. He helped her to her feet and kept her hand within his. ''I was in the stable loft,'' he said. ''Mathieu brought me through the postern gate the night after he had joined the garrison. For two days I watched the bailey yard from the loft and saw your dealings with Mauleon when he came to your gates. And by night—''

She pulled her hand from his grasp and made a show of shaking the leaves from her skirts. ''And by night?'' she prompted.

''By night, I moved between the sentry posts, dressed in Mathieu's tunic. When I came to you, it was from the battlements. By rope.''

''I saw the rope. And the blood upon the sill.''

''An old wound,'' he said.

Old wounds did not open unless they had gone rotten and the victim was close to death. The mercenary Payen could not have managed to climb Rochmarin's walls in that state.

''How old?'' she asked.

His gaze hardened. ''Do you propose to bind it, madam?''

She stepped back from the hostility in his eyes. ''I—''

''Do not trouble yourself,'' he said. ''A wool merchant's daughter would know nothing of treating wounds taken in honest combat.''

Chapter Six

The widow Malebis rode in silence the rest of that short autumn day. Three miles past the standing stones they turned from the forest onto a narrow road that took them, in a confusion of forks and returns, past the steepest of the foothills that lay north of the abbey.

Twice they passed travelers, humble folk walking slowly with no pack animals to carry their burdens. Though they had little to fear from these farmers, Payen did not risk their reports to others; he waited, each time, until the strangers were out of sight and led his party once again into the forest.

The widow Malebis made no attempt to speak with the farmers they passed and kept her face well hidden in the hood of her cloak. Payen gave silent thanks for her steadiness; she must have been anxious, even frightened by their encounter at the standing stones, but she had not wavered in her decision to trust and to travel with him.

By late afternoon her silence had begun to worry him.

They reached the river Rance before nightfall and began to

look for shelter. The lady Johanna seemed indifferent in this matter and did not demand the crowded public lodgings that would have given her opportunity to leave Payen's company and make her way to Dinan alone. Instead, she rode past three inns at his side, without visible regret.

At last they reached a sturdy bridge that spanned the narrow river between a small, silent village and the bare, wind-robbed branches of a wide orchard. Across the water a wooden mill rose from half-ruined stone foundations, nestled hard against the bridge; a waterwheel hung swaying in the sharp evening chill, its wooden chute closed to the river current. Beyond, from a small house at the edge of the orchards, came the smell of roasting meat.

Mathieu smiled. "I say we could do worse than a miller's board."

Payen saw the broad cleared space before the mill and a shuttered opening through which a sentry might watch the bridge. "It's a good place."

The widow Malebis seemed content to pass the night in the mill loft. Payen had half expected her to seek the company of other women and try to bed down with the miller's large family beside the warm, untidy hearth; he had rehearsed his refusal in his mind, seeking the words that would keep her at ease yet convince her that she dared not sleep far from his side. But those words were not needed; she seemed content to stay at his side and did not gainsay the miller's assumption that she was Payen's wife. Only later, when the lady Johanna answered with difficulty the miller's simple invitation to join him at his hearth to share the roast pig and newly harvested apples, did Payen remember that the lady had lived at Rochmarin but a short time and that she had only begun to learn the Breton tongue.

She had eaten in silence at the miller's board; only when Payen rose to his feet and thanked the miller's wife for their meal had Johanna attempted, in broken words, to bargain with the miller for one of the precious tapers he kept safe in a small box beside the hearth. The miller's woman had been worried that the dry chaff in the loft would ignite and had tried to dissuade the lady Johanna from taking the lighted taper with her. Payen had translated the woman's speech and added his own words of caution. Johanna had nodded and accepted a shallow pottery bowl into which she might set the candle to keep it from the wooden floor, but she would not give up the costly light. She had held the taper to the fire and had set it in its own melted tallow within the bowl. Holding the light before her like a warrior's shield, she had followed Payen and Mathieu across the small clearing to the mill.

As irritating as the morning's aggressive questions had been, the woman's silence was worse. They had two days' travel before them to reach the coast, and Payen intended to have the lady's account of her late lord's dealings. She might know how he had come to ambush Payen, whether it was the message from the true heir of Rochmarin that had angered the man—or simple greed. Had the young fool thought so well of his skinny sword arm that he had grown ambitious and believed that he might betray a disinherited Breton without risk to himself? Had he ever, from his first courteous message up to the day he had left for Nantes, intended to deal honestly with Payen?

The Malebis widow, though young of feature and clear of eye, seemed older in wisdom than the young fool who had wed her. Had she taken a small part in her husband's plot to kill rather than accept Payen's bribe in honor? Had she understood why her young lord had died at the whorehouse in Nantes?

Payen took the taper in its bowl from Johanna's hands and carried it for her up the loft stair.

The last harvest was two fortnights gone; the mill was idle. Below its walls the dark waters of the river were low and barely challenged the barriers that had closed the sluice gate for the season. The great wheel hung graceless in its place, moving fitfully in the cold night breezes.

Mathieu followed Payen's gaze to the widow Malebis and frowned. "I'll take the first watch," he said.

The lady Johanna raised her head and seemed about to speak but turned away before uttering a single word. Payen sighed. He would need to get her talking now, before she became accustomed to treating him with silence.

He nodded at Mathieu. "Call me when the moon is high," he said.

Mathieu picked up his sword and descended the steep wooden stair to the floor below, where the great wheel of the mill had its hub; Payen followed, and helped him carry a grain chest to barricade the door. Mathieu took up his watch at the arrow slits that those who preceded the miller had placed prudently over the river landing.

Payen climbed back to find that the woman had shifted to sit with her back against the wall, near the small square pit of the loft stair. She had taken, once again, to keeping her right arm across her waist and her hand buried within the border of her mantle, where she must have hidden her dagger. She shifted again under his scrutiny, and he heard the dull weight of coins sewn into the green hem of the mantle. The woman was carrying more silver than he might find in one of the goldsmith's shops she had spoken of and had her puny arsenal to protect it.

If she didn't sleep this night, and sickened before they reached the coast, he would have her death upon his conscience, weighing more heavily than the killing of the young lord who had been her husband. Payen cleared his throat. "If I offended you about the gold, I am sorry for it."

She looked up in surprise. "You did not offend." The taper's light upon her hair cast a soft yellow sheen upon the shining honey-darkness.

He attempted to ignore the silken tie at the end of her braid and did not imagine loosing it to free her hair. "Your advice was kindly meant. If I had the faith you do in goldsmiths, I might have considered leaving my wealth with them. But a mercenary cannot be sure he will be welcome to return to any place upon God's earth; what may be an ally's town one month may be closed to Mercadier and his army the next."

"You are Mercadier's man?"

Payen nodded. "I fight for Mercadier when the pay is good."

"And when it is not? What then?"

If she moved closer to the stair pit, she would fall and break her neck. Payen attempted to smile. "I am no assassin, madam. I earned the gold you saw in clean combat, in honest wars and skirmishes. My steel has never struck a man's back."

The callow lord Malebis had been struck once in the gut and finished with a sweeping slash across his throat. He had died, Payen believed, before the second blow had fallen.

The woman regarded him as if she could hear his thoughts. She had good nerves and was doing a fine good job of keeping her trembling hands hidden within the mantle. When the taper's flame faltered in the cold drafts, she did not flinch.

"Why did you come to Rochmarin?" she asked.

Again the question she had asked, in many less obvious ways, since Samhain night. "To warn you," Payen said.

"Why?"

Her eyes, an odd, commingled brown and green by daylight, were a rich gold in the light of the small flame sputtering within the bowl. "I do not kill women," he said. "I have told you this before, and you have good reason, madam, to believe it."

She closed her eyes briefly and nearly quelled the small note of fear in her voice. "Why did you take the trouble to ride to Rochmarin to warn me? To refuse the killing is one thing, to warn the victim another."

The lady was watching him with an intensity Payen had seen in sentries of hard-besieged fortresses. "Once asked to do the killing," Payen said, "I took care not to be blamed for your murder. The next man might have agreed to do it, but the rumors might have named me.''

Her gaze continued unblinking upon him. ''Do you not believe me?'' he said at last.

''I think you spoke the truth,'' she said. ''But there is more, is there not?''

Payen shrugged. Small wonder the watchmen of Rochmarin had loosed their arrows upon this woman. To some Bretons the lady's level stare would bespeak witchery. ''What do you mean?''

Her hand reached within the mantle. Did she intend to stab him, with Mathieu on watch a few steps below them? Did the woman realize how hard it would be to slay a man with the slight dagger she carried?

''My husband and six of his men-at-arms died at the hands of brigands,'' she said. ''I believe he was lured to Nantes and murdered. Perhaps by assassins paid to do the job.''

With effort Payen kept his face empty of emotion. ''I swear to you, madam, that I was not hired to kill your husband.''

There was silence for a time. Beyond the wall the idle waterwheel creaked as it moved in the rising breeze. ''What lured him to Nantes?'' Payen asked.

''An old debt.''

''He carried gold?''

''Not when he left. There was a debt owed to him,'' the woman said. ''An old debt to be paid at last, with gold taken from the wars in Palestine. My husband rode to Nantes with a dozen men-at-arms and took eight with him to the meeting place. Two escaped the ambush and brought the others to find him at dawn. He was dead of many wounds, and his men fallen beside him.''

Payen closed his eyes. It was as he had guessed. The bastard Malebis had never intended to give up Rochmarin. He would have returned to the land with Payen's gold and none would have doubted that it was his own wealth, a debt repaid. Malebis had never intended that Payen live past their meeting.

Payen had guessed the facts during his long, painful march to Mercadier's camp. To hear them from Malebis's widow was more painful yet.

He opened his eyes upon the lady's silent regard. The golden eyes had turned dark in the dimming flame. "And you believe I killed him," he said.

Her gaze did not waver. "I believe you and Mathieu and others were hired to kill us both. You decided to spare my life, and came to warn me, after Nantes."

"And if it were true, would the others—those who would have shared the gold with me—would they have been content to let me ride ahead, to bring you out of Rochmarin?"

She shook her head. "It is not possible that an enemy of Rochmarin would have hired an assassin for me alone, and not for my husband. It is the same matter. Someone wanted my husband dead, and my murder was to follow. It might be the debtor—the man who lured him to Nantes. Who was he, the man who bought my death? What is his name?"

Payen shook his head. "I told you. I was given no name."

She leaned forward. "It must be the same man who killed my husband, then paid you to—"

The rising breeze came stronger through the unchinked timbers of the loft. Payen moved the taper out of the draft. "Your enemy believes that you were the one who bought your husband's death, madam. That is all I know of him."

Her breath caught in one short, soft sound. "Is that what you were told?" she asked at last.

Payen nodded.

"Did you believe—"

He stretched his legs before him upon the chaff-strewn floor. "I believe little of what is said of such intrigues. Those who bring their troubles to Mercadier's assassins seldom speak the truth. Their words may be lies—saving only the name of the man—or woman—who must die." He reached for the wineskin and offered it to Johanna. "And even then the name often proves false."

She refused the wine.

Payen drank again. "I am a soldier, not an assassin," he said with deliberate clarity. "Nor have I ever harmed a woman. I came to you to save your life and to ensure that none, knowing that Mercadier had offered me the task, would blame me for your death."

"And my husband?"

Payen set his jaw. "I have said already, madam, that I was not paid to kill him. Do not speak of it again." He softened his voice. "Do you trust me to get you safe passage home? Will you cease your talk of Dinan and find a ship in another port?"

"Which port?"

Payen shrugged. "I care not. We might ride north to Aleth—"

"Then we would pass Dinan on the way. I will need to send a message to one who would help me, who would find passage for me in one of his ships. If you would take word to my uncle's friend, then I would ride with you beyond Dinan to the seacoast and wait there for the ship he will send."

It was too easy. Payen smiled. "Done. Who is the man who would help you?"

She fidgeted with the hem of her mantle; the weight of coins was evident and would deceive only the most witless of thieves. "One who buys wool from my uncle."

"Wool trade?" He frowned. "So that is how your family could afford to wed you to Malebis."

She closed her eyes and rested her head against the wall. "Walter Malebis was a costly husband, for Rochmarin needed repairs. My dowry bought them."

The walls of Rochmarin had withstood a fortnight's siege and the fast-flung stones launched by Henry Plantagenet's siege machines. When the Normans had broken through, a full quarter of the outer defenses had fallen. Those who had been in the bailey yard when the gate frame had collapsed—

She had stopped speaking. "And then?" he asked.

The widow Malebis was watching him with new caution in her gaze. Payen attempted to smile. Remembering—remembering the fall of Rochmarin—was an indulgence he must not allow himself. The woman had enough to worry her without sensing his angry past.

She raised her chin. "I must thank you—you and your man. When I embark for England, there will be gold for you."

If he did not take her gold, her suspicions would rise again and flower during her sea passage to England. Later there would be trouble. "If you have gold to spare after you buy passage, Mathieu and I will take it. And thank you for it."

"There will be twenty coins."

Payen sighed. "We have ten from the harper lad who paid Mercadier the earnest money. Do not make the sum thirty. We have no wish to bring Judas's luck upon ourselves."

She smiled then, a timid curving of her fine, delicate mouth. "You and Mathieu need not fear Judas's shadow in your dealing with me. You have saved my life and will see a second reward at God's hand at Judgment Day."

He closed his eyes. "I am no saint, madam. And my fate at Judgment Day will not be a pretty thing. Keeping you from death this day may save me from the worst of it, but my sins are great."

"You gave alms to the monks," she said.

She had seen him pass the purse to Alain. With difficulty Payen kept the anger from his voice. "I give alms from time to time," he muttered. "It will not wash the sins from my life."

He closed his eyes and turned his face from her, feigning

sleep. It was as well that the woman wished to return to England, far from Rochmarin and the ears that would twitch if rumors of a crippled monk of St. Martin's abbey with a patron's gold began to cross the land. The widow Malebis might be the death of the three of them—Payen, Alain, and the hapless Mathieu—if she began to speak of what she had seen and heard this day. He would have to keep his wits about him to duck her questions, or be faced with the need to kill her after all.

Johanna sat against the wall and let her eyes close. Last night she had slept for a brief hour in her bed of leaves under the mists, but now, in the great, echoing loft above the mill works, she would not lie sleeping beside the brigand Payen.

She feared him still, but not as an assassin. The half-raveled mystery of his motives for taking her from Rochmarin did not trouble her so much as the pain she had seen in his eyes. Pain, and a kind of desire.

Two nights before, when he had come to her chamber, fear had been thick in the air, and she had barely managed to remember his words in the shadow of her terror. Now, after a day and two nights in his company, she had ceased to fear that he would harm her and believed the small part of the truth he had so grudgingly given her.

What she feared now was the effect of the soft growl of his voice upon her reason. Her blood sang at the sound of it, and only with difficulty did she remember, at times, that she must keep the words in her mind. He spoke to her of danger. Of life and death and betrayal. And all she kept, in the center of her mind, was the rich, hinted caress in his voice.

She looked back at the sleeping figure across the loft. "Payen?"

He raised his head. "Lady?"

"How many days to Dinan?"

"Three. Maybe four. Will you sleep now?"

She sighed. "I will."

He reached for the taper and pinched the flame to kill it. For a brief moment the wick glowed. Then all was darkness.

Chapter Seven

The hopper pole fell from its rack at dawn; the clatter roused Mathieu from his sleep and brought Payen pounding up the loft ladder. Johanna woke as the last echo within the empty grain bin died, and she shrank back against the wall at the sight of Mathieu's dark face and Payen's bright steel in the dim morning light.

The muffled squeal of mice retreated to the corner behind the hopper.

''Vermin,'' growled Mathieu.

Johanna staggered to her feet and cursed the weight of coins that dragged at her hem. ''How often—'' she muttered.

''What?'' Payen's voice had thickened in angry relief.

''How often will I wake to trip over your sword?''

Mathieu sank back upon his bedroll and flung an arm across his face.

''Twice—'' Johanna said. ''Twice in three mornings I have found your sword near enough to kill me just for waking.''

Payen rammed his steel into its scabbard. "And one night of three you lived only because I drew it in your defense."

"I was well past the bonfire when—"

"Your horse was shot, madam, and your watchmen set to put an end to your life. Tell me," Payen snarled, "that my sword had no use then."

Johanna crossed her arms to still the quaking in her limbs. "And now you draw it to defend me from marauding mice? I may lose my head for sleeping too near the stair, but I'll die in the certainty that the rats won't take me."

"The rats wouldn't dare. They would fear your temper, madam. Even in death."

Mathieu raised his head and grinned. "Payen's a good hand with a sword," he said. "There are none better. He never strikes without looking first."

Johanna sat down upon her bedroll.

"Now what troubles you?" said Payen.

Mathieu crossed his arms beneath his head. "I spoke the truth, lady. With Payen, you are as safe as—"

"What troubles you?" Payen shouted. "Do you still believe I'll take your life? After near killing myself upon the walls of Rochmarin to reach you, and dragging you halfway across the duchy?"

Johanna shivered. "No," she said. "You wouldn't take my life. I'll lose it on the edge of a careless sword."

Mathieu snorted. "Now, those are killing words. Payen with a careless sword? Take them back, lady—"

Payen silenced him with a small gesture. He walked to Johanna's side and knelt upon the bedroll. A small prickle of shame heated Johanna's cheeks. It was Payen's own bedroll, given to keep her warm as he had taken his turn to keep watch.

"I live by this sword," he said. "And I have some skill. Enough to keep you alive from here to the coast. Enough to keep from harming you when I draw it. Tell me, Johanna

Mercat, why you trust me less than a clumsy young squire would deserve?''

A clumsy young squire. Blood upon the dust of the garrison yard. Skill with a sword, to be passed to the young, could kill those closest—

''Well, madam?'' Payen's voice had gentled to a whisper.

If she did not put the vision from her mind, she would show weakness. She would weep, and this man would know where her fears lay. Johanna raised her gaze to his face. ''You may be skilled with that sword,'' she said. ''And no threat to me. But if you do not let me rest until the dawn is full, I'll slit my own throat to get some sleep. Can we not leave our words for the daylight?''

Mathieu giggled and pulled his cloak over his face.

Payen did not turn away. ''Give me your hand,'' he said. And took her with him to the stair and down to the grinding floor, where the great, thick hub of the wheel hung idle and shuddering in the wind, rattling the greased kingpin within its motionless works. He pulled her to the grain door above the landing to see that the horses were still there, huddled below them, in the lee of the river pier; only then, with her hand still trapped within his own, did he speak to her again.

''You will not sleep,'' he said. ''So you may as well hear what I would have you do when we reach the coast. It will put your mind at ease, for you will know I must keep you safe.''

Johanna withdrew her hand and stepped back from the door. Now it would come, the missing piece of this man's plan, the thing he would not tell her in their speech the previous night. Did this hard-scarred mercenary believe that he might gain her dead husband's lands by wedding her? Had he heard tales of the great dowry that she had brought to Walter Malebis, and had he imagined that he could gain as much for himself, as dowry or as ransom? And once enriched by her gold, would this man prove more dangerous to her than the Rochmarin watchmen from whom he had saved her on Samhain night?

"I want you to understand," he said, "that seeing you alive and on your way to England will benefit us both. I need to have you safe—and seen to be safe—for my own sake, that I not be blamed for the death I was hired to accomplish. When we reach the coast, I will take you to a village priest or to a monastery—it matters not—and have a cleric write that he has seen you living and without duress."

"And then?"

"And then I will see you embark for England. Have you not listened?"

"You will have taken much trouble, and risked much, to accomplish what you might have done by refusing the gold Mercadier gave you to kill me. You did not need the coins—you left far more than ten gold pieces buried yesterday."

Payen began to speak, then turned from her to look again at the horses. "Nevertheless," he said at last. "I have taken the trouble, and you have your life. All I ask in return is your word to a cleric that you are Johanna Mercat, widow of Walter Malebis, safe on the coast of this duchy, and embarking for England. He will write it, then, and keep the document."

"Against the day you might be accused of my death."

He nodded.

"And the cleric will not, once he has written that paper, offer to wed us, so that you might return to claim Rochmarin?"

In his gaze there was an intensity that could kill. "The king and his lords do not take mercenaries as vassals, madam. Even a wool seller's daughter should know that."

With effort Johanna managed not to shrink back from his dark regard and the insult in his words. In her brief months at Rochmarin she had heard enough slurs upon her uncle's trade to harden her to a common mercenary's disdain. "This wool seller's kinswoman knows of mercenaries. We hired men such as you to guard the cargo on my uncle's ships and to bring the gold back safe from Brittany, and from Flanders. My uncle kept them as far from me as he could, and told me never to trust their loyalty unless I had promised them enough gold to buy their swords and had enough wealth to make good the promise.'' She paused, and drew a quick breath into the sudden ache in her chest. Harald—young Harald had not heeded their uncle's words. He had admired the swords, mimicked the mercenaries' rough speech, and heard their tales of war and booty. And came to crave a life outside the wool sheds and counting house.

The man called Payen was speaking again. ''So your uncle had the right of it. And did he tell you that once sworn to a task, even a half-trained soldier would have the wit not to abuse the one who will pay him?''

Johanna turned her gaze to the dawn's light, away from the shadows in which Harald's bloodied face still floated. ''No. He did not.''

''Then he must have lived in fear of us all. And taught you to turn foolish green at the sight of a drawn sword. I have seen a ten-year-old princess of the realm less disturbed than you by the sight of weapons; even a child knows when a sword is meant to protect her.''

Johanna turned back to the ladder. ''I'll fetch your bedroll.''

''Mathieu will bring it.'' He moved to her side and placed his hand upon her arm. ''If there is trouble on the road—if we need to fight—do not run from me unless I bid you go. You might blunder toward danger and meet your death.''

''I am not a fool. I will not run.''

Johanna turned back to the stair; Payen's hand slipped from her arm, and he let her go in silence.

The loft was still, and Mathieu was once more asleep. Johanna knelt beside the thick woolen bedroll and began to fold it. Her strange protector still had not told her why he had come to Rochmarin to save her. A skilled mercenary had his choice of masters, his pick of tasks; why, then, had the man Payen taken her death gold? And having taken it, why had he decided to ride across Brittany to spare a woman he did not know, to whom he owed no loyalty?

She had pushed him as hard as she dared, but he had not answered. To be honest, she feared she would not like the truth when it came.

They followed the river to the hills above Dinan, where the narrow waters of the Rance began to flow wider, flooded with streams from the valley's walls, and fell steeply into a deep estuary that could carry a heavy ship north to the sea.

They found an open meadow beside an orchard and made a crude shelter from the twisted, wind-torn branches of the ancient trees. As Payen and Mathieu worked, Johanna found the last harvest of pinched, fallen apples and gathered a skirtful within her badly soiled kirtle.

The wind was colder upon the valley's frost-browned walls; the distant fires and torches shining from the town of Dinan shone crimson in the falling night.

They were far enough from Rochmarin, and from any who had seen their progress to the coast, to risk a fire. Before the night shadows had reached their hilltop, Mathieu had coaxed a spark from his dagger upon a rough stone and nursed the young flame with dried apple leaves and grass. When the fire burned strong, Payen came up the slope with a brace of fat quail and set to gutting and plucking the birds.

"How did you catch them?"

Payen grinned and took a withered apple from Johanna's skirts. "I slew them with the edge of my broadsword quite by accident as I was hobbling the horses," he said. "There's some use in having a clumsy swordsman traveling with you."

Johanna flushed. Their quarrel at the mill had mellowed into rough teasing, then to gentle banter. "Tell me," she insisted, "how you caught them so quickly."

"Temptation," he said, and pulled a handful of dried grain

from his money pouch. "Temptation and a swift hand to my bow."

"You are an archer as well?"

He shook his head. "I am often hungry, and for that I need a small bow. My skill, though you doubt it, is with my sword."

He spitted the birds and set them to roast above Mathieu's applewood blaze. "You will be safe up here, though cold. I will leave you my bedroll and cloak."

Johanna felt the cold breeze return to her shoulders. "You will not stay the night?"

Payen frowned. "There is still a moon—almost a full moon—to light my way to Dinan, and the road looks wide and well traveled. I'll start down after we eat and find your uncle's trader at dawn."

"Do you remember—"

"Yes," he said. "The timber house built upon the stub of the old keep, beside the riverbanks, close upon the churchyard."

"His name—"

"—is Guy. A white-haired ancient. Will you give me the password, Johanna?"

"I don't know it."

"Your uncle sent you to be wed in Brittany and he did not give you the password he used for business with his trader in Dinan?"

Johanna looked up at the sky. "The clouds will cover the moon, Payen. Could you not wait until dawn?"

"Why?" he persisted. "Will you trust me better at dawn?"

Johanna sighed. The man would not leave her in peace until he understood. It was a reasonable demand; Payen could not risk offending an important citizen of Dinan or rouse suspicions that he came unbidden to tap the Mercat wealth through their trading partners. By now the news of Johanna's disappearance might have reached Dinan, and old Guy would be wary of a man claiming to bring her greetings.

The shadows of the night advanced from the valley below

to the hilltop camp; only the cooking fire illuminated the wide meadow and touched the crude shelter built at the edge of the orchard.

"It was not a simple thing, my marriage to Malebis."

"You said your dowry was large. Was it paid through your uncle's partner in Dinan?"

"No, I brought it from Yorkshire. Guy had nothing to do with it."

"And your uncle did not wish to have your husband put his hand in Guy of Dinan's moneybox to divert the gold owed to Yorkshire into Rochmarin's treasury."

Johanna stiffened in alarm. The man she called Payen was no simple soldier. At times he displayed cynicism equal to her uncle's darkest moments. "That is possible," she said slowly. "It made no difference, for my dowry was large, and paid at once. In full. Walter Malebis had no need—"

"No right," Payen muttered.

"No need," Johanna insisted, "to ask for more. I doubt that he even knew of the trading with Dinan. He was not one to notice such things."

"Tell me something of your uncle, then. Something to convince this Guy of Dinan that I come on your behalf."

"Loki's Horn."

"What is *Loki's Horn?* An alehouse?"

"Just speak the word and say that you come from Johanna Mercat's side to ask for help."

"For all I know, it is your uncle's code for his partners to seize the man who utters the word and charge him with abduction."

Johanna smiled. "Then you will have to trust me, will you not? It is no less than you asked of me that night you came to Rochmarin."

He gave the spit a slow turn and lay back upon his cloak. "I came to you in generosity, with an offer of help."

''I have offered you gold.'' Johanna selected an apple and held it to the firelight. ''And that gold may be found in Dinan.''

Payen sat up and reached for the wineskin. ''Some gold may be found in the hems of your mantle, and in your cloak.''

Johanna's next words died upon her lips.

''When I carried you across the broken footbridge, when your horse balked in the storm at the ford of Cagarun, I felt the weight of coins against my legs. That, and the sound of your cloak upon the miller's wooden floor, told me all I needed to find your gold, Johanna.''

She felt her face redden in the firelight. ''It is silver,'' she said. ''And not enough to buy passage to England.''

Payen raised his brows. ''Would you care to show me?''

''And ruin my work hiding the coins?''

He shrugged. ''You wouldn't send me into Dinan without cause. I'll not ask you to prove your words.''

Shame was becoming a daily event in Johanna's dealings with the man called Payen. She drew the bezeled ring from her small finger. ''Here,'' she said. ''Show this to Guy of Dinan, and bid him help me in the memory of *Loki's Horn.*''

''An old god's drinking cup?''

Johanna smiled and accepted the wineskin. ''A ship. The ship that made traders of my father and his brother, my uncle.''

''Ah.'' Payen held the ring in his palm. ''The first of their fleet?''

She drank of the wine and managed not to spill it upon her cloak. In her years as a girl, and her months as Rochmarin's lady, she had not learned to drink from a wineskin. These past gypsy days had taught her much that her late husband would disdain. ''*Loki's Horn* was the first of their fleet. The ship was what brought them to begin to sell wool. There were raiders upon the Yorkshire coast when I was a child. Raiders from Jutland, in the north. They came to Gunndale many times in my grandfather's time, but the brigands who came in *Loki's Horn* never made it ashore to burn my father's barns.''

"Ah. So you did have one or two men about your farm who knew which end of a sword to grip."

She shook her head. "Not a one. Not one of them knew more than how to fling a hayfork at invaders before they ran into the hills. The raiders who came on *Loki's Horn* died in the sea when the ship hit the rocks offshore. For two days the ship lay wrecked within sight of land, her crew drowned in the surf. Then it broke free and drifted down the shore. My father and his brother followed it and claimed the wreck when it grounded a league from Gunndale. They promised half a summer's wool to the shipwright who repaired the ship and paid the other half to the Whitby men who sailed her to Flanders."

Payen frowned. "And the cargo? They had given away their wool for the year."

Johanna made an impatient gesture. "Their fellow farmers' wool was the cargo. They made a small profit that summer and more the next year. They bought a second ship and began to trade with Dinan."

"And when you were of an age, they bought you a Breton lord to make you noble."

She faltered. "Yes. They did."

Payen took the wineskin from her hands. "I marvel, madam, that they persuaded you to cross the sea and give your gold to a foreign lord. One whom you do not mourn, as I see it."

"I mourned him."

"For a few days."

"Do you think I wanted him dead? Do you return to the rumors brought by the harper who paid you to kill the wicked widow Malebis?"

Payen sighed. "I have not the valor to return to that subject, madam. I meant to say that I cannot imagine your uncle, however fierce he may be, compelling you to wed where you did not wish. Why did you come to Brittany, to Rochmarin?"

To oblige her beloved, foolish Harald, her brother, who wished to be a knight. To bring Harald to Rochmarin, to learn chivalry from his new marriage brother, Walter of Malebis. To bring Harald to Rochmarin's garrison yard, to lose his young life in the careless sweep of a broadsword in the hands of a drunken sot. To find, when three months a bride, that she was alone at Rochmarin with only her fool of a husband and his timid sister Agnes to understand her words, alone among the Breton folk who disliked their Malebis lords and disdained their awkward Yorkshire lady.

"I wanted my husband. I wed him freely, without duress." *And the sheep of Yorkshire would, one day, mate with gulls and learn to fly.*

A small smile twitched at the corners of Payen's mouth. As if he had heard her thoughts. As if—"

Johanna tensed. "Did you know my husband, sir?"

"No."

His voice had lost the warm, teasing tone she had come to recognize when he was at ease. The night became colder.

Payen stood and sought his saddlebags beside Mathieu's sleeping form. He nudged the bedroll with his boot and called to Mathieu to awaken.

"You will leave before these birds are roasted?"

He shrugged. "I'll take a piece and be on my way. I'll keep your ring safe, madam, and bring it to you tomorrow. Mathieu," he said, "keep watch tonight, and see the lady safe to the dawn."

He walked down the meadow to catch his horse and gave Johanna not another glance. Nor a word.

Chapter Eight

Old Guy of Dinan did not share his Mercat partner's reluctance to keep mercenaries to guard his wealth. Before dawn Payen had found them.

He had come to the odd timber house perched upon the base of a ruined tower and left Arsuf saddled and tied behind the lane. Then he settled beneath the overhang of a storage hut down the road to watch for the first sign of movement in the trading house. The old man's watchmen had proved they were as vigilant as they had been subtle, and came out to seize him before the morning light filled the narrow road.

Payen allowed the trader's men to bring him, unarmed but unbound, into Guy of Dinan's hall beside the quays.

Without a word Payen presented Johanna's bezeled ring to the old man. He waited in silence as the merchant dismissed his guards and closed the door behind them. With a finger to his lips Guy of Dinan brought Payen from the hall into his counting room, a small chamber lined with ledgers, hung with saddlebags, with a tall set of shelves to hold a number of small strongboxes.

"Where is she?" Guy whispered.

"Not far. And eager to find passage back to England."

The old man frowned. "I heard she was dead."

"She's alive, and begs your help—the name of a good ship carrying your goods and no passengers save Johanna, and gold to pay the master."

"I must see her first. Bring her here—"

"She would not be safe. There is a death mark upon her, bought by a nameless man from Mercadier. I cannot bring her here."

"Then take me to her—"

"And be followed? No, sir. You must agree."

"Then take some of my men to bring her here."

"Do you trust them? All of them? Is there no one here in the house who is new, still a stranger to you? Would you trust all in your house with Johanna Mercat's life?"

"I'll not give you gold until I know that you did not cut this ring from Johanna Mercat's finger. Alive or dead."

"Then help me in the name of *Loki's Horn.*"

The old man's features began to relax. "The name of a tavern, young man?"

"The name of the Mercat ship that made merchants of farmers."

Guy of Dinan was already crouched upon his knees, pulling a chest from the lowest shelf on the small chamber. "They have been here already," he said. "To tell me that Johanna was almost certainly dead, asking that I give the Malebises any gold owing to Johanna's uncle Mercat to buy mercenaries to search for her killers. I turned them away not two days ago."

Payen drew a long breath. "Walter Malebis is dead. Who came on his behalf?"

The old man placed a pouch of gold in Payen's hand and closed it over the coins and Johanna's ring. "His sister. Young rabbit of a girl, scared of her own shadow. Came with her betrothed husband, Adam Mauleon, whose lands border Rochmarin. Now, listen. My own cog, the *Broceliand,* will leave Dinan in two days and stop at Aleth to take on cargo before sailing across to England, up the north coast to Whitby. If the lady Johanna waits for it at Aleth, none will know she's there until she's safe at sea."

"Done." Payen hesitated at the door. "You were prepared?"

"Since Johanna Mercat first wed that young lordling Malebis. And when her young brother died, I expected her, but she did not come—"

"A brother died?"

Guy of Dinan shook his head. "In the garrison yard, training in the use of weapons. A sad accident, only days after he had begun to learn. The lady Johanna was overwhelmed with guilt."

"For sending him to be trained?"

"For making it possible. I doubt, sir, that she would have wed young Malebis had her brother not had visions of arms and glory before his eyes. In return for Johanna's dowry of Mercat gold, Walter Malebis was to take her brother into his household and train him for knighthood."

The old man shook his head and walked with Payen past the serving maid in the hall. "Will you break your fast with me?"

"I cannot. Johanna is waiting."

Guy of Dinan sighed. "Better she had stayed in Yorkshire and married a merchant. Or a sheep farmer. Anyone but that spendthrift fool Malebis. I wish her safe journey. Tell her that."

The old man's household had hidden Arsuf in their own stables and given him a measure of oats, but none had dared to come near enough to take the harness from his back. "When the widow Malebis is safe at sea," Payen muttered into one fine silken ear, "we will both have a day or two free of the saddle."

He rode unchallenged from the riverside back up the steep track to the valley headlands, to the high, desolate meadow where Mathieu watched over Johanna Mercat.

The woman had not told him of her brother killed within Rochmarin's bailey walls. From what the old man had said, the lad had not survived more than a few days of Walter Malebis's care. It was small wonder that Malebis' widow did not seem much grieved to have lost her husband, when she had suffered a greater loss, of blood kin, earlier in the season.

Payen shook his head at the thought of the stripling Malebis taking any lad, even the most callow, into his tutelage in arms. Though he had a few able men in his household—two of them had been handy with a sword, and damned hard to kill during that bloody ambush in Nantes—Malebis himself had been awkward with his foolishly jeweled weapon. No wonder his widow thought all swords a menace to her.

The old lord Malebis had, for all his sins, been a crafty and seasoned warrior. And for his sins he had begotten an heir with none of his sire's strength. Some of the cleverness had passed on into the son, but not enough to keep the fool from allowing greed to lead him into a conflict for which he had lacked the skill to survive.

Less than a mile from the orchard camp Payen guided his mount from the road across a stubbled barley field to a stand of beech lining a small tributary of the swelling Rance. He tied Arsuf to a sapling oak and moved to the edge of the copse to watch the road. Guy of Dinan had seemed a cautious, trustworthy man, but Payen had learned through long years of hard living that appearances and first meetings often deceived the unwary. And even though the old man might wish Johanna Mercat well, his household was large, and the younger servants might be in the pay of rivals of old Guy—and of his Mercat trading partners. The richer the merchant, the thicker the spies in his kitchens.

There was no movement upon the hillside track, nor sign of passage. Only the crows, seeking the last of the spilled harvest grain, gave a hint of life to the land.

Payen waited a moment more, then returned to fetch Arsuf. He rode back across the field, disturbing the angry crows, sending flocks of brown sparrows to follow. The old man's account of the Mercat lad's death continued to disturb Payen's thoughts. Had Walter Malebis's shallow store of cleverness led him to carelessness with the life of his wife's young brother? Had Malebis sought to win more, or all of the Mercat merchants' gold by killing one whose portion would then fall to Johanna? And had one of his fellow Norman lords—Adam Mauleon, or another as ruthless—decided, at Malebis's death, to see his widow die in order to seize Rochmarin?

Payen gave Arsuf his head and allowed him to canter on the higher slopes at the narrow head of the valley. The gelding had been impatient, keeping to a walk for the days they had traveled with Johanna Mercat and the palfrey bought from St. Martin's abbey. "Only two more days," Payen spoke aloud. "Then you and I, Arsuf, will have done with the slow pace of women and their baggage."

As he spoke, he heard the foolishness of his words. Johanna Mercat carried no baggage save the silver sewn into her hems. The woman was not as much trouble as she might have been.

In the distance, above him on the hillside, Payen saw the pale smoke of Mathieu's campfire beside the untended orchard. The tension in his spine relaxed: If Mathieu had fed the flames, all must be well at the hillside camp.

"Watching the track will do no good," Mathieu said. "Payen is too smart to follow the road when he fears your enemies may follow him back to you. He'll be riding behind the fields and go back to the road only to see whether he had pursuit.''

Johanna nodded and turned back to the view of Dinan's deep valley. As nervous as the man called Payen had kept her these past four days, he had made her more frightened by his absence. Last night, huddled within the rude apple-branch shelter, with only the solid bulk of Mathieu's shoulders between her and the creatures who stared with bright eyes from the darkness beyond them, Johanna had come to know how much she had depended upon Payen's cold, far-seeing eyes and his war-hardened body to keep her from the perils of their travels. For as much as he frightened her by his quick, unsleeping responses to the sounds of the night, she trusted him to strike in her defense.

Mathieu pulled an untidy cloth-wrapped cheese from his saddlebag and began to pare the greening rind. ''One time, Payen deceived Saladin himself with his back-tracking games.'' He paused to sniff the pale golden heart of the cheese and smiled. ''It took nerve, what he did, for had the Saracens turned back when they lost Payen's trail, they would have found him, and he would have had a dozen knives at his throat. He would not have lived to bring us across the duchy, living rude and eating near-rotten cheese.''

Johanna took the bundle from Mathieu and began to slice away the mold. ''It's not bad cheese. Any kitchen maid knows that summer cheese goes green in the rind by early winter.'' She paused and tried to keep her voice level. ''Payen fought Saladin in Palestine?''

Mathieu shrugged. ''He did some fighting and spied as well. With his dark looks he near passed as a Saracen, if he didn't talk. He was working on the heathen speech and had nearly learned it when Ascalon fell, and King Richard brought us out of Palestine.''

Johanna kept her eyes upon the cheese. ''He was King Richard's spy?''

Mathieu chuckled. "That would be too simple for Payen. No, he fought for the Templars, and spied for them whenever the fighting ceased."

She dropped the knife upon the dry grass and offered the cheese, neatly sliced and cleaned, to Mathieu. "Payen is a Templar?"

Mathieu choked upon a half-swallowed mouthful of apple. "Payen a Templar? I think not! The Templars are a stiff-necked lot and won't take any but knights with names to them, good names. No, lady. Payen fought for the Templars for gold and was better off for his low station than many sworn to their order. For he could leave when the fighting was done and take his gold home when he pleased. They paid well, the Templars did. They hired only the best and had plenty of gold to tempt them to stay."

So that was the source of the coins Payen had hidden throughout the duchy. Heavy Templar gold, earned in combat and deceit. Johanna shivered. "So he came home with his wealth and hired himself to Mercadier? Why did he not buy land and take his ease? Surely there are few lords so dainty they will not accept a former mercenary as a vassal." She pointed to the wind-fallen apples below the tangled, untended limbs of the orchard. "Look there. The lord of these lands has no vassal to set men to tend this orchard. I have seen many fallow fields and ruined manors between here and Rochmarin. Payen could find a lord willing to accept his service in return for land, and he has the wealth to arrange it."

A shadow passed over Mathieu's features. He rose to his feet and began to prod the fire. "He didn't care to. Many do not."

Their speech had ended with those words, and Mathieu continued silenty, as if he had wedged an iron-bound door shut between them. Johanna resumed her watch over the valley track and saw, at the edge of her vision, Mathieu's flushed face beside the small campfire. The man looked guilty. Did Mathieu live in such fear of Payen's displeasure that he regretted his brief recital of the man's past?

A whistle, brief birdsong from the tangled depths of the orchard, announced Payen's return. Johanna looked from Payen back down to the valley road. "I never saw you. How do you manage that?"

"Years of practice," he said. His smile was broad and carefree, his features happier than Johanna had seen them. He pulled a loaf of bread from his saddlebags and tossed it to Mathieu. "We had good fortune this day. All of us. No one followed me from Dinan, there's bread and cheese from a farm at the edge of town, and you, my lady, have a place on Guy of Dinan's sailing cog—safe passage to England from Aleth, two days from now."

These were welcome tidings. Johanna had expected to feel more than a dull, shifting ache within her breast.

Payen was smiling still. "Well, Johanna? Did I not tell you we would find a way to get you home?"

She formed her mouth into a smile. "I thank you, Payen. And Mathieu." Johanna looked beyond Payen's wide shoulders to the orchard, and back down to the distant town of Dinan, and to the green river that flowed to the sea. The smoke of the hard applewood was fragrant upon the cold November wind, and she longed to return to the bedroll within the small, dry shelter Payen had built for her.

"Will we sleep here?" she asked.

Payen laughed. "Have you found a taste for a gypsy's life? No, Johanna, we'll ride around Dinan and go up the river closer to Aleth while the weather is still fine. There are shipyards down the river—and shelter for those who have crossed the sea. We will sleep under a roof this night, God willing."

Johanna cast a last look at the campfire.

"Let it burn down while we eat," Payen said. "And I will tell you of your old friend Guy."

"He believed you?"

Payen sat beside the dying fire and opened his money pouch; upon his outstretched palm Johanna found her ring. "Your jewel was helpful but not enough to make the old man trust me. It was good that you gave me the name of the *Loki's Horn,* for it sweetened his manner and opened his strongboxes. I have gold for you, Johanna. Enough to take you home twice over."

Much as Johanna had disliked Payen's brooding caution in the tense, early days of their journey, she found his present good spirits as irritating as salt in an open wound.

"I will give you the part I do not need, then," she said. "In that way, you will not need to wait to make your celebrations that your task is done. Besides," she continued with curiously benumbed speech, "I do not know how I would have sent the gold to you from Whitby. A mercenary, after all, must go where he pleases, and leaves no trail for his masters to follow."

There was silence from the other side of the fire.

Mathieu cleared his throat. "You know, my lady, that we work for Mercadier from time to time. If you ever needed to send to us, you could tell your messenger to find the camp of Mercadier—the old queen Eleanor, King Richard's mother, always knows where Mercadier has moved."

"A wool seller's daughter in Yorkshire would find Queen Eleanor more elusive than your friend Mercadier," Johanna said. "I could send word to the jester in the moon more easily."

"Then we will have your gold, and drink your health, and say our farewells before we reach Aleth," Payen said. "And should I discover, one day, the name of the man who sent your death gold to Mercadier, I will find a scribe to write his name and send it to you, to the Mercat yard in Whitby."

"If you do," she said, "I will send you more gold. Have the scribe tell me how to send it to you."

Payen shrugged. "It would be hard to predict, as you have said. I'll send word to you nonetheless, and freely. You may keep your gold."

They ate in silence. Mathieu lay back and closed his eyes.

Payen sat unmoving and glanced up at her from time to time with curiosity plain in his gaze.

Johanna ignored them both and did not look back at the orchard. The day had become, of a sudden, much colder.

Chapter Nine

They did not reach Aleth that day, nor did Payen wish to press on to the coast. A short mile from the harbor, near enough to taste the salt in the strong sea winds, they halted at an inn well used to traveling merchants and noble folk returning from sea voyages to foreign lands. There were bedchambers in the place, with fine pallets that a man with gold would not be forced to share with strangers. Payen paid three silver coins for two such chambers on the warm, noisy floor above the common hall and gave the innkeeper to believe that Johanna was his wife. By nightfall word had spread among the merchants and drunkards in the hall that the lady with the soiled kirtle of a wanton and the stern features of a northern queen was wed to the hard-eyed mercenary and would be approached on peril of a man's life.

From the chamber window Johanna watched Payen lead their mounts across the inn yard into the great stable and saw him stop to speak with a serving maid, a woman with raven-black hair as dark as Payen's own. Johanna watched them together until her eyes became reddened in the sharp wind rising from the distant sea; she hesitated, and held the shutters open to see Payen touch the woman's shoulder and smile down upon her glossy head.

He pointed to the chamber window and smiled again.

Johanna drew a long breath and blinked her salt-stung eyes. There was no need for Payen to spend the night without a woman to warm his bed. As was his custom, he would spend half the night in wakefulness and sleep only when Mathieu awoke to guard their small party. There were more than enough hours in half a night to—

Johanna slammed the shutters closed and looked down at her mud-spattered kirtle and the wide, damp stain that rose from the hem of her cloak. In touching her hair, the inevitable leaf came to her hand, and she loosed her braid to shake the dust of the road from her unremarkable brown tresses. At home at Gunndale, before she crossed the sea to this dark, foreboding land, she had gathered herbs each fall, and used them when she bathed, and kept her hair as shining as—

As shining clean as the braids of the woman in the inn yard.

A second despairing pass of Johanna's hands through her hair yielded two more leaves and a small twig—a bit of an apple tree, snared in her braid as she had gathered the bittering, windfallen fruit beneath the dying trees above Dinan.

Johanna broke the dead twig and crushed the fragments to dust and splinters.

For the first time since her husband had died, and for the first time in her life, she considered that she might be barren.

She bit her knuckles to take the pain from her chest and breathed deeply to rid herself of the sorrow. It was foolishness—nothing but weak, puling foolishness—for a widow to think of the children she would never bear. She had never heeded Walter Malebis's implication that she was robbing him of the heir he desired of her body; when she thought of his complaints at all, she had imagined what a Malebis child might have become, and a brittle indifference settled within her mind.

Why now, with freedom so near at hand, did she think, at last, that a child—even a child of Walter Malebis's—would have been a blessing?

She was young. She might wed again. Any one of the Whitby lads who had apprenticed to her uncle over the years would make a decent husband, one who would understand how to help her sell wool when her uncle entered his dotage. And at Gunndale there were freemen, skilled herdsmen and farmers, who would think it an honor to wed a Mercat woman.

If she had the sense of a young hen, she would save her broodings for home, when she could turn her mind to the future in the safety of Gunndale, or within the busy confusion of Whitby.

From the passageway came the sound of footsteps and a trace of a serving maid's foolish giggle. There was a quiet rapping upon her door.

Johanna set her jaw. If Payen wished to tumble the serving maid, he would not compel her to lend her own chamber for his sport. It was Mercat gold that had paid for the two chambers, and she would

The door opened, and Payen frowned from the framing post. "You should have barred the door," he said.

"No one has troubled me," she said. "Until now."

He stood aside and gestured for the maid to enter. "This is Ursula," he said.

Johanna became aware that she was still in her muddy cloak, and her unbound hair was not yet free of dust. She crushed the remains of the apple twig into her fist and thrust it beneath the sodden cloth.

The maid smiled and made a timid gesture toward Johanna.

Johanna rose to her feet. "This is my chamber, Payen."

"Of course. I'll leave Ursula with you; she has agreed to sell us her dowry clothes for a purse of silver."

"They're not as fine as yours," the maid said, "but they're clean. My lady," she added in haste.

Johanna sat down and placed her hands upon oddly quaking knees. "I thank you," she said.

"It's your silver," Payen answered. He turned to leave but paused after the first step. "Are you ill?"

Johanna shook her head. "Thank you," she repeated. And dropped her gaze to the dark, sodden line of her hem upon the planked floor. She would need to keep the cloak, and the kirtle as well, for there was too much silver within the damp hems to pluck free in the waning light. Johanna raised her face and smiled at the nervous maid with the splendid raven hair.

"There is more silver for you—two pieces," Johanna said, "if you will find a bathing barrel and fill it for me. And an extra coin, as well, if you would find me herbs to clean my hair."

"There's just what I use in the washhouse—" the girl began.

"That will do," Johanna said. "Yes, that will do very well."

Beyond the door came the sound of more footsteps and Payen's voice speaking of sentry hours with Mathieu. The ache in Johanna's chest became a warm, radiating joy. A sudden joy, with no cause to it, as far as she could imagine.

Payen would not permit her to eat in the common hall, for there were many travelers under the innkeeper's roof; if any had come from the parish of St. Martin, they might recognize the lady of Rochmarin and spread word of her presence before she was safely at sea. Instead, Payen sent Mathieu to eat in the hall, to see the faces of the others who would sleep in the inn, and to hear the gossip at the board and, if possible, in the kitchens.

The maid Ursula, content with enough silver to buy clothes more splendid than the ones she had brought to Johanna, and proud of the transformation in appearance and manner that she had brought about for the sad, tired lady she had found in the inn's best chamber this day, had taken a platter of roasted meat and bread to Johanna's chamber an hour after nightfall. She had tarried a moment to admire the lady's newly washed hair and to braid it afresh before Johanna sat down at the small hearthside table to eat her first unhurried meal in days.

The maid disappeared as quickly as she had come; Johanna set the chamber bar in place and turned back to her table. There was enough meat heaped upon the platter to feed a small army; the kitchen maids must have imagined Johanna was as starved as she had been filthy from her journey.

"I brought wine," came a familiar voice through the barred oaken panels. "Will you open the door?"

She allowed herself the space of two long breaths to smooth the foolish smile from her face.

Payen stood silent as Johanna stepped back from the doorframe and looked beyond her to the small table. "They believe we are man and wife," he said at last. "There would be no harm in making the tale appear truthful"—he moved past her and set an earthen jug beside the hearth—"as far as sharing our board."

"No harm," Johanna answered, and wished she could find words to fill the silence that had bloomed between them.

Payen walked back to the doorway and returned with a small bench from his own chamber. He set it beside the table, a good distance from the edge, and sat upon it, an arm's length from Johanna.

"The innkeeper has good wine," Payen said, "brought from the south by sea to Aleth."

Johanna accepted a low cup from Payen's outstretched hand, taking care not to touch the strong brown fingers that held it. She raised the drinking bowl to her lips and smelled the richness of the wine; her thoughts drifted, of a sudden, to the way the sun had shone upon Payen's dark hair when he had come back to fetch her in the meadow above Dinan.

''Your hair—'' he said.

She stiffened in dismay. Had she spoken aloud, and all unwitting, had she told him her thoughts?

''Your hair is the color of honey.''

Johanna touched her ribboned braid and frowned. ''My hair is too dark to be—''

''The honey of Palestine is as dark but shines gold in the firelight.''

Johanna set her cup beside the platter and stilled the small tremors upon the bloodred wine. ''When we began this journey, you said my hair was as brown as the bark of a tree.''

Payen shrugged and set his cup beside hers, to touch it. ''A young tree bathed in honey.''

The fire blazed as warm as a summer day. Johanna shifted uneasily within her newly bought kirtle and wished she dared unlace it to cool her skin.

''Southern wine is strong,'' Payen said. ''You must drink it slowly at first.''

''My uncle has such wine,'' she said. ''He trades some wool for wine each year and sells it from Whitby over each winter.'' And he had warned his niece, when she was of an age to drink unwatered wine, that she should stay clear of the costly, seductive drink of the south lest she lost her wits and her virginity in the bargain. Her wits she had kept, and she had lost her virginity in the sweat-soaked bed of a husband with the raw appetites of youth and the skill of a blacksmith set to wrest a song from a harp. In the months she had passed as Malebis's bride she had wished many times for her uncle Mercat's southern wine to bring her through the nights at Rochmarin. And now, a widow with no need to warm her blood, Johanna had a great ewer of that wine upon the hearth, and a man to pour it into her cup.

Payen was speaking of her uncle Mercat. ''And he might sell it at twice the price to those who believe the tales of its powers.''

Johanna raised a deliberate, questioning brow. "What tales?" she asked. She would not be led to admit that her thoughts had reached that far.

Payen made a dismissive gesture. "When I was in London at Lammastide, the wine merchants were selling tuns of this Provencal wine as a potion for lovers—to provoke lust, and to make it more intense."

Once again Johanna set her drinking cup back upon the table. "Why have you have brought it here to me?"

He grinned. "There is no other in the inn. It is wine like any other, of better savor than some; but it has no magical properties to inflame the senses. The tales arose," Payen said, "from the songs of the trouvères and the richness of life in the south. The men of Provence court their women with delicacy and song, and will do so for all time, whether they drink this wine or the waters of the Rance."

The heat of the fire had bloomed of a sudden across the chamber and touched Johanna's face with crimson splendor. She raised the cup to her mouth and drank deep of the wine.

Payen's broad smile had returned. He tore bread from the golden loaf and offered it to Johanna. "The wines of the south," he said, "are best drunk with food."

She took the bread from his hand and held it. "You are not a man of Provence," she said.

"I am a Breton, as I have said. But I lived in the south for a time."

"Fighting?"

"Not there. I would not have the will to bring those cities low. When there is war in Philip Augustus's southern lands, I take my sword elsewhere."

"But you would kill for gold in the north, and in England?"

He shrugged, undisturbed by Johanna's barbed question. "If the cause was not repugnant to me."

"If you have always chosen your causes, and refused to fight where you have seen fault in the cause, then how did you come to have so much gold?''

His eyes focused in sudden intensity upon her face. Johanna had forgotten, in the warmth of the fire and the heat of the wine, that the man across her table was a predator among men and not to be provoked by foolish attempts to win his secrets.

''You do not know,'' he said with deliberate calm, ''how much gold I possess. I am a soldier, lady, who has sold his steel in many places and chosen not to draw it in others. There are many such men in Mercadier's camp; we are not ungoverned animals to be loosed upon any prey that crosses our path.''

''Mercadier's reputation is other.''

''Your knowledge of two of Mercadier's men is, I trust, as I have said.'' Payen reached with slow precision to bring Johanna's loose braid to rest upon the laces of her kirtle. ''If I were an ungoverned beast, Johanna Mercat, you would not be sitting as you do now, with the table to keep me from you, and your bed standing cold within this chamber.''

She held herself unmoving beneath the warmth of his hand. ''The tales of the wine hold truth, then.''

Payen's mouth curved in a lazy smile. He took his hand from her hair and sat back.

The delicacy of his gesture sent a shock of longing through Johanna's body.

''One does not find lust in wine,'' he said. ''One finds truth.'' He looked across the chamber to the smooth, undisturbed pallet and raised a regretful brow. ''I bid you good night, Johanna Mercat.''

''You have not eaten,'' she said, and wondered at the quick, heedless words that had come from her mouth.

''I will find all I need in the hall, when Mathieu has eaten—when he takes up his post outside this door. There will be one of us out there all night, my lady. You should sleep well, for you are safe.''

She rose and gave him her thanks, and they spoke no more

of wine and lust and prey. When Payen had closed the door, and Johanna had barred it upon the night, she shut her eyes and imagined how it would have been if he had tarried longer.

He had left her alone with nothing but his words to warm her. His words alone would keep her wakeful this night.

If she had been any other woman, the widow of any man but Walter Malebis, Payen would have asked her to take him, for a night, into her bed. Would have won from her, in the long hours of darkness, her willingness to join with him in white-hot glory he knew they would find.

There had been a moment, that last moment in which he had found the will to leave her hearth, when Johanna Mercat had been willing. He had seen the color rising from the laces of her kirtle to cast crimson upon her fine neck; he had watched the shades of curiosity darken to imagining in her eyes. He had left her, then, before he had brought them both to folly.

He stood in silence outside her door and knew that she had not moved from it. Only a thickness of oaken planks was between them—that, and the bloody ghosts of Rochmarin.

Payen closed his eyes and conjured, once again, a vision of Walter Malebis's corpse upon the brothel floor. That ghost, of all the slain people of Rochmarin, would alone bring death to the fire Payen had seen in Johanna's eyes. And the others—a generation of Rochmarin warriors, slain in treachery by the old lord Malebis—would cry out in Payen's dreams to bring him from the widow Johanna's bed.

From the trembling of her hand upon the door, Payen knew that Johanna Mercat had watched his leaving with as much relief as regret. Why, then, did he stand outside her chamber like a lovesick youth, unable to walk away from the woman he must not touch?

The maid Ursula was willing, and had said as much when she had accepted the Dinan silver from his hand. Payen turned his back upon Johanna's door and walked to the open stair above the innkeeper's hall. He watched the maid's trim body as she moved between the board and the hearth and saw the firelight upon the dark glory of her hair. She swatted away the bold hands of a drunken singer beside the broad firepit, bringing an abrupt end to the lout's whining lament about a faithless lady of Dinan; across the hall, women's voices rose in tittering rebuke.

The black-haired maid smiled up the stair.

Payen shook his head and walked back to his cold chamber to watch the widow's door.

If he stayed in Johanna Mercat's company much longer, he would sicken from unmatched lust. It was as well he would see the last of her tomorrow, upon the quays of Aleth.

Chapter Ten

An hour after dawn, when the sea mist began to lift, they could see the port of Aleth a mile beyond the inn, and two longships heading for the quays, their oars flashing in sunlight above a cold, windless sea. Above the shrill confusion of twenty travelers leaving the inn yard with their well-laden packbeasts, the maid Ursula offered Payen a surly farewell, and Johanna Mercat ignored the encounter with an indifference that set Payen's teeth to grinding.

At the gates of the inn's stable yard, a pack mule laden with covered panniers balked at the passage and scraped his load against a post, giving brief freedom to the young hens confined within their wicker walls.

Payen helped Johanna up to her saddle and handed her the reins. "Where is Mathieu?" he muttered, and turned to beckon him.

He looked back to the stables and swore a soft oath. Mathieu was there, his face as red as a Lammastide apple, in speech with the maid Ursula.

The mule backed into a hayrick, then broke from the gates, scattering plump birds beside the track: Its frantic owner bolted after, spurring a reluctant piebald horse. Mathieu rode past the distracted Ursula and reached the open road.

Payen, Mathieu, and Johanna rode down the Aleth track, careful not to overtake the recalcitrant mule and his despairing master.

"You have the gold," Payen said.

"Half in the pouch upon my belt, and the other half beneath my—in my kirtle," Johanna said. "Why would you not take the half of it?"

He ignored the question. "And your silver?"

She patted a tight bundle of cloth balanced before her on the saddle bow. "Still in the hems of the old mantle," she said.

There was little time left to them, and there were questions he had not yet asked. "You had already sewn the coins in your clothes," Payen said. "You had done it before I came to Rochmarin."

The widow Malebis faltered, then regained her smile. "Yes," she said. "I had thought of traveling alone to the coast. It would have been harder than I expected, alone. I see that now."

Payen shrugged. "Without the Samhain uproar, you might have made it. Why had you planned to leave? Had there been threats?"

Her determined smile disappeared. "It was time to go."

"Was there a threat? An enemy?"

"Not one. A great host of them, none of them like to strike me down, but all of them careless whether I lived or died. It was the people of Rochmarin who drove me away. They hated my husband, and they hated me."

"You had done nothing against them," he said. "I heard no complaint of you when Mathieu and I were at Rochmarin."

"They wished their Norman lord and his English wife would quit Rochmarin, and leave them as they were before the rebellions. If my marriage-sister, Agnes, had shown any understanding of this, I would have asked her to leave with me. But she was blind to it all and obsessed with the lord Adam Mauleon. He will wed her in the spring; I pray he will keep her safe before.''

Payen winced at her words. How many ears had heard Johanna's plans? Had the watchmen at the bonfire been paid to stop her? Had their arrows been shot in craft rather than in panic? It was a miracle that the woman had survived the night. He lowered his voice and attempted to keep it level. ''You spoke with Malebis's sister? Did she know of your plans to leave?''

''No, she would not have listened and might have tried to stop me,'' said Johanna. ''I pray she will wed Mauleon soon and go with him to his own lands, where he lives in greater peace than the Malebis lords managed.'' She turned to him, and for an instant her smile faltered. ''Will you send word to Agnes, once I am gone, to tell her I am safe? I had thought to send for her once I had reached Dinan, but since she had traveled there and beyond with Adam Mauleon, I knew I'd never find her before I sailed.''

Payen nodded. ''I will send a message to her when you have gone.''

''Thank you,'' Johanna said. ''Agnes must be worried.''

Payen managed a smile to match Johanna's poor attempt. ''Do not pluck out the coins from your cloak aboard the ship,'' he said. ''The crew may notice you working at it; no matter how well chosen and well paid, the crew must not be trusted. At least one man in twenty—''

''—will be a former brigand, no better than a murderer.'' Johanna sighed. ''I was listening, Payen. I will remember your words. And you must remember,'' she added, ''that I am a wool seller's daughter and know what to expect from the crew of a trading cog.''

''See that you don't let them have what they expect, then,'' Payen muttered.

Johanna Mercat smiled again in sudden sweetness and extended her hand to Payen as he rode beside her. "I will be careful," she said. "And I will remember Mathieu's kindness and your care of me. And before next spring I will be sure to send gold to Guy of Dinan's trading house for you. Do be sure to fetch it, for I want you to have some reward for all you have done."

They rode in silence until she turned to him again, her brow marred by sudden concern. "Your document—we must find a cleric to leave a record that I embarked to England—"

"You find one when you reach Whitby. Send it with your next shipments to Guy of Dinan."

She protested again that they must make the record clear before she left and delay her sailing if it came to that. He dismissed her objections with a few curt words and bade her mind the road ahead, as she must not, for any reason, arrive at Aleth too late to sail on Guy of Dinan's ship.

Payen kept his own gaze fixed upon the road to the port. He had learned, the night previous, that the widow Malebis could bring greater disaster than an accusation of her murder upon his head: She could, all unwitting, tempt him to stay by her side and take his place in the bed of the one woman in all of Brittany whom he must not love.

After one swift, questioning glance, the widow Malebis began again to chatter of her homecoming and of the riches she would send in gratitude for Payen's care of her. He watched her smile broaden as they approached the port of Aleth, and he marveled that she could put such a carefree face upon their parting.

It must have been the wine, last night, that had put a hint of tears in Johanna Mercat's eyes as Payen had left her bedchamber; this morning, the woman seemed as if she wanted nothing more than to board a ship for England, and to end, with a late winter's gift of gold, any obligation she felt to her rescuers, to her companions of the past four days. To the man who would have wished, above all else, to cover her delicate body with his own, and lose himself in the glory of her sweet scented flesh.

To the tortures that the widow Malebis had already inflicted upon Payen's secret desires, she had added, on this cold morning, the cruelest of all: Johanna Mercat rode beside Payen and touched him when she would, and urged him, with each expression of her gratitude, to answer her. Smiling into the face of Johanna Mercat's contentment to part from him was more difficult than Payen's first battle and no less painful than the wounds he had taken on that long-ago day.

If she did not cease her bright, determined smiles, she would drive him mad with the folly of wanting her.

Payen turned to Mathieu. "When we reach the harbor," he said, "you must stay with the lady. I will speak with the boatmen and see that all is in order."

Johanna's smile did not falter. It must have hurt that fine mouth to hold it in such full and rigid delight the whole morning long. "You will come back to say your farewells?" she asked.

"Mathieu will stay with you and see you safely into the ship's tender," Payen said. "You will be safe enough." He'd be damned for a fool if he said his farewells upon a crowded landing place before the eyes of all.

"Payen, are you angry?"

At last the widow's too-brilliant smile had become smaller, and a trace of regret crossed her features. It was only decent that she rue their parting as much as Payen himself, for she, too, must have felt the nearing of passion in their dealings the night before. A man without scruples might have had her, and might have her still, tempting her away from a return to England, keeping her at his side in the long winter nights.

Payen rubbed his brow. He must be ill. The inn's food—the meat may have sickened him. The innkeeper's filthy kitchen may have poisoned them all, leaving them prey to fits of fancy. Once free of the widow Malebis, and miles from Aleth, Payen would thank his Breton saints that he had not taken the woman to his bed.

The quays were crowded with merchants and fisherfolk selling the morning's catch. The *Broceliand*'s master, seeing the crowds and confusion, sent them to a narrow beach at the edge of the settlement and bade them wait for his rowing boat to fetch Johanna from the strand and take her out to the ship.

Payen said a brusque farewell and left Mathieu to wait for the small boat to ground upon the heavy, damp sand; Mathieu would lift the widow Malebis into the bow and feel the fine curve of her waist beneath the folds of her cloak. Mathieu alone would stand and watch the lady's boat take her beyond reach.

Payen turned from his last sight of Johanna Mercat and looked back to the port. No one had followed them from the crowd upon the seawall, and no one overlooked them from the track that wound from the beach to the hills above Aleth. His task was nearly at an end, and he had lost nothing but his heart, and his wits, in the process.

She was in the boat now, waving farewell to Mathieu; the oarsmen were pulling the little craft parallel to the shore, a few feet from the shallows, making for the nearest quay, where the ship's master waited to be ferried to the broad, black-tarred cog anchored beyond the quays, where the green waters of the Rance met the gray tides of the English sea.

At the end of the beach the rider of the piebald horse was shouting at his still-rebellious mule. The beast broke free of the reins and headed for the open sands.

Anything, even dealing with the renegade mule, was better than watching the widow Malebis leave this land forever.

Payen raised his reins and sent Arsuf in pursuit of the mule. He overtook the bucking, braying animal and led it back to its bald-headed, gesticulating master.

"I'll slay that young scoundrel who told me the beast was trained to the pack frame," the farmer raged.

Payen made a brief reply and turned back to look at the sea. The small boat was halfway from its beach landing to the quay, still skimming along the shallows, well out of the swift river current that would have carried them away from the anchored cog and out to sea. Johanna had settled upon the bow bench and was looking away from the shore to the open water.

"What use is a fancy riding mule to me if it won't carry my chickens on market days? What fool would train it for the saddle and not for burden?"

Payen turned back to the sidling mule and its raging owner. The beast was handsome, its coat as well curried as—

As the harpist's fancy black riding mule at Mercadier's camp.

"Where did you get it?"

The farmer broke off his tirade and made a small gesture of conciliation. "I'm sorry. And I thank you for stopping the beast. I didn't mean to anger you. Sir—"

"Where did you buy it?"

The farmer caught the mule's reins and cringed away from Payen's question. "I did not steal the mule. It's mine. Good silver, I paid. The lad with the harp will tell you."

Payen reached down and silenced him with a hand to his throat. "Tell me where you saw the man—the harper—where is he—"

The farmer's voice rose in fear. "At the inn. Last night, sir—at the—"

"Johanna!" Payen released the man and sent Arsuf pounding across the beach, straight for the boat carrying Johanna to the quay.

The oarsmen faltered, then panicked when they saw him riding for them and tried to turn out to the deeper water. They were too slow for it and too nervous to heed his bellowed order to beach their boat.

He had to hack the ends from two oars and knock one of

the boatmen on the pate before they heeded him and gave him Johanna back. But he got her, and kept her from reaching the ship which might or might not have carried a second assassin, hired with gold from a harper lad's master.

She had been weeping. Unreasoning, unexpected, and undignified tears had streamed down her face, robbing her of a last sight of Payen upon the beach. It had taken all her will to smile during the interminable mile she had ridden with Payen and Mathieu from the inn to the port of Aleth, and the effort of it had taken all her strength.

Spared—denied—final words with Payen, Johanna had said her farewells to Mathieu and turned her face away from shore, hiding her sudden hot tears from all but the portside oarsmen.

The sound of angry voices came across the water; one voice rose above them, and Johanna heard Payen call to her, then bellow her name.

She wiped her eyes upon her mantle hem and turned to see him riding straight for her, shouting and spurring Arsuf to greater speed. His mount slackened its pace only an instant when it reached the water's edge, then plunged into the swell, sending two long fountains of white foam from his black shoulders, bringing Payen into the sweep of the panicked boatmen's oars.

He bellowed again, then drew his sword and hacked down at the nearest oars, severing the shafts as if they were grass before the scythe.

"To me—" he called. "Johanna, to me."

She looked at the naked sword in his hand and saw that he was reaching with his other arm to bring her from the boat to his saddle. She tried to speak, but the words would not come.

In that moment the larboard oarsmen crowded away from Payen and fell upon the others, filling the port side with their frantic weight. The boat lurched and listed; green water began to pour over the submerged top plank, keeping the small hull from righting.

Johanna moved to the high side, up the slippery bench, away from the flailing limbs of the oarsmen seeking to steady themselves. Payen's hand closed over her arm, and she took a shaking step up to the highest plank, and then to Arsuf's saddle. In the moment she stepped away, the boat overturned in the shallows, spilling the oarsmen into the white maelstrom of cold water and roiled sand. The sputtering boatmen rose in waist-deep water and sent curses to heat the cold November morning as they sought, without success, to stop the weed-slicked curve of the overturned boat from drifting down the beach.

The enraged cries of the crew and the sound of Mathieu's shouting followed them back to the dry sand of the dunes and to the rocky track above the beach until they reached the highest point of the hill and could hear them no more.

Johanna slipped from the saddle and steadied herself against the wet, brine-streaked shoulder of his mount. Payen looked back down at the figures of the crew, then up the river to the Dinan ship still anchored in the wide flow of green. He lifted his sword from the scabbard and began to wipe the saltwater from the steel. "They may have found you," he said. "The harper—the one who took your enemy's gold to Mercadier—was at the inn."

For a foolish moment she had imagined that he had wished her to stay for his sake. That he had felt the pull of her sorrow and come to make her his own, if only for a night.

He looked back down to the beach and below them to the narrow track that had brought them to the vantage point. There was no pursuit; none who had seen the force of Payen's sword had dared to follow him from the strand.

"Let me go back to tell them I have decided not to sail." Johanna said. "If I ride with you now, they will call it abduction, and—"

"Let them say what they will." Payen looked past her once

again to the efforts of the crew to drag the small boat ashore, far below them upon the gray sands. The shouting had ceased.

"Tell me," she said. "Did you see him in the port?"

"No, but the harper is near, and so may be his master. The lad sold his riding mule this morning to a farmer at the inn."

"The same—"

"Yes," he said. "The inn where we slept." He uttered an oath, a fulsome oath that brought color back into Johanna's face.

Johanna turned away and saw, in the distant shallows beyond the beach, a stain of deeper color. "My cloak—" Johanna said.

"Forget it."

"The coins in it—and your money pouch—"

"Leave them. We cannot go back."

"Could Mathieu—"

"He's disappeared, or should have. He'll find us soon if he can."

"And then? Will you take me back to Dinan, to Guy? His household is large and has many guards. I'd be safe there until my uncle can send help."

"Help? You have help, madam. And I will not take you back to the old man. You have been betrayed, Johanna. The harper did not find you by chance; there may be one—or many souls in the old man's household who spoke of you to the harper or to his master. Gold may turn a man from his oaths. And from loyalty."

"And I have no gold to buy the loyalty of a river barge's crew, let alone a ship that could take me home. Without Guy's help—"

"Gold is not a—" Payen's words broke off as Mathieu came in sight, riding from the far side of the hill, leading Johanna's palfrey by the reins.

"How did he do that?"

Payen shrugged. "He's a good man in a fight and a better

one in retreat. He disappears as quickly as a Breton wizard. Better.''

''If we stay here in sight,'' Mathieu shouted across the salt-withered grass, ''they may find the wits to come after us. You had good reason,'' he asked, ''to wreck the boat and steal the lady?''

They rode east until the thin, cloud-shrouded sun was high above them, and bought food from a cattle herder's saddlebags to eat on a cold hill above the long, white sands of the ocean shore.

''I must find a ship,'' Johanna said, ''at the next port. No one has followed us, and I'd be safe—''

''You will wait here,'' Payen said, ''while I go back to see whether we are followed. And to speak with the harper.''

''If I take ship soon, before they find us again, it would put an end to their pursuit. At home, none would harm me.''

''Are you frightened?'' he asked.

''No,'' she said, and wondered why it should be true. ''But I will go back,'' she said with greater conviction. ''I cannot spend the winter here, hiding from all who might recognize me.''

''You must not go back to your home, where any who seek you may find you, without knowing who put the death mark upon you. If it is the Bretons of Rochmarin, they will be content that you have gone from the land, and leave you in peace. If not—''

''If not, it is a matter in which my uncle must help me, for it extends beyond my husband's lands, and beyond your concern.''

Mathieu half rose to his feet at the sight of Payen's darkened face.

Johanna ignored the signs of displeasure. ''You have taken much care to keep me alive, but I must release you from my troubles, lest you be blamed for my flight by those who will remember our passing.'' She drew a long breath and looked away from Payen's face, appealing to Mathieu. ''And if the weather does not hold long enough for the passage home—if the ship should not reach England—and I should die nameless with it, you will need your document to prove that you brought me this far in safety.

Payen muttered a soft curse. Still Johanna did not look at him. ''Mathieu,'' she said. ''I will go down, this day, to the coast and find a cleric to write of my presence, and I shall give you the document. I have enough gold left to buy passage. You and Payen must leave me.''

''Mathieu is a fool,'' growled Payen, ''if he tries to compel me. You are going nowhere, madam, until I find the harper and discover who sent him to Mercadier.''

''I am going today—''

''You are waiting here until nightfall.'' Payen rose to his feet and with one hard glance brought Mathieu to his side. ''Mathieu will keep you here. You think, madam, that I should not concern myself with you beyond this day; instead, imagine how I would mislike to discover—after these days spent in your rescue—to discover you dead in some village port, your throat cut and your body thrown into the midden of a fishermen's inn.''

He turned from her and began to saddle Arsuf.

''Payen—'' Mathieu had hurried after him. ''Payen, let me go.''

''Wait with her.''

''Payen, the innkeeper's maid Ursula will help me get to the harper. I saw him too, at Mercadier's camp. Let me seek him.''

A smile touched Payen's mouth. ''I saw you speaking with her this morning in the inn yard. Go then, but do not tarry in her bed.''

Mathieu flushed and lowered his voice. ''She asked of you,

Payen. I promised her I would bring you back that way once the widow had sailed."

His words were not soft enough to die before they reached Johanna's ears. She kept her face still, as if she had not heard.

Payen shrugged and mounted Arsuf. "Then I will go, and if I cannot find the harper, I'll seek the maid's help." There was nothing in his expression to tell Johanna whether he had welcomed Mathieu's tidings.

Chapter Eleven

‘‘He told the maid Ursula his purse was empty, and that he sought a lady he had expected in Dinan. He had given up waiting, he said, and followed the odd rumor to Aleth. He said that the lady, when he found her, would restore gold to his purse. Two days ago he spent the last of his gold on lodging for himself and a place in the stable for his mule. This morning he sold the mule and told Ursula he would wait three days longer before walking back to Dinan to trade his songs for a living, until he could find the lady.’’ Payen closed his eyes. ‘‘He must have been seeking you, Johanna, and may have intended to kill you himself, to have the reward for himself. It was only through luck, and the possibility that he did not know your face, that he did not try to kill you last night in the inn.’’

‘‘He was there last night?’’

‘‘He was. Following rumors from Dinan.’’ His voice softened. ‘‘Where would he have learned them, save from Guy of Dinan? And why would he follow them, but at Guy’s bidding?’’

Johanna turned from him, and began to pace from the small

fire to the shadows beyond. She turned back, her eyes smarting from the wood smoke. "Guy of Dinan is my uncle's most trusted trading partner, here in Brittany or elsewhere. And he was my father's friend before. He would never betray me. He has no enmity, now or from the past, toward my family. And he would not betray me for gold. He needs none—"

Payen caught her arm and brushed her face lightly with his palm.

"I am not weeping," she raged.

"I trusted him too," he said. "Old Guy was cautious of speaking about you and reluctant to help a stranger in any matter touching you. But his household is large, and some of his servants young, their loyalty untested. There may have been a traitor among them." He took his hand from her arm. "Tomorrow," he said, "we'll ride for St. Michael's port to find a ship."

Johanna nodded.

"But tonight," he said, "I would have you look upon the harper's face. It may be that he came to Rochmarin, or to the abbey when you were there. You may remember him, and who was his master."

Johanna shivered and looked into the darkness beyond the loom of the campfire. "You brought him with you?"

Payen stepped from her and seized a dry branch from Mathieu's woodpile. He thrust it into the flames and held the small, swift-burning torch between them. "He is in the church, just east of the inn. We can reach it in less than an hour on the main road."

Mathieu rose to his feet "Payen?"

He shrugged. "The man is dead."

"You killed him." Johanna's words were a small, strangled gasp in the darkness.

Payen turned back to her and shook his head. "I did not. Though he deserved it for seeking the life of a woman, I did not kill him. He died at midday, when the inn was quiet, and there was no mark upon him, the maid Ursula said. It may have been poison. Or fright."

"Who else was there? Did she remember?"

"A few travelers who asked for a meal and continued soon after. Two or three parties, Ursula said. None of them remarkable."

Mathieu muttered words Johanna could not hear. "Is it wise," he ended, "to go back?"

"The inn was empty when I arrived and was still when I left. The church is small and the approaches clear, easily seen. Only the priest lives near." He turned back to Johanna. "The priest will bury the man tomorrow, and none may discover, after that day, who he was or the name of his master. This is your last chance, Johanna, to see the face of your enemy. His looks are not Breton, they say. If he is English, and from Whitby, you should know it before you embark." His voice softened, and he touched her cheek again. This time she did not deny that she was weeping.

"Can you do this?" he asked.

"I will have to," she said, and turned her face from his gaze.

Johanna had seen the dead before—in the wind-scoured hilltop church above Gunndale, and in Whitby there had been two men from Mercat ships brought back from the sea dead of wounds taken in fighting brigands in a Flanders port. Those dead, seen resting upon their biers in the small stone chapel above Gunndale, and in the larger church in Whitby with the sounds of commerce beyond the open doors, had seemed small—more effigies than men—in their lifelessness.

Even Harald's young body had seemed, as it had rested in the chapel at Rochmarin, to be unreal, a shrunken husk rather than the remains of a recently living boy.

She had attended but not looked upon the body of Walter

Malebis when he had returned from Nantes, a bloodless, shrouded corpse in a narrow wagon.

The body of the harper, the stranger who had brought the death mark to Johanna, seemed to fill the small sanctuary in its cold mystery. From the trees at the edge of the church clearing, Johanna saw only a glimpse of white, humped linen through the sanctuary window, and knew that this dead, of all she had seen in her young life, would hold the greatest warning, and the most powerful remembrance of her own mortality.

They had waited, their crude torches extinguished, in the darkness without the church for the hour it took Payen to circumscribe the church and the priest's house in two slow passages to be sure there were no sentries set to guard the approaches, no enemies waiting in the night.

At last Payen returned to watch with them the small, flickering lights of the tapers showing from the unshuttered embrasures of the church, at the head and feet of the sanctuary's cold guest.

"The priest will be there," Johanna said.

"He will not. The harper is a stranger to these people, and the priest said prayers enough before nightfall. The corpse rests alone, and the priest is in his hut, sleeping."

"The shutters are open," she said. "There must be someone within."

"The soul must go forth from the church," Payen said. "If the shutters are closed, the spirit will stay and haunt the living."

"I have never heard—"

"You were not raised a Breton," Payen said. He turned to her and touched her arm. "Are you ready?"

She reached down in the darkness and set her hands upon Payen's shoulders to light upon the cold ground. Mathieu caught the reins of her palfrey and promised, in nervous, short words, to keep their mounts safe and to bring the beasts to the church door and call Payen should he hear sounds of men or horses approaching the churchyard.

Payen held her arm through the uneven ground of the churchyard and drew her closer still as he opened the narrow door of the chapel. "There is no mark of violence upon him," Payen said. "He will look as if he sleeps."

He drew her with him across the bare stone floor. Johanna had been in darkness for more than an hour with only the distant taper lights to attract her gaze. Those same candles burned bright as suns to her blinded eyes, and she faltered in the light of them.

"We must be swift," Payen said. "Turn your face to me, and I will bring you to—I will bring you there."

There was no smell of death, only the scent of hot wax wafting in the breeze from the unshuttered windows. Their footsteps were loud in the small space, louder than the slight, sibilant wind passing through the chamber and the hissing of the wax fallen to the dusty floor.

She felt a slight movement from Payen and saw that he had uncovered the face. It was a young face with the down of late youth upon the smooth skin. He had been a handsome lad with regular features that might have seemed an angel's visage, save for the long, indulgent mouth that had puckered, for all eternity, in an expression of satisfaction.

"Look again," Payen whispered. "Do you know him?"

Johanna shook her head. "There were minstrels, harpers among them, at Rochmarin many times before my—"

"Before?"

"Before my brother died there." Johanna looked again at the young face; only the pale, blue-tinged color of the lad suggested death. But for that, he would have seemed only to sleep. "I never saw this man among them."

"And elsewhere?" Payen's voice was low and demanding and did not permit her to turn from her purpose into old griefs. "Think again, not of minstrels and harps, but of the past few months at Rochmarin, and of faces from home. Have you never seen him?"

She would have remembered that long, undisciplined mouth so prominent in the thin, youthful face. "Never," she said.

Payen moved the linen back to cover the harper's face. "We must be gone," he said.

The darkness was deeper now as she turned from the taper-lit sanctuary and stepped into the night. She stumbled upon the last step down to the churchyard and felt Payen's arm keep her from falling. "Sit," he said. "Sit here and put your head upon your lap."

"I am not faint," she said.

"Of course." Payen whistled, sending a brief note of bird-song into the night. When Johanna raised her head, Mathieu was there, holding Arsuf's reins. Payen lifted her onto the saddle and mounted behind her. Mathieu left them for a moment, then reappeared framed in the soft light streaming from the church door.

"My horse—"

"Mathieu will lead her," Payen said. "Tell me if you sicken, and we will stop."

The night had turned colder, and the sea wind rose strong as they rode back to the coast. Johanna slept briefly in Payen's arms, but she woke when the dreams began and kept awake by watching the dark, star-pierced sky above them. The two men and their mounts seemed to know where the road was in the darkness, and Johanna ceased to worry that they would reach, too soon, the high cliffs beside the small camp where Mathieu had built their fire only hours before.

They were nearly upon the camp when they turned and brought Johanna to the low-burning fire, than gave her a bedroll to sit upon as they brought night-gathered brush to feed the fire.

"Well, that was a fine waste of time," muttered Mathieu.

"It was," Payen said.

"No." Johanna rose to her feet and bent to untie the bedroll. "It was necessary, and might have been the end of my worries if he had been a familiar face. Payen was right—I had to see him.''

Mathieu shook his head. ''I recognized the young scoundrel. He was in the common room last night, drunk as a lord at harvest time, hanging about kitchen maids' skirts, singing with a voice that would curdle new milk. I should have heeded the words, for he whined of a lady in Dinan.''

Payen returned to the fire. ''He sang of her?''

Mathieu shrugged. ''He sang of a lady with—''

Johanna raised her head. ''With what?''

''A lady none too careful with her favors,'' Mathieu muttered.

They listened in silence to the crackling of the fire. ''It must have been an old song,'' Payen said.

''Yes,'' Mathieu agreed. ''An old song.''

Johanna broke the sudden silence. ''You think I was to be murdered for adultery?''

Payen did not move. ''Might you have been?'' he said at last.

''Believe what you wish,'' Johanna said. ''But adultery is not among my sins.''

''And your late husband, madam—did he think you faithful?''

''He did,'' Johanna whispered. When he thought of her at all. She raised her voice and looked Payen full in the face. ''You told me, days ago, that the harper claimed I was a murderess, that I had paid to have my husband killed. Did he mention adultery when he hired you?''

Payen dropped his gaze. ''No,'' he said. ''Mercadier said nothing about your virtue.''

Mathieu cleared his throat. ''It must have been an old song the harper sang,'' he said. ''Not about you.''

Johanna shrugged and pulled her cloak about her shoulders. She felt Payen's gaze return to her, and she felt the memory of the southern wine and the warm shadows of the previous night's bedchamber come back to tinge her cheeks with sudden heat. If Payen had thought her a faithless wife, a lecherous widow, would he have turned back at her doorway and touched her? And would he have closed the chamber door again, shutting out the world, and come back to her hearth, and then to her bed, and would he have stayed with her through the night? How would it have been had he thought her a wanton and had taken her to him for all the hours of that long autumn night?

As if in answer, Payen's hand touched her shoulder. "Lie with me," he said.

The bedroll was before them, crushing the sweet, dried grass, the close-woven wool flung open to the heat of the fire. "I'll keep you from the chill," Payen said. "Nothing more."

"I am not a wanton."

"You are not a wanton," he agreed. "But you are trembling, and the night is growing colder. You will sicken if you sleep cold this night."

If the message of his gaze had held pity, she would have answered with all the harshness she could summon. But there was something more within the cautious warmth in his eyes, a care that went beyond duty, an acceptance that told her better than words might that he believed she had spoken the truth.

He dragged the bedroll a few feet from the fire, away from the straying sparks that reached into the darkness, and lay down upon it. He held the harsh woolen cloth open with his arm and brought it about Johanna's shoulders when she folded herself into his embrace.

Against her back his body was large and warm; she no longer felt the sharp north wind that rose from the distant sea to pass over their desolate hillock. He made no move to draw her closer against him, but kept his arm about her shoulders and his chin against the top of her hair.

Mathieu rose and stretched; Johanna watched his boots disappear beyond the loom of the low flames. "The fire," she said. "They will find us if they see the fire."

He shifted slightly and brought his arm more closely about her. ''It could be one man only who traveled to keep the harper from speaking of his mission. I doubt there are many, for there was no fight when the lad died, nor had he run from the inn.''

''There may be more than two, and they will come in the night and kill us all.''

She felt him shrug. ''I doubt there are many. And they would have searched this place before now if they knew you were here. Mathieu is watching, but I doubt he will hear anything bigger than a wolf this far from the road. And the fire, Johanna, will keep you from wolves and the cold.''

''How do you and Mathieu not sicken when you pass each night half waking, never sleeping without the other on watch?''

''A soldier sleeps well when he reaches a safe place. When this—when this is done, and you are safe on your way home, I'll eat a fair dozen of those game birds and sleep for a fortnight.''

The fire blew flat in the rising wind, sending pale smoke to follow its light into the darkness. Never had Johanna appreciated walls, even the walls of the smallest hovel in Gunndale, as much as she did then. Without Payen's body to keep the chill from her own, the sea wind would have cut chill into the marrow of her bones. Winter would come close upon these brief autumn days, and they must, each of them, find shelter before the snows. Her own haven was so far away, across the dark sea, and beyond the cold hills of Yorkshire.

''Where will you go for your fortnight's sleep?''

His breathing stilled. ''I'll go to the Templars,'' he said at last. ''To their preceptory near the coast.''

She smiled. ''You'll be safe to sleep there. Few would dare approach them in their fortresses, even with good reason. Will they let you stay?''

''They will.''

Something in his tone made her hesitate. ''You know them?'' she asked.

''They taught me to fight.''

The unrelieved black he wore had been a signal she had not understood. ''You are a Templar?'

''No.''

''Were you a Templar, before—''

''Before I began to fight for gold? No.'' He sighed. ''The Templars will not take into their order any man of common blood, or a man not of legitimate birth.''

''But they taught you to fight?''

''Yes, when I was a young lad with no future but the sword, they taught me to fight, and later, when I had paid them back, they gave me gold to add my sword to theirs when they needed more soldiers than the order could muster.''

Only the darkness, and the impossibility that he might turn his gaze upon her, gave Johanna the courage to continue her questions. For she wanted, more than she craved his goodwill, to know how the man Payen had come to his life of blood shed for gold, of death accomplished in cold efficiency, for the causes and vengeance of others.

''And you left the Templars' employ for Mercadier's army?''

His voice held no anger at her persistent questions. ''I never left either. When King Richard took his army to Palestine, I was among the Templar army. There were many of us, hired to add our swords to those of the ordained knights. And when we returned, there was more work to do in the matter of King Richard's imprisonment.''

''You tried to free him?''

He shook his head. ''No, but I took the old queen's negotiators to treat with the Austrians who took him. She paid well, as did her emissaries. Then I went back to Mercadier for a time.''

''Where you heard there was gold to be earned at Rochmarin.''

Payen brought the blanket close about her shoulders and muttered a swift blasphemy. ''If you will not sleep, madam,

I'll set you to watch in Mathieu's place. Will you be silent, now, and let me sleep?''

Johanna nodded and fell silent. Her last vision, before sleeping, was of the embers of the fire, flaring hot and crimson as the north wind carried their heat into the vast, empty night.

He held her against him, warming her in the cold autumn night, until he heard her breathing lengthen to a cadence of sleep and felt her body soften and accept his closeness.

If he had not known that Johanna Mercat had been a wedded wife, and that she had slept, each brief summer night, in Walter Malebis's bed, he would have thought her an untried virgin. However long she had been wed, and however complete her understanding of the ways of men and women, she showed no knowledge of the subtle language of nearness without passion and touch without demand. Though he had expected that she might, as a chaste widow, object to lying at his side, he had imagined that her body would seek the animal heat of his own. But the widow Malebis seemed ignorant of the simple expedience of sharing warmth on a cold autumn night.

Payen could not put from his mind the image of Walter Malebis's dead face. Though not a youth, and not innocent, Walter Malebis had not seemed, in death, to have the features of a lord in the healthy flush of manhood. There had been a petulance, an almost childish anger upon that dead face turned to the dust of the whorehouse floor. What manner of husband had he been to the subtle, self-possessed Johanna Mercat? And how had he comforted his young wife when her brother died in the Malebis garrison yard? How often had he thought of holding her, when passion's play had done, to warm her in the night?

Payen felt the heaviness of arousal at Johanna's nearness. He was no better than the deceitful lord Walter if he could not offer the warmth of his body without turning his mind to sin.

He turned his gaze to the stars and began to count the jewels in thc great warrior's belt, and the number of pale lights that shone along his sword. The bright, lusty star of Venus had set long ago, or so he hoped. He did not wish to look to her portion of the heavens.

Chapter Twelve

She woke to the sound of their voices and the soft, nervous whicker of her palfrey. All but Payen's bedroll and the newly nourished fire before her was gone, dragged to the short picket line where the horses had passed the night. At her feet, wrapped in thick layers at the bottom of the woolen bedding, were smooth, fire-warmed stones.

Arsuf, Payen's great black gelding, was resisting Mathieu's efforts to cinch Payen's saddle; Payen was attempting, with more success, to heap Mathieu's saddlebags and bedroll upon Mathieu's saddle and tie them over the plain wooden bows.

The gray palfrey that Payen had bought at St. Martin's abbey for Johanna was already saddled and burdened with a single bag; the mare had backed as far as she could from the confusion surrounding the larger mounts.

"Keep a steady hand to the reins, and do not let him turn back to nip your leg," Payen was saying. "He'll settle after the first few miles. If you can, ride him all the way and lead your own mount. Arsuf dislikes to be led and will break free if he can."

"Don't worry—I'll get him to Mercadier's camp and wait for you there."

"Don't sell him to Mercadier. I refused him a good price two months ago, and he may try in my absence—"

"Your devil beast will be there, as vicious as he is, waiting for your return. I swear it, Payen."

"And take care of your own skin, Mathieu. Don't find yourself in a war you didn't choose."

Mathieu emerged from the far side of Arsuf's powerful shoulders and walked with deliberate caution to the glossy black head. "If I manage to get this black beast back to Mercadier without losing my boots, nothing I find in that camp could harm me."

Payen picked up the reins and handed them to Mathieu. "Arsuf," he growled. "You learned to carry an extra burden of skirts, old friend. You won't object to Mathieu?"

Long, yellow teeth in an equine grimace answered Payen's question.

Johanna crawled from the bedroll and found her boots. "Don't leave," she cried. "Mathieu—"

"I'm taking the horses ahead, my lady. Payen will see you onto a ship."

"Must you go?"

Payen held Arsuf's head as Mathieu climbed into the saddle. "We might be recognized," he said, "if we appear at the next port together. Arsuf alone would attract notice and prime the memories of those who saw us at the inn."

Mathieu was holding his own against Arsuf's efforts to nip his rider's boot. "Farewell, lady," he called. "May you find a good ship and be safe home before the snows come."

"Mathieu, farewell. I thank you for—"

With a brisk shout Mathieu called for the leading rein of his own mount and attempted to keep Arsuf from backing him against the hillock's single, wind-bowed oak.

Payen turned from the sight of Arsuf's mischief-livened progress down the hill to the coastal track. He returned to the campfire and began to roll the woolen blankets into a long bundle.

"I'm sorry," Johanna said.

"You have done nothing to regret," he said. "There's the last of the innkeeper's bread beside the fire. Can you be ready to ride soon?"

"You have given up your horse for my sake."

"I'll have him back. Mathieu will keep him safe."

Johanna looked back at her lightly laden palfrey. "Will she carry us both?"

"No," said Payen. "I'll walk. It's not far from here to the coast."

"I still have the pouch I wore beneath my kirtle. It's half the gold from Dinan."

Payen shrugged.

"We could buy another horse," she said.

"No need. We dare not look as if we can afford a second mount. If we attract too much notice in the first village, we'll have to sell the palfrey as well and continue on foot."

"You do not look like a poor man, Payen."

He drew his cloak from the palfrey's bag and drew it across his shoulders, then let it fall to cover his well-used scabbard and the plain, workmanlike hilt of his sword. "None will notice me as we pass," he said. "They will see you."

Johanna looked down at her dusty, sleep-rumpled cloak and the wide, irregular salt stains upon the kitchen maid's best kirtle. She sighed. "They will not see a prosperous woman."

Payen walked to her side and pulled the hood of the cloak to cover her hair. "They will see a beautiful woman," he said. "Let us take care they will not, if questioned, remember the color of her hair, or the odd green in her eyes."

They had been alone before, when Mathieu had taken his turn as sentry, a distance from their sleeping place; and they had been alone and away from scrutiny in Johanna's chamber only a night ago at the inn. Never before had they been alone so far from others and out of the hearing of Mathieu. Johanna could shout and none would heed her. They could sit beside the remains of the fire a little longer, turn to each other for warmth or something beyond creature comforts, and none would see them. None would ever know.

He had called her beautiful. Payen had said that when she passed, men would see a beautiful woman. Johanna looked into his gaze and saw that he had meant those words.

"Johanna—" he said.

She looked down at her newly freckled hands. At the inn, with clean garments and in the comfortable light of the hearth, he had not spoken of her beauty. Now he had spoken to distract her from their worsened lot.

"Will you not eat the bread? You have miles to ride before we reach the next village."

The vision of that bedchamber and the soft firelight vanished with his words. "You should have the bread," she said. "You are walking."

He returned to scatter the embers of the fire, then wrapped the bread in its cloth and placed it in the saddlebag. "There is a stream beyond the track," he said. Together they led the palfrey down to the swift-running water and filled the two waterskins Mathieu had left them.

Johanna found at the bottom of the bag the small wooden comb that she had bought from Ursula at the inn. She who had crossed the sea with a dowry of gold and chests of fine wool and silk would leave Brittany dressed in a kitchen maid's clothes, with only a crude comb to burden her.

The length of corded silk with which she had tied her braid was gone, lost in the darkness the night before, among the sad ruts and mounds of the churchyard where the harper would find eternal rest. Johanna took her small dagger from the dust-darkened broderie of her sash and cut a narrow piece from her mantle's hem to bind her hair. She returned to the stream and knelt upon the mossy bank to bring the cold water to her face, then scrubbed her cheeks with the newly cropped corner of her cloak.

Payen turned back from his inspection of the mare's hooves and cleaned his hands in the numbing cold of the stream. He lifted Johanna into the little palfrey's saddle and left his hand upon the beast's withers as he walked beside her, down the hill.

These were settled lands, with orchards and fields as close as the salt would allow them to the sea. They passed two villages before they halted at a fishing settlement close upon the broad white sands of a small cove. Johanna pulled her hood forward and took the palfrey into the grove of beeches between the village and the sea; Payen bought bread, apples, and a bowl of milk from an untidy hovel at the edge of the clustered huts.

"We are well on our way," he said. "If the weather holds, and we move fast, we'll find safety ahead, and comfort, before nightfall."

Johanna shivered. "It's colder. I'd rather an inn full of thieves than another night beside the road."

"It's safer than an inn—where I will take you. The Templars have a house above the port near here, and lodgings where their shipwrights and merchants may live when they do business."

Johanna shook her head. "They would not allow me there," she said. "When I came to Brittany, there was trouble with the high winds, and my ship put in to shore before it reached Dinan. Though there was a Templar house in the harbor, they would not give me a bed for the night."

Payen smiled. "The black knights take care to seem, to the eyes of outsiders, as shy of women as they are modest at their board. But to those they know well, they sometimes show a decent welcome and a bit of the luxury they conceal from the king's eyes."

Johanna did not smile back. "I do not want to go to the Templars," she said. "They are cold souls and bring fear to everyone who deals with them."

"They frighten outsiders," Payen said, "when it suits them. They tolerate me because they find me useful when they need an extra sword. If I bring you with me, they will not harm you, Johanna."

She looked down at his hand upon her saddle bow. "How old were you, Payen, when you learned arms from the Templars?"

"Twelve years old," he said. "Far past the age of fostering."

Only noble families sent their sons to be fostered by those who could teach them of the world and the use of arms. It was an odd phrase for a mercenary to use.

He was looking up at her, frowning at her reticence. "They treated me well enough," he said. "Without them I would have starved."

He must have come from peasant stock, perhaps the baseborn child of a woman who had taken a knight into her bed, then birthed a warrior son—

"How old was your brother when he died at Rochmarin?"

She had been lost in her speculations and heard his question as if in a dream. An instant later she drew a quick breath and turned from his regard. If he had struck her, the blow would have pained her less than those words. Johanna began to wind the reins about her fingers. "He was fourteen years old and as tall as a man," she said. "He had never been fostered and had not learned the use of weapons."

"Was he sickly?"

With effort Johanna kept her voice level. "He was full of health and stronger than this horse."

"Why had you waited to foster him?"

She pulled the tangle of leather from her hands and began again to wind it about her palm. "Harald had learned my uncle's business and had begun to help in his accounting. It was his wish,'' she said, ''to be a knight, to have skill in arms. He pestered us all until I—''

''Until you wed where he could get it?''

She drew herself back from his gaze and bit the inside of her mouth to keep it from trembling. Others had spoken the words that had, for a time, become Johanna's obsession. When Payen uttered them, they became as weapons close upon her soul.

She willed him to be silent. ''My uncle is a rich man,'' she said with deliberate hauteur. ''He has many trading interests abroad. He had his reasons to wed me to Malebis, reasons too subtle for you to comprehend. My wishes and Harald's ambitions figured small among them. Such decisions are not as simple as you might imagine.''

She managed not to wince as she delivered her rebuke to the baseborn Payen, who would have spent his life at labor in the orchards and fields of Brittany had the Templars not taught him to fight. She had chosen words to stop Payen's questions, but her insult was a hollow thing, fashioned only to offend. Payen's imaginings, Johanna suspected, would not be simple or lacking in subtlety.

A short indrawn breath was his reaction. He took his hand from her saddle and placed it upon the neck of her horse. Upon the horse he had bought for her with the gold he had won in the battlefields of the east.

''I'm sorry,'' she said.

''You seem to be full of regret for many things this morning.''

''I have been much trouble for you, more than you must have expected, when you came to Rochmarin.''

He muttered something blasphemous and began to untangle the kneaded mess of reins from her fingers.

''I am grateful to you,'' she continued, ''and will see that you have more gold for your help than you would have had from fighting, these days you have spent in my company.''

He straightened the ends of the reins and gave them back to her. "Do not trouble yourself, Johanna, about offending me. We are different, you and I, and cannot treat together without some strife. You were born rich, and I went to the Templars a penniless and orphaned child. We have both made our way as best we could. Beyond that, there can be little understanding between us."

She must have made a small sound of dismay. He looked up and smiled. "There may be, and should be, goodwill between us. We have lived through some troubled days together and survived the time well enough."

Johanna leaned forward and covered his broad hand with her own. "We have, Payen. We have survived well enough because of you."

He drew his hand from beneath her fingers, then hesitated, and brought it back to cover them. "You have not been so much trouble," he said. "I have known much worse."

"Women?" The word escaped before Johanna could stop it.

Payen's smile broadened. "Women," he said. "And a fat merchant or two. There have been many, Johanna, who were worse fellow travelers. You have complained little and kept your fears to yourself."

She smiled back. "I had little fear with you and Mathieu at my side."

He shrugged. "There were times, I thought, when you feared the ally you knew more than the enemy you did not."

"You were my—" Johanna hesitated. "I did not fear you."

Payen laughed. "I pray you had some small, hidden portion of fear that night I came to you at Rochmarin. Only a madwoman would have been as composed as you managed to appear."

"You left, I remember, before I was fully awake. For a moment after you had gone, I thought I had been dreaming."

"You were sleeping as deeply as the dead when I came to

you." He raised one brow. "Did you know, as you wakened, that I had called your name many times? I was close beside you, ready to stop your scream, speaking to you before you roused. Had you taken poppy juice to make you sleep?"

"No."

"I haven't seen you sleep so soundly since you left Rochmarin. You must have learned, in our journey, to sleep with one ear to your safety. You were restless and woke many times last night."

"It felt strange, last night, having another so near as I slept."

He looked at her in swift surprise.

"I had forgotten," she said, and felt shame that the short year of her marriage had left so few memories. She had been wed, and should have remembered the feel of a man's warmth in her bed; she had slept beside Walter Malebis for nearly a year—the awkward, cold nights after the Yuletide feasting, the damp, mist-laden nights of spring, then the long summer months, and the harvest season.

"When did you wed?"

"Last year, before Yuletide. My husband left me, on that journey to Nantes, after the second harvest was in. He died ten days later. They brought his body back in a wagon—" Johanna sat straighter and turned her mind from that day. She had begun to babble as much as the old Gunndale crones at shearing time.

Payen walked in silence for a time. "The second harvest was not long ago. Are you with child?"

A knight, whether Norman or Breton, would have asked that question with more courtesy. A wool seller, however lowborn, would have prefaced those words with an apology if the woman to whom he spoke was not of his household. Johanna waited for Payen to beg her pardon.

He turned to her and frowned, waiting for her answer. There was nothing in his face to show that he meant disrespect or had heard the boldness of his own words.

Johanna sighed. The man had crossed the duchy to save the

life of an unknown woman; she would not fault him for his rough speech. "If I had been with child," she said, "I would have lost it by now."

He recoiled as if she had raised a sword between them. "Have you come to harm? Yesterday, on the beach—"

She shook her head. "No. There is nothing wrong—and there is no child."

"You are young, Johanna. You will wed again, and there will be children." Hearing no answer, he touched her hand. "You will wed a good merchant in Whitby and never again leave your home or have a sword drawn within your sight. This journey will seem as a troubled dream that grows more distant with each passing year."

"Is it so with you? Do you forget all the killing—do you forget what you have seen?"

Payen shook his head. "One never forgets his own deeds, good or bad. Merciful or bloody. They stay with you and come back to you in your sleep." He sighed and looked ahead to the next curve of the seashore. "Wed a merchant, Johanna, if you would have sleep of a night."

Her blood flared hot in her veins as his words echoed again in her mind. Wed to this man, she would sleep but briefly in the long winter nights. There would be visions, and none of them dreams.

Too late she remembered that Payen had seemed, at times, to hear her thoughts. Johanna pulled her hood to cover her hair once again, then lowered her gaze to count the threads of the plain saddlecloth upon her palfrey's withers.

She dared not look again at his hand, browned and gentle, upon her palfrey's neck.

They left the road not far from the Templar port, for Payen had gold buried nearby. The man must have sowed his wealth across the duchy, to have passed two such hiding places by chance in this journey he had not planned. He found his second cache, as far as Johanna could observe, as easily as a hungry, winter-bound animal might find food hidden in the summer past.

Johanna waited upon the palfrey as Payen paced the site of an ancient beacon fire and watched as he found a landmark in the cracked, blackened circle burnt into the stone. From that flat granite rock Payen sighted past a second, small boulder and moved beyond, to claim his coins from the cold earth.

Johanna looked back, away from Payen's cache place, and saw what the low scrub trees had hidden from her sight: There was a pattern to the crooked, frost-heaved stones that lay near the beacon place. Once again Payen had found his gold undisturbed within a stone circle set in place by ancient hands. Payen returned, bearing an earth-damp leather sack weighted with coin.

"I will bring it all," he said. "And I'll get you home in safety; if I need to buy a ship to take you home, I will do it."

The man was eager to be rid of her and would squander a pouchful of gold to see her leave Brittany's shores.

"Are you not pleased? A woman should smile to know that her safety might be bought by this much coin."

Johanna looked away to the farthest of the ancient stones. "Are you not afraid," she said, "to use these old circles to hide your treasure? At Rochmarin the Breton folk stayed clear of such places."

He moved to her side and opened the saddlebag tied to the palfrey's saddle just below Johanna's knee. "You did know that they go to the old stones at midsummer, and at the planting time, and after the harvest?"

"There was no gathering to see—"

"They would have concealed those visits from you and from all outsiders. The stones do not stand unattended every night of the year. And your Breton folk at Rochmarin would have held no fear of them by day." Payen retied the saddlebag and led the palfrey by her bridle strap back down to the coastal track. "You have such places in England, where the stones were set in place by the ancients. Your people do not neglect them."

She shook her head. "There were flowers on May mornings, and milk poured upon the stones at midsummer. Nothing more."

He laughed. "I wonder, then, how your family came to be so rich. You would have little help from the old gods if you treat them ill. If you cheat the old ones of their due, no weight of gold to the almshouses and monasteries will bring your luck back."

Johanna crossed herself. "A man who lives as you do should not speak blasphemy. You might die unshriven."

He shrugged. "A woman who rides with a rough soldier should not be so dainty of his speech. She might find herself alone."

"I—I am well able, as I have said, to go from here on my own—"

"And such a woman should learn when her foul-tongued escort is teasing her." He looked up and sighed at her silence. "I'll not leave you, Johanna. Not until you're safe, back in Yorkshire, ignoring your old gods and offending them with your paltry gifts of weed blooms and sour milk."

"Well, what do you give them? Not your gold, for you take it away again and—" She broke off as the meaning of Payen's first words reached her mind. "You are coming on the ship?"

He patted the saddlebag. "I have enough gold to buy my passage as well."

"You cannot—it is too much."

"I'll bargain hard with the ship's master. There will be gold to spare."

"It's not the gold I mean. You cannot—you have your duties—your—Mercadier."

"I'll find his army when I come back. Mathieu knows where to send word to me—to a place where I will get his message."

The image of Payen with the crippled monk came to Johanna's mind. She would wager half the Mercat fortune that St. Martin's abbey sheltered Payen's kin, and that it was the only place under God's hand where Payen might be reached in troubled times—through his cleric brother.

Payen looked up at the clouds moving above them. "The wind is strong from the west," he said. "I'll be to England and back again before Mercadier finds his next war."

He was not teasing. Payen meant to come with her all the way to the coast of England. A pain rose and grew within Johanna's throat and did not allow words to pass.

She would not be alone when she crossed the sea. She would not be alone— "You must not come with me."

"Are you not pleased? Are you—" Payen's voice faltered; then he uttered a low oath. "You are crying?" he asked. "Come, madam. I'll not charge you more than my passage money. You'll not lose your Mercat gold by paying me what I'm worth."

"Damn the gold."

"By St. Petroc's little finger, madam, is this a merchant's daughter speaking?" He placed a warm hand upon her cold, fisted knuckles. "Calm yourself. This is the road to St. Michael's port. If a Templar patrol should find us, they will think I have abducted and ravished you. Can you not stop crying?"

"I am not crying."

"Then keep the tears from your face. It makes you seem as if you weep."

"Can you not be silent?" she cried. "I have a mote in my eye."

"Then I pity the mote, for it will surely be drowned."

She began to laugh; the tears came again, and more laughter. Beneath her, the palfrey sidled from the track and stopped.

It seemed a small gesture, and right for the moment, to touch his shoulder and then to take her knee from the saddle bow and turn to look full upon his upturned face. She did not remember the small slide from her saddle into his arms, nor did she know which of them had first sought the brush of lips upon palm, then upon eyes closed in longing.

His palm rose to cup her chin, to bring her mouth to meet his kiss. The sea wind against her cheek moved upon the deep flush that rose where he had touched her and could not take the heat of passion from her face.

The silent, fleeting touch of his mouth upon her skin turned her mind from the sudden fire within her. She was as a leaf before tinder, without thought or choosing, and only his touch and the deep, hoarse words he uttered could bring her back from that fire to keep her from blazing into dust.

He took his mouth from her lips and held her close before him, murmuring words she could not hear for the cruel drumming of her pulses.

His words continued beneath that swift cadence, running low and insistent, unheard in the rush of heartbeat, blood, and desire.

It was only when she tried, in her desire, to bring his face back to her own that she opened her eyes and saw, in his gaze, that he was not lost to that same drumming and had used his words to quell it. Again and again he spoke them, and her mind returned from that place where words had no power.

"You do not want this," he said.

And Johanna knew that these were the words he had told to her, again and again, as he had held her to his body.

"You do not want this," he said once more, and saw that she had understood at last.

He closed his eyes and brought her head to his shoulder, beneath the strong stubbled line of his jaw. Behind her, the dappled warmth of the palfrey kept the wind from her back.

It was enough to be wrapped within his arms, his heartbeat steady beneath her cheek. To stay as they were might be enough.

''You do not want this,'' he whispered against her hair, and was silent at last. There was bitter resignation in those hoarse, final words.

And she understood, as if he had spoken it, that as he drew his hand along the line of her jaw, and down the pulsing of her throat, that he meant it to be the last touch. That he meant to remember the feel of her in that moment, for there was to be no other touch. No more—

She seized his hand and brought it back to warm her face. ''We are free, you and I. In these days until I am once again Johanna Mercat, the wool seller's daughter, we are free. Can we not—''

''No. You do not want this.''

''I am no fool, '' she said. ''I need no one to tell me what I want or want not.''

He sighed. ''You are no fool, but you are ignorant of much that would turn you from me.''

''I was a wife,'' she said. ''I am no maiden in need of a guard for my virtue and a mentor to think for me. I know you, Payen, as I never knew my husband. Do not tell me that I am ignorant.'' She paused to draw a painful breath. ''Tell me, instead, why you turn me from you.''

He began to speak, then muttered a foreign oath and looked past her to the road. ''It would be a poor end to our journey,'' he said, ''if we stand here speaking of lust where our enemies may find us.''

Lust. Never in Johanna's short time as a wedded wife had Walter believed her capable of lust.

''And this night?'' she asked. ''Will you turn from me this night with your talk of ignorance and your belief that you know, better than I, what I should want?''

''This night,'' he said, ''will be a living hell.''

He brought his hands within her cloak and down her body, and for a blessed moment Johanna felt a lover's delight in his touch. But he closed his hands about her waist and lifted her back to the saddle.

She stopped herself from touching him. "Do you believe," she said, "that a single kiss has put us on the road to hell? And that we would be damned if we came closer?"

"Yes," he said.

"Then tell me why."

He looked at her, and Johanna saw that his desire was as great as her own blaze of wanting. "When we are with the Templars, and have bought passage to England, then I will tell you. Not before."

"You will tell me before you buy passage." She met his gaze and looked beyond the plain desire to the secrets he had kept from her. "You have not told me why you traveled across the duchy to save my life. There was something more in your mind—not just the fear that having heard the harper's offer, you might be blamed for my death. To have brought me this far was an act of charity that might redeem you from the flames of hell. To go with me to England would be more than charity, and I am not such a fool that I would accept your company without knowing your purpose."

He shrugged. "We will speak, then, at the Templars' port." Payen's frown lightened, and the corner of his mouth twitched. "You are hard woman, Johanna Mercat, and not given to extremes of gratitude."

"When it comes, my gratitude will bring you gold to match your deeds."

"Then add a silver coin or two for my boots. You will owe me new ones by the time we reach the coast."

Chapter Thirteen

They reached the sea again and looked across a vast, clouded bay to the east. Below them, a small port crowded with trading cogs and fishing boats nestled into the rocky shore. Upon the narrow beach, the shell of a half-built longship lay braced by timbers dug into the sand.

"Where are they?" Johanna asked.

Payen pointed to a small rectangular fortress overlooking the village, set well back from the sea. "It's shelter," he said, "and a refuge from assassins. Try not to frighten the sentries with your frown."

For a woman who had been reluctant to approach the Templars, Johanna Mercat showed an admirable ability to deal with them. She waited in silence as Payen asked for lodging in the small house set aside, within the walls of the settlement, for travelers; she made no gesture of dismay when Payen, pressed by the gatekeeper's questions, told the man that Johanna was his wife.

When Payen returned from the stables, he found that Johanna had managed to find and bargain for a length of cloth to replace her bedraggled mantle, and had begun to persuade the sergeant locking the storehouse door that he had been foolish to buy goods of coarse Cornish wool when fine Yorkshire fleeces were nearly as cheap.

He stood in the thin sun of that Breton afternoon and gave thanks that they had managed to reach the one place in all the duchy where Johanna could move at will without fear of attack. The Templar monks, for all their ill-concealed pride and well-concealed mysteries, would take up no secular causes, and would assist no lord, however influential, in matters of vengeance and intrigue. They were steady in their loyalty to the princes of the Church, and to those few temporal kings who had gained the Templars' respect through deeds of warfare and hard justice; all others, however well landed, however influential in the courts of Christian kings, would fear to speak of their own petty disputes before the black-clad Templar knights. The knave who had sent a harper lad to arrange Johanna Mercat's death would be unlikely to come near to the Templars for his next attempt.

When Johanna had finished her discussion of wool and extracted a promise from the storehouse sergeant to buy from Guy of Dinan, Payen walked with her across the well-swept bailey yard and carried their single saddlebag up to the high gray chamber that had been given them.

There were few other travelers lodging at the fortress, for the weather had turned bitter cold and the Templar houses, though well built and shielded from the worst of the intrusive sea wind, offered little of the warm cheer of the roadside inns with their loud gaming and their heady smells of ale and hot brandywine.

Though the house would offer no sly maids to inflame the senses and press strong drink upon him, Payen saw that the spare comforts of the lodging house held a more serious temptation: He and Johanna would be nearly alone within those thick, mortared walls when night fell upon the settlement.

Payen dropped the saddlebag beside the bed and cleared his throat. "I will return before long." And without waiting for Johanna's answer, he went to seek the master's quarters, and old Hamo Strongbow.

The months since the old knight had returned from Palestine had not dealt kindly with Hamo. When Payen appeared, Hamo roused himself from uneasy slumber in a high-backed wooden chair, the only object of luxury in a cell as gray and cold as the chamber opened for Payen.

Hamo raised his brows and gestured to a low bench against the wall. He waited for Payen to settle, then looked to the arrow slit that pierced the western wall; there was a narrow view of the bailey sentry post. "I saw you arrive, Payen of Rochmarin. You have taken a wife?"

"No," Payen said. "I have brought a fugitive; I protect her by that falsehood, even here."

The old man sighed. "And have you used the guise of a Templar in this journey?"

"No."

"Then I am content, for I would not have rumors of Templar knights bringing their mistresses and trumpery wives to these walls." He looked back to Payen, then resumed his watch over the bailey gates. "My English fellows tell me that you have, quite recently, worn a Templar surcoat in your travels."

"I did so," Payen admitted. "For a good reason, in a cause close to your great regard."

"And that reason, I trust, is no longer a problem?"

Payen smiled. "I got the bishop Hubert Walter to his meeting place in Spain and back to Canterbury. He treated with the Hashishin messenger; there will be help, of a subtle kind, in assuring King Richard's release this winter."

The old man shifted and turned his bright gaze upon Payen. "There would be a place for you in our ranks, as you well know, when you cease to hide your name and your blood. Your name has honor to it, though the lands are gone."

"I cannot."

"Your name could be spoken in secret and another used when you come into the order."

Payen shook his head. "I have not the calling."

"You have the ability and the skill at arms. And you have not, from rumors that have reached me, given yourself to more than the usual pursuits of the flesh. There would be occasion, and opportunity, to satisfy your craving for women from time to time."

Payen sighed. "I would be a poor Templar, sir. I could not give you complete loyalty."

The old man sat back. "Ah. You have not given up your ambition to take back the lands."

"I will see my brother in his place as lord of Rochmarin, if I can." In the early evening light Payen saw that old Hamo's face had paled. "How goes it with you?" he asked.

"Well enough, save when the weather comes from the north. On those days my bones ache so hard that if Saladin himself came calling, I'd be hard pressed to lift a sword." The old eyes focused upon Payen's hands. "You have seen combat, I think, since Palestine. Is Mathieu still with you?"

Payen frowned. That diversion was meant to draw his mind away from Hamo's health. It did not.

"Has Mathieu yet paid his debt to you?" Hamo asked.

"There is no debt," Payen said. "Only in his imaginings."

"Saracen raiders at Mathieu's back were no imagining. No one but you, Payen, would ride out to get him, foolish as he was."

Payen frowned. "Why should the foolish die when the crafty of the earth hide behind their gold? Mathieu has repaid me many times over since Palestine."

"And the woman? Another foolish soul who will owe you a debt of loyalty?"

Payen felt his face darken. "She owes me nothing, nor will I take her gratitude."

"You will take the lady, I think. I saw how you looked at her. Now or later, you will have her gratitude as well as her gold." Hamo began to cough. "It's near winter, and my bones are crying out for the sun of Palestine. Small wonder that men leave their hearths for pilgrimage. There is no heat on God's earth like that of Christ's own lands."

Payen moved to the hearth and prodded the wood to blaze hotter. He cast two great wedges of oak into the flames.

Hamo sighed. "I thank you, Payen. But it's not age nor the cold that plagues me. It's the scars, and the crooked bones healed in the saddle, and the flux that never left after Ascalon." He covered Payen's hand with his pale claw. "If you will not come into the order, then put aside your sword long enough to find a place in the world. Do not spend the rest of your years fighting, Payen. Stop before you have too many scars, before your body is ruined from wounds sewn poorly and bones healed ill."

"It is what I do."

"Well, ask the woman to find you something more. She will do it if any may. Did you see her, calling young Paul to task? She had him in retreat as I watched. That one, my friend, does not fear to speak when she sees the need."

Johanna had bargained with the young monk at the storehouse and won, for two silver deniers, a fine length of wool that she might wear as a mantle. She was pleased with her small triumph and seemed content to see Payen come to find her in their cold, remote chamber. But for the small tremor in her voice, Payen would have believed her unconcerned about the night to come.

She folded the mantle with slow, distracted precision, then turned to Payen. "You said you would speak of your past."

"I will sleep below and leave the chamber for you," he said. "I want you to know that before we speak."

"Do as you wish," Johanna said. "There is nothing between us but an embrace, and that done with misgivings. Yours," she said. "Not mine."

Though he carried a brand to light the wood that waited in the small wall hearth, Payen did not progress beyond the doorframe. "There is everything between us," he said. "And every reason we should never again touch."

She sat down upon the pallet, a crimson-skirted island of warm, dismayed sensuality in the bare stone chamber.

"Do you remember," he asked, "how the watchmen stood back when I rode into the firelight and cursed them for attacking you?"

"I will never forget," she said.

"Did you understand why they heeded me?"

The wariness left her eyes. She must have thought that this confession was to be a matter of brigands, warlocks, and Payen's own tattered past. He paused then, savoring the last moment in which Johanna would look at him as something other than an adversary.

"They took you for a ghost," she said, "or a living man with a reputation too unsavory to ignore?"

"They took me for my father," he said. "They took me for the last true lord of Rochmarin."

He walked past her then, to hold the burning brand to the kindling. Light and heat and a rush of flaming sound filled the chamber.

Johanna watched him as he tossed the brand upon the new flames; when he turned back to her, she was still frowning. "You are some kin of Walter Malebis?" she asked.

"The last true lord," Payen said, "was no Norman. He was Alain of Rochmarin, and I am his son."

"The Malebis—"

"Came to claim the land after the rebellions, when my father and my mother lay dead in St. Martin's abbey. The Normans would not allow them to rest in the chapel at Rochmarin."

She raised her gaze back to his face, her questions as plain as if they had been spoken.

"The first of the Normans to come, after the last skirmish, was your husband's father. Your husband was the next lord after him. The people of Rochmarin had not seen my face for two decades and remembered me only as a child; but some of the men about the watch fire would have remembered my father. And most could recall his curses, uttered in the Breton tongue as he fell beneath a Norman army thrice the size of the Rochmarin garrison. I inherited his face, Johanna, and remembered his curses. I used them both to fright the watchmen."

Johanna spoke at last. "You are the heir," she said. "The lands would have been yours had the Normans not come."

He shook his head. "It would be a simple decision between us if I were the heir. You are the widow of Walter Malebis, who died without an heir, and none can be sure, this early, that you do not carry a Malebis child. Wed to me, you might have an early child of our union; if a son, and if he came soon enough, he might inherit Rochmarin. If you brought him into the world in Yorkshire, no Breton could tell the precise day of his birth. And if none could tell with certainty whether he was my son or Malebis's child, he would still have the right to inherit the lands—because of me, and because you were the last Malebis bride at Rochmarin."

"You want me because of that child?"

"No. Fate never brings a plan as simple as what I described. I am not the heir, Johanna. If my family returns to the lands, it should be my brother, if he is able, who will be lord of Rochmarin."

"If he is able—" She hesitated. "Your brother is at the monastery? At St. Martin's?"

"You saw, then? You saw his face."

She nodded.

"His name is Alain, as was my father's. The land should be his."

"He is a monk; he will have no children. He is—"

"—quite capable, they say, of begetting his own heirs despite the injuries that left him a cripple at the fall of Rochmarin. He is no monk, but a novice only, and will be until he dies, or leaves St. Martin's to take his place at Rochmarin. He will be free to wed should the lands come back to us."

She raised her chin. "And do you believe the lands will come back to your kin after all those years? Walter Malebis held them from the young duke, King Henry Plantagenet's grandson. Brittany's lords in this generation are Normans, or Bretons who have done homage to the Plantagenet duke. Walter's sister will wed Adam Mauleon, and their children will inherit."

"Do you want Walter's sister to inherit? Do you wish to see Rochmarin added to the lands of Adam Mauleon?"

"It would be better," she said, "than to bear your child knowing that you wanted me only as a second chance to put your blood back at Rochmarin, if your brother could not take it."

He closed his eyes and repeated the words with which he had stemmed the passion between them on the road to the sea. "You do not want this," he said. "Now you see the truth in my words. You might have wanted Payen, the mercenary with nothing to gain but pleasure from bedding you. Payen, the cast-out son of Rochmarin, is not a man you should touch."

"And what do you want?"

"What I want," he said, "does not matter."

"What do you want?" she said again.

He closed his eyes. "I want to take you this night and keep you as my leman until this inconvenient passion dies between us. I do not want you for the child, not for that alone. If I did, I would not have stopped you from giving yourself to me beside the road this day, when your blood was hot and your reason overcome."

She had not moved, nor given any sign that she agreed with him. "Then why did you stop me?" she asked at last. "Is your blood colder than mine? Was it my desire alone that brought us this far?"

"You have had enough sorrow in this land without finding, in your last night before sailing, a trap woven of lust and the past. You do not want Rochmarin; but you would be trapped there if you bore my child and my brother begat none."

She rose to her feet and fixed him with a gaze colder than the winter sea. "If I bore your child," she said, "I would not allow it to bear your burden of old ills and vengeance at Rochmarin. I would raise him at Gunndale, as I was raised, and teach him to make his way without killing—not for the lands of Rochmarin, and not for the causes of others. You would not take my child where I refuse to go, nor teach him to want the life that killed the child who was my brother. There are other ways—better ways—to live."

Payen felt an unreasoning mirth rise within him. Johanna stood amid the gray shadows of a cold Templar chamber, her face aflame above the vivid rose of her kirtle, her small fists closed upon her skirts, and denied him, before he had so much as touched her soft young breasts, the rearing of a child who might, next midsummer day, have suckled upon her.

She was furious, and she was right to be so.

He collapsed against the doorframe and gave himself to mirth.

She recoiled as if he had cursed her. "Is it so hard to believe that Rochmarin is not the end and beginning of my hopes for a child of mine? Are you content to bring a child of yours into the same game of blood vengeance as you must have played since your parents died? Is it so difficult to believe that I would not share your obsession with that demon-ridden land?"

Her face was bright red now, and her hair seemed to stand

out as if a storm were coming. He sat down in abrupt collapse and tried to turn his mind from mirth. It was hopeless. He had not laughed so since the day he had taken Alain to the abbey.

She made for the door and pulled the skirt of her kirtle aside to step around his booted legs.

He caught her hand and asked her to stay. And he fell back, once again, in helpless laughter.

She stepped back into the chamber and slammed the door shut with a force that reverberated down his spine. "Why," she asked, "should I remain to watch you laugh at me?"

"Because," he gasped, "it is not you alone. We are both—"

"What? We are both what?"

With great effort he kept laughter at bay long enough to tell her. "We are quarreling about a child not yet conceived, and we have yet to do more than touch our lips. This—prudence, lady, goes far beyond anything I imagined when I dreaded the hour I would tell you these matters."

"This prudence," she replied, "has been days in creation. For I had thought, Payen, that we might make a child together. And I had imagined that I must—if you stayed long enough—that I must tell you that no child of mine will follow your life; my child will not die in a garrison yard or return fluxed and scarred from the king's next battles in the Holy Land."

He seized her hand again and brought her down to rest upon his doubled knees. Payen took her cheeks between his hands and spoke into her flushed face. "You are telling me that if we bed together, and if there is a child, you do not expect me to stay to see it grow?"

"I did not imagine you would. Your life—"

"My life is harsh, as you have said. But you had imagined you would bear a child of mine and raise it in Yorkshire? You wanted this?"

There was no laughter in either gaze. "I want a child. If it happens now, before I return to Yorkshire, it will seem to be my dead husband's babe. And I would not need to wed again."

He took his hands from her face and drew back to look at her. "You do not want to wed again?"

"I do not want my life, or my child's life, to be under the shadow of another's trials or foolishness. If I wed again, it will be to a man who will not bring my kin into danger. I will live at Gunndale and Whitby, and no one will take me from home again."

He sighed. "Your late husband did not distract you from your homesickness. Was he no comfort to you?"

She started to rise. "I will not sit on a cold floor with night upon us and discuss my dead husband."

He pulled her down to rest once again upon his knees. "No, we will sit here and quarrel about the child neither of us has demanded—the child we are too angry to conceive."

Laughter and anger had gone; there remained, in the chill air of the chamber, their last words. The sudden madness of half-truths and desires had offered a turning place where folly might be found.

Johanna's boldness, the spirit that had offered Payen more than kisses by the roadside, in the full light of day, had vanished; in the sudden stiffness of her back, and the absence of color upon her cheeks, Payen sensed that the moment of freedom, of possibilities, had passed. He took his hands from her waist and willed the wild pulse of his heart to slow.

She looked to the hearth. "You might have told me days ago that you came to Rochmarin because you feared your family would be blamed for my death."

"I did not intend to tell you. It was only when you showed me—kindness—" he said, "that it became necessary to tell you."

"If you had told me, I would have been less trouble for you. I thought, at first, that you had been with the brigands who slew my husband."

Payen's heart stopped. If Johanna Mercat came to know the worst of his secrets—that the disinherited lord's brother, a notorious mercenary, had agreed to meet Walter Malebis in Nantes, and had slain him there—she would possess a weapon that could destroy both Payen's hopes and Alain's sanctuary. If the widow Malebis let slip, by mischance or in anger, that it was no common brigand who had slain Walter Malebis, the wrath of the Plantagenets and their Norman lords in Brittany would fall upon Payen, his brother, and all their distant kin. He must not, for their sake, give Johanna Mercat that weapon, however much he trusted her.

Johanna touched his face. "What will you do when you leave me in England? If Adam Mauleon has wed Agnes, will you demand the land back from him?"

He covered her hand with his own. "No, he'll keep it. If Mauleon can hold it, I'll have done with Rochmarin."

"And your brother?"

"—tells me he is content at the abbey. There are worse fates, as you have said."

She sighed. "Is it for my sake that you may give it up?"

If it were that simple, Payen would have answered her. But he did not wish to lie to Johanna Mercat, and he had not the heart to tell her that he had known, when he saw Walter Malebis's body upon the brothel floor, that Rochmarin might never be his.

He drew her hand to his mouth and inhaled the sweet scent of her skin. "The land is gone," he said. "You shun it, and I know that my kin may never return."

Beneath his lips her hand trembled. "What we have, Johanna, is this chamber and this night. There may be other nights, but not many. In England we must part."

"And if there should be a child?"

"The child would be yours to raise as you wish. I'd send you gold for the child, but I'll not draw it into my life."

Chapter Fourteen

She rose to her feet but left her hand in Payen's hold, cradled against his cheek. If there were words to speak to a man whom she would take to her bed, without the blessing of wedlock, Johanna did not know them. Nor did she, in that first moment of uncertainty, meet his questioning gaze.

Then he was beside her, close beside her, bringing her hands to his lips, teasing the fine, sensitive skin of her wrists with kisses so soft they might have been her pulses, given in a ragged cadence of desire.

''Are you cold?'' he murmured.

She shook her head. It had been easier, sitting upon his knees with his face level to her own, to speak with him of this night, and of desire. Now he had risen to stand beside her, over a head taller than Johanna's good height, and it was impossible to read his features without raising her face to him and inviting his mouth to close upon her own.

He took his lips from her and pulled his tunic over his head; he cast it into the shadows beyond the pallet. His hands moved to the laces of her kirtle, and she stood quiet under that slow, deliberate touch upon the cloth that kept her body from his gaze.

The firelight upon his arm showed scars and a wound only recently healed. She touched him beside the crimson weal and sighed. "Does it pain you?" she asked.

His hands stilled. "No more," he answered. He took his hands from her kirtle and turned from her to open his saddlebag. Johanna stood in the firelight, uncertain how to respond to his sudden movement. He drew the wineskin from his saddle pack and turned back to her.

He took her hand and led her to sit beside him upon the pallet. He offered her the leather flask. "To forget," he said.

She took it and drank the rich red wine that the maid Ursula had found for them at the inn. "What would you forget?" she asked.

He drank then, and he looked at her with hot desire in his gaze. "The past," he said. "I would have this night, Johanna, without the past to torment us."

She looked again at the heavy scars upon his arm—upon the dense, well-formed muscles of his sword arm—and felt his frown follow her gaze. "The past," she said, "holds much for which I must be grateful to you."

He drank again and set the wineskin aside. "I meant what I said, Johanna. We have nothing, you and I, but this chamber and this night. And a few more nights if we are lucky. We have dealt with the future, so let us leave the past outside this chamber as well."

He reached for her again, and she tensed against the moment when he would take her kirtle from her and send it to sprawl in the darkness beside his tunic. But he drew it down her shoulders, freed her arms from the sleeves, and took the thin cloth slowly from her breasts, covering each slow revelation of flesh with the warmth of his mouth.

She understood, then, that if there were to be haste, it would be her own desire that brought it.

In Walter Malebis's high bed at Rochmarin, Johanna had not known the luxury of slow lovemaking. In the breathless space of time Payen had taken to free her breasts into the firelight, and to warm them within the careful torment of his mouth, her husband would have spent his seed in her and collapsed into sleep.

In the spare comfort of a Templar house, in the touch of a man who had earned his bread in war and killing, Johanna had found a gentle spirit offering her the freedom to love as she wished.

Payen must have sensed the drift of her mind; he took her face between his hands and looked into her eyes. "There is no past for us," he said. "This is to be our own time, and all is new. Everything is possible. Tell me what you desire."

"Everything."

He smiled. "What first?"

She lowered her gaze. "I want to choose the time."

He drew back slightly; the slight crease between his brows would have been a frown had he not attempted to smile. "Not this night? It is your choice as you have asked. It always was, Johanna."

"Tonight," she said. "I want to choose when we begin."

He drew her kirtle back up to cover her breasts and placed her hand upon the laces. Then he settled back upon the pallet, his hands behind his head, and looked at her. Though the smile had vanished, there was no rancor in his gaze. "We must use words, then," he said. "I had imagined, just now, that you had given consent."

Johanna shook her head. "I meant, I want to choose when you—"

"When I come into you?"

"Yes."

"And you will tell me, in words, when the moment comes—when you agree?"

"Yes," she said. "That is what I want above all else."

His frown deepened; Johanna steeled herself to deny him. "You believe we need words?" he asked.

She nodded.

His smile returned and grew into laughter. "You are an odd lady, Johanna Mercat." He reached for her arm and drew her down to rest upon his chest. He began to toy with her hair and to draw the tresses from her braid. He moved his fingers among the strands and brought them to cover his chest, to lie amid the dark, whorled pelt beneath her cheek. "I could lose myself," he whispered, "in the silk of your hair."

His chest moved in silent laughter. "Have I your consent, Johanna Mercat, to lose myself in your hair?"

She raised her head and frowned down upon his mirth. "That is not what I meant," she said. "Do not mock me."

"It is not a mockery matter," he said. He brought his hands within her hair and turned her face to his gaze. "Promise me, lady, that when you give your word that I may come within you, you will speak without regret."

He kissed her then and set her from him. "There is a limit, Johanna, to the curb I can place upon my need."

There had been no curbs, no restraint in what Walter Malebis had done with her. To her.

Payen raised his brows, waiting for her answer.

"There will be no regret," she said.

He smiled and crossed one long leg over the other; he began to study his boot with comical intensity. The firelight upon his arms brought the dark scars into prominence and cast its light upon the well-formed breadth of his shoulders. With slow, careful grace he caught her hand and brought it to rest upon his chest. "Touch me as you wish," he said. "Tonight I will ask you for no restraint upon your own wishes."

Johanna stilled her hand. "And after tonight?"

He smiled then, and shifted slightly beneath her palm. "After tonight," he said, "we will be at sea. We will negotiate." He brought her other hand to rest beside the first and drew them closer to his black, silken pelt.

She began with timid fascination to stroke the hard muscles beneath her hands. With a murmured question and a smile he brought his hands back into her hair and drew her face down to his own.

His mouth opened beneath her own and began to tease her with small, sucking nips upon the fullness of her lips. He brought a gentle finger to her lower lip. "Have I your leave, Johanna, to come within?"

She opened her lips and nipped his finger as he had done to her, then lowered her mouth once again to him. Beneath her his lips were closed; she felt them curve in a small smile.

She raised her head.

"I have promised," he murmured. "Until you say that I may enter, I will not come into you."

"You are cruel," she said.

"I am sworn," he answered.

"Then yes," she said. "Oh, yes."

He brought his palm to rest beneath her chin and drew his thumb along the line of her lower lip. When she opened to taste the smoke and salt of his skin, he sat up and brought his mouth to do what his hand had begun. With shallow, skillful passes his tongue brought a shock of pleasure to her mouth and sent subtle waves of heat into her belly.

She had not felt, before that moment, how rough was the cloth of her kirtle, and how heavy it lay upon her body. The room blazed with heat, and she longed to be rid of the encumbrance of her robes.

At her slight movement Payen took his hands from her body. He smiled, then, to see her frantic haste to draw the kirtle down, to free her body to the warmth of his gaze. The kirtle was still with her, fallen about the stem of her waist. Above its many folds, her breasts were bathed in firelight.

He moved his hand within a feather's touch of one yearning peak, then drew away. She saw, in the crook of his brow and the slow smile that curved his mouth, what she must do.

Johanna lifted the curve of his broad palm and traced a small pattern upon the callused skin. "May I come within?" she asked.

"Yes," he muttered. And muttered again, his words a sustained, incoherent oath as she brought his hand to her breast and moved within his gentle touch. His lips went to take what his palm held, and she felt his broad, open hands move to her back to hold her close against his face. Slowly his mouth began to draw pleasure from her soul and bring it to crest in the tender flesh beneath his lips. There was a long pulse of wonder, a strange aching need below her belly, then a moment of sudden loss.

Johanna fell back against Payen's arms and felt him lower her to the cool linen of the pallet. Her kirtle had come up to pool above her calves in a heavy mass that covered her from waist to knee.

The chamber was cold once again. The intense heat that had consumed her body was ebbing, and she began to shiver. She reached for Payen's arm, drew him down upon her, and sought the heat of his long body.

His lips upon her throat brought the flames back to spread, in violent swiftness, and to burn again within her woman's flesh. She moved beneath him to draw the kirtle from her hips, and felt his hands move down in a long, delicate caress to take the robe from her and cast it into the shadows.

She opened to him as she had been taught to do. And waited, as she had been taught to do.

His hands moved to the laces of his chausses, then back to rest beside her waist.

"May I come within?" His voice held the low intensity she

had heard that night at Rochmarin. In Walter Malebis's bed. In the moonlight—

There was a limit, he had said, to the curb he could place upon his need.

"Yes," she breathed, and tensed against the rough linen of the pallet.

His hands began to trace the line of her hips and moved to caress, with slow, subtle care, the delicate pulse within her woman's flesh.

"Yes," she said again, and felt the exquisite pressure of his hand as it moved closer to her need.

He was breathing hard, and the long planes of his back were hot to her touch. At his waist, the laces of his chausses were loosened; with one bold motion she drew them down and cried out in frustration when they would not be freed.

His hands stilled her effort, and he moved from her to stand at the pallet's side. His gaze moved from her mouth to her hips, and back to look into her fire-dazed eyes. He held her gaze and with a smile that came near to mischief lowered his chausses over the great bulge of his desire.

"Say yes," he said at last. "Say yes, my lady, or I will die from needing you."

She smiled and held her arms to him, and felt the heavy promise of his body cover her wanting flesh. She opened as she could and arched against the hard, silken warmth of his manhood. "Yes," she whispered. "Yes, oh, yes."

He moved within her, and thrice again. He took his mouth from her lips and worried sweat-beaded skin of her shoulder.

Johanna sighed. "It was good, Payen—"

His head came up. "Is something wrong?"

"No, it was wonderful."

He let out a long breath. Deep within her, Johanna felt him grow larger still. "Must we stop?" he asked.

"Stop?" she asked. And began to understand.

Sweat stood heavy upon his brow. In a strangely gentle voice he spoke again. "I still stop if you need to."

"There is—"

He kissed away her words. "There is more," he said in a whisper laced with desire. "Are you willing?"

"Yes," she said, and moved against him, feeling, with dawning wonder, his strength.

Time disappeared. For an eternity Payen would still his desire and keep her waiting until she pleaded for his deeper touch. Then, in the space of a single hissing spark from the crimson hearth, he would bring her back to unreasoning pleasure, and hold her still against him, waiting for her need to grow again.

She began to cry out each time he ceased to move; he covered her mouth to silence, with deep and demanding kisses, her rising voice.

At last he abandoned restraint and brought her to completion, and added his own hoarse cry to the frantic keening that she recognized, with surprise, as her own voice.

Payen collapsed upon her, then took her in his arms, rolled upon his back, and held her upon him. He reached for the rough Templar blanket that they had cast upon the floor and brought it to cover Johanna.

She shook her head and cast it aside; Payen drew it back again. "It's freezing cold," he said. "In a moment you will begin to feel it."

"Never again," she said. And lowered her cheek to his shoulder to fall into a deep, satisfied slumber.

Payen held Johanna Mercat close to him that long, cold night and did not let her go. He watched, with indifference, as the fire burned low and did not move from the sweet touch of her body curved so perfectly upon him. He pulled the heavy coverlet closer about her and knew that she would sleep warm within his arms.

Her legs, sweetly parted upon him, left the warmth of her womanhood nestled around his rod, and he woke twice to find himself as hard and hungry as he had been at his first sight of the full delicacy of Johanna Mercat's breasts. She had begun to wake each time, but he had whispered her back to sleep and let her rest. Had she not been exhausted from days of hard travel, and had she awakened far enough to speak of desire, he might have taken her many times before the light of dawn reached their bed.

One night was not enough.

Payen smoothed Johanna's hair upon his shoulder and smiled at the memory of her confusion in those first hot moments of coupling. He had barely begun to move within her sweet, narrow passage when she had stilled and thanked him, as if they had reached completion after a night of hot love play. Her surprise, and the expression of her face in the firelight as she had greeted each renewal of their long passion, had brought him close to laughter and near to early completion.

And when they had done, and he had taken his weight from her, she stiffened in his arms as if she thought he meant to leave her to sleep untouched after all the fine coupling they had shared. She had seemed happy enough, once she understood his intent, to be drawn with him to rest upon his chest.

Walter Malebis had been with them all that long night. Within Johanna's mind the memory of what must have been short, cold coupling had been a shadow upon the early moments of their bed play.

And later, as Johanna had met their long, slow games with surprise and then delight, the specter of Malebis's dead face and that long, indulgent mouth had come to Payen's mind, and he felt a secret anger that Johanna Mercat had been wasted upon a callow lordling who had not troubled himself to show her the courtesy of gentle lovemaking.

One night was not enough to bring the lady the pleasure she deserved but had not known.

One night was not enough for Payen to love the exquisite body and the timid, emerging mischief of the widow Malebis.

When he stirred again, he thought he heard her heartbeat against his cheek and wondered that it was so irregular, and so swift. He came awake then and knew that it was the sea he had heard.

This far from the shore, the surf should not have sounded loud enough to wake him. With care Payen set Johanna from him and tucked the heavy woolen blanket around her. He moved to the narrow shutters across the arrow slits and felt a chill wind pierce the chamber.

The sound of the sea was louder now.

Payen closed the shutters and began to collect his garments from the far corners of the chamber. He prodded the fire, set fresh wood to burn upon it, and stood grinning at the sight of Johanna Mercat asleep in the Templar pallet.

For once in his life Payen was grateful that the bite of the north wind, and the force of a northern gale, would keep him from leaving port.

With luck, the gale would blow for many days. And he would have a few long nights, God willing, with Johanna Mercat.

His smile grew broader still. Northern gales had been known to last a fortnight. If his luck held, this one would keep them in port for a long, long time.

Chapter Fifteen

Payen did not sell the dappled mare but kept her from sight in the Templars' stables. He rode out each day mounted upon one of Hamo's bay geldings and counted it fortunate that his beard had grown to the point that he might be taken for one of Hamo's knights. Few of the travelers who had seen him before Aleth, riding Arsuf in the company of a fair woman, would think him the same man.

Nor was he.

Never, since the fall of Rochmarin to the Normans, had he known the fear that followed him as he rode forth, dreading to hear Johanna Mercat's name spoken in the taverns, and fearing even more that he would hear nothing and be unable to find her enemies before they found her.

The northern storm had kept the port useless; any ships that staggered under bare masts down the long, cruel swells of the English sea toward Brittany had chosen, if they could, to make landfall west of the Templar port, where the wide mouth of the river Rance offered a safer haven.

One ship, guided by a fool, or unable to choose another port, had tried to make for the small harbor below Payen's vantage point. It had met its end before his eyes in the white bar of breakers over a mile from shore, and none of the small, flailing figures had managed to cling to the spray-flung wreckage long enough to get past the rocks and reach the pummeling surf that swamped the harbor quay.

Payen had seen, far below the hill, four Templar shipwrights attempt to drag a small carrack into the sea. The hull had overturned upon the men before they had pulled themselves within the craft; the black-clad figures fought hard to claw their way back to land. When the small crowd upon the beach had turned their attention once again to the distant wreck, the small, helpless figures vanished beneath the white water.

Too far above the harbor to reach the shore in time to help, Payen had forced himself to watch the distant tragedy and had imagined that he heard the cries of the doomed borne to him upon the cold November wind. Death in battle—hot battle with blood madness to cloud the mind—was preferable to such a helpless, cold fate. The victims had no choice, no way of turning from their doom, no chance to use their wits to live past the hour the ship had foundered on the rocks.

At Rochmarin, Johanna Mercat had been as doomed as those drowning figures beyond Payen's reach. By her name and her marriage to Walter Malebis, Johanna had been caught in just such a trap, and might, but for Mercadier's casual words over his wine on an idle October night, have faced assassins and died, never knowing why they struck, nor how she could have saved herself.

Payen shuddered as the early winter wind passed over the distant wreckage and reached the hilltop.

Years ago Rochmarin had held within its walls many doomed and innocent souls. Payen's mother and young brothers had been trapped at Rochmarin when the Normans came, confined within those unlucky walls with as little chance of survival as shipwrecked men.

Payen turned from the sight of the cold sea. If Johanna Mercat could be persuaded to regard with tolerance those men who lived by steel, she might find herself a husband who could keep her safe and allow her fine spirit to survive the hard years to come.

He could not be that man.

Payen's mount shied beneath a savage oath.

Even if he had been willing to put aside his sword and learn to count fleeces in the Mercat storehouses, Johanna Mercat must never take him into her life. One day there would be a man who knew his face, and would ask Johanna how she had come to wed a man who had been used to taking all he required through bloodshed. And she would begin, one day, to wonder where Payen had been the night Walter Malebis had died in the whore's house in Nantes.

And should the truth be discovered, Johanna herself would be suspected of paying Payen to kill her husband. Already there had been rumors that the widow Malebis had bought her husband's death; already the tale had reached Mercadier's camp, given as a reason the widow Malebis should die.

He pulled the sidling mount back onto the narrow track to descend from the foothills to the coast. That life-devouring storm that had broken the longship and taken its crew to die in the sea had given Payen the gift of time—it would be many more days before the Templars would send their ships north. Payen and Johanna had no choice but to wait in relative safety within that high gray chamber where none could hear their love games.

A few days had been added to the only brief paradise Payen would ever know.

Already the thought of Johanna Mercat, waiting beside the small hearth, the door barred against all but Payen, sent his blood rushing through his body. Not even a last cold sight of the distant, hopeless wreckage could stem the need he felt for that widow lady with her fine, pale Yorkshire skin.

Once she was safe in her cold land, given into her uncle's keeping and never to return to the dangers she had left in Brittany, he would set her from him and kiss her once in friendship, and try, in the long journey back to the Breton coast, to forget the feel of her, to forget the way her hair had shone upon his shoulder each dawn, tangled from their lovemaking, fragrant in the chill air of the chamber. He would forget, for all time, the way her odd green-flecked eyes had turned gold in the light of the fire and glowed with all the colors of the flames.

She was not in the chamber when he returned.

For the first moments, before he saw that the fire was banked and the pallet neatened, he feared the worst. Then he forced himself to take notice of the obvious order of the bedchamber and the absence of Johanna's cloak.

If he was breathing during his desperate search of the empty rooms, it did not ease the pain within his heart. When he crossed the bailey, his constricted throat could not bring forth the words to ask whether the stable boys had seen her.

He found her outside the walls, standing in the lee of the Templar fortress, looking out to sea. The trapped wreckage of the longship was before her, its narrow bow tilted skyward, as if still attempting to escape the distant black teeth of the reef.

"I heard them again last night," she said.

He saw that she was shaking. "Come back inside," Payen said. "There was nothing we could have done."

"I will kill us both if I go home before spring."

"We will both live to see Whitby," Payen said. "When the storm blows by, it will be safe to sail."

"I don't want you to come," she said. "I'll go alone. Promise me you won't follow."

"I won't follow," Payen said. "I'll be at your side."

She shook her head. "Don't play with my words. I don't want you with me."

He took her arm. "You're cold. Come back, Johanna."

"If you won't stay behind, I cannot sail. I'll stay until spring, no matter—"

He pulled her to his side and began to draw her with him to the gates of the fort.

"I heard them, the night before they died, and they were calling again last night."

"They were far out at sea the night before it happened. They struck at dawn."

"I heard them, Payen—"

He stopped and drew his cloak along his arm to cover her shoulders. "All right," he said. "You must have heard them."

"Do not speak so. I knew they were coming. It was a warning. If we sail, there will be death—" She broke off and looked at him. "Don't you believe me?"

His laughter surprised them both. "You are asking a demon-ridden Breton, my lady. A man of the race that tends the ancient spirits of the stones and brings the scorn of a Yorkshire woman upon him when he speaks of the old ways. If the sea demons spoke to you last night, Johanna, who am I to deny it?"

"It was so real, the first night I heard them, and in the morning you were gone, and the bell was ringing, and the wreck was there."

They had passed the sentry post and turned to the narrow house where they had slept. "That night the watchmen saw a fire out at sea and called their fellows to watch it pass. I heard, and went down to speak to them, but by then the light had disappeared. They were not sure how close it was, and there was no chance of rescue in the darkness. You must have wakened then. It was no dream, Johanna, and there was no warning. When the sea is calm again, we will sail—together."

"If you should come with me, and you are drowned—"

"If I do not come, and find myself a local skirmish to pass the time, I might die in the fighting. Then how would you feel, Johanna Mercat, knowing that you had left me to die?"

She passed the edge of her mantle across her face and turned to him with reddened eyes. "I would think you were a sorry, cruel knave to have spoken so, and would squander a fortune in gold buying masses for your soul. It would take the profits of two good shearing seasons to buy you out of hell's fires."

He laughed again and took the mantle from her shoulders. "Indeed, Johanna, you must love me well, to be willing to part with so much gold to save my soul."

"It is not a matter for jesting."

It was not. If Johanna lost the small battle with her tears, and began to cry in earnest, Payen would be undone. He glanced at the chamber door and cursed himself for his cowardly wish to flee.

He kissed the tears from Johanna's eyes and set her from him only when she had begun to protest that his beard was scratching her face, making her seem to weep.

She moved from him, set more wood upon the fire, and draped her mantle across the settle bench to dry.

"That was not a Templar ship out there." Payen said. "When we sail, it will be aboard a Templar supply ship, taking wine to sell to the English. There will be none but Templar crew with us—no others paying passage money. We will leave when the weather clears, heading first for the southern ports, then up the coast to Sandwich and then to Whitby. If the storms return before they reach the north, and the crew decides to winter in an English port, we will leave and ride north together. It is your best chance, Johanna, to leave your enemies behind. They won't know you sailed. Hamo would never speak of your leaving here, and even he does not know your true name."

Johanna nodded and turned back to watch the flames.

"We each of us have our fate to meet, Johanna, but I doubt we'll find it in shipwreck before we reach England, not aboard a Templar ship. The knights pay skilled seamen to man their vessels; King Richard would have no others to take charge of getting his army to Palestine."

She shrugged. "They lost him on the way home. I have heard the stories. They were shipwrecked, and gave King Richard to Leopold of Austria's men."

"The king left his escort and hired a pirate to take him from Cyprus. It was the thief's boat that foundered."

Johanna shrugged again. "The Templars did not bring him safely home, and the ransom tax will ruin us all."

Payen sighed. He should have left her to weep. The woman had a mean way about her when she was trying to keep herself from tears. "Madam, the Templars would not dare lose you, or allow the ship that carries you to be wrecked, for you would torment them with your words, whether living or from the grave."

She stood and crossed to the door. "I want to speak with your old Master Hamo. Will you bring me to him?"

He did not rise. "What do you intend?"

Johanna raised her brows. "You do not trust me with your friend Hamo?"

"No."

"Then I will have to find him myself."

Before she could lift the bar, he was beside her. "Tell me your intention, and I will ask Hamo to see you."

"You have forgotten," she said, "that you need a scribe to write you a document, and a cleric to sign it, to show that I reached the coast in good health in your company, and that I sailed for England of my own volition."

"And you have forgotten that I no longer want your name known by any on this coast. I have told you, madam, that I will get the document in England. Now, not even Hamo knows who you are, and if I need to keep you from his presence in order to preserve the secret, I'll do so."

"The whole purpose of your helping me was to ensure that your family would not be blamed."

"And the whole purpose of your leaving a document with Hamo is to rid your conscience of the matter, so that you may attempt to bribe your way onto a Templar ship without me. It will not work, Johanna. They will not do that for a woman."

"We had a plan, Payen—"

"And the death of the harper changed everything. You have been betrayed, Johanna, and if you flap about the bailey yard shouting your name to all who would listen, you will undo all my efforts—days and nights on the road, all for nothing. You might as well have waited beside the harper's corpse and shouted for his murderers to come back and get you."

Her eyes were darkened, the green of them vanished in the anger of her gaze. "I do not flap about," she said. "And I doubt your Master Hamo is as indiscreet as you describe him."

"Johanna—"

"I do not flap," she muttered. "And I do not shout. You do enough for the both of us."

Payen leaned against the door and managed not to answer.

"You leave me no choice," she said, "but to scream."

"None will come," he said. "Half the knights in this fortress fear women, and they all fear me."

She retreated to the shutters and began to open them.

"You have two choices," Payen said. "Sail with me on the wine ship, or stay here with me and wait for your enemies to get wind of two guests in the Templar fort. They will hear by Yuletide, I imagine, and come for us before Twelfth Night. They will come as guests to the fortress and lodge within this house. One night we will wake to find smoke pouring through the floor and half the planks in flames. Then I will have two choices: to push you through the arrow slit, hoping that you won't break your neck, hoping that the ones who find you on the bailey ground won't kill you; or I could kill you myself, to spare you the wait, in the infirmary, for the assassins to finish you.''

Her hands dropped to her sides, and she stood without moving, her head bowed.

He had gone too far, and spoken to her as a soldier would reason with another.

''Tell me—'' Her voice was thin but steady. ''Are there signs that they have found us?''

''No. I would have told you.''

She turned, then, to face him. Her color had gone, but there was no sign of tears in her eyes. Payen took a step forward.

''Promise me,'' she said, ''that you will never lie to me.''

''Promise me,'' he asked, ''that you will not send me from you before we reach Whitby.''

She nodded and let him take her into his arms. The sound of slow footsteps, and the voices of the those returning from work upon the longship growing upon the shore, came muffled through the oaken shutters. ''No one knows,'' Payen murmured, ''the hour of his death, or the manner of it. We must plan your return as best we can and keep a sharp eye to danger. Beyond that, Johanna, it profits us nothing to think of what we will face.''

''I forgot—for a time.''

He smiled. ''As did I, for a time. Last night, before the moon rose, I found a sweet freedom unlike any I had known.''

Johanna tilted her face to look at him with a frank, careful gaze. ''I believe, Payen, that you have had other nights of sweet freedom—many of them.''

''None like our night,'' he said, and kissed away the doubt at the corners of her mouth.

She took her mouth from him and placed a finger upon his lips. ''You need not say that. For me it was revelation. For you—''

He took her hand within his own and kissed her palm. ''For me,'' he said, ''it was paradise. Never doubt that, Johanna.''

She smiled, then, and looked at him with a gaze lightened by pleasure and curiosity. Beneath that bright promise, Johanna's cheeks were pale.

Payen found her other hand and drew her with him to the door. "Will you stay here and wait for me? I'll find a servant and bring food from the refectory."

The shadow of concern vanished from her gaze. "I'll come with you," she said. "If we are to appear as man and wife, it would be better if I did not hide here in the chamber."

He smiled and set her from him. "Any who saw you come through the gates with me would understand that I would be eager, on this day of storms, to keep you near the hearth, and in my bed."

She glanced at the hearth. "Then you should ask for more firewood. And two buckets of water to set beside the fire." Johanna smiled. "It will complete their visions of our love nest."

Payen grinned. Their imaginings would not come close to the splendor of it. "Wait here, and bar the door until you hear my voice again. And cover your hair with your mantle before you take the bar down."

"I'll be careful."

He turned back. "I'll ask old Hamo to see us together this day, and you may ask what you like about the wine ship. Ask anything you wish, but do not tell him your name."

She brightened at his words; it took all his strength of will to close the door upon the sight of Johanna Mercat's smile.

Unlike their chamber in the solid, spare house for guests, Master Hamo's quarters possessed a confusion of color and riches Johanna had not seen since leaving her uncle's house near the Whitby quays. These tapestries and plate were not set out to tempt the interest of traders, but were prizes won from the Saracens vanquished by the order in Palestine.

"In my youth, dear lady, there were victories, and prizes to be brought home from Palestine." Hamo sighed and gestured to an imperfectly repaired helm upon the wall. "All I brought home from King Richard's war with the Saracens was a great hole in my helmet and the good luck that it had rolled from my head before a Saracen stone went through it during the siege at Acre. In all the months that followed," Hamo continued, "I had no booty worth the cost of a good smith to mend it. Our armorers were swift to repair it but not as skilled as the Saracen who made the helm."

Payen raised his wine cup to admire the intricate carving upon the smooth horn surface. "Now, Johanna, Master Hamo will tell you of his Saracen helm, and how he came to receive it, and the trouble he took to have the crown of it flattened, so his own men would not mistake him for Saladin in the heat of battle."

Hamo shook his head and turned to Johanna. "Payen has told the half of it already. No, lady, I would hear of you and your troubles. You have no wish, I heard, to remain in Brittany this winter."

"No, Master Hamo. I would return to England."

He smiled. "I hear something of the north in your voice, lady. But I shall think no more on it, for I should not learn your destination, nor your family, nor your own name. I am an old man, you see, and may forget what may be told, and what must not be told, if any come looking for you."

Johanna smiled and leaned across the table. "I have no doubt you would keep my secrets, Master Hamo. But Payen has said that it would be less trouble for you if we keep you free of the need for falsehood."

"Indeed. Payen has acquired the mind and manner of a courtier, then, since last we spoke. He has lacked, in the past, the ability to save his friends from such trouble. Indeed, his exploits have caused us, at times, considerable trouble."

Johanna could not hide her delight. "What trouble?"

"Do you see how his beard has thickened in the past two days? Payen has taken the guise of a Templar knight when it pleased him in the past, and he has deceived even members of the order with his disguise. If he crops his hair, lady, then look for a Templar tunic in his saddlebags. He wears a Templar surcoat when he pleases, and uses the deception to speed his journeys. When he crops his hair and wears a beard, he could be one of us."

"Hamo—"

"Should be one of us," Hamo muttered. "He may be one day."

Payen reached for Hamo's wine cup and filled it from the high jug on the board. "Drink again, old friend, and you may have me Master of the English Commanderies by the end of this meal."

Hamo drank and fixed Payen with a grim look. "I would have you a Templar by the end of this meal if I could. And master of this preceptory after me, when my day is done." He turned to Johanna. "That is what he was created to do. A finer knight could not be found in all of Henry Plantagenet's empire, yet he is no knight, but follows that old vulture, Mercadier, taking gold for fighting, never caring who pays him."

Johanna saw the shadow upon Payen's face. "I have heard that the brigand Mercadier pays well, and has King Richard's goodwill. For a man not born to a noble family—"

Hamo winced. "Payen is good enough for the order."

Of course—old Hamo had trained Payen soon after the fall of Rochmarin to the Normans. Hamo knew the family and its former station. Johanna looked at Payen. There was sternness in his face, and a kindness that would not permit him to insult old Hamo.

Payen set down his cup and took Johanna's hand. "We thank you," he said, "for the wine, and for your company. I am weary, though, from days of travel. Good night, Master Hamo."

"Will you return here and become a knight of the order?"

she asked as they neared their chamber. "It would be better than returning to Mercadier if there comes a time when your duty to your brother is finished."

"It would not be a simple thing, restoring my brother to Rochmarin. We are the only ones left, now, of all our kin. If Mauleon weds the Malebis girl and will not cede the land to us, King Richard will do nothing in our behalf. And if we ever regain the land, we would need to hold it against Mauleon and others who would move in at a sign of weakness."

"Your brother cannot lift a sword."

"But I can, and I will. I will hold the land for his sons until they are of age. And there will be lords of Rochmarin once again—"

"And what will there be for you?"

"Justice."

"That's a cold reward. And a temporary one. Your own sons will be left to fight for the king or for Mercadier's successors."

"My sons will find lands of their own and hold them fast."

"As you would do if you did not have your brother to protect?"

Her words had gone right to the quick of his long-hidden pain. He turned upon her, and saw with bitter satisfaction that she had backed away from his regard. "I care not for any lands but Rochmarin, and they are for my brother's sons. If I sire bastards upon the women I bed, they will have gold enough to feed them and train them to make their own way in the world, and if they prove worthy of their keep, they will find their own lands and not hang about at their cousins' board, asking for scraps of Rochmarin's bounty."

Her gaze did not waver before his anger. "And where will you be while your bastard sons are learning to be men?"

"My bastards will learn from the Templars, as I did."

"And if their mothers will not send them?"

"Then they may keep my gold and buy rings for their fingers and find some other occupation for their bastards."

"As I must do."

"As you have told me you will do whether I will it or not."

"You vowed that if I get with child from you, you will give up all claim upon it?"

"I have said it," growled Payen.

"And if your brother should die without sons, you will not come to Whitby to take my child."

Small wonder the watchmen at Rochmarin had thought Johanna Mercat a witch. The woman could lead a man to perdition, using his own words to draw him to doom.

Payen opened the bedchamber door and held it for Johanna to pass. "If your son had your stubborn tongue and your will to drive me to anger, I would leave him to you and wish you well of your young wool seller."

Chapter Sixteen

The wind was down on the third day, and by nightfall the heavy line of surf had disappeared from the offshore rocks. The wine ship had suffered no harm in the days of the storm; after a half-day's inspection, the shipwrights gave their blessing to the journey, then spent a brisk two hours bailing the long, shallow bilge. By nightfall, seventy fat tuns of wine were lashed to the lower strakes beneath the rowing benches; a low-roofed timber shelter nestled within the high, sharp curve of the bow awaited the two travelers who had paid Master Hamo in heavy gold to cross the English sea.

Payen and Johanna embarked in the dark hour before dawn, setting forth from the quay in a small carrack with four men to row them out to the anchored cargo ship. It was still dark when the anchor stone thudded into its frame aft of the bow shelter. With a petty dispute about their food supply and its stowage, Payen was able to distract Johanna from the sight of the unlucky wreckage as the wine ship rowed clear of the offshore rocks.

They had agreed that the smaller of the two waterskins that Johanna had filled at the Templars' deep well should rest beside the narrow entrance to the shelter, near the cloth bag containing two loaves of bread and a half wheel of cheese. The larger waterskin and the three wineskins were tied to the great timber post that held the shelter firm against the bow stem, secure but harder to reach.

When they emerged from the shelter, the great shards of the ruined ship were far behind them, barely visible above the dark, rolling swells.

Payen turned back and drew a large leather garment from his saddlebag. "It's for you," he said.

"It doesn't look it," she said.

He raised it over her head and drew it down to cover her woolen robes. "It's a hauberk, or the beginnings of one. The armorer hadn't yet begun to sew the mail upon it, and I thought it would keep the spray and the cold from you."

Johanna looked down at the incongruous garment and touched the thick, supple leather. She smiled.

"It's not so heavy, is it? It will keep the water from you."

"I thank you," she said. "I'll give it back when we reach shore, and you should have it finished. It must have been costly."

He shrugged. "Without the mail it wasn't too much. I traded the palfrey to the armorer for this hauberk and some silver."

Johanna smiled again and moved to the rail to view the vast stretch of sea before them. Payen stood beside her and thought that he had not experienced such a fine, cold dawn in many years. There was a long, deep swell running from the north but no danger in the smooth green surface of the sea. The white teeth of the storm waves, capable of rending a longship into flotsam of planks and ruined spars, had disappeared with the wind, leaving only great, glassy hills for the wine ship to climb, and long, shadowed valleys into which the high bow must slide.

From the bow Payen watched the Templars' oarsmen pull

the creaking, protesting ship into the remains of the storm seas. The light wind following the storm was against them, and the great striped sail remained unused, rolled and tied snug to the boom, and set along the passage between the oarsmen.

The first bench of rowers had craned their necks to see Johanna's odd attire, remarking upon the sight of a hauberk covering a woman's mantle. Johanna had scowled and returned to the cold shadows of the shelter to fall asleep, her pale cheek resting upon the single saddlebag that held the few new garments Payen had bought from the Templars.

He had covered her with his cloak and left the shelter to watch the coast of Brittany recede from sight, the dark cliffs and mist-clad hills visible only when the ship rose to the crest of each swift-running swell.

When the land was gone from view, and the bow faced a landless expanse of gray water, Payen began to regret that he had insisted that Johanna eat a great hunk of bread before leaving the fort, and that he had joined her in the hasty meal to be sure she had sustenance. The heavy, dark bread sat ill in his gullet, and the straining, slithering motion of the ship as it negotiated the swells had developed into an irritating pattern.

He took a few steps aft to the first bench of rowers and clapped a hand upon the youngest of the oarsmen to offer to spell the lad. It was good to work up an honest sweat at the oar, and the dull weight lodged within his gut was less trouble to him as the pull of the shaft began to distract him. With a quick frown over his shoulder he warned the oarsman away from wistful looks at the bow shelter; then Payen settled into the rhythm of the ship.

If the weather held as it was, it would be a slow voyage north against this soft wind. The oarsmen could not maintain their present speed longer than half a day, and there were few men to spell those who rowed. At the first landfall north of Sandwich, it might be faster to leave the ship and ride north. The snows might come within the month, but it would be safer to face them ashore, where he might find shelter for Johanna at the manors and inns that lay beside the great northern road.

It would be safe enough, once they reached England, to sleep in the inns, for the enemy who had set assassins to find Johanna in Brittany would have no way of knowing when she might ride north to Whitby. With luck, Johanna might have been given up for dead, and the pursuit called off long before she left Brittany.

Indeed, it would be prudent to leave the great northern road from time to time and use the smaller tracks as well, though it would slow their progress. To be honest, Payen would not mind a longer time with Johanna Mercat.

There had been a moment, two nights before, when he had believed that Johanna would not let her near him again. When they began their angry words on the subject of Payen's determination to devote his life to his brother's lordship of Rochmarin, Johanna showed her disdain for his decision. Once the argument had grown to encompass his vow to support his brother's heirs rather than any landless bastards of his own, Payen resigned himself to a series of cold nights spent on the floor outside the chamber door.

But the widow Malebis had turned to him after the final angry words had died and held her hand to him. "You are a foolish, noble man to give up your own good to set your brother in place at Rochmarin, when you know you will need to defend him for all time. Must we deny ourselves this time together as well?" She had smiled then, despite the odd, watery brightness in her eyes. "Having spoken so many bitter words about your bastard and my child, should we not give the poor soul a chance to be born?"

He had hesitated, then, at the thought of Johanna, full-bellied and alone in the next late summer, laboring in some remote Yorkshire manor to bring forth his child. By late summer the slender chance that Rochmarin might be won back might have disappeared, and he might go to Johanna to see her through her birthing time. He had put the thought aside as foolishness, for there might be no child; Johanna had been wed to Malebis for near to a year's time and had never quickened. Still, the image remained.

She must be a witch, a fair witch from the harsh north come to draw him away from his life's obsession. She had only to smile in her shy, hesitant attempt at seduction, and draw her kirtle from one exquisite, white shoulder, and Payen was lost. Blessedly lost—

Payen's hands tightened around the oar, and he pulled harder to bring his arms to the point of burning effort. If he continued to indulge in memories of Johanna in the fortress chamber, he would become so aroused that he would not dare stand to take the few steps back to the shelter. And he would be hard pressed not to draw Johanna into the farthest cold shadows of the crude walls and take her within earshot of the Templar crew.

He managed, with difficulty, to turn his mind from lust. That fine, fair woman had brought him near madness, and he would need to keep himself, for her sake, from unmannerly desires.

The young crew returned and touched Payen's shoulder to bid him give back his place at the oar. Payen stood and picked his way past the benches to the stern, where two burly men had braced themselves against the lapstraked hull to control the great steering oar. Worse than the other tasks was this matter of keeping the steering oar beneath the green water and raising it at the crest of each long wave to keep the sea from snatching it as the ship wallowed down the back of each swell. The kick of the long shaft could be deadly, as might be any failure to keep the ship square to the advancing waves.

From the stern, the bow seemed too narrow, almost fragile as it cut into the heavy, lumped seas. If it should lose a plank, and the seawater came in—

Payen made his way forward to the shelter, muttering brief

words of apology as he trod, once again, upon an occasional toe of the men who labored at the oars. Johanna was sleeping, just as he had left her, but not so pale as she had been. If he could keep her gullet filled with bread and water, she might not fall ill from the motion of the ship.

"Johanna," he muttered. "Wake up."

Her eyes were green now, as green as the sea. "Is something wrong?" she said.

Payen pulled the food sack to his side and found the cloth-wrapped loaf of bread. "You must eat," he said. "Eat often, while you can, and you may escape the seasickness."

She nodded and sat up.

Payen opened the cloth and saw, with a wrenching pain in his gut, that he had taken cheese from the bag. "It's not the bread," he said.

She looked at him with that odd green gaze and smiled. "Then I'll have the cheese," she said.

"No. The bread—"

Johanna took the cheese from Payen, opened the cloth upon her lap, brought her small knife from its sheath at her sash, and began to slice into the yellow mass.

"Wait. Bread is better—"

"It's good cheese your Templars make. None better." Johanna cut a thick slice and held it for Payen to take.

"No," he said.

"There is more than enough—"

"No," he said, and escaped from the shelter to draw long, cold breaths of air into his heaving chest. He managed to get to the rail, and clung to the top strake as he hung his head over the side.

Below his squinting gaze, the green water surged past the hull, and the foremost oar flashed in and out of his vision, pulsing faster than the hard, driving ache at his temples.

A hand descended upon his shoulder, and a second reached for his arm. "Back off," he growled. "Or I'll spew my guts in your face. If you want to help, keep an eye on the woman.'' He sucked in a long, desperate breath and closed his eyes. ''Make sure she doesn't fall into the sea.''

''She won't fall unless you make good that threat about your guts,'' came the firm voice of Johanna Mercat.

''Stay back,'' he muttered.

A cloth moistened with fresh water passed over his face and returned to wipe his brow. ''Go ahead, do it,'' Johanna Mercat urged. ''I'll be right here.''

As from a great distance, Payen heard an oarsman cough.

With as much speed as he could muster, Payen set Johanna from him and lurched across the ship to the other rail, and left his morning meal upon the smooth green surface of the sea. He swallowed from the waterskin pressed into his hand and spat into the sea. The cool cloth returned to his brow. ''Now can you lie down?'' Johanna asked. ''I'll help you into the shelter.''

''I meant it,'' he muttered.

''What did you mean?''

''Back off,'' he said. His eyes focused upon the cloth in her hand. ''By St. Helen's filthy moneybags,'' he said, ''it's the cheese cloth.''

''No, it's not—''

''It's the cursed cheese cloth.''

''It is not the cheese cloth, Payen.''

''Must you speak of it?'' he said.

The sickness receded. Johanna's face came into focus, pink as a flower, healthy as a dairymaid at midsummer. ''I could hate you,'' he said, ''for your color. And your good cheer.''

''I know,'' Johanna said. ''Now, can you walk back to the shelter?''

He shook his head. ''Bad idea.''

''I'll put the cheese out.''

''Wise woman. You are a wise woman.''

It was a good thing it was a Templar ship, with a crew of

men whom Hamo had said they could trust. For if one of them had come into the shelter to steal the widow Malebis, Payen would have been hard pressed to lift his sword to defend her.

He had little recollection of that day, or of the long night that followed. He awoke many times to see the low afternoon sun streaming in narrow assault through the shelter's small entrance, and later to find himself in darkness. Each time Johanna Mercat had been at his side, the waterskin at hand, and his own cloak spread to warm them both.

He opened his eyes at the second dawn and saw that there was a following wind, and the great painted sail raised to catch it. Upon the benches, and below the bung-plugged oarlocks, the rowers slept; their long oars lay glistening of salt in an orderly stack down the single passage through the benches. There were new helmsmen now, as burly as the first and straining hard to keep the longship steady before the wind.

"Where are we?"

"Off the big islands. The wind rose while you slept, and the steersmen gave up and turned east to ride before it as far as it would take us. There were fires ashore, Payen. Great fires to show where the islands began."

He put a hand to his brow and shut out the light. "And I slept through it all." In the small, dark space of the shelter, his muttered curse became an awkward blasphemy. "Your pardon," he said. "I had not expected to sleep so long."

"I had," she said. "Since Rochmarin, you have slept but little. And after Mathieu left us—"

He attempted a smile and allowed it to broaden, as it did not pain him overmuch. "After Mathieu left us, I would have been a great fool to sleep away our nights."

She brought the wineskin to his mouth and fussed about the cloak. "Say what you will, but I was worried that even a fierce mercenary needs some sleep, and I was glad to see you resting."

"You were not frightened?"

She shook her head. "No one approached me or said a word. Only the master steersman came forward and asked if we needed food. He hasn't come back."

Payen lay back again and stretched his arms. "By St. Radegunde's knees," he said. "It is a wonderful thing to be among ones you trust, and able to sleep. It has been weeks—"

"Where were you before Rochmarin?"

Had he spoken aloud in his sleep? Had Johanna begun to think back on her husband's death and connect it to her own death threat? Payen shrugged as best he could. "With Mercadier," he said. "And Palestine, before that."

And Nantes, if the truth be told. At Nantes, in the house of a whore, slaying Johanna's husband.

Her face, backlit by the morning sun, sanctified by the aura of rich, brown honey hair about its pale beauty, showed no sign of suspicion. Payen appealed to St. Radegunde of the pretty knees and all the other saints he had offended since leaving the fort. Please, he prayed. I'll never sully your names or your attributes by my oaths again if you would keep Johanna ignorant of that one deed in my past that would drive her from me.

Chapter Seventeen

The seas continued to run high, whitened by the new wind that had come up from the west. At noon on the second day, the master took the great steering oar for an hour, then gave it back to the helmsman and came forward to speak with Payen.

"He sleeps," Johanna said.

"Tell him, then, when he rouses—we'll not make for the southern ports, but go as far as Dover while we can."

He pointed to the dark, lumpish land that had appeared on the port-side bow. "We should have reached the coast last night, but we were slow, rowing across the big seas."

Behind Johanna, Payen stirred and rose from the bedroll. "Trouble?" he asked.

"We'll make for Dover and winter there if the weather continues so cold. Master Hamo gave us leave to choose where we'd sell the wine, and orders to winter on the coast if the snows come early. There's a Templar preceptory at Ewell where they'll take us in and sell you horses." The master took a small pouch from his belt. ''If we don't make it all the way north to Whitby, I'm to give you your silver back—all but ten deniers.''

The deck shuddered beneath them as a rogue wave crossed the northern swell and struck the Templar ship in a fountain of green water and heavy spray. The master turned back to the crew and bade them cut free the outermost of the wine barrels and lash them along the narrow passageway between the empty rowing benches.

Johanna turned to Payen. ''Could you eat bread?''

He smiled. ''I could eat two loaves, and that cheese as well. The sickness has passed.'' With a brief touch to her arm, Payen moved past Johanna to help roll the largest of the tuns up the yawing deck to the centerline.

The new wind grew stronger as the crew worked, and there was sober agreement that the rowers' benches would be unused until the longship reached port. Johanna watched as the last of the barrels was hauled from beneath the benches and wedged into the passage walk. Payen looked up and made his way, stepping from bench to bench, to stand beside her. ''You're cold,'' he said. ''It's your turn to use the bedroll.''

Johanna reached to steady herself against the shelter posts. ''Will there be trouble?''

Payen's smile did not falter. ''If there is, we'll be sure to cut one or two benches free, and they'll float us clear across to Frisia, and we'll winter there.''

The great sail shook above them, and the mast rumbled deep in its socket. The shower of rainwater that shook free of the boom to fall upon the deck carried with it a delicate burden of ice shards.

''Do you think—''

Payen shook his head. ''This is a Templar ship, built for supply runs, safer than most.'' He pointed to the flat slate stone set below the stern post. ''And the crew has been prudent to the point of denying themselves a cooking fire. They'll bring us to port.

"We should share the shelter," he said. "The crew would have warmed themselves in it in turns had we not bought passage."

Johanna hugged the incongruous leather hauberk close about her and nodded.

Before darkness came, the master took sightings of the islands fast disappearing behind the stern and announced that if the wind did not veer, the ship would be safe to run before it during the long hours of night.

Johanna slept sitting between Payen's legs, held fast in his arms within the far corner of the shelter. Twice during the night the crew who had crowded into the dark refuge woke and changed places with those who had been outside, tending the sail and dealing with the odd tun of wine that had worked itself free of its lashings. In the crowded space of the shelter, all who slept were huddled close together; only the steersmen had room given them to lie prone and sleep without cramping.

Twice she woke to the sound of voices calling to her, but when she emerged from sleep found that it was the sea running beneath the strakes that had spoken. When she woke at dawn, there was no longer a rhythm to the rush of the waves past the bow; the sea now hissed and beat upon the oaken planks in angry spasms, seeking to break them.

Then another whispering began, speaking in soft cadences, bringing warmth to her cheek. Payen had enfolded her in the warmth of his arms and had kept her from the worst of the bruising motion the sea had brought to the Templar ship.

At dusk on the third day they sighted the great beacon fire at Dover, burning high above the strand, spreading rose and crimson through the mist that held to the shore. The wind was southerly now but carried no warmth in it. To turn and reach for Dover, exposing the length of the ship to the full force of the wind and the swift-running waves, would bring disaster.

So they ran before the rising gale, and watched, as darkness fell, the fires of Dover recede into the night.

Payen drew his wineskin from the saddlebag and offered it to Johanna. "Drink slowly," he said. "It's brandywine."

Johanna choked down a mouthful of the potent drink. When the fire in her throat had gone, a fine, hot languor remained. For the first time since dusk, she lost the need to hug her arms to her chest. "As good as a hearth," she said.

"And better than imagining a warm bed at Dover's port."

"I had promised myself," Johanna said, "not to think of hot food and hearths until we make landfall."

"And I had vowed," Payen said, "not to think of warm beds and firelight upon your hair."

There were six snoring crew in the bow shelter, and a score more gathered at the steersman's side, discussing the likelihood of navigating the broad mouth of the Thames by night.

Johanna brushed Payen's lips with her fingers. "Hush," she said. "If you speak so, I'll begin to shiver."

He caught her hand and nipped her cold-numbed fingers. "Come," he said. "I'll keep you warm, so that you may dream of whatever you desire."

And he led her out of the wind, and settled into their corner of the thin-walled refuge in the bow.

At dawn Payen tucked the bedroll around Johanna and urged her to stay out of the weather. The wind had continued strong during the night, and there was no way to know how far past the mouth of the Thames they had sailed. A heavy mist marched along the shore, its dull gray taking color from the sea and from the cold lands beyond view.

To turn west to seek the estuary would be to risk running aground. Until night fell, when the beacon fires upon the long coast would burn again, there was no way to know where, in the gray mass west of them, a safe harbor might lie.

When the pale noon sun was above them, and before the Templar crew changed watches, Payen shut them out of the shelter, urged Johanna to sleep again, and went out to take his turn beside the steersman, adding the strength of his arms to the pilot's efforts to keep the longship running straight before the wind.

When she woke again, she was alone, and daylight streamed through the timbers of the shelter to reach the tangled bedroll and two sodden cloaks left to warm her. Above the whining of the wind came the percussive struggle of the oars in their tackle and the clash of ill-timed blades colliding above the spume. The solid thunder of the anchor stone rolled past; the ship's motion changed from a lurch to a wallow.

Payen's voice rose above the din, and soon he was beside her. "We are safe," he said.

"Anchored?"

"And soon to row up to Orford port, when the tide turns."

Johanna sat up. "Orford? North of the Thames?"

"Well north of the Thames. It's better for us," Payen said. "Fewer port masters to ask questions."

Johanna rose to her feet and shuddered in the cold breeze piercing the timber walls. "Last night, in the worst of the weather, I vowed twenty gold marks to St. Caedmon's shrine in Whitby. Now I think he deserves forty."

Payen took her in his arms. "We have enough gold to buy horses from the greediest ostlers in England—and to buy shelter every night from here to Whitby. And if it's not enough, I—"

She made a small gesture of futility. "You have a sack or two buried near this place?"

"And no need to call upon goldsmiths and wool merchants to give it to me. It's there, hidden in the honest earth, with no one to mark my passage when I take it. And none save my lady Johanna to mark the number of coins."

Johanna turned from the sight of the low, rain-slicked land

that had appeared beyond the long bundle of sailcloth tied to the cross-spar. "How many caches have you hidden, Payen?"

He shrugged. "A few."

"How many in England?"

Payen raised his brows. "A greedy question, madam. Do you plan to hold me to ransom?"

She ignored his attempt to jest. "How many?"

He sighed. "A few—five, maybe—along the coast."

"And in Brittany?"

"More. Most of them near ports."

"You are rich," she said. "Few landed lords have that much gold, and few merchants. I wonder that the old queen hasn't demanded the better part of it for King Richard's ransom."

"A landless man has no tithes to pay," he said. "And as for King Richard's captivity, none could say I have been indifferent."

"Your master Hamo said something about the ransom—"

Payen took his heavy coat of mail from the second saddlebag and frowned at the hint of rust upon the edges. "Not here—I'll tell you on the road north, if you want to have the tale." He tied the two bags together with a length of cord and frowned. "If you're willing, we'll leave the ship when they come near shore at dawn, before they row up the river to Orford."

Johanna nodded. "I don't care where we go, as long as there's warm food and a bed."

"Better chance of comfort in the villages. Richard's castellan at Orford had a stingy board when last I came this way."

They lay at anchor that night, the beacon burning north of them at distant Orford Ness and the narrow mouth of the river Ore opened before them. When the moon rose and the tide turned to flow behind them, the crew ran out their oars, took up the anchor, and pulled the ship upstream to anchor once again near the fishing village tucked into the shelter of the long spit of mudbanks offshore.

At dawn, a series of small blows and scrapes to the hull

announced the arrival of two rowing boats from the settlement. The master and the oldest steersman went ashore, leaving the crew to wait in the lowering rain.

When the master returned, Payen and Johanna said their farewells to the crew and went ashore in the fishing boat.

When at last they stood upon the shore, Johanna had to turn her face from the sea to gain her balance. Payen caught her about the waist and sat her down upon the small heap of bags he had carried from the boat. "It will pass," he said. "Just sit and wait for the land to stop rocking."

"I will never leave England again," Johanna said.

"A pity," he muttered.

She looked up at him, shading her eyes from the thin light streaming down through the sea mist.

"You have a gullet made for sea voyages," Payen said. "This land sickness will pass within the hour."

"Nevertheless, I need never step upon a ship again," she said. "Nor should you, for you seemed sick unto death that first day."

"I managed."

"I nursed you."

"And when you began to take the cold to your bones, Johanna? Who kept you from sickening?"

She sighed. "You were stronger when the cold weather came. In good weather, sailing in a better season, we might deal well together."

Payen's gaze became as cold as the sea wind. "As you have said, there will be no more journeys for you. Once at Whitby, you will never stir from home."

"I'll not leave England, but I'll go to York."

He smiled. "All the way to York?"

"And to London. My uncle is too old to go alone to London."

"Ah."

"There is no need to be discourteous."

He shrugged. "If we begin to discuss my lack of courtesy,

we will never reach Whitby.'' He picked up the saddlebags and walked to the strand to watch the Templar ship pull into the Ore. Above the damp tidal line he made a hollow and emptied his mail coat into the depression. With slow deliberation he spread the mail, buried it below a layer of dry white sand, and began to walk upon the surface with heavy steps.

Payen pulled the mail from its shallow burial and frowned. ''Rust from the sea will eat through good mail in a fortnight,'' he said. ''I should have oiled the bag.''

''And your sword?''

He drew the dull steel from its scabbard and let it fall back. ''Not a mark. I worked on it at dawn.''

Johanna shivered in the sea breeze. Payen threw the mail over his shoulder and picked up the saddlebags. ''Come,'' he said. ''I can't have you sicken of the cold now.''

They ate their first warm meal, a rich pottage of barley, herbs and fish, at the hearth of a fisherman's hut. There were no horses to be bought in the village, but the fisherman's son offered to row upriver to a freehold farm owned by a man who had bought a palfrey for his handsome young wife.

An hour later they had finished their pottage and stretched their feet out to the small hearth. They had begun to doze, when the lad returned with a fine roan palfrey and a narrow-eyed yeoman with a long dagger strapped to his side. An hour later Payen's money pouch was lighter of two gold pieces, the palfrey was theirs, and they had learned that lodging might be bought from the nunnery five miles to the west, along the old paved road set in place by the ancients, in the days when the old gods had walked upon the earth.

The nuns had objected to a man and wife lodging together beneath their roof, and had sent Payen to sleep in a storehouse loft near the gates of the abbey. When night fell, the warm food and dry garments purchased from the nuns had not stopped

Johanna's shivering; Payen had spoken again with the hard-eyed abbess and dropped two silver deniers into the alms box to win the right to stay in the small chamber where Johanna would sleep.

The expression on his lady's face was enough to send Payen back to the storehouse loft.

"I came to be with you in case you sicken in the night," he said.

"You should go back."

"The abbess has agreed."

Johanna sighed. "It is not necessary."

Payen dropped his saddlebags upon the rough timber floor. "I will not touch you, Johanna. Not with the abbess prowling past the door."

"That's as well," she muttered.

He sat beside her upon the narrow pallet and pulled the coverlet about her shoulders. "Have I made you angry? Why do you shun me?"

When she spoke, there was a quaver in her voice as if she were still aboard the Templar ship, the cold sea wind in her face. "You have done nothing," she said. "You would be better off in the loft, for this pallet is hard, and too narrow for us both."

"You are ill," Payen said. "I'll ask the abbess to send a woman to you."

Johanna shook her head. "It will pass."

He stood up.

"It is often like this," she said.

Payen shook his head. "In all the nights we slept without shelter, and in the days on the ship, you were never like this."

Johanna turned her face from him and spoke to the wall. "It is my woman's time," she said. "I always feel the cold on the first day. Now will you go?"

"Do you want me to leave you?"

"Yes." She turned back to him and spoke in a softer tone. "A few days from now—"

A few days from then he would not dare to touch her, for a child conceived now would not be born until the first harvest beyond next summer. No one with fingers to count the months would consider that child the legitimate son of Walter Malebis.

"Of course," he said.

She touched his hand. "Do not be angry. But leave me now."

He dragged his saddlebags into the corner. "I'll return at dawn," he said.

"You are not angry?"

He managed a smile. "No. Do you want the brandywine?"

"No. You take it."

Payen left all behind him and took only his sword when he crossed the abbey yard. By the small flame of the cresset torch at the gates, he saw that the light rain was starred with sleet; the snows would be upon them early this year.

As he settled upon a bed of straw and drew an empty wool sack to cover him, Payen prayed that he would find a second palfrey early in the next day. They would need to move fast to get to Whitby before the coming snow and ice made the journey dangerous. As for the other danger—that Payen would forget his resolve and get the widow Malebis with a child too late to seem her husband's—a swift journey would bring an early end to temptation.

The abbess saw him emerge from the storehouse at dawn and turned upon her well-concealed heels to make straight for the alms box in the chapel. She tucked the small coffer beneath her arm and marched back to him with defiance blazing from her dark eyes. "It was a donation you gave me, sir. If you chose not to return to the chamber we gave your wife, that is none of my concern."

Payen looked from the shabby box to the abbess's florid cheeks and back to the coffer. "It was not my intention to take back the silver," he said. "As you said, it was a donation given for the poor of this parish."

"Then we are agreed," she said.

"I would count it a kindness," he continued, "if you would allow my wife to stay in that chamber and abed this day while I ride forth to find a second mount."

"Your palfrey is known to us," the abbess said.

"I bought it from a freeman on the coast."

"Indeed. And you will pay good silver for another?"

Payen took his gaze from the abbess's pursed mouth. The woman spoke as if she thought him a thief. Mayhap there had been other travelers, honest folk, who had resorted to theft rather than negotiate with the abbess and endure the woman's cold eye. "Of course," he said. "I will pay for a good beast if it be gentle and sound."

"I have such a mount," the woman said. "But would not part with her for all the gold in your pouch."

If there was to be thievery this day, it would be done by this nun, for she had begun to bargain hard for Payen's coin. "There is enough silver here to buy two horses," he said.

"You would need that many coins in gold, not thin silver, to buy a good sound palfrey such as my Hrothswitha."

Payen shrugged. "All I ask is that you allow my wife to wait here while I find a second mount and bring it back. I'll return by matins. How much," he asked, "should I donate to the poor in gratitude for that kindness?"

The abbess tucked the box more firmly beneath her arm and extended an open palm to Payen. "There is a harsh winter coming, and the poor of this parish will need coats to warm them."

Payen thought back to the great, bulging wool sacks hanging in the storehouse loft, long past the season when it might have been washed for winter spinning. "I understand," he said.

"I am moved to sell my mare to clothe the poor," the abbess continued. "I would consider selling her to you for fifteen deniers, as a kindness to your young wife."

"And how old is your horse?" Johanna's voice joined the chaffering. She emerged from the abbey hall, graceful once again in woman's clothes, the long hauberk no longer hiding the sweet curve of kirtle and mantle drawn across her pretty breasts.

"Five years."

Johanna raised her brows.

"I bought her five years ago," the abbess continued. "She's a fine mare, white as the snow."

"I had a white mare years ago," Johanna mused. "She was a fine-looking beast—"

"The lady Katherine Bigod will ride only white mares—"

"—until the day she died of old age. It was impossible to see the marks of age upon her. Only when one saw her teeth—"

"There is much sand in the earth, this near the coast, and Hrothswitha grazed in such pasture as a colt. It polishes the teeth and evens them, but wears them down early."

"—if one could manage to look without losing a finger. White mares are always bad-tempered. I would fear to ride one across country without a good solid bridle, and a well-secured saddle—"

Payen drifted away, unnoticed by the two women who had met their matches in chaffering and parsimony.

A kind-faced nun beckoned him into the hall and gave him a bowl of pottage and a cup of ale, and a place beside the long fire pit to sit and warm his feet as he ate. It was a good feeling to have the heat of the flames before him, and a meal eaten without an eye to the door, fearing attack. Though Richard Plantagenet's England was as fearsome as any other land in the known world, Payen had no enemies on this side of the water, and the lady Johanna might have left hers behind in Brittany.

Payen placed the wooden spoon back into the empty bowl and set it beside him on the bench. Yes, it was a good feeling to have left Brittany for a time, and an even better feeling to have a pretty woman to do his bargaining with the old raven-eyed abbess, and to ride at his side on the way north. It would be the devil's own torment not to touch her again, but he could not, despite the temptation to folly, wish her gone from his side.

Payen drank the last of the ale and went out to the stables to rescue the old abbess from Johanna's stubborn wit.

Chapter Eighteen

Payen emerged into the cold sunlight to find Johanna upon the back of a fine young palfrey with decent harness and a woman's saddle, an elegant construction with both stirrups and a good sturdy ledge upon which a woman might rest her boots while perched atop the seat. From the bow and cantle came flashes of silver and green as the dainty cream-colored mare trotted across the abbey yard.

Johanna brought the little mare to a stop beside Payen and held her arms forth to let him lift her from the saddle.

"How much?" Payen asked.

Johanna smiled. "Put me down and saddle your mount. We should be on our way."

"How much?" he asked again.

"I will give you the gold when we reach Whitby."

The abbess was making her way across the yard. "I will have to give her something," Payen muttered. "Tell me how much."

"Twenty deniers."

He set her down. "Twenty?"

"She's a good beast, and so pretty—I'll keep her and ride between the farm and Whitby twice a year, and she will be useful—"

"She may be a fine mount but not worth twenty deniers."

"The saddle—"

"The saddle will attract thieves as gulls to a fish market," Payen said. "Could you not find a price without the saddle? I'll find you one as good—"

"It's not jeweled," Johanna said. "It's only paint and gilt on the bows."

"Tell that to the thieves when they run at you from the woods, and send them back to wait for the next gaudy traveler."

The abbess was at his shoulder, smiling in expectation. Payen closed his eyes and gave her his money pouch. "You may take it all," he said. "The pouch as well—if you will give my lady a simple length of cloth to put over the saddle, to hide the—richness—of it."

He had scarce finished speaking as the woman dropped his pouch in the alms box and retreated into the abbey. A moment later a grinning novice emerged with a length of brown wool. "It's good stuff," she said, "woven for our habits."

"And now to adorn a saddle once built for another sort of woman," Payen muttered. He turned back to Johanna, who was rubbing the mare's neck and crooning into her ear. "I thought a sensible lady with a merchant uncle would know better than to let that tough old woman cloud her wits with a harlot's saddle."

"It came at a good price with my mare," Johanna said. "It fits her to perfection."

"Is this how you managed your silver at home? I cannot believe you had a sou left for your dowry—"

"No," Johanna said. "This is the first time."

There was something in her voice that made Payen look more closely at her smiling face. "The first time?"

''The first time I spent silver on something to please myself.'' She began to smooth the mare's silver mane upon the richness of creamy hide.

''You wore silk and broderie wool—''

''As befit my station. Had I wished to wear plain garb, my uncle would have objected, and my husband would have taken it as an insult. This mare,'' Johanna said, ''is beautiful to gaze upon, has a sweet look to her, and I bought her because it pleased me.'' She turned to him in sudden embarrassment. ''I mean to pay you at Whitby. You said you have coins hidden nearby.''

Payen smiled and nodded his head. If she wanted the gaudy saddle for her little mare, he would manage to get it past the roadside thieves and safe to Whitby. ''It's as well, is it not, that I thought to leave a cache on the northern road, not far from here? And that we won't need to ride into Gipeswic, past taverns filled with horse thieves, to fetch it from some drunken silversmith who might or might not remember that he keeps my coins?''

She smiled back. ''It's as well. I vow, Payen—if gold grew upon trees, your caches would have bloomed by now into orchards from which the country folk could pick their fortune.''

Even in their bedchamber in the Templar fortress, Payen had not seen her smile with such careless delight. He placed a hand upon the mare's fine neck. ''Did you jest, Johanna? You have never bought anything, before this mare, just to please yourself?''

She shook her head.

''But you are rich—and took a great dowry to the Malebis—''

''And never saw such a waste of coin in my life. Had my uncle poured the gold into the sea, I would have been happier. So now,'' Johanna said, ''I will buy a thing when it pleases me, and I'll have no more coffers of gold waiting for the next hungry lord who comes to Whitby. If I wed again, there will be no dowry."

Payen touched her shoulder with a hand made awkward by his recent resolve.

Never again would he bed Johanna Mercat; she was not for him, and he would not risk leaving her at Whitby with a bastard child and no hope of giving it a name. One day she would wed another, a man who would live the life Johanna had chosen, a man who should count himself lucky to have Johanna with or without her Mercat gold.

At that moment Payen would have given all the gold he had buried in God's good earth to be that man.

They rode forth from the abbey that day, though Payen had told Johanna they should delay. She seemed in good spirits; wrapped as she was in two cloaks, she did not suffer from the ever-increasing assault of the wind as it whistled down the north road. Her Breton hauberk, dried, oiled, and tied behind the cantle of her saddle, was ready to use should the weather turn colder still.

Payen had cause, in those early days of the journey to Whitby, to bless the gaudy little mare Johanna rode, for the obvious value of the beast gave him reason to spend his nights near the stables to turn away thieves. In this way, he removed himself from the temptation of Johanna's bed without speaking of his purpose in leaving her untouched.

When they had been four days on the road north from the abbey, Johanna told Payen that her woman's time was past, and offered, with a shy apology for her coldness at the abbey, to share a bed at the small manor where they had sought lodging.

Payen watched the faces of the servants who led them to their lord and saw no sign that they or their master recognized Johanna or thought them anything but a merchant and his wife traveling north after selling their wool to the London mercers.

He made certain that Johanna would be safe for the night in the small alcove set into the thick walls of the manor hall, with the servants sleeping beside the fire pit and their master and his lady in their great bed behind the high wooden screen.

When night fell, and Payen had followed Johanna into the alcove where she would pass the night, he felt such lust at her nearness that he turned from her and tried to imagine a great, strong wall between them. It did not help.

He took up his saddlebag and told Johanna that he would sleep in the stables, guarding their mounts and harness. Before she could speak the question he saw in her gaze, Payen cautioned her to open the shutters above her pallet and call to him should she need him; then he left her without looking upon her again. He bathed in the black cold of the river that curled wide about the manor fields and returned, when the heat had begun to forsake his body, to sleep in the stable loft.

He sought monasteries and abbeys for lodging each night thereafter and found his excuses easier in those places. Johanna had not spoken again of her willingness to have him return to her bed. By day she continued in good spirits, speaking with ease and smiling as if they were old companions with years of friendship between them. But at dusk each night, when they passed the simple luxuries and warmth of the inns bordering the northern roads and found instead the stern security of religious houses, Johanna would fall silent, and her smiles, though steady, would be forced.

One day past Wetherby the road became crowded with folk heading to York, and Payen began to mislike the looks of a few of their fellow travelers. An hour before dusk they headed for the relative quiet of an abbey set back from the road, surrounded by ragged turf, where the country's brown sheep grazed in huddled, anxious groups.

Tired of abbey fare and mistrustful of the pilgrims who had watched Johanna's approach with unholy interest, they had turned back from the wind-scoured monastery to turn north once again. Near dusk they found a squat tower set so close upon the road that it seemed to block the way.

"I remember this place," Payen told Johanna. "I came here once, on Hubert Walter's business."

Johanna frowned at the bulging stone walls. "It looks as if a giant carried off the better half."

"It was a keep, they say, in the time of William Rufus. One or two of the chambers are as secure as the old lords must have built them; we'll bar the door and be safe enough."

Johanna turned to him in cautious surprise. "You will share the chamber and leave our mounts unguarded?"

Payen shrugged and attempted to ignore the question in Johanna's gaze. "I'll promise the ostler a gold piece if the horses and their harness are there for us in the morning, then we'll barricade ourselves within the chamber to stop the innkeeper from coming up to rob us by night. There are worse scoundrels than horse thieves abroad in these parts."

They conducted their business with the innkeeper from horseback, and descended to stand upon the sodden ground only when Payen was satisfied that the man would attempt a semblance of honesty in his dealings. Together, they took their mounts to the low-roofed byre and showed the color of their gold to the crosseyed ostler.

"He won't fail us," Payen said.

Johanna hesitated at the wide timber stair that led to the high-set door of the old keep. The door had long since disappeared, and the round hall in which the inn's guests sat at the greasy board was open to the elements. Payen took a torch from the bracket in the wall and tilted his head toward the steep, precarious stairs cut into the thickness of the old keep walls.

The talk in the hall ceased as they walked through the firelit hall and became a brittle silence when Payen turned at the foot of the stairs and held his torch high, as if to illuminate their faces before his gaze. As he had expected, the group of travelers who sat surrounded by their panniers and bedrolls beside the hearth looked away in immediate fear. After a space of time the two brigands occupying the crooked settle before the fire turned back to their ale cups; a murmur became speech, then the hall sounded once again with the voices of men in an hour of idleness.

Johanna began to climb the stairs with Payen's outstretched arm at her side to keep her from slipping and falling the dark distance to the crowded floor below them.

As promised, the chamber was theirs alone, and as clean as might be expected; it was for gentle folk, the innkeeper had said, and never offered to those who would as soon sleep ten to a hearth. The straw in the tick rustled when Johanna put a hand to it, and there was little sign of damp upon the walls.

Payen held the torch high above his head and saw that there was no visible break in the timber underside of the roof. A wooden stair no longer reached the old trapdoor to the tower top; its ruins had fallen against the wall into a precarious heap of splintered wood. The widest of the broken planks stood wedged into the single arrow slit, blocking the night sky and muffling the sound of the ever present wind.

''I'm glad,'' Johanna said, ''that you left the horses to the ostler's care. This is not a place where I would sleep alone.''

Payen gave the torch to Johanna. ''Bar the door until I return,'' he said. He made his way back down the ledged stair to bid the serving maid give him a jug of ale and the inn's black bread—a single long loaf with a false miller's grit roughening the crust.

He shook his head at the smoked meat and cheese the woman offered, for in the saddlebags they had cheese without the bloom of mold upon it, and meat a season younger than the hard, sooty pork hanging from a hook upon the hearth wall.

When he turned back to the hall, the men upon the settle avoided his gaze. As before, the worn and scarred hilt of Payen's sword and the marks of battle upon the scabbard had turned away all but the most foolish or ambitious of the inevitable roadsidc brigands.

Two decades earlier in the Templar preceptory at Ewell, old Hamo's first lessons to the green, orphaned lad Payen had been to teach him the demeanor of a warrior. Those lessons, as much as the training in arms, had preserved Payen's life by honing his awareness of furtive moves within range of his sword. Sensing his watchfulness, only a few of the common brigands who had ever considered robbing Payen had decided to risk their lives in the attempt.

It was fortunate that the thieves at the hearth did not know that the widow Malebis had made a shambles of Payen's watchfulness. Though he kept fierce vigil over Johanna's safety, Payen feared that his mind turned too often to the memories of her touch; if he continued to lose sleep each night in hopeless longing, he would soon be useless as a protector.

He had allowed himself to come close to her, to desire her, and then to take her though she was the one woman in all of Brittany whom he should not have touched. What should have been a single night of bed sport, a cure for his foolish lust, had become a memory so rich and compelling that to look upon the woman was to imagine himself within her once again.

There was only one way to turn her from him, to damage her trust so completely that she would never again look upon him with her odd green gaze and smile into his eyes. If he told Johanna Mercat that the sword that now protected her had first taken her husband's life, there would be an end to her smiles.

He stopped halfway up the stair, looked down at the firelight upon the bedrolls in the round hall below him, and banished from his mind the image of Johanna Mercat descending the stair in the darkness with tears of anger obscuring her sight. To tell Johanna now that she had coupled with the man who had slain her husband would deliver Payen from temptation, but might send the lady from his side and into danger.

Payen reached the chamber and called to Johanna, and tried,

in the moment before she unbarred the door, to imagine that he did not want her.

She was still holding the torch. ''There is no hearth—no place to rest it without risking fire, and no bracket upon the wall.''

Payen took the brand from her grasp and held it high. If there had been a place for light and warmth in the chamber, the traces of it had long since disappeared. The torch sputtered in the draft and sent a small ribbon of sparks into the air; if dropped upon the ancient planks, the brand would turn the high chamber into a funeral pyre.

He made his way past the tangled ruin of the truncated stair and pulled the wedged timber from the arrow slit. The rush of the night wind through the narrow opening was balm upon his lust-darkened face

Payen thrust the grip of the torch into the embrasure and set it upright to hold its flames within the narrow stone frame. ''I'll leave it there while we eat,'' he said. ''When we finish, I'll wedge the timber back to keep the wind from you.''

''I don't mind the cold,'' she said. ''We have been so long upon the roads that I have become a creature of ice. When we reach Whitby, and stand beside my uncle's great hearth, I may melt.''

In his arms she would become a creature of flames and melt in the sweetness of desire.

Payen brought back, as a desperate attempt to keep his gaze from her face, the vision of the long, dark stair without the chamber and the fall into darkness that awaited the unwary. He crossed to the place where he had set down the ale and the bread and dragged his saddlebags beside it.

Johanna came to sit opposite him, beyond the bag. ''Is there brandywine?'' she said.

Brandywine would heighten the senses and cloud his resolve. Payen found the wineskin and passed it to her. He watched with an odd burning in his belly as she drank and offered it to him.

"No," he said, and flinched at the expression in her face. "No," he said more gently. "I don't dare sleep well this night."

"I think," she said, "that you have not slept well since we landed on the east shore."

He looked up, saw the uncertainty in her gaze, and cursed himself for causing her to doubt that he wanted her. "Johanna, we cannot—"

"It does not matter."

"I will not risk a child. Not now. It would be born after the first harvest next year, and none would believe it to be Malebis's son."

She looked straight into his eyes, as if seeking an answer to a question she dared not speak. "No one knows," she said, "the day of Malebis's death. Not here, so far from Rochmarin."

That fortnight after Nantes—the road east to Mercadier's camp, then the long, painful ride to Rochmarin—were deep in Payen's memory, carved with the precision of an artisan's knife. He knew the day of Malebis's death too well.

She watched him still, with a gaze made golden in the torchlight. Had she heard his thoughts, she would have known him, at that moment, for the killer.

Johanna dropped her gaze to examine the hard bread set upon the saddlebag. The flickering light of the torch moved over the unruly glory of her hair, compelling Payen to smooth the firelit strands from her temples.

She twisted the loaf and offered him the larger part. "I might be wed by then," she said.

A blow to his gut would have been kinder. "So you might," he said. "And your new husband would not be content to find you already with child when you say your vows."

She did not look up. "It depends upon which man I wed."

If he said nothing, would Johanna Mercat's gaze darken and remain dulled by the knowledge that she had coupled with a landless Breton and found, a fortnight later, that he would not speak of marriage with her, or return to her bed?

"You said you would not wed again."

She made a small gesture. "I might, if I could choose the man."

"Choose him with care," Payen said. "Few men deserve to seek marriage with you—and fewer still would merit your kindness."

She raised an impassive face to Payen and frowned as if puzzled by a trifle, by words of no consequence. "I am weary," she said. "And have begun to speak foolishness. The pallet is small, I think. Could we manage not to disturb each another if we lie down together?"

Payen looked away, as if considering the width of the straw tick. "We could manage."

Johanna raised the jug of ale and held it between them. "There are no cups," she said. "I'll drink first."

When she was done, he drank from the shallow spout as Johanna toyed with her bread, rubbing the grit from it. He watched her rise and lie upon the pallet, one cloak wrapped about her and the other pulled over her shoulders.

The still-smoldering stub of the torch had begun to smoke as it died. Payen tossed it out through the arrow slit and wedged the timber back in its place, shutting out the wind and the stars. Fearing that he might need weapons close at hand should the innkeeper or the ruffians in the hall decide to try the door, Payen took his sword from its scabbard and placed it upon the floor beside the pallet. The scrape of steel against the hard leather scabbard brought Johanna's head up from the pallet.

"If there should be trouble, roll to the floor and lie on there, between the pallet and the wall." In the darkness he heard her indrawn breath, and a slow rustle as she lowered her head to the wool-covered straw. "Only two more days of this," he said. "and you will be home, safe in your uncle's house."

Silence throbbed in the blackness of the chamber; only the

delicate sound of Johanna's breathing was between them, too rapid for sleep, too shallow for comfort.

He had not dared, since leaving the safety of Hamo's fortress, to sleep naked, as a man should do. In the cold nights spent in stable lofts and abbey storehouses, he had remained dressed, his sword within reach, ready for the unexpected hazards that stalked travelers by night.

This night the cold was too sharp and the brigands too near for Payen and Johanna to remove even the outer cloaks, which had warmed them in the thin northern sunlight. They lay without a coverlet upon the plain straw mattress, dressed for flight. It would be impossible, through the layers of close-woven wool, to feel the sweet heat of Johanna's body, or touch the fine, smooth glory of her limbs.

Payen turned to Johanna and drew her close against him.

Though she did not resist, though she turned her head to rest upon his shoulder, Johanna did not curl against him as she had in their long nights together in the Templar fortress.

"For warmth," Payen whispered.

"I know."

"Will you sleep? The brigands would have come by now if they dared. I'll wake you if I hear them on the stair."

She sighed and shifted upon the tick. Sleep came to her then, and soon the brittle tension that had kept a space between them disappeared. Beneath his chin her head moved against his throat, and her hair lay sweet and heavy upon his chest.

When her breathing had slowed into deep slumber, Payen brought her hair to his cheek and caught the scent of sweet herbs. He closed his eyes and knew that he would never lose the memory of that cold night.

Chapter Nineteen

Payen should have been pleased as they rode forth from the broken keep. Their mounts had been safe with the ostler, their harness untouched by thieves and as clean as the stable boy had cared to leave it. The two armed men who had seemed seasoned brigands by firelight were still deep asleep in the common hall, their slack forms sprawled before the ash-clogged hearth with the scent of spilled ale heavy about them.

Yet Payen showed no pleasure in the morning's good fortune, nor did he seem to realize that this day was fine for the season, and the track much drier than a northern moorlands traveler should expect.

After the first mile Johanna gave up her attempts to get Payen to speak to her as they rode. Only when the track narrowed at the crest of a small hill, and dispersed into a web of tracery paths that seemed more suited to sheep drovers than to horses, did Payen end his long silence.

He turned in the saddle and looked to the moors behind them, then pointed to the jagged silhouette of the broken keep from which they had come. "It's as well no one has followed us," he said. "It looks a slow way from here, and we may find ourselves lost by nightfall, far from a settlement. Whitby must be north and east of us, but beyond that I know nothing of the way."

Johanna frowned into the morning sun. "It looks like this for miles south of Whitby—no tracks larger than these. It puts me in mind of the land at Gunndale, though it's farther north, beyond the river."

"We will find no road?"

"Just cairns, on the higher places. When we reach the river, there's a track beside the banks going east to the port."

"That is all? Your Whitby must be no more than a village. How did your uncle come to be rich in such a place?"

"His father—my grandfather—found a ship."

"Loki's Horn?"

Johanna nodded. "Once they had a ship, the gold came as well. The farmers bring their wool to Whitby by wagon across the moors, and those who have ships sell it abroad. There's gold in ships, Payen."

He frown and turned from her to face the vast, undulating moorlands before them. "It's like the sea," he said. "The hills are no higher than the swells in the ocean, and they run long as the waves."

Johanna followed his gaze and saw, for the first time, that the land could be seen to move, its grays and greens seeming to shift beneath the morning mist. "I never saw it so, but today—it seems to move." She looked back to Payen and smiled. "You must not look while you ride—you may sicken."

He smiled back, and brushed her cheek with his hand. "You had a poor bodyguard at sea, but he was grateful for your care."

"And he told me so—gave me leave to back off, as I recall."

He took his hand from her, but his smile still warmed her face. "I don't remember that discourtesy."

"I do."

"Then I beg your forgiveness."

"Then I will see you through your moor-sickness, should it come."

Payen looked at the mist-clouded sun and back to Johanna. "If we ride straight north, will we find your river?"

She nodded. "This land begins to look like home, though I never rode far enough south from Gunndale to find the broken keep."

"A good thing you did not. A pretty maid might never get past the ruffians about the place." They nudged their mounts forward and chose a wandering sheep track that seemed more northerly than the others. "Speaking of ruffians," Payen continued, "when we're within sight of Whitby, I'll leave you to ride in alone."

Speaking of ruffians. Was that what he considered himself—a ruffian, a sometime bodyguard? Johanna drew a long breath. "There is no need—"

"If it's a port, there must be inns. I'll find a likely one, and sleep there. If you need me—" His voice roughened, and he began again. "If you should need my help, I'll be there for a night and a morning; I won't ride back south until tomorrow's dawn."

"You must have your gold, Payen. Come with me to my uncle's house and receive his thanks as well as the gold."

"You could send it to the inn. It would cause less talk if I ride south before you and your uncle announce your return."

"My uncle is a fair and just man, and he will want to thank you—"

"Your uncle, just or not, would see how things are between us."

"There is nothing between us. Not now. Not since—"

"Do you imagine it is a thing I can stop, as one would silence a song, or take a tapestry from a wall?"

"It is a thing you can stop, Payen, for you have managed to turn from me—many times."

He hauled upon his reins and reached for the bridle of Johanna's palfrey. "Do you believe those words? Do you believe I am content? My need for you has not ceased, and it will not, though I might never touch you again." He looked to the sky as if searching for words. When he turned back to her, his eyes were darkened and bleak.

"You uncle would see, Johanna, how much I want you—the sight of you, across a chamber. The sound of your voice. The scent of your hair—"

Johanna sat still upon her mare, fearing that her slightest motion might end Payen's words—and the exquisite pain they brought her.

What he had not said at her side in the darkness Payen was speaking now, in the soft morning light, with only the distant sound of birdsong to mar the small silences between his words.

"I cannot touch you," he said, "for if I did, my desire for you would overwhelm my reason. I love you, Johanna Mercat. Every night that remains to me in this life I will remember how it was between us, and that must be enough. For I will not touch you again."

The birdsong ceased, then returned with a new strain, as if someone were weeping far in the distance. "I may be barren," Johanna whispered.

"I doubt you are. When you are home, and wed to a man who can honor you in the way of peaceful men, there will be a child. You will look back upon our nights together and thank the saints that you did not bear a dark-haired son with a warrior's heart."

"My future is my own," she said. "Do not imagine that you see what I want, or how I will find it."

Though the light fell full upon Payen's face, he had managed to keep from his features any trace of the sorrow in his words. At Johanna's denial of his right to think of her future, Payen's eyes took on a fierceness she had not seen before, even in the desperate hours at Aleth. "You must live in peace," he said.

"I gave you your life when you might have lost it. You owe it to me, Johanna, to return to your homelands and live long and content."

"I owe you more than I can tell," she said, "but my life is my own, and I will live it as I choose."

"Then you will understand," he said, "that you cannot compel me to stay."

She managed not to look away. "I did not ask you—"

"You did not need to ask. I saw it in your eyes. And I will remember the sight all the days of my life."

And she would remember, all the days of her life, how Payen of Rochmarin had taken her heart and turned away from her—leaving her to live in peace, leaving her to remember and crave the touch of his scarred, war-hardened hands.

His gaze narrowed, looking far beyond her shoulder, back to the indistinct mass of the distant keep. Her little mare recoiled from Payen's sudden release of the bridle; he hauled his horse around to face south and stood in his stirrups. "Damnation," he muttered.

Two dark forms separated from the gray mass of the keep. Only the motion of the forms suggested horsemen riding north; at this great distance from the keep, with the sun still low in the sky, Johanna could see nothing more.

Johanna caught up her reins and turned the mare back north. She hitched the hem of her kirtle above her knees and swung one boot across the mare's neck, trying to find the idle stirrup, to ride astride. Her palfrey danced and sidled in confusion.

"What are you doing?" Payen's voice, though calm, held none of the warmth he had offered her only moments earlier. Though he might remember, as he had promised, the look of her eyes all the days of his life, Payen had already cast aside all his courtesy and resumed the brusque manner of a warrior with a novice squire at his side and a battle approaching.

"I can ride faster astride," Johanna said.

"Do not. We will ride as before, as if we had not seen them." He nudged his horse to her side and held her shoulder as she rose and placed her boots back together upon the side ledge of the saddle. He loosened the reins in her hands and placed a calming hand upon the palfrey's neck. "Ride on with me, a little faster than before, and do not turn to look back."

"They will reach us—"

"Much the worse for them. We will pick our ground and be ready when they reach us."

A dull ache throbbed in Johanna's throat. "They may mean us no harm, Payen. They may be simple travelers, as we are."

"I saw no such folk last night. But they will have their chance to show us what they want. Don't fear, Johanna. I have never killed a man outside battle unless he deserved it, and I won't become careless today."

His face darkened at his own words, as if he had, of a sudden, remembered some bloody struggle in the past.

She urged her mare to an easy canter, and Payen kept his own mount at the same pace. "Does it not worry you," Johanna called, "that if these are the ruffians from the common hall, you may face two of them?

He looked at her in confusion, and she repeated the question.

"No," he said at last. "If it comes to a fight with the two we saw sleeping at the common hearth, only a bad turn of luck would bring me down." A moment later he spoke to her again. "You won't see it, Johanna. You'll be nowhere near."

"I am no coward—"

"You'll be nowhere near. Cross me in this, and I'll give you to the gypsies, that you might plague them next."

Johanna spoke no more during their steady canter north, nor did she look over her shoulder at the horsemen far behind them. She used the silence to wonder, with some rancor, how Payen might have spoken those same orders to her had he not professed, only moments earlier, to love her beyond reason.

* * *

Payen seemed more concerned with the passage of the sun across the sky than he was to mark the progress of the riders following them. Each time they had stopped to water the horses at one of the rills that crossed the moorland, Payen frowned at the sun and looked ahead, attempting to gauge how low the sun would be when they reached the next tree-bordered stream, and the next beyond it.

Only once had he stopped to speak to her, when he had seen a small circle of stones upon the top of a rise, far to the north. ''Is that your landmark, the circle you see from your farm?''

Johanna looked and saw that the standing stones were smaller than the ones that stood watch over Gunndale, and not as crooked. ''It cannot be,'' Johanna said. ''We call the ones on our hill the Hags' Teeth, for they are long and crooked.''

''Tell me if we come near anything you recognize. Are there no folk living hereabouts? I have seen no one save our friends to the south.''

''The shepherds take their flocks down to the farms in the low ground for the winter. This is summer pasture, useless to shepherds now that winter is near.''

''Then Gunndale is on lower ground, near the coast?''

Johanna shook her head. ''No, it's on high ground, and the winters are harsh. It was a farm before my grandfather turned to wool selling and became rich. Now Gunndale is only a summer steading. There will be no one there.''

He looked to the south and uttered a curse more terrifying than any Johanna had heard before. ''Still they come,'' he said. ''Have those fools no better prey to follow? I think they are keen to die this day.''

To Johanna's eyes, the riders seemed smaller, more distant than before. ''Will we outrun them?''

''And face them again tomorrow? No, I'd sooner deal with them now and sleep soundly this night.'' He cursed again and shook his head. "How is it," he asked, "that your homeland, where your uncle grew rich without using a sword to win his fortune or to defend it, is home to such brigands? The men in the common hall last night were the worst mean-eyed louts I had seen since the Norman barracks in Palestine."

"I never traveled south," said Johanna, "before I was wed. It's the folk in the south who learn robbery at their mother's breasts."

Payen turned back to face the north. "Come, then, let's go a little farther along the track—and make ready to stop the small invasion behind us."

Johanna saw the night fall from a chilly perch far above the fire Payen had managed to light with a small whetstone, the blunt iron of his dagger hilt, and a handful of old straw he had pulled from the tick at the inn and carried in his saddlebag. One warm, luxurious moment after he had set the straw ablaze beneath a tangle of dried branches, Payen turned to Johanna and gave her a choice of three trees far beyond the fire, at the edge of the small wood that closed upon the banks of the Esk.

The branches were bare, scoured of their leaves by the winds from the moor. Reluctant to leave the fine blaze beside the river, Johanna had pointed out that no matter how high she climbed among the broad branches, she would be visible from the ground.

"They won't look up," Payen had said. "They will see my bedroll atop that log and your saddlecloth pulled over the pile of leaves and think they have found us both. And once the fire has drawn their eyes, they won't look beyond the light." He boosted her into the first fork of the oak and stopped to touch her hair where it blew against the first great branch. He muttered something she did not catch, then urged her to step higher, beyond the trunk, to sit with her cloak wrapped close, her boots upon the low fork. "I'll be near," he said, "and I'll know when they come. Don't call out to warn me, for even a whisper might reach them."

Johanna pulled her two cloaks tight about her shoulders and shifted as far as she could from the long dagger that Payen had brought up and set upright into the wide branch above her perch. "Use it if they find you and come up to drag you down," he had said.

"And if they use a bow to shoot me down?"

"I won't let them near you. But if the impossible happens, surrender first, and use that little capon-sticker you keep tied inside your mantle when you get the chance. Don't climb down with the dagger in your hand, or you'll fall on it."

"You aren't wearing your mail," she said.

"They would hear me move if I wore it. Silence is better protection in the night."

To Johanna's mind, there had been a maddening hint of cheer in Payen's voice, as if he had looked upon coming struggle as a diversion of little consequence. He was right to be more content than Johanna—he was the one nearer the fire, his presence made obscure by his dark clothing and the bed of leaves in which he lay; he was not watching from a distance, helpless to aid his companion should the thieves rush from the darkness with swords drawn.

Though the wind had ceased, there were sounds among the trees; the small animals that rustled through the fallen leaves were scarce louder than footsteps and caused Johanna to turn her gaze to search the darkness many times before the trouble began.

They were more skillful than she had expected—swift as they moved past her tree to the campfire, and quiet to the point at which they abandoned stealth and rushed forward to hack at the bedding Payen had left wrapped around the log to distract them.

With rising panic Johanna watched one of the thieves retreat into the darkness, leaving his fellow to deal with a sword caught fast in the log. From his covering of leaves Payen rose and flung a stone at the first thief, then ran past the sprawled, groaning form to wrench the sword from the gnarled wood. He stood considering the dazed man on the ground; he had not yet drawn his own broadsword but held the thief's smaller weapon at his side.

Payen appeared to have forgotten the second man. Had he seen only the one from his hiding place?

From the woods to her right Johanna heard the second thief moving back toward the camp and saw his shape pass the tree in which she had hidden. Still Payen seemed not to hear the man approach; he prodded the fallen man with his boot and asked a gruff question that Johanna did not catch.

She was not to call out. Payen had told her so, and she understood that if she made a sound and the unharmed thief doubled back to find her, Payen would have to turn away from the fallen man and risk a knife in his back.

If Payen would raise the thief's sword and put an end to the wretch, Johanna could call out and tell him to beware of the second man. Why did he hesitate?

The shape of the second thief grew smaller and more distinct as he crept closer to Payen, nearer the campfire. Could Payen not hear him? He was at Payen's back, not twenty paces away, and his short sword was ready in his hand as he rose from a crouch and stepped forward.

Johanna tore the dagger from its place above her, slid down to the lowest fork of the oak, and dropped to the ground. It was luck and nothing more that kept her from falling upon the blade in her hand. With a little more luck she would reach the second thief before he rushed Payen.

Of course the thief heard her, and he glanced back before he charged into the clearing with his sword raised above him, heading straight for Payen's unprotected back.

Johanna screamed a warning, ran after Payen's attacker, and overtook him at the moment he reached the campfire. She screamed again and drove forward with Payen's long dagger raised high, then brought it down when she was within a long stride of the thief.

There was a grunt, a sharp cry, and a hand upon her wrist, pulling her back from her prey. "No," said Payen. "Step back, don't come near them."

The first thief was still on the ground with Payen's boot upon his gut. The second, who had fallen when Payen twisted aside, lay beside him, the end of his fellow's sword through his shoulder as he begged Payen to free him of its bite. Blood welled bright in the firelight and shone wet upon the mottled iron of the rogue's sword. It could have been Payen's blood upon the cold ground. It could have been Payen. And if he turned from them, they would try again to kill him—and might succeed.

"Do it now," Johanna said. "Don't wait. They'll kill you."

Payen did not take his gaze from the pair. "Kill me?" he said. "How would these clumsy louts manage it?"

"Do not jest," she pleaded.

He glanced at her and turned back to the thieves. "Go closer to the fire and sit down before you faint."

One of the men raised his head in surprise. "Not you," Payen snarled.

She had begun to tremble. "I will not faint," Johanna said. "I know what you have to do, and I won't be the cause of hesitation. They tried to kill you, Payen, and they'll try again. I understand that you must—"

"Kill them? For a wool seller's daughter, you are uncommon bloodthirsty." He smiled. "And brave as well, Johanna."

Johanna's teeth had begun to chatter. "I—"

"Take the straps from the saddlebags and bring them to me. Then go sit by the fire and put your head down."

There was a sound from the trees and red staring eyes beyond the firelight. "Their horses," Payen said. "The saddlebags, Johanna. Give me the straps and get back."

She did as he asked and sat with her back to Payen as she listened to the shuffling grunts of the prisoners. He was going to hang them, then, so that she would not see him raise his sword to them or see their blood flow wide upon the frost-covered ground of the clearing.

He was speaking to them in a low voice. "And if you open your mouths to beg, and keep us from rest, I'll kill you where you lie." Payen was standing beside the bedroll, holding up his ruined cloak. "I should kill you anyway for hacking through my bedding. You can thank your hordes of vermin that I won't rob your saddlebags to replace it."

Payen had bound the thieves together; whatever would happen, it would not take place this night, under the early winter moon. When Payen shook the bedroll free of leaves and brought the mangled pieces to her, Johanna was nearly asleep.

She awoke at dawn to the pitiful cries of the thieves and Payen's gruff order that she must turn her eyes from the sight of them. She hid her face in the bedroll and stopped her ears. There was a low shaking of the earth beneath her as Payen ran the thieves' horses out of the camp, and more shrieks from the prisoners.

The sound of Payen's sword drawn from his scabbard caused Johanna to cover her ears once again. When she raised her head, there were no bodies, no blood upon the fallen leaves. In the distance, between the stands of young oaks, two naked backsides ran stumbling from the grove and into the thin mist of morning.

Payen looked up from his frowning inspection of the thieves' swords. "They couldn't kill a chicken with these edges," he said. "Their only chance would be to ask the birds to sit still for bludgeoning. I doubt those fools have many men's deaths on their souls."

Johanna shivered. "They cut through your bedroll."

He smiled. "So they did. Shall we save the swords for your uncle to cut open his wool sacks?" He lifted them and frowned down the lengths of steel. "They were hammered true enough. With a little work they might be worth selling."

"You did it for me. You risked letting them live because of my squeamishness."

Payen shrugged. "They weren't worth the killing. There would have been no honor in it, and there was no need."

"In the past—"

"In the past, I never killed without reason. In war I slew my share. In peace I have killed some, but not without honor." He turned and looked at her with bleak intensity in his gaze. "Will you remember that, Johanna? Will you remember that I have never killed without honor?"

She smiled then. "I will remember."

He nodded and placed the thieves' swords beside the fire. He did not smile back.

Chapter Twenty

By midafternoon the Esk had widened and flowed deep enough for small boats to float in its stream. Two rowing craft were upon the water, carrying close-huddled travelers bent against the gusts whistling up the river. Payen and Johanna rode along the well-cleared track beside the water with only the naked trunks and spiked branches of the river grove to shelter them from the cold wind from the sea.

When they neared the town, the great walls of its abbey rose above the river, and Payen could see banks of sea mist beyond. They found the last of the moor's small manor halls and paid the kitchen maids for a meal and hot water to bathe their faces. Johanna drew her comb from the saddle pack and sat beside the cooking fire to loose her hair and smooth it before plaiting it once again into a secure, straight fall of shining brown.

Payen had refused the maids' offer of more hot water and a straight knife to shave his beard. It would be a long, cold ride to retrace his journey across the moors, and he might be grateful of a heavy beard to keep the ice from his face. So he waited at the buttery door, watching Johanna twist her shining tresses into submission, telling himself that this time was no different from the other days he had watched her, and that there was no need to remember this final sight of her unbound hair.

He turned from her, walked to the stables, and brought a brush to the manor yard, where his gelding and Johanna's palfrey, still saddled, were eating oats from the stable boy's bucket.

Payen began to clear the tangles and burrs from the mane and tail of the little mare. He shouldered aside his jealous mount, continued to work on the mare's silver-hued mane, and began to stroke her neck.

When Johanna rode into Whitby, and when she arrived at Mercat house, there would be interest in her journey and questions about her manner of travel and her companions. If she managed to hide the signs of their nights abroad on the moors, it would be easier to deflect those questions.

"You need not do that."

She was standing beside him, her hair arranged in perfect symmetry and covered by a thin veil he had not seen before—a delicate length of linen that would have long since been blown to shreds had Johanna worn it at sea or on the journey across the moors.

Tomorrow, amid the opulence of the Mercat house, she would no doubt weight her veil with a fine silver band; today, drawing upon the small store of finery she must have bought from the serving maid at Aleth, she had tied the veil in place with a length of braided wool of three colors.

He brought the brush back to the mare's warm neck. "Your horse must not look like a wild creature when you ride into Whitby. You would look as if you have been sleeping on the moors without shelter for the mare."

"I have."

He continued to pull the brush through the mare's silver

mane. "You need not give your uncle more to worry about. He'll be angry enough that you had to flee Rochmarin."

She placed a hand upon his arm. "He will be grateful to you, Payen. And he will understand that the journey was difficult."

He turned to reply, but the words fled when he looked full upon her. Tucked beneath the neatened hair and the short, precise veil was the woman he loved; and he wanted her back. Payen closed his eyes and wished himself back in Aleth, with all this long journey before him and Johanna at his side. And their nights in Hamo's settlement would be still to come, in all their mystery and splendor—

Johanna raised her hands to her veil and adjusted an invisible imbalance in the set of it. She had drawn it low upon her forehead, covering the fine speckling the sun had left upon her brow.

This was the Johanna Mercat who would ride into Whitby and take her place in her uncle's house, among the clever, prudent men who would soon begin to turn her thoughts to a clever, prudent marriage. Her other self—the woman who had come north at his side, heedless of the sun upon her face, careless of the wind that had plucked her hair from its braid and sent it shining in a great tangled halo about her—was gone.

"Well?" she said. "Is it still not straight?"

She must have been speaking of the veil. He reached to touch it but feared he would mark the delicate cloth with his hands. Payen drew back. "It will do," he said.

He took up the brush and gave the mare a last pat. "I'll take it back to the stable boy," he said. Payen retreated across the yard to the welcome darkness of the low-roofed stable, where the cold wind did not intrude. Still, he could not rid himself of the pain that reminded him, with each ragged breath, that the journey home would hold no joy for him.

Last year, before Acre on the shores of the Saracen sea, one of King Richard's minstrels had sung of a knight who had died for his love of a woman not his own. The fool in the verses had not died from wounds in the lady's defense, but from heartsickness in her absence. Payen had laughed at the tale and asked for a better song, of war and lust and all that should matter to a man.

Now, in the gray north with winter soon to come, and the cold pain of parting weighing heavy upon his heart, Payen understood that song. He wished he had listened to the final words.

She had been at the point of asking him to remain in Whitby for the winter, to ask him, if he needed a reason for staying, to advise her uncle where he might find trustworthy mercenaries to guard his cargo boats.

Within weeks the southern ports would be unreliable, and Payen might find himself in England until the worst of the winter gales ceased to ravage the coast. Why should he turn back to cross the moors this late in the season, when he would have comfort and gold for his trouble in Whitby?

He would not stay near her—he had made that plain enough on many occasions since they had set out to ride north. There were places he might live—chambers he might take, and women who would wish to warm his bed—in the cluster of houses along the Esk. The town was large enough that Payen could live apart from Mercat house, and Johanna would not observe, from her large square chamber overlooking the mouth of the river, Payen's comings and goings at Mercat house.

It was a reasonable plan, and she had rehearsed it many times as she sat combing her hair and plaiting it beside the kitchen fire. Payen had come to glower at her, to tell her they must leave; she had put down her comb and turned to speak when she saw him turn from the sight of her and stalk through the door as if he could not wait to leave and put these last few miles behind him.

She had followed him to the yard and found him brushing

her palfrey, the sleeves of his tunic pushed high upon his powerful arms, his skin still darkened by the distant sun of Palestine. Though he was frowning, impatient to be gone from the manor yard, his hands upon the little mare were gentle and skillful in taking the burrs from her mane without tugging that fine arched neck.

He had looked at her as if she wore a demon's horns rather than the veil she had saved in her saddlebag since Aleth; he had spoken, then, of concealing that they had traveled alone together in their long journey north.

And when she had drawn a bold breath to speak to him of wintering in Whitby, he turned from her and muttered of the stable yard, and of oat buckets. And when they rode forth from the manor gate, Payen wore an expression of grim resolve that had kept Johanna from trying once again to speak of the future.

Payen's hard-eyed displeasure kept the few travelers on the river road from tarrying to speak to them. When the first familiar face appeared in the trickle of riders from the town, Johanna saw that old John the shipwright wished to speak to her; when John opened his mouth to speak, he looked askance into Payen's dark gaze and retreated from them without uttering a word.

"Must you frighten them?"

Payen shrugged.

"He wished to speak—"

"But he thought better of it, it seems."

"There was no need—"

"Do you not want to make Whitby by nightfall? No prudent man would wish to keep you out here, talking, when you should be safe at home before the night comes."

Payen pointed to the painted saddle, revealed to sight this day; the novice's brown wool was rolled and tied behind the cantle, no longer draping the bows to hide the gaudy splendor from strangers' eyes. "Blame the saddle if you wish, but I still look for thieves, even this near town. When I leave you at your uncle's house, you may be as foolish as you wish. I'll not have to watch it, nor will I know.''

The harshness in his voice set Johanna back in her saddle. She bit the inside of her cheek and vowed that she would not provoke more anger from Payen in their last hour together. In all the days of their journey, even when the sleet had begun to fall upon them when they were far from shelter, Payen had never spoken to her with such anger in his voice. Now, at the end of the journey, he seemed eager to cut his life free from her at last.

She bit down harder upon the soft flesh inside her cheek. To cry now would be shameful and would likely make Payen's temper more foul.

There would be no talk of the winter now, not while Payen's eyes gazed down the road as if he would throttle the life from the next man who passed them.

And there would, of course, be no talk of desire or of love. They had left such words behind them, in the mist that had closed in their wake upon the moors.

Too soon, the streets of Whitby were before them, and the time of parting had come.

''We have spoken all that can be said between us, and your uncle's house must be near. It would be best, I think, if you ride on now.'' Payen's face was empty of emotion; if he had managed to look full into her eyes, Johanna might have believed him indifferent to their farewells.

''Your gold,'' she said. ''Where shall I send it?''

''Tell me the name of an inn.''

''John the shipwright keeps an inn east of the abbey, near the sea.'' Johanna looked down at her sun-speckled hands. ''He's the old man we passed not an hour ago. His wife will be at the house to give you a bed.''

''I'll find it. Go now, Johanna.''

"I—"

"You must go—" His voice softened. "You know you must go."

"I hope, Payen of Rochmarin, that beneath your hard face there is some part of you that will understand that I—"

"Do not say it."

"—that I am grateful, and that the gold I will send is only a portion of my gratitude."

He relaxed then, and smiled. "Tell your uncle to keep you from harm, and thank him for his gold."

And because she was slow to turn her mare down the lane to the riverbank houses, Payen did not wait to see her go. He bowed his head in brief farewell and rode on.

Johanna thought, as she rode the short distance to her uncle's house, that she should not have rebuked Payen for his hard looks at passing horsemen outside the town. Now that she was near home, and there were many who stopped to gawk at her and a few who approached close enough to speak a few words, Johanna found that she, too, wished to avoid speech; her face must have shown her indifference.

The sun was low behind her, streaming along the eastern flow of the Esk; it touched the choppy water where the river met the sea, sent its brilliance against the small facets of the waves, and cast its light back to Johanna's stinging eyes.

Against the glittering, restless water, the Mercat house was a dark silhouette pierced by deep-set, narrow embrasures.

There was no smoke coming from the solid chimney and no firelight within the wastefully unshuttered windows of the long kitchen built onto the hall. The new serving maid, the farmer's lass who had come to the Mercat house only a month before Johanna's wedding, must have become careless in Johanna's absence. Even now the foolish child must be down the lane, begging a pan of embers from the baker's wife to start the fire again.

The cook and the scullery maids must have gone as well, leaving Uncle Hugo alone in the twilight in a cold house. It was as well she had come back before the snows came, for Hugo would not stay in good health with such carelessness about him—

Johanna reined her mount to stop at the turning of the road and slid from the saddle. There was no ship anchored off the quay and no boats drawn up in the mud of the riverbank below the Mercat warehouses. She dropped the reins and began to run down the hill to her uncle's empty house.

Payen was careful to hide his connection with Johanna Mercat. He rode up to the high ground of the abbey and straight beyond it to the sea, where he found the narrow track worn into the turf above the wind-driven water. He waited there for a good hour, ready to move on if he should be seen, waiting until the sun had moved low in the sky before he mounted his palfrey again and entered Whitby from the south. The shipwright's house was near the abbey, as Johanna had described, and had no other travelers in the two small chambers off the common hall.

Payen had paid the kitchen maid to put two kettles of water on the hearth and had rolled the deep bathing tub from its corner beside the stable-yard door. The maid offered to bring the shipwright's best linen washing cloths for Payen, and tarried in forthright invitation while he stripped and settled into the steaming water.

When he narrowed his eyes and looked askance through the fine mist rising from his bath, Payen could imagine that it was Johanna, not the kitchen maid, who stood staring at him from the hearth. With the firelight behind her, and the ends of her hair catching the color of it, the woman would have been a temptation had she been Johanna.

Payen sighed and let his head rest back upon the rim of the oak-staved tub. There would be time, tomorrow, to find a woman. And if the weather stayed clear and he rode south tomorrow, he would wait and find a clean whore in the first town he reached. Or he might wait for Nottingham and find the brothel where he had bedded a skilled, friendly whore during the fortnight he had spent as a bodyguard for the royal emissaries collecting the Saladin tithe for old King Henry, two years before King Richard had taken his armies to Palestine.

And if the women in the Nottingham brothel were jades, he would find better in London, or— Payen whispered a round curse and sank lower in the water. He must find a woman—soon—and cease his yearning for the lady he must not have. If he thought upon Johanna Mercat again, if he allowed himself to remember the way her body had looked in the firelight and the candor of her smile, he would find her in her uncle's house and bed her, and never again let her stir from his side. And for that act of selfish lust he would deserve to burn in hell's hottest corner.

For his lady's sake, and for his sanity, Payen resolved to find a woman to turn his thoughts from Johanna Mercat.

As if she had heard his thoughts, the kitchen maid advanced from the hearth bearing a cup of ale with the laces of her kirtle's neck askew and a determined smile upon her face.

If she had stayed across the kitchen, her face in the shadows, Payen might have continued to imagine she was Johanna and might have come to a state of acute desire before she approached. But she hastened to come near him, and her smile was not Johanna's.

Payen looked upon her and felt his desire grow colder than his swift-chilling bathwater.

There was a thing he would have liked from the maid; with difficulty, Payen managed not to ask the woman for news of the wool sellers of the Mercat house, and the health of all who lived there. If news of Johanna's disappearance from her husband's keep at Rochmarin had not yet reached Whitby, it would be foolish to inquire about the family and begin rumors of a Breton mercenary who had appeared on the day Johanna Mercat had come home.

So Payen began to speak to the maid, asking her of the town, and of the sailors and the wool traders who had come to the old shipwright's house. With unconscious perversity the woman chattered of every merchant living in the sturdy houses along the riverbanks—every one of them save old Hugo Mercat.

At last, when the water was cold and his patience at an end, Payen dried himself and dressed in the clothes the maid had set before the fire, and had set out on foot to see the manner of house to which Johanna had returned. It would do no harm to look upon it from a distance.

It was as if robbers had come to the house and stripped it to the walls of all its comforts and riches. The long kitchen was empty even of firewood, and the hearth was full of ashes, caked into a foul, dense mass from days without a fire to keep the damp away.

Johanna forced herself to go up to the sleeping chambers before the daylight disappeared. The rooms seemed small without the fine chests and beds with which her uncle had furnished them; as in the kitchen and hall below, the bedchambers offered no sign of a struggle, nor wounds in the walls to record haste in the removal of the great chests that had held her uncle's clothing, and the coffers that had held the wealth of the Mercats.

Footsteps sounded in the hall and echoed in the cold air above. Johanna came down the narrow stair and for a brief moment thought that it was her uncle Hugo who stood gawking from the kitchen passage.

A wheezing cry came from the figure. "Is it Johanna Mercat, come back from the dead?"

Johanna stepped back up and placed a steadying hand upon the wall. This was a sailor, from the look of him; and he was not one of Uncle Hugo's shipmasters. "I am Johanna Mercat, and not a ghost."

"Then you must give me my wages."

"Where is my uncle?"

The man fell silent, then hacked and spat upon the floor. "He died, of course. And his heirs took away the gold that next day, before I could ask for my pay that's owed me. It wasn't your uncle's way to leave a man unpaid."

Johanna sat down and put her hands to her temples. Across the room the shipmaster shifted from one foot to another. "The abbot said he'd write to them to tell them what was owed me."

She lifted her head and tried to focus upon the man's words. "Who?"

"I'm Mark, master of the Flanders ship."

"No—the heirs you spoke of. Those who came here. Who are they?"

He considered the toe of his boot and spat again. "Must be you are the heir. That would be just. They were wrong, then—you aren't dead."

"Who came here? Who are the heirs?"

"Your kinswoman and her husband."

"I have no—" She had no kinswoman. Only by marriage—

"The abbot said as the woman was your sister by marriage, and her husband was King Richard's man, he gave leave for them to take the gold, leaving a tax for the abbey to give the king, if he asks."

Agnes. Agnes and a husband had come here, presuming her dead, and taken all she possessed. And her own kin—her uncle Hugo— "How did Hugo Mercat die?"

The stocky figure bowed, then, into an attitude of thought. "Hard to tell. Some say he sickened at the tales of your death, and your soul gone, carried away by the Samhain devils. He was old, Mercat was, and given to bad temper, and short of breath last spring when he hired me. He's dead, I say, whichever way he came to it. And he'll rest easier if you give me the gold that I'm owed."

"I'll find it."

The man turned and stepped away. At the end of the passageway he turned back. "Have you sickened too? It's a cold night coming, Johanna Mercat."

She wiped her face upon her sleeve. "Where did they go? The others—"

He shrugged. "The old ones went back to the country."

"To the farm? Did they go to Gunndale?"

The shipmaster shrugged. "The Mercats don't tell me what they want."

"And the ships? Where are the ships?"

"Gone south with your kinfolk. The abbot will say they're yours now. If you can find them."

At the top of the road she found her little mare grazing upon the last of the withered summer grass above the river. Johanna led her to a large stone and mounted into the fine saddle Payen had bought for her a lifetime ago, before her world had fallen to ashes around her.

If pride kept her from going to Payen now, she might never find him again. Johanna rode up the hill toward the abbey, and beyond it to the shipwright's house.

Payen got as far as the mouth of the river and looked along the banks at the merchants' houses as they bloomed with windows of firelight at dusk, then darkened again as their shutters closed upon the night.

In a moment of cold reason he turned back to the shipwright's lane and vowed he would not sully his clean parting from Johanna with a chance meeting on the merchants' road. After a few steps he had halted and thought again. It was full night and no decent woman would be abroad upon the streets; even if he spent the night beneath Johanna Mercat's window, she would never know he was there. Payen doubled back to take up his vigil over the uneven roofs of the wool sellers' houses, secure in his belief that no harm would come of it.

The moon rose and showed the way past the merchants' row, and Payen followed its white path along the river street, walking slowly, listening to the indistinct voices that came forth from behind well-fitted shutters. At the end of the road, near the place where Johanna had said her last farewell to him, Payen turned and retraced his steps, vowing that he would pass by only once again, and slowed his progress to be sure that he might consider each house in turn, and miss nothing that might be seen. His shadow loomed tall before him in the moonlight, and he began to imagine that he might frighten any who walked his way.

At the end of the road, near the meeting of the river and the sea, the last house still wore its shutters open; the fire within the hearth must have been a pauper's low blaze, for the light of it did not reach the street. There was an old man standing at the door, muttering some madness of abbots and kinsmen and ships gone south without him.

Payen passed the fool, then turned back to ask him if he knew where, among the river houses, one could find the wool sellers.

''Ask Alice,'' the shipwright told Johanna. ''She was making eyes at him, and bathing him in my kitchen, and bragging of the good bedding to come this night.''

Johanna stiffened. ''The man is with your maid?''

''He's in his chamber, no doubt. It's the far one, where the passage makes a turn. Knock on the door.''

Payen had not lost time to suffer grief at their parting. Even now he might be coupling with the kitchen maid a few steps from where she stood. Johanna turned to the door and saw that a light snow had begun to fall upon her mare's saddle.

John the shipwright inclined his head to the door. "It's a deep frost coming, and a snow to cover it. I'll give you the other chamber."

If she did not find him tonight, Payen would be gone from Whitby and from her life by morning. Find me tonight if you need me, he had said. And he had told her that if she wished to give him gold, she must send it here, to John the shipwright, for Payen would not come to her.

She owed it to him to tell him why there would be no gold for him this night. And she wanted, more than shelter and a fire to warm her, to speak with him, to tell him what she had found in her Mercat house.

"Give me a taper," she said.

"I'll give you the chamber and put your horse in the stable."

"No. Just give me the taper."

"Now, Johanna Mercat, you cannot disturb a man at his pleasures, no matter who he is, and this is a fierce one. Stay clear of him—"

She took the taper from the shipwright's hand and carried it to the first bedchamber door. All was silent within.

"Payen? Please come out to speak with me."

He did not answer.

She rapped upon the door, then kicked it twice for good measure. Then she set her hand to the door and pushed it open. "I must speak with you," she said to the rushes upon the floor. "Will you send her away just for a time?"

Silence answered her. There was no kitchen maid. And Payen was not in the bed, nor poised behind the door to deal with an intruder. He was gone, but he had left his saddlebags behind, slung across the pallet.

Johanna touched the stained, scarred leather and sat upon the bed. Payen's few possessions in their saddlebag had been, for Johanna, the only familiar objects in the inns and camps where they had slept for the past two fortnights. For one elusive moment she let herself believe that this was a night like so many others in their journey, and she could imagine that she would sleep in this room, safe in Payen's arms.

This night, though, Payen would not come to her and keep her close. He was in another chamber, in another woman's bed, and would not be found this night.

The weeping came upon her then, and she allowed herself a little time before she dried her face and went out to give old John his taper, and to take her mare back to the cold, dark stable beside the empty house beside the river.

She would not see Payen again before he rode south at dawn. It was possible that he might send to her, one day, for the gold she had offered him. If he did not, she might never discover where he had gone, or what had become of him.

She led the mare into the stable, took the saddle from the little beast, and rubbed her dry with old straw from the moonlit manger beside the door. There was no reason to prefer the empty house to the stable; Johanna pulled the rest of the straw from the manger and lay down to sleep upon it.

The shipmaster had told Payen that the Mercat house was empty, old Hugo dead, and his kinswoman like to seek help from the abbey, where the wrong heirs had left some Mercat gold for the king to take in taxes in the spring. Old Mercat's fellow wool merchants would be no help: Two had gone south with their ships to pass the winter among the rich merchants of London, and the last of them had gone down to York to see his son wed.

Payen had walked through the house and the stables and found no sign that Johanna had done more than turn from the sight of the stripped rooms. The stable door was open, and the

Mercat stock long gone. Johanna had left nothing behind her, not even a saddle cloth, to show that she might return.

He had run through the moonlit night to the abbey and hammered upon the abbot's door until they had opened it to send him away. He believed the abbot when he said that Johanna Mercat had not come to the place; in the cleric's face Payen saw obvious disbelief that the report of Johanna's death had been false, and plain doubt that Payen was in his right mind.

As he ran through the darkness to the shipwright's house, Payen thought that the abbot's doubts might have been close to the truth.

Chapter Twenty-one

The cold had been a blessing, had kept her mind upon survival, had kept her from naming, again and again, the kinfolk whose voices she would never hear again. The cold had taken her tears from her, turned them to shards of ice upon her face, and roused her fears of death in that long night. The cold had given her, in the numbing of her senses, a distance from the pain of losing Payen.

In that long, waking night she had made her decision: to ride to Gunndale before the deep winter came. Though she might find a welcome in many houses in Whitby, Johanna did not wish to winter in the town; Mauleon might find her there if he came back in the spring. And if Mauleon brought her death, there would be none left to remember old Hugo Mercat's kindness and the bright green of young Harald Mercat's eyes. And she would lose, with her passing, the hope that one day she might see Payen again.

She paced that long night through, across the earthen floor of the small stable to keep the cold from her limbs. And as she walked from door to wall and back again, Johanna tried to make some sense of what she had learned. She did not know the purpose of Mauleon and Agnes's journey to Whitby, but she found the haste with which they had dismantled Hugo Mercat's household to be frightening. Was Mauleon the one who had sent gold to Mercadier to order Johanna's death, and had he wed Agnes in order to have the right to Hugo Mercat's wealth? Had Johanna been wrong to leave the girl to wed Mauleon, and should she have compelled Walter's young sister to leave Rochmarin with her?

Most frightening of all was the question of Hugo Mercat's death. How had he come to die when Mauleon was in the house, ready to seize the Mercat ships and wealth?

Before dawn the snow began to fall through the moonlight outside the stable door. Exhausted from her pacing, Johanna allowed herself an hour upon the bed of straw and gathered her strength for the journey ahead.

When she rose again, the dawn had not yet come. The cold had slowed her blood, and the sharp pain in her legs was a warning that she dared not sleep again until she reached Gunndale. Temptation returned; she considered again the possibility of seeking shelter in the house of a merchant whom her uncle had befriended. When she had walked through the pain of the cold and her knees had ceased to hurt with every step, she renewed her resolve to leave the town. She must not do the expected thing and burden another house in Whitby with her troubles—or the danger she might face from Mauleon.

The servants had gone back to Gunndale, where the old bonds between Johanna's family and their fellow farmers extended back into the old times, before the Normans had come north to rule them. The manor was small and held by distant kin to the Mercats. At Gunndale's smaller steading, on the land from which Johanna's grandfather had taken his first bags of wool to send abroad on *Loki's Horn,* there was a small house that would be empty for the winter. If Mauleon came back to

Whitby, no one in the town would think to send him to her at Gunndale; and if he came to Gunndale, the manor folk would never betray her to him.

Payen would have held the same opinion. He would have traveled with her to Gunndale if he had come home with her to find Hugo Mercat's house empty and the servants gone—

Johanna shook the straw from her cloak and resumed her pacing. Payen had brought her in safety across the sea and along weeks of the hard northern roads to reach Whitby, and if he did not ride south this day, he, too, might be trapped by icy ground and snow upon the moors and be compelled to stay for the winter months.

To return to the shipwright's house, to seek Payen and tell him of her plight, would be the act of a coward. He had given her the chance to live; she must give him freedom to return to Brittany, where his brother and his duty waited.

From the river came the sounds of boatmen readying their craft for the day. With luck, there might be a barge crossing the water at this early hour to bring Johanna and her mare to the north shore, where the long track to Gunndale's lands began.

Johanna led the mare to the stable door and lifted the saddle to rest upon the two thick blankets that had kept the beast warm for that long night. The morning had brought a deeper cold, and despite her brisk pacing, the blood had not quickened in Johanna's fingers; the task of securing the saddle girth and the straps of the mare's bridle was slow and painful.

With a last glance at the empty house Johanna led her mare past the gates of the yard and down the snow-whitened riverbank to the deserted quays where Hugo Mercat's two vanished longships had once loaded their cargoes of wool.

Beyond the quays to the east, there were barges large enough to take a horse across the river. The bargemen would know her, and might take her across despite her lack of coin. On the other side Johanna would trade her fine saddle for food and a warmer cloak. At Gunndale she would find all else that she needed.

The old shipmaster who had told the tale of Hugo Mercat's death was nowhere to be found when Payen returned to the narrow street of houses upon the riverbank. The moon had moved halfway across the sky during his frantic search for Johanna, and Payen began to fear that he would not find her before dawn.

He walked back to the shipwright's house and took his saddlebag from the chamber. In the kitchen he found the maid sleeping upon the bench beside the hearth and felt a twinge of shame when she awoke and offered to go with him to his chamber. She sighed when he told her that he could not tarry, then accepted his silver for the shipmaster and gave him a bundle of cold meat and bread for his journey.

On horseback he rode through the narrow streets of Whitby, making his way by the light of the setting moon to the Mercat house. Though he had no torch, he went through the house once again in case she had returned. In the stable he found the straw drawn from the manger and spread upon the earthen floor, then swore a great string of oaths as he saw the faint tracks of small boots and a horse's hooves leading down to the river.

The tracks ran east and ended in a dark, muddy place where boats drawn up upon the shore had kept the fresh snow from the earth. In vain he searched for a sign that Johanna had turned back toward the town.

The moon was near setting and the eastern sky still dark. Upon the far shore there were torches moving and the distant sound of voices. Payen bellowed across the river for a boatman to come and cursed the slowness with which the drowsy crew poled and rowed the barge back to him.

Though the bargemen agreed to take him and his mount over

the water, Payen could not compel them to tell him whether they had taken a lady across the river before him. In the light of the small cresset lamp on the deck, the boatmen's narrowed eyes and hard faces told Payen that they sought to protect the earlier traveler from a stranger's interest.

The kinswoman of the late Hugo Mercat of Whitby might inspire that attitude of protection. Payen began to hope that his decision to cross the river would lead him to Johanna.

He had given the boatmen their deniers and led his mount from the barge before he noticed the little painted saddle upon the landing.

"Where is she?"

The bargemen looked to one another, then lowered their stubborn gazes to the deck. Payen was half tempted to show them the edge of his steel to prod their memories, and half grateful that the men wished to protect Johanna Mercat from rumors of flight from town with only her saddle to barter for her needs.

"That is Johanna Mercat's saddle. Did she sell it to you?"

The smallest of the boatmen raised his head, then ducked again. "Nah."

Though the snow would show her tracks at dawn, the morning sun might melt them. Payen needed to know how to reach Gunndale, for Johanna must have decided to take refuge at the small farm.

Payen pointed to the saddle. "I'll buy it."

Heads rose and the red, torchlit gazes became narrower still.

"Sell me a warm cloak and that saddle and tell me which way the lady rode, and you'll have silver for your trouble."

The short boatman cleared his throat and began to coil the mooring rope.

"The snow is coming harder, and she has no saddle to help her stay on the mare's back," Payen said. "Which way did she go?'' He took his money pouch from the saddlebag and began to count silver into his palm as he waited for the bargemen to conclude their muttered parlay.

When she reached the steeper ground north of the river, Johanna rode astride to keep from slipping from her mare's back. The beast was nervous without her saddle and had turned skittish when a low-flying merlin had crossed the snow-dappled ground before them. Before her, Johanna had placed the saddlebag; she rode with one hand to the reins and one to the bag, for if it slipped to the ground unnoticed, neither Johanna nor her little mare would have food to strengthen them in the long, hard ride ahead.

Though she had only her horse, three thick woolen cloaks, and a sack of food to call her own, Johanna's heart rose to the prospect of reaching Gunndale. Her cousins would be at the small manor house, and Hadwen with the other servant women. And beyond the manor, beyond the high ridge where the Hag's Teeth stood vigil, she would live in the long, low hall of undressed stone where her ancestors had made their home in the days before they had left the land to sell wool across the sea.

Johanna did not allow herself to think of the long fire pit and the thickness of the walls. And she banished from her mind the image of Payen of Rochmarin beside her in the hall, his eyes burning gold and azure in the firelight.

Her palfrey sidled away from a clump of furze rattling iced and frozen in the wind; Johanna calmed the beast with a hand to her neck. The snow-laden gusts were increasing; Johanna's legs were cold above her boots, and it was impossible, riding astride, to keep her cloaks wrapped about her knees. The mare snorted and wheeled around to face the east wind. With some coaxing she turned back and trotted for a distance, but the next frigid gust brought her around again to face east, with her ears pricked forward against the wind.

It was too soon after summer for the wolves to hunt a horse and rider. There were tales of desperate predators coming after travelers in the deep cold after Yuletide, but never this early in the winter. Johanna gripped the reins with hands sweating despite the cold and left her saddlebag balanced before her to stay or fall as it would. If it was a wolf her mount had sensed, Johanna could not afford to slip from the mare's blanket-covered back. Once down, she might never rise.

The merlin hawk swooped low again, and in her white wake there was another shape—dark, four-legged, and approaching fast from the east.

The mare tossed her head, and the saddlebag slid to the ground. Johanna narrowed her eyes against the driving wind and saw that it was a horse coming toward them—a horse and rider.

The mare would not turn but began to trot forward, toward the rider from the east. Johanna hauled back on the reins and set her boot to the mare's right flank to turn her, but to no effect. The dark-clad horseman was closing fast and would soon be upon them.

A voice called to her, a voice distorted by the wind to seem—

Johanna dropped the reins and let the mare trot forward to find her stablemate.

"I brought your saddle," said Payen of Rochmarin.

Johanna nodded.

"Your legs will freeze if you ride astride with your kirtle flapping in the wind."

She nodded again.

He dismounted and walked to her side. "And if you weep in this wind, your eyes will close from the ice, and we will never find Gunndale."

He lifted her from the mare and held her close against him, muttering a litany of oaths and curses and words of love. Her tears burned hot beneath his kisses; he drew back to brush the ice from his beard and took her mouth beneath his own.

"Will you not speak to me?" he said at last.

"I gave you your freedom," she said, "and you did not take it." Johanna smiled, then, and drew his face back down to her. "The cold has robbed you of your reason."

He smiled back, set her from him, and began to untie the high, lumped bundle behind his saddle. "Brush the snow from the blankets," he said. "We'll bring you home upon your gaudy saddle."

He hefted the saddle into place and worked with swift precision to tighten the girth.

"My saddlebag," Johanna said. "It's just ahead on the ground. There is food, and grain for the horses."

He lifted her onto the saddle and tucked her cloaks around her knees. Leading the two horses, Payen retraced the mare's path, frowning as he saw that the small hoofprints were vanishing in the snow-scouring wind.

Payen tied the bag to Johanna's saddle and remounted. "I saw no cairns—only your track. Do you know the way?"

"I do," she answered. "We'll need to ride hard to reach the farm before nightfall. It will be a close thing with the ice coming." She hesitated. "I risked it for a reason," she said. "My uncle—"

"I know," he said. "You were right to get out of Whitby. Better to face the ice than be trapped in town, to wait for Mauleon's next move."

They rode on, the gale at their backs and the sleet blown hard across the turf. Though the bite of the rising wind was sharp, it kept the snow from staying on the higher ground, and Johanna was able to bring them from landmark to landmark, making slow but certain progress toward home.

* * *

He had never been so far north, nor felt cold so intense. When the wind increased, Payen feared that it would be the death of Johanna, and he began to look for a likely place to shelter until the storm passed.

Johanna, remembering her uncle's tales of wintering in these moorland heights, insisted that they continue, for the cold would seep into their bones if they stopped their journey, and they would be found, come spring, sleeping the long sleep upon a hillside.

They rode without speaking, for the wind caught their words and hurled the sound into the distance. They stopped once to eat the near-frozen bread and hold the bag of oats before each horse in turn. The smoked meat had frozen solid; Payen set it aside, saying that it would make them a good meal when it had set for a time beside the fire they would find at Gunndale.

Unspoken between them was the fear that they would not reach shelter before night and never again feel the heat of a burning hearth.

The wind dropped in the late afternoon; the snow lay as it fell upon the turf and grew deeper as Payen and Johanna rode. To avoid the worst of it, they turned their mounts to higher ground and rode just above the floor of the long valley that would lead them to Gunndale's manor, where Johanna's cousins would welcome them.

The moon was full that night and rose soon after the snow had stopped falling.

They must have strayed higher than they had intended in order to avoid the deepening snow, for when the moon's light shone full upon the land before them, there were stones standing in their white path and darkness to either side, where the hilltop sloped away. Upon its high ground the ragged circle threw shadows of confusion—some canting as if drunk, others split and shattered by ancient frosts, and a few still upright, bearing white crowns of snow.

"The Hag's Teeth?"

Johanna lowered the woolen cloth she had tied to cover all but her eyes. "Yes," she said. "The Hag's Teeth. We're nearer the old hall than the manor. It's not far, Payen. We can reach it."

"Where?"

Johanna pointed to the south, to a shallow dale set into the larger slope. Huddled close to the earth, a long, low roof shone straight in the moonlight. They had found shelter in the shadow of the Hag's Teeth.

There was a narrow door, wedged shut with a small log set against it, and a wider door beyond, barred with a length of timber set into brackets. Johanna touched Payen's arm and pointed to the larger of the two. "That one," she said. "It's for the animals. Get them in first."

They left the doors open to the moonlight, for the house was colder than the snow field upon which it stood. The end of the hall that Johanna called the byre was open to the rest, with only a low wooden wall to keep the horses from straying into the earthen-floored section, where a long fire pit and a scattering of stools and a trestle board lay stored against the rough stone wall.

In the moonlit shadows they worked for a long, agonizing hour to bring wisps of straw into flame with sparks from Payen's dagger hilt upon the rough stones of the pit; from a rotten bench in the shadows they broke wood to feed the small fire. When at last they had a struggling blaze curling about a splintered plank, Payen climbed onto the roof to move the flat, stone-weighted cover of the smoke hole. With the flat of his sword he sent the snow rattling from the slope; with his hands he broke the ice from the timber panel and heaved it aside to reveal the jagged, soot-blackened opening in the roof.

Below Payen, the fire was a scrap of crimson warmth in the

darkness. And Johanna's hair shone as dark honey in the light of it.

When he returned, she was beside the fire, her cloaks still wrapped about her, sound asleep.

He opened the saddlebags, gave the last of the grain to the horses, and placed two more bench legs upon the small blaze; then he took Johanna in his arms and held her as they slept beside the fire.

Chapter Twenty-two

When she woke, daylight shone through the cracks in the shutters and in the door, and the fire blazed bright beside her. The horses stood beyond the low wall, content in their shelter; the saddles rested at the end of the fire pit and the bags lay open. The smell of smoked meat drifted upon the air.

There was a bump and scrape at the door and the sound of boots upon the wood. The door opened in a flood of brightness, and Payen's form appeared within the frame, laden with firewood.

Payen shouldered through the door and leaned to shut it upon the cold. He added the wood to a small heap in the corner and stood smiling at her. "I have found a use for the thieves' swords," he said. "With a little sharpening, they proved near as good as an ax."

She frowned at the fragments of old hewn timber. "Where did you find the wood?"

"Down the slope, in a ruined hut."

"There is no hut."

Payen frowned back. "It's old and ill built. You must have seen it—"

She took a piece of wood from the pile. "It's the sheepcote."

"Johanna, it was but a heap of rotten wood inside a fallen hovel, with the snow coming through the roof."

"It's the sheepcote, with the folds stored for the winter. I'll need it come spring."

"Without firewood we'll not live through the coming night."

Johanna placed the wood upon the fire and went to his arms. "I'll ride over the hill, to the manor, and ask for help."

Payen watched the fire blaze higher and frowned up at the smoke hole. "Will we need to go to them? Your kin should be at the door before long, for the sky is clear now and they'll see the smoke."

"They wouldn't bother to ride here. They might think us travelers who needed a night's shelter."

"And they wouldn't worry that thieves had come to your hall?"

Johanna laughed. "There's nothing to steal and no harm to be done unless the hall burned. Since my grandfather took to selling wool in Whitby, this house has been shelter only to the shepherds who bring the flocks to the high ground for the summer."

"And if we were brigands planning to attack the manor? Would your kin not want to strike first, to turn them away?"

"My kin? They would deal with an attack if it came. They never look for a fight. Their weapons, when last I saw them, were gathering soot on the walls; they haven't taken them down since the William the Bastard conquered these lands. They tell the tale as if it happened yesterday, and credit the Normans with keeping the Scots from raiding this far south." Johanna picked up a second broken plank and placed it upon the fire. "Their wealth is in their flocks, Payen, and in a few silver coins they bury beneath the hearthstone. If brigands come, they find little to take with them."

"And if thieves gather the sheep and run them south?"

"They lose their patience, slaughter a few for their cooking pots, and my cousins find the rest a few days later and bring them home. My cousins talk a mighty streak on vengeance, but they cannot follow thieves when the flocks are scattered about the hills."

Payen laughed. "I'd make little gold if I tried to sell my sword to your kin."

Johanna shrugged. "It was only when my grandfather found *Loki's Horn* and became a wool seller that we began to need guards and strong houses. Before that there was no gold and little silver to protect."

The smile vanished from Payen's face. "I'll get your gold back for you, Johanna. Next spring I'll go south and find Mauleon. If the king has returned, I'll beg his help to restore all that was stolen from you. The gold, the ships—"

She placed her fingers upon his mouth. "Do not. All this long journey north I have thought of that gold and little else—"

He nipped her fingers and smiled. "Little else?"

"Listen to me, Payen. When I thought on it, I decided that the Mercat gold has brought me and my family nothing but ill luck."

"Gold brings what you make of it, Johanna. It brought you that good house in Whitby, and fine clothing, and the promise that your children will never go hungry." Payen looked about the firelit hall. "Do you propose to live here, tending sheep?"

"If those old raiders had not lost their way in the fog, and if my grandfather had not salvaged the ship and begun to sell wool, my family would have continued here, in this hall, with a few small fields and the sheep. There would have been no gold, and no chance for my brother to become a squire, to lose his life at Rochmarin."

He took her hand within his own. "Johanna—"

She shook her head. "Listen to me, Payen. Without the gold,

Malebis would not have wanted my dowry for Rochmarin, and I would not have wed him. I might have died at Rochmarin, as did my brother, had you not come. You, Payen, are the only joy that my Mercat gold ever brought me."

"You would give up what you had, then, and live here as a sheep farmer?"

Johanna smiled. "I have done it, Payen. And I'll need the sheepfold come spring."

A slow smile spread across his face. "Then I'd best not hack the rest of it into firewood. Where is the manor?"

"A few miles north, on the other side of the hill, beyond the Hag's Teeth."

He brushed her forehead with a kiss. "How many cousins?"

"Twenty. None of them near cousins, but all of them as good as kin."

A frown creased his brow. "Twenty are too many. I would have you to myself, Johanna, if I could. We might stay here, alone together for the winter."

She pushed back and looked into his eyes. "You said you could not bear to have me near. A child, you said, would bring us both disaster. Do you propose that we live apart from my kinspeople, as if we were man and wife?"

His gaze did not drop from her question. "A child might bring disaster. To part might bring disaster. The risks are there, whatever we decide." He reached to touch her cheek and brought the smell of wood and smoke to her senses. It was the scent of a winter house, and life-giving fire. "I am weary of living as if the lands of Rochmarin and your Mercat gold should be waymarks for us both, to send us apart. I was a fool, Johanna. Last night, when I could not find you, and thought I might never find you—"

"But you did. And if I leave the Mercat gold and ships to Mauleon, I'll never be lost again. Stay with me, Payen, and I will never be lost again."

* * *

Stay with me.

Standing straight upon the earthen floor, her green mantle vivid against the gray walls of the steading, Johanna was a promise of spring in the winter. Her oak-brown hair falling smooth in the firelight glowed with rich color, and her eyes, turned green above the mantle and taking gold from the light of the flames, were life itself.

He began to tell her this but did not have the words. He looked to the fire pit and saw, in the flames, faces from his past and the harrowing of Rochmarin.

Johanna's face paled, and the green life dimmed in her gaze. "It is too soon for promises and oaths. We have the winter, Payen; that will be enough."

"No." He lowered his voice and began again. "No, there will be more than a winter. Much more, God willing, than a winter. But I must leave you in the spring and cross the sea again. I must make certain of my brother's safety and his place at the abbey, for that is all he will have."

Johanna's gaze did not waver. "I would not have you choose between your brother's needs and my love, Payen. If my own brother had lived, I would have given everything I owned, and my life as well, to keep him from harm. Do what you must, Payen, and come back to me if you can. We will have the winter, and if you return—"

"I shall return."

"I will be here, at this hearth, waiting for you."

He drew her close and looked into those green eyes that spoke of the future, and the return of spring to this land of ice and snow—to his cold, war-burdened life.

Narrow shafts of sunlight pierced the planks of the door and fell in lines of warm gold upon the dark green of her mantle. Her hand moved to the clasp of it, then dropped to her side.

''The manor is an hour's easy ride from here in summertime,'' she said. ''With the snow on the ground—''

She was his now. There would be a winter of long nights and days of solitude for them. Payen sighed. ''Then let us ride now and return before nightfall.'' He looked to the door. ''If this were paradise, Johanna, we'd not leave our fire for a fortnight.''

Johanna smiled. ''When the heavy cold comes, you'll call it paradise.''

He smiled back. ''And how shall we pass the time before the deep winter comes?''

Her delicate brows arched high above the green of her eyes. ''We'll haul firewood from the grove below us, beside the river. And we will repair the sheepfold panels. And—''

''And?''

Her smile deepened. ''We might not need so much firewood after all.''

Gunndale's manor was a large hall built in the same way as Johanna's low house beyond the Hag's Teeth. Upon the doorposts, unpainted and rubbed smooth by the passage of many hands, were carved faces of somber and Nordic feature.

The Gunndale folk had nothing in common with those fierce, scowling faces upon their doorposts. They were as Johanna had described: hardworking, prosperous sheep farmers, slow to anger or to fear, and untroubled by the news of their Norman king's long absence from England. Though Payen had learned to speak the English tongue in his years with King Richard's army, he had difficulty understanding the odd, gruff accent of the people of Gunndale's manor, and he used the delays to slow his answers to the inevitable questions that needed no language to express. Johanna dealt with them.

Old Rolf and his kinfolk had heard, when they sent their taxes to the king's agent at the abbey, that Hugo Mercat had died, and that Johanna had died abroad in Breton lands. The latter claim they had not believed, for there was no marking stone at the abbey church.

With a frown and a nod old Rolf promised Payen that if any should come to Gunndale to seek Johanna, he would say that he knew nothing and would send word in secret to the steading beyond the ridge. ''And will you get Johanna's gold back from those thieving Bretons?'' Rolf had asked Payen.

''It was thieving Normans who took it,'' Payen said. ''The same thieving Normans who robbed my Breton father.''

In a wide-mouthed display of yellow teeth, Rolf had laughed and called his sons near to hear Payen's words. ''It seems Payen's kin had the same trouble our folk did with the Normans,'' Rolf wheezed. ''Are they never content with the lands they have?'' The old man reached for Payen's sleeve and drew him near enough to hear Rolf's hoarse whisper. ''Each Samhain morning, as my grandfathers did, I go up to the Hag's Teeth and leave her grain and ale for our dead, and ask her to keep the Normans from returning here. And in my lifetime, she has. See that you do it too, for your lady's sake and your own.''

Beyond the matter of the Mercats' fall and Johanna's safety, Rolf and his household seemed indifferent to news outside the small valley in which they lived. They welcomed Payen among them at their board but did not ask, in his hearing, how he had come to be traveling with Johanna.

They were not Mercats and seemed to call themselves by none but their given names. Though they could name with precision their forefathers for ten generations back, there were no deeds of war to distinguish one from the other, save the one who had fought the Bastard's Norman invaders and lost his life on the hillside below the Hag's Teeth. After that day the small manor at Gunndale had been all but invisible to any but the Norman tax collector at Whitby.

The women treated him as if he were wed to Johanna; Payen

had said nothing to deny their belief, nor had he claimed she was his wife. After the first hour of cautious speech the men began to question him of his past and spoke of his fighting skills with the same calm demeanor with which they told him how Johanna's sheepfolds might be readied for the spring.

The Gunndale folk were generous and sent two wagons filled with food and tools from the storehouses that stood in a tidy square beside their manor hall. Smoked meat, grain, ale, and slabs of dried peat made their way that afternoon across the ridge to Johanna's hall. "It's owed you," the old Gunndale patriarch had said. "Hugo Mercat never kept his profit from our Gunndale wool sold in Flanders but gave us everything it earned, save the wages of the crew on the ship. He did it for friendship's sake, for we had helped his father find the means to repair that salvaged ship that started them selling wool. So, for friendship's sake we'll see you through this winter and count ourselves still in your debt."

The men followed them back to Johanna's hall with the two wagons heavy with supplies, cutting deep grooves in the sun-washed snow. They helped carry the salt meat and grain bags to hang from the low rafters, and rolled a tun of precious foreign wine to rest in the far corner. A wide straw tick, and cord and tools to build a plain bedframe came next, and then a deep, well-staved ale tub.

For a woman who had, until the Samhain past, possessed gold enough to buy the Gunndale manor many times over, Johanna seemed uncommonly pleased with each bag of grain, each thick woolen coverlet that came from the wagons. She had, it seemed, already forgotten that her family had ever owned anything more than this low hall beneath the Hag's Teeth.

For a man who had never thought to have a hearth or a woman of his own to care for, each woolen coverlet, each cooking pot carried from the wagons bespoke a life more foreign to Payen than the Saracen tents of Palestine. Payen watched the cold, bare refuge become a warm haven where the woman he loved would live at his side in the long winter to come.

They watched the small convoy leave, their palfreys tied to the wagons to return to Gunndale's sturdy stable and deep stores of oats for the winter. In all the broad snowy field upon which the low steading stood, there was no other living creature but Johanna and Payen. The small warmth of the afternoon sun crossed the snowfield to reach them as they stood before their door.

It was the happiest day of Payen's life.

Johanna's face was pink with happiness, and her eyes shone leaf green in the low sunlight. If there was a goddess of the spring who lived in these moors, far from the new religion, Johanna was her handmaiden and carried in her strong, slender body all the life and magic of which the ancients had sung.

She smiled at Payen and bent to plunge her hands into the soft, drifted snow blown high against the wall. She spread her mantle before her to catch the snow, and ran to the fire pit to empty the cold burden into the ale tub. She seized a bucket, turned back to the door, and cast it into the same drift; she pulled it out and started back to the fire pit.

Payen took the bucket from Johanna's hand and carried it for her. "Have you some magic, to make ale from melted snow?"

Johanna laughed and took up a second bucket. "Who would want to waste the tub on ale, when by sunset we could have a great tub of water melted beside the fire pit, and Hadwen's dried roses to sweeten it?"

"You might chill and sicken—"

"Not if I have a warm mattress and Gunndale coverlets to keep me from the cold. Not if I have—"

Payen caught her hand and kissed it. "Careful what you touch, Johanna. You shall have what you want, and sooner than you imagine."

She laughed and drew back. "Not before the tub is filled with snow."

He dug the bucket into the snowdrift and reached the tub in two long strides. "I'll have it full in the time it takes you to find the coverlets."

Johanna shook her head, beset with sudden shyness at the end of their waiting. She trembled at the nearness of Payen. "They gave us an ax," she said. "Will you cut the wood we dragged from the grove? And I will—"

The wind gave a soft whistle from the dark rafters and sent the plump bags of grain spinning slowly in the shadows.

"I'll broach the barrel first," said Payen, "and give you wine. An hour from now, I'll return."

"There's not so much wood out there—"

"When I've done, I'll walk up to the Hag's Teeth," Payen said, "and take your old gods a skin of wine to thank them. And then I'll take my turn in that tub and sleep at your side. If you are asleep, Johanna, I'll not wake you."

She turned away and began to search the small bags of herbs from Gunndale. "I did not mean to turn you out."

"And I did not mean to demand anything but a warm bed."

Johanna turned back to smile upon him. "It had gone beyond wishes and demands between us before we took ship. It was a long journey, and we are not, I think, the souls we were in Brittany."

Payen nodded and made no move to touch her. "Do you regret that you have taken this stranger to your hearth?"

"No more than you regret giving up Brittany to follow this stranger—to live in a steading so small that your head hits the rafters." She moved to him and placed a small, cold hand upon his cheek. "By spring, Payen, we will be strangers no more, and you will know all my secrets."

He kissed her then, a gentle kiss that left her free to draw back and speak again. "And I," Johanna continued, "will know all your secrets. All of them, down to the last Saracen lady who taught you the skills that left me breathless. All your secrets, Payen. A winter's worth of secrets."

Secrets. Secrets would kill him in the end.

It would have eased his soul to tell Johanna Mercat the last of his secrets—the last that mattered. That he had slain her husband and left his body bloody and cold upon the floor of the brothel in Nantes.

Knowing Walter Malebis's young cruelty, Johanna would understand that Payen had had no choice. Knowing Walter Malebis's greed, Johanna would know that the Norman lordling had gone to Nantes with no intention of accepting Payen's bid to take Rochmarin back in exchange for a fortune in gold. Knowing Walter Malebis's ruthlessness, Johanna would know that he had intended, from the moment his men had armed themselves to ride with him, that Payen and any who arrived with him should die, and that Payen's gold should go into Malebis's money pouch as quickly as his body would go into the mouth of the Loire.

Payen made his way to the largest of the Hag's Teeth and stood before the great stone that kept vigil upon the steading below its slopes. Walter Malebis had died with more than betrayal upon his soul. From what Johanna had told him, Payen believed that Malebis had put young Harald Mercat in the way of death in the garrison yard at Rochmarin. No knight, however inexperienced, however negligent, would set a new squire to train with any but blunt swords, nor would he place sharpened swords in the hands of those who taught him.

Days ago, in the small grove beside the Esk, when Payen had held the thieves' ill-kept weapons in his hands, and had said to Johanna that they were scarce fit to slaughter a chicken, the truth had come to him. Johanna's brother had died, she said, of wounds taken in training on the third day of his time at Rochmarin. The third day.

It was no accident. It was murder, done to ensure that Johanna and her husband would inherit all the ships and gold of Hugo Mercat. And having watched his men-at-arms slay Johanna's young brother, Walter Malebis had saddled his horse and set out for Nantes, to take Payen's hard-won gold and give him death in payment.

Payen brought his fist against the great stone and cried out a curse. No matter how foully the young lord Malebis had lived his life, no matter how many murders he might have countenanced in his greed for gold, the man had been Johanna's husband. And Johanna did not know that she had taken to her bed the man who had made her a widow.

She did not know. She might never know, if they spent their lives there, in the shadow of the Hag's Teeth. She might not discover Payen's deed unless he spoke of it in sleep, or in fever, or by chance one day when the canker of his secrecy would make its way forth into Johanna's hearing through a careless word.

He unstopped the wineskin and poured a crimson flow upon the stone. He owed God and the saints and the old ones of this place his gratitude that Johanna's life had been spared and that they had come to have a life together. And he asked forgiveness from them all—old gods and new—that he would keep two secrets from the woman with whom he would spend his life. Either of them, if revealed, might take the light from her eyes, and diminish the small share of happiness she had craved—to live in this poor place, to do the work of a shepherd wife, and to turn her back for all time upon the riches she had known and live in peace with the man she loved.

Payen watched the wine congeal to crimson drops within the small crevices of the stone. He was a coward, of course. The first of his secrets—Malebis's likely murder of the Mercat lad—he had kept for Johanna's sake alone, to spare her further grief. The second—his slaying of Walter Malebis—he would keep both for Johanna's sake and because he could not bear to see the desolation that would come to her if she learned the truth.

He was a coward, then. And he would make a good job of it for Johanna's sake.

Payen took up the empty wineskin and turned south to look down upon the roof of the steading where he would, for these winter months, find his own kind of paradise. The setting sun shone upon the snow-laden roof and brought to life the thin curl of smoke that rose from the hall. If it were possible to send his memories from him, to set them adrift in the cold black sky with only the moon to mourn their oblivion, he would give his life for the deed.

God and his saints, and the old ones who watched from the Hag's Teeth, had offered him no way to scour the memories from his soul.

Chapter Twenty-three

March, 1194

The new palings for the sheepfold lay ready within the store hut, and a month's supply of firewood was stacked beside the hall.

"You will live in Rolf's household until I return," said Payen for the hundredth time.

"I'll move as soon as the shepherds bring the flocks over the hill."

"You will not stay here alone."

"Or—?"

"Or I'll drag you to Rolf and tell him that Johanna Mercat has lost her reason and must be watched lest she run straight into the arms of her enemies."

Johanna looked to the small squares of greenery that had risen from the earth beyond the western wall of the steading. "The herbs need tending."

"They survived despite your shepherds' neglect for two

generations,'' Payen said. ''The damned things will live until I return. Get your cloak, Johanna. We are going to the manor.''

She smiled and began to take her mantle from her shoulders. ''The river ice has broken, Payen. And the sun is warm. Too warm, I think.'' She pulled two leaf-laden twigs from the clump of winter savory and held them before Payen's nose. ''Let us stop quarreling and go down to the river. The effects of savory upon the skin are wonderful.''

He seized the small branches and tucked them behind Johanna's ear. ''The effects of your delay are, as always, the stuff of wonder. I am serious though. If you will not go to Rolf's household, I cannot go to Brittany. And if I delay the journey, and become stranded over the water next winter, I will grow mad from desire and drown off the coast one night, trying to reach you.''

She snatched the savory from her hair and began to remove the small leaves one by one. ''I will not say farewell at the manor with Gunndale's great crowd watching us.''

Payen took the twig from her fingers. ''Let me help,'' he said.

Johanna cried out in rage. ''Will you not cease your jests and listen to me? This leave-taking is a difficult task, Payen, and you are not making it easier. I will not go to the manor to see you ride away. You must go to fetch your horse and ride back here to get your saddlebags. When you have gone—'' She swallowed quickly. ''When you have gone, I'll walk to the manor and stay there until you return. On fine days I could ride across the ridge—''

''—with young Rolf to protect you—''

''—with young Rolf to protect me from the Hag's Teeth and see that the shepherds are looking to their duties as they should.''

''And each night, without fail—''

''I will sleep at the manor, with twenty folk snoring in

the common hall, and Hadwen's chatter to keep me from my sleep.''

Payen smiled. ''I hadn't noticed you so eager to have undisturbed sleep, madam. Only three nights ago I found my own sleep broken by your restlessness and I was hard put to quiet you. Hard as a—'' He stepped back in a mock cringe from her blows, then came forward, of a sudden, to catch her wrist.

He kissed the soft white skin beneath her wrist, where the sun and the small scratches of her weeding had not reached.

''Come back to me, Payen.''

Her eyes were shining with unshed tears. Payen kissed the corner of her mouth, where her smiles must begin. ''I will come back, I promise you.''

''And you will not fight?''

Payen closed his eyes. By then, if all had gone well, King Richard should be ransomed back from Austria, as Payen had reason to know. ''I have no lands, Johanna, but I swore an oath of loyalty to King Richard. If he is threatened, then I must fight.''

''The king still lives, does he not? Even at Gunndale we would have heard—''

''Likely the king lives, and must be free by now, and on his way home. If not, Count John will move again to take the throne, and the lords loyal to young Prince Arthur will fight to get him the crown.''

The twig snapped between Johanna's fingers. ''And you would join the young prince's side, as he is Breton born?''

Payen took up the broken pieces. ''No, I'd leave both sides on their path to hell and come back to defend this place.'' He smiled then, and touched Johanna's hair. ''Don't worry,'' he said. ''King Richard will return, and though he loves this land scarce better than the meanest of his estates in Normandy, still he will serve England well by living, so that there will not be war between his heirs. There may be peace in this land for many years to come.''

"If the king does not need your sword, you will come back by midsummer?"

"For anything but the king's causes—for Mercadier's sieges, or the fate of Rochmarin itself, I will not fight." He kissed her then and tasted the savory upon her lips. "If the king's brother has the courage to raise a rebellion again, so soon after last year's disasters, he's a greater fool than I thought him." Payen placed his hands beside her face and raised her gaze to meet his own. "The rains have not begun, and the roads will be good. With luck, I'll be at the south ports before a fortnight is gone, and I'll find the first ship crossing to Brittany. Another fortnight should be enough for all I have to do for my brother. Before Easter, Johanna, I might be home. Now you must promise—will you be here, waiting for me?"

She smiled then. "No, I'll be sitting at old Queen Eleanor's knee, stitching with my soft white hands."

"Johanna, you will not ride to Whitby—"

"I'm not a fool—"

"—even if I am late returning, and you seek news of events in the south?"

He raised his brows. "You will send young Rolf instead and wait for him to bring you news?"

She frowned. "Young Rolf can't remember the name of his own betrothed after visiting the alehouses of Whitby."

He slid his hands down to her shoulders and held her fast. "Nevertheless, will you promise me?"

"I'll not go to Whitby. Not even if I hear that Mauleon is there, selling the house stone by stone as ballast to Flemish ships."

Payen looked up at the sky, then smiled down upon her face. "I believe it's not yet noon, Johanna. There's time enough for a look at the river."

"For a swim in the river?"

He growled into the softness where the grace of her neck met the exquisite line of her shoulder. "You would unman me,

Johanna, in the new-melted ice? How would I sit a saddle, having frozen my—''

''As easily as I might, Payen, after lying with you upon the riverbank—''

He had unlaced her kirtle and begun to nuzzle it from her breast when they heard the shouting and looked up to see a horseman calling in the distance, from the Hag's Teeth, far above them.

Payen pulled Johanna's kirtle together and thrust her behind him, his hand upon the hilt of his sword.

''It's young Rolf,'' said Johanna. ''And he's sure to tell the tale of what he saw when he's back at the manor. I'll never hear the end of it in the weeks you will be gone.'' She tied her laces and stepped to his side. ''Payen, call him down. We'll never hear him from this distance.''

Even from the far hilltop Rolf's face showed deep crimson beneath his shock of bright red hair. He walked his mount down the hillside and reined it to a halt a safe distance from them. ''There's a man come to Whitby,'' Rolf bellowed. ''He's looking for Payen and knows your name as well, Johanna Mercat.''

''Mauleon,'' Payen snarled. He beckoned Rolf to come closer.

Rolf was not reassured. ''I'll stay my distance,'' he called. ''What do you want us to do? The man's lodging at John the shipwright's house and says he won't go back south until he speaks with you, Payen.''

Johanna gasped. ''Does Mauleon know your name, Payen?'' She walked forward and took the bridle strap of Rolf's mount in her hand. ''Who saw him? Is he tall, with pale hair?''

''John himself told me the man's of middling size, not a youth, with a red beard. He's a drunkard, or so John believes, for the first night in Whitby he went down the streets bellowing for Payen, or those who had seen Payen, to come forth and speak, and was shouting for a Matthew as well. He did that for two nights, in three alehouses, and gave the abbot a hard time yesterday with his questions. Many times he asked John where the Mercats had gone, but John told him nothing, as we had warned him.''

''Matthew? The man was calling for Matthew?''

''It might be Mathieu,'' Payen said, ''calling my name, and giving his own.'' He nodded to Rolf. ''I'll be over to Gunndale in an hour to get my horse and ride into Whitby to see this loud drunkard for myself. I'll not ride south until I'm sure the man in the alehouses, whoever he is, is not bringing trouble for us.'' He turned back to Johanna. ''My lady, it's time for you to go to Gunndale, and I'll hear no more talk of crowds and snoring.''

She had managed to smile. ''It must be Mathieu.''

Payen nodded. ''I pray it is.'' He looked back down the slope, past the greening hillocks, to the bare trees clustered about the river. ''In the summer, Johanna, I'll come back to you.''

''And the trees will be in leaf, and the grass high beside the river.'' She turned to him and placed her hand upon his heart. ''I'll be here, waiting for you.''

Even if the women's end of the common hall at Gunndale had not been crowded, and if Hadwen had not talked half the night of her daughter's journey to Whitby and the wonders she had seen, Johanna would not have slept that night at the manor. She lay awake listening to Hadwen's long, drowsy narrative, then attempted to count the number of deep nasal voices snoring at the far end of the hall. And tried not to imagine what Payen might have found at Whitby.

If it was Mathieu seeking Payen, he might bring news of some fresh war to which Mercadier had invited his elite warriors, or it might be bad tidings of Rochmarin, or of Payen's cloistered brother.

By dawn Johanna was sleepless, and it pained her to open her reddened, weeping eyes to the morning light. She lay abed past Hadwen's rising and endured the sly hints of women with child who had begun to lie abed past dawn as soon as they had quickened. That had brought on a second spell of silent weeping imperfectly concealed against the deep straw tick where she slept.

She rose at last and put off Hadwen's fussing by claiming it was dust from the tick that had set her eyes to streaming. Hadwen's indignant words followed her out to the privy and back to the washing bowls set out beside the morning bread.

Johanna tarried in the storehouse yard east of the hall, making herself useful in the woolshed, sweeping the last of the previous year's dust aside, joining Hadwen in counting and repairing the great wool sacks that would hold the coming June's shearings from the rafters. From the woolshed door she was the first to see Payen and Mathieu ride down the hillside to Gunndale in the company of a well-swathed figure on a third horse; she was the first to run from the manor yard to meet them halfway down the snow-sodden hill and to discover that Payen and Mathieu had brought a priest to Gunndale.

"So I came to find Payen, to be sure he was not stranded up here in the north, and to bring him back to put down the rebellions." Mathieu smiled at Johanna. "Any man who seeks the king's favor in the years to come had better be ready to tell King Richard where he was when the royal armies reached Nottingham to end Count John's uprising."

Johanna drew a painful breath. "Mathieu, you might have left us in peace. Payen does not need—"

Payen covered her hand with his own. "Johanna, I must go. This is my king fighting to keep his crown—"

"And why should he keep his crown? He's brought us nothing but taxes and said to my uncle's trading partners that he would sell the city of London, and gladly, to the devil himself if the price were high enough to buy him a larger army for his next wars in Palestine. Payen, you won't need to join the king's forces?''

Payen moved his hand to Johanna's arm and smoothed the sleeve of her kirtle. ''Whether or not the king would see me in his ranks, I'll go south to fight for him. I gave him my oath, when we set out for Palestine, to fight for him until he was back safe upon his throne. Even Mercadier would not turn from him now.'' His voice softened. ''And in my oath to you, Johanna, I said that I would take up my sword only if the king had need of it. The time has come.''

''And you brought us a priest to say masses for your soul while you're in the south?''

Payen winced. ''Can you not imagine the reason?''

Johanna looked from Payen's watchful eyes to the shivering figure huddled beside the Gunndale fire pit. ''We had agreed,'' she said, ''that we could not be wed, for your name and the fact that I live would become known hereabouts, and the risk was too great.''

Mathieu laughed. ''Payen found himself a priest who had sailed north on the ship that brought me,'' he said. ''The man's headed up to the borders and won't have a chance to speak of the marriage in Whitby.'' Mathieu lowered his voice to a whisper. ''Won't have a chance to speak of much at all if the Scots get hold of him.''

Johanna sighed. ''If he's a foreign priest, he'll need to say banns for a fortnight to discover whether you, Payen, have six wives still living, and whether I keep a bawdy house and consort with imps.''

Payen sat back and smiled in lazy satisfaction. ''This priest has need of gold, Johanna, and Mathieu has enough in his money pouch to bribe the man. We have already settled the matter of banns. Now, do you wish to wed me before I go south?''

Johanna looked from Payen to Mathieu.

Mathieu rose. ''I'll see to my horse.''

From the far end of the hall, Hadwen and the serving maids were watching and giggling over the ale tub. Mathieu strode past them with a dismissive gesture for their questions. The priest rose from the fire to fill his cup again and turned his back upon the chattering women.

Payen cleared his throat. ''Though he is far from his chapel, the man is a priest—a true one, known to Mathieu from years past. He has a parchment with him, and could give you the record of our marriage to keep here, or back at the steading. We could take it to the abbey and place it in the abbot's keeping when our troubles are done.''

Johanna glanced again at the watchful group around the ale tub. ''It would be ridiculous to wed here, when these folk have accepted us as wed and never asked—''

''They knew, I think.'' Payen's smiled faded. ''Johanna, if there should be a child—''

''There is no child. By now there would have been—''

''Or if I should meet death before I can return, there may come a day when it would do you some good to be known as my wife. No—listen,'' he said. ''This is not a time to pretend that death is for others and not for me. Listen, Johanna—King Richard has reason to be grateful to me, for a journey I took on his behalf last fall, before I came back to Brittany. Hubert Walter, the new archbishop, knows it all. If I should not return, and if you have need of the king's favor one day, you could take the marriage paper to Hubert Walter, and he will help you.''

''I will not wed you for that.''

Payen drew a long breath. ''It is all I have to give you, Johanna. Will you not accept it?''

There was nothing in his face to show the intensity Johanna had heard in those words. Nothing but the pain that darkened his azure eyes.

"Yes," she said. "I'll wed you, but not here."

Payen's eyes lightened in relief. "Not at the Hag's Teeth. I'll not wed you in the old crone's maw."

"At the steading," she said. "I'll say my vows at the steading, with only Mathieu to witness."

Payen glanced down the hall. "And Hadwen? There should be a witness from Gunndale, and the woman seems ready to burst from curiosity. Have pity, Johanna, and let your Hadwen come with us."

The small wedding party rode past the Hag's Teeth on their way to Johanna's hall, and Hadwen insisted that they stop and pour ale upon the largest of the stones.

Payen watched from his mount's back and did not approach as Hadwen turned her broad, blond features to the tallest stone to make her prayers to the old ones. He imagined that he saw the stain of the crimson wine he had offered last winter, when he had sworn to keep Johanna free of the burden of knowing that she had bedded her husband's killer.

He had taken that deception, that sin upon his soul, and he would add another. He would wed her, and bind Johanna to him for all the days of their lives, without confessing to her that one secret, that one part of his past that would mar the joy in her eyes and darken the days of her waiting.

She would have loved him still, had she known. Johanna would have loved him still but felt the deep torture of guilt within her soul each day she remained at his side. He would spare her the pain, and spare himself the chance, however small, that she might have sent him from her.

They said their vows before the south side of the hall, standing in the late winter sun upon the newly thawed earth. The priest, who had complained that he rode to Gunndale expecting a chapel in which to wed the fearsome black-clad brigand to the green-eyed lady, had seen the menace in the ruffian's eyes and agreed that in the absence of a consecrated church, one hillside was as good as the next, and the ceremony as valid in a shepherd's hall as in the manor at Gunndale.

Old Rolf sent the newly married couple on their way with gifts of ale and bread and meat and bade them return at morning for a small feast before Payen and Mathieu left on their journey.

So they were wed upon the hillside looking down to the river and the trees that had not yet shown the promise of spring. Hadwen had stood at Johanna's side, with a kerchief to her face to conceal what might have been amusement, tears, or both. Mathieu had stood closer to the priest, with a hand ready to clutch the cleric's arm lest an excess of ale cause the priest to lose his balance and topple down the hillside.

Mathieu had stood over the priest watching him write, in large letters upon a good piece of tanned calfskin, the record of the marriage of Johanna Mercat, widow of Walter Malebis, to Payen, once of Rochmarin. He offered the vellum to Johanna. "Can you make it out? Did the priest write your names true? Did he write that you are wed?"

Johanna had read it and pronounced the lines well written. With a flourish worthy of a royal gift, Mathieu emptied his money pouch into the priest's hand, then frowned as he took back a few silver coins for the journey ahead. Then he herded the unsteady priest and a weeping Hadwen back to their mounts and rode with them over the ridge.

Payen and Johanna stood watching the three riders pass through the Hag's Teeth.

"Are you happy?"

Johanna smiled. "I have another night with you, Payen."

He took the vellum from her hands and held it to the waning sun to see the last of the ink dry. "And you have this, Johanna. Will you place it in the wall behind the loose stone?"

She shook her head. "I'll take it to Rolf when we ride back to Gunndale. It will be near at hand while you're away."

Payen smiled. "Then you agree you'll not come back here until I return."

She turned to him with an uncertain smile. "I could not. I'd weep the spring away with the memories."

"I'll come back to you, Johanna, and there will be a lifetime more of memories for us." He took her hand and drew her with him to the door. "And a few still to make before I ride south." Within the hall the flames blazed long and bright and extravagant in the fire pit, and the sacks of food from Gunndale were set out upon the low trestle beside it.

"My only regret at the fall of the house of Mercat," Payen said, "is that Gunndale will no longer have its gifts of wine. Old Rolf was unhappy that the last of it is gone."

"He gave us one of the last tuns on the first day we were here." Johanna filled two cups with ale and set them upon the board. "When you return, Payen, it will be ale for us both, for the rest of our lives."

"There will be gold, Johanna, when I come back from Brittany. I'll take your advice, at last, and recover the caches I left along the coast and bring back what my brother will not need."

Johanna began to take Hadwen's bread and smoked meat from the sacks. "Then hide it well, and don't let King Richard discover it should you find yourself fighting for him. My uncle Hugo said that our young king has greater hunger for gold than his father and all the abbots of the land together and a bad temper when he sees a rich man keep his coins to himself."

Payen laughed. "Are you suggesting, wife, that if there's fighting, I should bury my gold in a safe place? You once told me I'd be foolish not to bring it all to a silversmith."

Color flooded Johanna's face. "In times of unrest the silversmiths must give the king what he demands and not complain overmuch if they don't see their gold again when peace comes.

There are a few clever ones—I would have given you their names—who know how to keep their patrons' gold safe."

"In a hole in the ground, no doubt." He set his ale cup upon the board and began to toy with the rim. "When I return, we'll hide our gold where we can find it—if my wool-seller wife will agree."

"I am no wool seller. Not now. I'm a sheep farmer."

Payen took the food sack from her hands and set it aside. "We will see, when we've had a year of living among the sheep." He brought her hand to his lips. "Why are you putting food on the board, Johanna, when our bed stands empty and the fire is hot—hot enough that we might shed our clothes and not feel the cold?"

"It's not yet night, Payen."

"All the better. Did you never, in all the long winter nights, wish we might lie together without the cold waiting, just outside the coverlets, to nip us?"

"If I recall, we did enough sweet nipping beneath the blankets that we wouldn't have felt the bite of the cold."

He drew her with him to the pallet and pulled the tunic from his shoulders.

"And is it warm enough, in your northern summers, to lie upon the grass and pleasure each other?"

"If you don't mind a few hundred sheep watching." Johanna reached to hasten the flight of Payen's chausses to the far corner, where his tunic had fallen.

Her kirtle soon followed Payen's clothes and landed in the shadows beyond the fire pit. "Then we'll find a place where the sheep don't graze and make it our own."

"There is no such place." Johanna pulled the coverlets from the bed and sat upon the smooth linen cloth that covered the straw tick. "You will have to get used to the sheep, Payen, if we couple upon the summer grass."

"The ewes might learn your practices," Payen whispered.

"And run in fright from yours."

He sat back in mock indignation. "They'll learn to cry out like a cat in season if they study you, wife."

"And the rams will—"

"Yes?"

"The rams will see that there's a creature lustier than they." Johanna lowered her gaze and smiled. "And better endowed than the best of them."

Payen caught her to him and rolled her onto her back. "I think a shepherd's life will not be a bad thing," he said, "as long as you permit us to scandalize the sheep from time to time."

"As often as you like," she murmured.

"Then let's count the ways we'll put a blush on their faces."

"Sheep don't blush."

"Ours will. Believe me, Johanna. Ours will."

"Then we had better begin to count, husband."

An hour before dawn, when the moon was setting in the west, they walked together down to the river and bathed in the clear, newly melted water from the snowfields in the higher moors to the north.

"It's not as cold as you said."

"It's freezing, Payen, but the fire pit and a night such as ours would heat the blood past feeling the ice."

He picked her up and carried her from the riverbank. "Then if you're willing, wife, we'll go back and warm ourselves again."

She tugged the pelt upon his chest with a delicate precision that brought him to a state of sudden need. "I'm willing, Payen. But after all we have done, can you—"

He stopped and let her slide, inch by intimate inch, down to the ground, to stand nestled against him. "I see," she whispered. "I see."

"Come summer," he said, "we'll leave our bed and come back to this hillside, and couple here, in the moonlight."

"Do you promise?"

"I promise."

For a moment he feared she would begin to weep. Johanna drew a long, ragged breath and managed to smile as she reached up to tug his chin. "And will you have your beard, sir, when you come back to me?"

He put a hand to his chin. "Should I?"

She turned from him to run up the hill, to the firelight moving within the hall. "Surprise me," she said, and reached the bed mere seconds before he caught her again.

Chapter Twenty-four

She did not go home to the steading after Payen left. Even when the Mercat and the Gunndale flocks were driven over the ridge and up to their spring pasture, Johanna did not return to the little hall where each small detail would remind her of Payen and of his absence.

They had agreed with Rolf that the old fields where Johanna's ancestors had grown barley and oats near the steading should remain uncultivated, and they had accepted Rolf's offer to continue the exchange he had made with Johanna's grandfather when the Mercats had left their land for Whitby. The old Mercat steading would give summer pasture to the Gunndale sheep and shelter to the shepherds, and Gunndale would give back a portion of its crops and winter fodder for the Mercat flocks.

"Your man chose a good season to leave you here at the manor," Rolf had said. "You and your man would have misliked the company of eight shepherds and their dogs when the flocks went over to your land—after your winter alone, with your man so eager to have you far from others, and none but the two of you at your hearth." With a wheezing giggle Rolf had pointed south. "Before next spring, your man had best put up another hut for the shepherds, lest he turn them out in the rain when the craving comes upon him."

"He would never—"

The wheezing lengthened into laughter. "After Yuletide, when the two of you bolted from the hall at dawn after the Twelfth Night and waded through the snow to reach your steading, I said to Hadwen that your Breton was as finicky as he was lustful. If we all needed an empty hall to couple with our wives, there'd be damned few marriages. Are they all like your Payen in Brittany?"

Johanna had shaken her head. "There are none like my Payen. Anywhere."

Hadwen had come forward to place a gentle hand upon Johanna's shoulder and halt Rolf's speech with a well-deployed glare. "Your man will come back before the shearing's begun, Johanna. And if he drives the shepherds from your hall, we'll hear no ill of it. Those lads are bawdy in speech and could do with a good dousing of rainwater from time to time."

Surrounded by the crowded cheer of old Rolf's household, it was easy to imagine that she had come to the manor for the day and that Payen was just beyond sight, on the south side of the hill, waiting for her at the day's end.

Johanna set herself to work in the Gunndale fields, walking the furrows with a pannier of barley seed tucked against her waist, sowing the earth between the rain showers that moved across the valley.

Only at night did Johanna allow herself to think of Payen. From her pallet set among the sleeping women she could see past the side screen to the great open hall and watch the embers of the fire pit fade and flare with each draft from the smoke hole. And when the nights grew warmer and the rains began, she would hear the hissing of rain upon the low fire and wonder how far south Payen had gone, and whether he slept without shelter beneath the cold spring sky.

She had imagined, as she had watched Payen ride south, that the nights would be the most difficult hours of waiting, but she found that she could close her eyes and set her cheek against the bolster they had shared, and imagine that he was with her. Those were the good hours, when in a state of wakeful dreaming she would hear his voice; at dawn she would wake to the sound of her own whispered answers.

A fortnight after Johanna's waiting had begun, the rains came in earnest, flooding the furrows and setting stray seeds floating in the long black rivers of mud. Johanna had retreated to the hall and sat beside the fire pit, hemming a length of winter-woven linen for Rolf's board. It was Hadwen who looked up to see young Rolf speaking with his father, shedding rainwater from his cloak onto the planked floor.

"If you had the brains of a gosling, you'd not stand in your wet mantle, warping your father's fine floor with your foolishness. If you should sicken, I'll say you were—" Hadwen rose to her feet, spilling hanks of broderie wool from her skirt. "What? What is it?"

Johanna looked up and saw that young Rolf's face was gray with worry and his father's features grim. She set the linen aside and stood to face them. "Payen. It's Payen. Tell me. Tell me now."

Rolf shook his head. "We don't know it's Payen."

"Tell me."

Young Rolf cleared his throat. "I rode down to Whitby yesterday to speak to the wool sellers, as your uncle"—he drew a quick breath—"as your uncle is gone, and we will need to find another to buy our fleeces. The talk was of you, Johanna Mercat. A ship had come up from Sandwich with news of your death."

Hadwen made an impatient gesture and bent to retrieve her broderie hanks. "That's not news, young fool. They thought

Johanna dead last autumn, and took her gold south before she returned."

Rolf shook his head. "The master of the ship said that he saw a Mercat ship at Sandwich, and the talk of the crew was that the Norman who had taken the ship, the husband to Walter Malebis's sister, had joined King Richard's army to put down the rebellions. At Sandwich, before they began the march to retake Nottingham, the Norman lord had charged a man among the soldiers, a mercenary from Mercadier's men, with Johanna's murder."

Johanna reached young Rolf a moment before Hadwen and seized the front of his mantle. "Where is he? Tell me he lives—"

"He's with the army. Word is that the king told the Norman lord that he needed every sword he could find to take back Nottingham Castle from Count John. The accused gave his parole that he would stay with the army until the rebellions had ended, and he would answer the charges at Nottingham. And the Norman lord swore that he would not raise his sword to the accused until the battles were won and the king's justice done."

Hadwen took Johanna's hands from the mantle. "Come, child. It may not be Payen."

She gave the Mercat flocks to old Rolf despite his protestations and accepted his gifts of a bag of silver coins, a strong packhorse to lead behind her own, and the company of his two sons on the trip south to Nottingham. Within the hour Johanna, young Rolf, and Edwin were riding south through the pouring rain.

They reached the river Esk before sunset and found the waters rising at the fording bridge. Johanna had forced her mount into the water and emerged on the south bank no wetter than before, but chilled to the marrow. Rolf's two sons followed her through the flood and could not persuade her to stop and build a fire to dry their garments and saddle packs. Grim-faced, they rode at her side until the chill of nightfall was upon them.

They found a small manor at the edge of the moorlands and rode through the timber gates of the crude stockade. Johanna used none of the caution she had learned when traveling with Payen; she and Rolf's sons were weary and hungry and soon to sicken from the cold spring winds upon their sodden clothes. They could not afford to slow their journey with illness and would treat with thieves and murderers, if necessary, to buy what they needed.

Johanna offered silver deniers for beds and a meal for the three riders and made it clear that neither she nor the men who traveled with her would have patience with thieves who might try to take more than she had offered. And she promised the point of her dagger to any who came near her and her companions as they slept beside the hearth.

Because she knew that the journey must be fast and difficult, and that she would need her wits about her when they reached Nottingham, Johanna did not lie awake considering the likelihood that their hosts would come to rob them in the night. And to preserve her sanity, Johanna did not allow herself to imagine what she would find at Nottingham.

Having made her threats to their dumbstruck hosts, Johanna fell into a deep sleep until dawn.

By noon they had gone past the soggy ground and reached the long, steep slope that divided the trackless moorlands from the gentler lands to the south.

Young Rolf and Edwin had broken their long silence as they saw the green hills before them.

"We'll sleep better tonight," Edwin said. "If the rain holds off, and the roads stay hard, we'll make another ten miles before the sun sets."

Johanna nodded.

"And it would be best," young Rolf said, "if you left the chaffering and the warnings to us."

Johanna glanced to her companions and saw ill-concealed expressions of exasperation. "Are you saying that you want to carry the silver?"

"Not the silver," Edwin said. "But it's not right for the woman among us to speak of knifing thieves and for her to sit sharpening her dagger before strangers."

"It worked. They left us alone and didn't steal from the saddle packs. And our mounts were still there for us at dawn."

After a time Edwin spoke again. "It would be better if you let us do the threats. It looks unwomanly for you—"

Johanna shook her head. "I care not whether they think I'm a she-wolf come to eat their lambs. We must do what we need to keep these people from robbing us, and if a woman preparing to use a dagger gives them cause to hesitate, then the men who dare to travel with her will seem doubly fierce." She glanced again at their frowning faces. "Go on. Tell me what you're whispering."

Young Rolf brought his mount up to pace beside Johanna's palfrey. "It's not as simple as you think," he said. "The freeman at the manor last night asked me, when you slept, whether you were a madwoman, and like to murder him in his bed."

She nodded again. "You see? It kept him from larcenous thoughts of his own."

"In fact, Johanna Mercat, the freeman said we were not to bring you back by way of his lands. If you frighten others, we may find ourselves unwelcome on the way home—with Payen, of course."

"When I have Payen safe at my side, I'll not care how we get back to Gunndale. If you wish, I'll use the rest of old Rolf's silver to buy us a little house in Nottingham, and I'll tell Payen we're never to stir from the town."

Young Rolf laughed, and after a quick glance at Johanna, Edwin dared to join his brother.

"Laugh as you will," Johanna said. "But once Payen is safe again, I'd live in the streets of Nottingham, if it came to that, to keep him from harm."

Edwin sighed. "And who will keep us from harm when Payen learns that we brought you south, to a city under siege? He'll kiss you in greeting, Johanna Mercat, and then turn his sword upon us for daring to risk your safety."

"We'll get him back and wonder later how to deal with his anger."

Edwin sighed again. "What will you do if the king doesn't believe you are Johanna Mercat? If he believes you are a woman hired to speak for Payen—"

"I won't let him believe that. And if Mauleon is present, I doubt he would refuse to recognize me. He has always, thus far, been careful of his honor."

"I'll pray it happens as you say. But if it does not, you had best leave your dagger with us when you speak before the king."

Johanna could almost hear Payen's laughter beside her. In his cause she had managed to wield a dagger to threaten the freeman, and had done it well enough that Rolf and Edwin now feared bloodshed in King Richard's presence. She was not the same woman who had fled Rochmarin that Samhain past.

Ten miles from Nottingham they met the first of a dense crowd of Nottingham folk fleeing the final occupation of the city by King Richard's forces. The line of wagons and the folk who walked beside them stretched far into the distance, and the more talkative among them were unable to predict what the king's next move would be.

The siege had been short but acrimonious, and the king

enraged that his Nottingham subjects had not recognized him at their gates. The townspeople had been loyal to Count John; when they had heard the trumpets and horns in the king's train, they believed the count's men who told them that it was but an impostor at their walls, an army of rebels led by a charlatan paid by the count's enemies to impersonate Richard.

Johanna heard the accounts of the king's men shot dead before his tent by the bowmen on the walls of Nottingham, and the terror of the soldiers when they discovered that it was their king, and no impostor, who had watched his men die only a few feet from his tent. When the king had wrenched bow and quiver from the corpse of his nearest archer and had stood in full view of the battlements to hail insults and arrows at the defenders of Nottingham, the citizens feared that their angry sovereign would permit a massacre once the gates were breached.

That morning a truce had been negotiated, and hundreds of Nottingham folk poured forth from the city, fearing that Richard Plantagenet's blood lust would endure longer than the peace.

Johanna heard the tales with single-minded calm. The city had surrendered at dawn, and with luck, King Richard would have had no time to hear the details of the accusations against Payen. That Payen might have fallen in the siege, Johanna refused to consider.

When they saw Nottingham's great castle rock, and saw the gallows outside the castle gates, she gave way, at last, to tears. Mauleon's accusations and the king's justice might already have claimed Payen's life.

There were twenty bodies hanging from the gallows, the smoke of the smoldering ruins of the city gates drifting past them, obscuring their dead faces in ashen mercy to the living who must look upon them. A score of ravens sat upon the crossbar, eyeing all who passed, and calling a harsh dirge through the smoke.

At the end of the road, where the way became steeper upon

the great castle rock, a woman in a bedraggled silken surcoat stood speaking to the dead upon the gallows, her words an impossible confusion of endearments and threats.

The woman turned unseeing eyes upon Johanna and gave a garbled answer to her questions, then turned back to address the corpses upon the gallows. And Johanna saw that there were more than these twenty executions; there were more gallows set before the walls of Nottingham and bodies already cut down and heaped beside the hastily built frames. Many had died at the hands of the vengeful king—too many to count.

Johanna gave the woman her cloak and forced her palfrey to ride through the burnt ruins of the gates. If Payen was among the men upon the gallows, she would not care whether the cold spring rain took her own life with a fever.

They rode through the smoking gates and found the narrow streets of Nottingham in confusion. The king's men-at-arms were gathered before the narrow hovels built against the castle rock and stood with weapons drawn before the ancient cave-mouths that pierced the sandstone base of the castle. At sword-point, the citizens of Nottingham were carrying forth the small treasures they had hidden within the caves and setting them upon the mud and stone lanes.

A mail-clad soldier stepped from a cleft in the castle rock and reached for the reins of Johanna's mare.

"Stay back," she shouted to Edwin and Rolf.

"Nottingham traitors won't need horses," the soldier snarled. "Count yourself lucky you're not hanging outside with the other traitors."

"We're not—"

Johanna raised her voice to distract the soldier from Edwin's protests. "I am here to see King Richard," she shouted. "We are here on the king's business."

A ragged-edged sword came up to her throat. "If you lie," came the answer, "I'll have your mounts and your lives before the sun is down." More men-at-arms closed about them; the stench of blood and sweat and smoke sent Johanna's throat into spasms of disgust.

"I must see the king," she managed to say.

"He's busy, lovey. Busy hanging traitors."

"These men and I are here on a matter of the king's justice. On the matter of Payen of Rochmarin and the lord Mauleon's accusations against him."

Within the crowd of men-at-arms there was a muttered response to her words.

"Does he live? Does Payen of Rochmarin live?"

An ugly wave of laughter rippled through the onlookers. The man with the sword lowered his weapon and spat upon the ground. "If he's kin of yours, you should think again before pleading for mercy. He slew a woman, and the dead lady's people are here to see justice done. You'll not save him, and you'll end by owing blood money to the victim's kin."

Johanna slid from her saddle and seized the blood-flecked mail of the soldier. "But he lives? He still lives?"

The man gestured for his fellows to seize the other mounts and pull Rolf's sons from their saddles. "He lives, and I'll take your mounts as payment for taking you to the king."

Again Edwin's voice rose in protest.

Johanna silenced him with a burning glare. She turned back to the mailed thief. "Do you swear upon all saints and your hope of salvation that you will take us to the king?"

He spat again. "Aye," he said at last. "And it's no favor I'll do you. You were warned, lady. Follow me now, or be damned."

And because she saw no better way to reach the king, Johanna followed.

Chapter Twenty-five

Men-at-arms crowded in the bailey yard, shouting and milling about the wagons of captured arms. Hearing their voices, Johanna feared that the soldier had led them to a place of butchery, where the fighting still raged. Had her courage failed her, she could not have turned back, for the soldiers who had taken the three travelers in charge had seized their horses and weapons.

Behind Rolf's sons, through the gaping bailey gates, the streets of Nottingham were a confusion of overturned carts, protesting merchants, and armed men demanding entrance to the narrow houses clustered in the shadow of the castle. Johanna and her companions would not have passed unmolested through the city to the far gates.

They turned from the sights beyond the bailey gates and watched a group of mail-clad archers push a cartload of weapons and armor into the yard and begin to sort the bloodied swords and hacked mail into piles upon the higher ground, raising their voices in argument as the last of the broken blades were apportioned among them.

The foot soldier who had seized Johanna's mare left them in the yard with a curt, blood-chilling threat should they think of leaving the place and disappeared into the keep. His fellows took the horses across the bailey and tied them to a collapsed cart; there was little chance that the palfrey and Rolf's beasts would see Gunndale again.

"Look at them," Edwin said. "They made a two-day siege, had a few hours of fighting, and they're carrying away enough swords and armor to make them all rich."

"Not all," Johanna said. "Some won only death in this place."

"Not this lot. They'll have weapons to sell and our horses to carry them. And that's not their own blood upon them." Young Rolf nudged Edwin. "See the one beside the siege machine? He's got only three fingers to his hand, but he carries jewels in the hilt of his sword. If I had the chance, I could—"

Johanna stepped before them. "King Richard has no place in his army for two young shepherds untrained in arms," she said, and gave a silent prayer that she was right.

Young Rolf dragged his awe-struck gaze from the king's men-at-arms. "My father said as much when he sent us south with you. We must bring you back in safety, he said, or he'll call us cowards both."

Edwin watched the soldiers move nearer to the Gunndale horses. "Do you think they would give us back the saddlebags? If they find the silver—"

"Hush," Johanna said. "I have it laced into a pocket in my hem."

The lads turned to stare at her mantle. "You can see where it pulls the cloth down," Rolf said.

"If you wouldn't talk of it, and stare at my kirtle, I might be able to keep it hidden," Johanna said. She held her mantle to cover the panel and prayed that none would notice the weight of it dragging the hem down.

If Payen still lived, and if the king did not release him before nightfall, Johanna would use the silver to bribe his jailers to let him escape. That it would be difficult to keep the jailers from robbing her and slaying Payen in his cell was a problem Johanna had considered; when she had the chance, she would remove the pouch of silver coins and press it into the mud beside the stone walls. She would make good her bribe to Payen's guards when he was free.

"No one's listening. They've forgotten us," young Rolf muttered. "We could stand here until nightfall, and they wouldn't take us to the king. Why should they? They think they have everything we owned. Johanna, if you offered them the—"

Rolf gave his brother a swift elbow in the ribs. "She said not to speak of the coins. Johanna will know when to offer them to the Normans."

She glared at the two and stood straight, holding her silver-laden skirt out of the mud. "I'll decide when to use it. And if you see me drop it, don't, for pity's sake, pick it up again. Leave it where it falls."

A smile crossed Edwin's face. "I see. I see what you'll do. But don't let the soldiers see."

"And what will this lady do?"

Two knights stopped behind them, and had heard their exchange. Johanna crossed her arms across her chest and turned to address them. Beneath the blood and dust of the field of siege, the two wore good mail and surcoats that had recently been new. These were not common soldiers.

Johanna hugged her arms tighter in an attempt to steady her voice. "We have traveled from Whitby to see the king," she said.

The elder of the two knights frowned. "The king has much to occupy him, as you can see. Come back two days from now, when his council will meet; he might hear your petition at the end of the day.''

''It will be too late. A man's life is at risk.''

He raised his hand and pointed to the heap of scavenged mail in the bailey yard mud. ''A good many men had their lives at risk today, and many lost the wager. Is your man among the traitors King Richard found when he took the city?''

Johanna saw a heavy ring upon the knight's hand and sealing wax limning the deep-cut cross in the stone. She looked again and recoiled from the sight; it was dried blood, not wax caught in the carving.

He followed her gaze and passed the ring across his cloak to clean it. ''Even a man of God must fight for his king,'' he said. ''And an archbishop's ring may be bloodied in the king's service.''

Edwin and Rolf retreated to the wall, silenced at last.

Johanna looked from the ring to the dust-stained, weary face of the man who wore it. If this man spoke the truth, he must have influence; an appeal to this warrior bishop might be her safest move to get to the king.

''My husband is accused of murder,'' she said. ''He fought for King Richard's cause and was to be judged when Nottingham was taken. If I could send a message to the king, it would save my husband's life.''

''How?''

Johanna drew a deep breath. ''He was accused of killing me.''

''There is a Breton accused of killing a woman.'' There was curiosity in the archbishop's gaze, and pity.

Johanna began to dread the cause of that pity. ''He lives?''

The archbishop sighed. ''He lives.''

She stepped back to clutch Rolf's arm in relief. ''I am the woman whose life he is accused of taking,'' she said. ''When the king hears my name, he will understand that the charges against my husband are false. I am Johanna Mercat, and the man called Payen is my husband."

The tall knight sighed again. "I am Hubert Walter, Archbishop of Canterbury, and chief justiciar of this land. I have spoken with Payen of Rochmarin, who has admitted that the lady Johanna Mercat is dead but denies having killed her. You, madam, are either a foolish, kindhearted woman, or someone paid by Payen's man Mathieu to try to free him. Either way, lady, you are an impostor. I would advise you to leave while you can, before you attempt to speak falsehoods before the king. He is not of a tolerant mind this day."

She raised her hand to keep him from turning away and quickly withdrew it when he turned from her in annoyance. "Was Adam Mauleon killed in the fighting?" she called after Hubert Walter. "Does Mauleon live? He knows me."

The bishop stopped and turned back to her. "Mauleon is Payen's accuser. He lives, and could tell us whether you are Johanna Mercat, for he is the dead lady's kin by marriage. I pray you will give up this falsehood," he said, "for you will accomplish nothing but to send Payen of Rochmarin to the gallows with greater speed. The king has no patience for liars and their kin." He looked beyond her shoulder and shook his head.

Johanna turned to follow his gaze and saw the figure of a woman walk past the bailey gate, her head bent, weeping into the folds of her traveling cloak.

Edwin gave a strangled gasp, then slumped back against the wall. "It's your cloak," he said. "It's only your cloak, and the woman at the gates."

She looked again. It was the woman who had wept beside the gallows; she was wandering without purpose, wearing the cloak Johanna had given her, mourning her man. Johanna shuddered; the figure might have been her own had she found Payen dead before the walls of Nottingham.

Hubert Walter still stood before her, frowning pity in his

gaze. "It would grieve me to see Payen of Rochmarin suffer a murderer's death. He is loyal to the king and has been useful to me in the past in the king's cause. Take care, madam, that you take no false steps and turn the king's mind against you both."

"I am no impostor," said Johanna. "And Mauleon, when we find him, will tell you I have spoken the truth. Please, sir. Please take me to the king."

As he had sworn to do, Payen had given his sword into Hubert Walter's keeping when the fighting at Nottingham was done and waited now for the king to call him for judgment. In the light of the small cresset lamp the guards had placed in the cell, Payen saw that the king's favor had given him more than an accused murderer might expect: a small pallet, a jug of water, and a hunk of smoked meat upon a trencher of bread. It was more than many of Nottingham's panicked folk could hope to have on this day of reckoning and surrender.

Of the outcome of his own hour of judgment, Payen had no doubt. Though he had Richard Plantagenet's respect and Hubert Walter's gratitude for past deeds—honest deeds done in the light of Palestine's sun, and others kept secret in the dark times of King Richard's imprisonment in Austria—Payen knew that the past would not save him from his present dishonor.

He might have saved himself by revealing that Johanna Mercat had not died on Samhain night at Rochmarin. Indeed, he had come close to telling the truth to Hubert Walter, for the bishop might have protected Johanna from Mauleon. But he had thought again, and realized that if Mauleon wanted Johanna dead, he would find a way to kill her; only if Mauleon believed his victim was long dead would Johanna be safe.

Johanna had realized the truth of that when she had decided to give up her claim to her own family's wealth and live in obscurity at Gunndale, taking a hard living from her small moorland fields and tending sheep. What Johanna had decided to do, Payen would make possible by refusing to tell his accusers that she lived.

So he had remained silent, and King Richard had demanded his word that he would remain in the hastily assembled army marching north to put down the rebellions at Nottingham, and if he lived through the battle, present himself for judgment when the city had been taken.

Mathieu had joined the march two days before Nottingham, arriving with a score of Mercadier's men, carrying messages to warn King Richard that he had rebellions to put down in Normandy after he had won back his throne in England. Payen had managed to reach Mathieu before his old friend had heard of the charges against Payen and had compelled him, for the sake of their friendship, to swear never to speak of Johanna's successful flight from Rochmarin.

There were footsteps beyond the heavy oaken door and the scrape of the bar being lifted by the guard. The door swung open upon many torches and the sound of angry words. A familiar silhouette appeared before the light. ''Idiot. You idiot.'' Mathieu came forward, then turned to curse the guard who slammed the door shut upon them.

Payen sighed. ''What have you done to merit these lodgings?''

Mathieu crossed his arms and frowned at Payen. ''Nothing. I'm here to speak with you, and had to pay five deniers for the privilege. Now, listen, for I have only a short time.''

Payen began to pace. ''Pay them five more, if we speak too long. I'll make good the debt from my caches, if you would—''

''Damn you, Payen, I'll let your money bags rot where they lie and the gold stay buried until Judgment Day. If you're stupid enough to be hanged for the murder of a woman who isn't dead, then—''

Payen turned and seized the throat of Mathieu's tunic. ''You promised, old friend. No word of—the woman. I'll haunt you, Mathieu, every day of your life if you speak of her and she loses the life I'll win for her."

"You damned idiot." Mathieu sighed. "I swore I'd keep your secret, and I'll make good the vow. But since you're determined to have your lady counted dead by all here, I've been looking for another way to save your idiot neck. There are caves below the castle—"

"This is one of them."

"And there are others that are more than cells—there's one that leads out, Payen. Right out to the streets of Nottingham."

"The guards are not fools. They'll have the way blocked."

"Not these guards. They're the king's soldiers, like us. Saw this place for the first time two days ago. The garrison guards are dead, or turned out of the city."

Payen stopped pacing.

"Who are the present guards? Can they be bribed?"

"Norman lads, all of them. None that I know. As for bribing them, I could try. A knife to the throat would be quicker. And more discreet."

"Have I come to that? To slay the men who fought beside us?"

"I have," growled Mathieu. "Because you're too much of a love-struck idiot to tell the king your lady lives. Think of it, Payen: it's her secret, or the lives of two, maybe three guards when I come to get you out of here. It's one or the other—" Mathieu broke off. "You idiot."

"So you have called me, many times."

"You're risking all upon the king's mercy? Damn you, Payen. It's either ending the secret, or escape from here. I won't let you throw your life away." He sighed and slumped against the wall. "How did this happen? How did Mauleon accuse you?"

"It was Mauleon's army—men from his own lands, and from Rochmarin. There was a young Breton who had been at the Samhain fire. He recognized me and went to Mauleon.''

Payen turned from the sight of Mathieu's anguish. ''You should go. We'll speak of this again.''

''When? When you're standing at the gallows with the noose about your idiot neck? I won't wait, Payen. If I can't bribe the guards, then they will die.''

''Swear to me—''

''Payen, I've done with vows and oaths and swearing. You turn them against me and force me to watch you die—''

''I have no wish to die. God knows, I have reason to want to live—more than most men. But if you want to help, Mathieu, then stay clear of me. Nothing will happen soon, for the lords called to council haven't arrived, and the king will hunt tomorrow.''

''The king won't use his council to decide your fate. He'll do it himself as soon as that bastard Mauleon gets him to listen. Payen, they might speak of it tomorrow, while hunting, and the king's mind might be turned against you before you have a chance to speak. How can you sit here and let it happen? How can I listen to them speak your fate, knowing that all has been decided before—''

''You won't hear it. You won't be there, Mathieu. I won't permit it.''

Mathieu gave a short, bitter laugh. ''From where you sit, Payen, you're in no position to tell me whether to watch your sacrifice.''

Payen closed his eyes. ''There is more, Mathieu. Mauleon has accused me of Walter Malebis's death. He says that among the men he brought from Brittany to fight for the king, there are two who were with Malebis at Nantes—the two who escaped the fighting. If they see you, Mathieu, they'll charge you as well—''

''If they live that long—''

''And if they charge you, and show the king that my fellow

member of Mercadier's army was there at Nantes, it will seal my own fate."

"I'll kill them tonight, before they speak."

"And if you fall, I will die in despair, knowing that there is no one to go to Johanna, to keep her safe. Swear, Mathieu, that you'll not be there when I'm judged, nor move against Mauleon. And—"

"What?"

"And that you'll not tell her—ever—that I would not escape the trap for her sake. Say that I died in the siege. Tell her that I died in the fighting."

Mathieu slammed his fist against the door. "I've sworn not to speak against the lie you are using to destroy yourself," he raged. "And I've sworn to find your gold and give it to the two people for whom you have lived and died. And I'll swear not to go before Mauleon's witnesses and put my own neck in the noose. But to lie to your lady about the manner of your death"—Mathieu landed a second blow upon the door—"I'll give you no more vows, you cursed madman."

"Mathieu—"

The guards had heaved open the door. Mathieu turned back with a bloodshot gaze. "I thank you," Payen said.

Mathieu took a wineskin from his belt and set it upon the floor. "Brandywine," he snarled. "For your last hours." And the door closed upon his rage.

Payen slumped against the wall. Many times in the brief siege he had been tempted to venture close to the archers on the walls and allow himself to be shot down in the field. Had death come to him in that way, he would have been spared the hearing before the king and the falsehoods he would need to speak in order to ensure that Johanna's safe obscurity might continue. And Mathieu would have been spared his bitter oaths to allow Payen to carry through his sacrifice.

But Payen was a warrior, and loyal to Richard Plantagenet, and he had not managed, in the end, to waste his life when there was fighting to be done and a throne to win back for King Richard.

And because he had lived through the fighting to take his place in a cell cut into the stone below Nottingham's castle, Payen would have a few hours of solitude and silence in which he might think, at last, of Johanna.

In all the long years of his manhood, Payen had imagined that death would come in battle, by a swift stroke of a sword, or in a lingering end from a poisoned wound. He had imagined those fates, and held them as harsh, familiar waymarks in his troubled dreams. To die on the gallows would be worse than any of those familiar visions of the end; he feared the noose as he had never feared the bite of cold iron.

If, at the final moment, he could keep his thoughts upon Johanna, and see, in his mind's eye, her green gaze upon him, he would manage the gallows well enough.

Of the long winter nights he had spent in splendid isolation with his lady, and of the years he might have spent with her, had he survived his journey from Gunndale, Payen could not allow himself to think. To know that he would never see Johanna again, to know that he would never again touch her shining hair, or hear her voice, was the hardest thing, worse than death itself.

Payen stood and began to pace the rough walls of his small cell. Mathieu's wineskin lay where he had left it, near the door. Payen picked it up and set it beside the small pallet that the guards, through the king's favor, had given him. He would drink it all, and gladly, after the king had heard his case. For that meeting Payen would need his wits about him; he must be sure that he did not, with a careless word, destroy the silence he must continue for his wife's sake.

Chapter Twenty-six

Hubert Walter had bid them wait for him in the bailey yard, and Johanna managed in his brief absence to drop the money pouch onto the ground beside the gateposts and press it deep into the soft mud with her heel. When Edwin called to her that the bishop had returned, she looked up to find a tall, battle-weary knight at his side.

Adam Mauleon, straight from the field of siege, with bloodstains upon his blue surcoat and upon his hands, stood an arm's length from Johanna.

Upon his features, incredulity became a tentative smile. "It is you," he said, and reached a cloth-wrapped hand to touch her.

Johanna heard, as if another had given it, her own stifled cry of alarm.

Mauleon drew back and held his injured hand against his chest. "I did not believe it would be you. The Breton—the man called Payen—said you were dead, that he had seen you buried. How—"

"You must release him." She turned to Hubert Walter. "As you can see, I am no impostor and Payen is no murderer. You will release him now?"

Mauleon and Walter exchanged a long look.

"The king bade him to judgment," Hubert Walter said. "And the king will release him when the time comes."

Mauleon looked about the crowded bailey and back to Johanna. "Will you come into the keep, Johanna? My men have made claim to a house not far from here; when they return, I'll send you with them to shelter."

In the faces of Rolf and Edwin, Johanna saw silent but unmistakable alarm.

Mauleon sighed. "I mean no dishonor," he said. "My wife will be here by sunset; she travels with the king's mother, who comes to hear the great council summoned to Nottingham." His gaze turned its cold light upon Johanna's indecision. "Agnes has been much troubled by your disappearance," he said. "She will want to keep you near."

Agnes. She would see Agnes, who had wed this hard-eyed man despite Johanna's cautions. With luck she could persuade Walter Malebis's foolish sister to leave this man, to take refuge with Queen Eleanor until the matter of Adam Mauleon's honor had been settled.

Johanna drew a breath. "I will come," she said, "if you will swear to the archbishop, upon his holy ring, that you never sought my death. That you never sent a message to Mercadier's camp to offer gold to the man who would slay me in the forest of Rochmarin. Will you swear this, Adam Mauleon? And will you also swear that these two men and I will be safe under your protection this night?"

Mauleon's gaze became a shaft of ice, hurtful as it reached her. "What foolery are you speaking? You say that Mercadier was to slay you?"

Johanna took a small step backward. "It is how I came to leave Rochmarin. The man you have accused is the one who saved me from the scheme. He came to me before Samhain to warn that a nameless lord had sent a messenger to Mercadier to buy my death."

"And you believed him?"

"Not then; but on Samhain night, as I fled Rochmarin, he saved my life. From that night I knew that he had spoken the truth." Johanna turned to the archbishop. "A trouvère had gone to Mercadier's camp to hire a man to kill me and had promised more gold when the deed was done. Payen heard of this, warned me to leave Rochmarin before the appointed time, and brought me home in safety. And now, for his trouble, he is accused of murdering me."

Mauleon's features had gone pale. "This is an impossible tale."

"But true."

"It was a lie told to you by a man who wished to take you from Rochmarin and wed you to regain the lands his father had lost."

"It was no lie. Someone paid ten gold marks to Mercadier to hire a killer and promised more when the deed would be done. The trouvère might have told the name of his master had he not met his death before we left Brittany."

Maulcon raised his brows. "A convenient death, which ended your questions."

Once again Johanna turned to Hubert Walter. "We are speaking of a murder that never took place. Whatever his reasons were, Payen of Rochmarin warned me and saved my life. Will you not order his release now?"

Again the bishop's gaze sought Mauleon's. Again he shook his head.

"Tell me of the trouvère."

Johanna looked to Mauleon and caught her breath. His face was set in stark misery, as if word of the trouvère's death had come hard upon him. Despite her fear of Mauleon, she felt an odd sympathy for the man. Had the singer been his messenger, and had Mauleon not known his servant was dead?

Mauleon's mouth was a tense, whitened line above a stubbled jaw. He seemed more shaken by this news than by the accusations against him. Had the trouvère been more than a servant to Mauleon?

"He was a young man," said Johanna, "and carried a harp. I saw his corpse laid out in a church near the road from Aleth."

Mauleon turned from her and fixed his gaze upon the lowering sky. A muttered oath drifted to Johanna's hearing.

"Will you swear?" she said. "Will you swear before the archbishop that you did not seek my life?"

He looked to Johanna as if seeing her for the first time. "You humiliate me," he said at last. "I am your late husband's kin—Agnes Malebis's husband—and you ask me to swear I won't shed your blood. This is an insult beyond forgiveness."

Johanna waited.

Mauleon turned to Hubert Walter. "I swear," he said with tight precision, "upon your ring of office and upon my immortal soul, that I never sought this lady's death, and will protect her as a Christian knight should do, and as her kinsman should do."

Hubert Walter looked from Mauleon to Johanna. "Are you satisified, lady?"

Behind Johanna, the sounds of strife and looting had not diminished. If she did not accept Mauleon's protection, she and Rolf's two sons would have to seek lodging in the conquered city and might not survive to appear before King Richard.

She looked into Mauleon's cold anger. "I will be content to go with you," she said, "if I may keep my two men with me."

Mauleon turned his dead gaze to Edwin and Rolf. "Bring them when I send for you." And he turned from them to go back into the streets of Nottingham.

Bishop Walter stared after the tall, battle-weary figure. "I pray you will not provoke the lord Mauleon further. He has sworn he means you no harm; do not test his temper by doubting him."

"If you would free my husband now," Johanna said, "there would be no need for me to trouble the lord Mauleon. Will you not release Payen? You have proof he has done no murder—"

Hubert Walter sighed. "It is not a simple matter"—he held up a hand to stop Johanna's next words—"and I will say no more of it. But when Mauleon returns for you, tell him to bring you to the chamber the king has taken, above the great hall. He has called me there to decide what he will demand of his English lords when his council assembles. If he is willing, the king might hear your plea this night, before the curfew."

Johanna closed her eyes in relief. "Thank you."

The bishop sighed. "I pray all will go well for you." He looked again at his ring and once again rubbed the large, flat stone upon his cloak to remove the blood of Nottingham's defenders from it; then he walked to the keep without a backward glance.

Young Rolf and Edwin ventured from the wall. "I don't trust him," said Edwin.

Rolf looked at his brother. "Which one?"

"Neither of them. Did you see the way they looked to each other when the archbishop refused to free Payen?" Edwin touched Johanna's sleeve. "Is it time, now, to bribe the Normans?"

She shook her head. "If the sight of me, alive and well, cannot free a man accused of my murder, there is more trouble here than we know." Johanna glanced to the soft mud that hid the pouch of silver from their sight. "Leave it. We must trust to the king's justice now."

Johanna gathered the skirts of her mantle about her and walked with Rolf's sons across the bailey yard. Somewhere within the gray stones of Nottingham's surrendered keep was her husband, and the king who could, with a single word, put an end to Payen's imprisonment.

What had begun as a journey to show that she lived, that the man accused of her murder must for the most obvious reasons be innocent, had become a half-revealed maze of deferred justice and mystery. Why, when Mauleon had admitted her identity, had the bishop not freed Payen immediately? And what had Hubert Walter's silent, frowning glances to Mauleon signified?

Richard Plantagenet, called by his army the Lion Heart, was by name and by repute a young predator—a golden, full-shouldered warrior with the tawny eyes and grace of a lion.

The king whom Johanna saw surrounded by his knights in the large chamber above the great hall showed too well the effects of his months in Leopold of Austria's prison. It was a hungry, hard-eyed wolf, scarred from adversity, who had returned to England's throne.

At first Johanna did not find the figure of the king among the Normans gathered near the great wall hearth, for there was nothing of their garments to distinguish one weary warrior from the next. At second glance she saw that there was one man seated at the fire—a lean, rigid figure before whom the others stood, attending each of his carefully spoken words. The knight looked too old to be Henry Plantagenet's golden son and his face too thin and exhausted to be the visage of the most powerful knight in Christendom. His features, tense and watchful, framed eyes that glittered with a feverish intensity.

He might have been a winter-harried brigand, or a beast of prey scenting trouble upon the north wind.

Bishop Walter stepped before the seated knight and addressed him with a tone of both familiarity and respect. "Sire," he said, "here is Adam Mauleon, and the widow of Walter

Malebis—the woman whom Payen of Rochmarin was accused of killing."

Richard Plantagenet raised his narrow, bloodshot gaze to look upon Johanna. "Payen said he saw her dead and her coffin placed in the earth. But it seems the lady lives. And her husband? Has he joined her in this miracle of resurrection?"

Hubert Walter cleared his throat and frowned at the king. For a terrible moment Johanna feared that the churchman would take the king to task for the hint of blasphemy in his words.

Richard Plantagenet sank against the back of his high, carved chair. "Have you made sense of it all, Hubert?"

"Walter Malebis is dead, sire. This lady is his widow; Adam Mauleon has sworn this lady is Johanna Mercat, wed to the late Malebis."

The king's gaze shifted to Johanna. "Well, madam? Mauleon told me that you were last seen at Samhain, carried from Rochmarin by the man called Payen. Did you go with him willingly?"

"Yes," she said. "He warned me that there were those who sought my death, and took me home to Whitby. I wed him a fortnight ago." Johanna stepped forward, ignoring Hubert Walter's warning frown. "Will you release him?" The royal gaze narrowed. "Sire," Johanna finished lamely.

"So he knew you lived and he wed you," said Richard Plantagenet. "Yet Payen told my justiciars that you had died."

Something was wrong. Something was terribly wrong.

Johanna watched the king's gaze move about the chamber; her breath caught within her chest and burned to escape.

The pale golden gaze moved back to Johanna. "You are the widow of Walter Malebis."

Was the king so battle weary that he could not remember her words? "Yes, sire," Johanna said.

"It is Malebis for whom Payen is accused."

Johanna looked to faces of the king's men. There was no surprise in their features. "Sire," she said. "I am Johanna

Mercat, widow of the lord Malebis. It was my death for which Payen was accused.''

The king shifted with impatience. ''And the death of your husband, Walter Malebis, is also in question here.''

''Payen did not kill him. He knew nothing of my husband.''

At Johanna's side, the archbishop made a small hushing gesture.

Richard Plantagenet reached for a cup of ale and drank it with greedy thirst. ''Payen of Rochmarin was accused of killing your late husband, Malebis, and of abducting and killing you. He wanted to take Rochmarin back for his kin. I had forbidden him to touch Rochmarin's Norman lord, yet he moved against Malebis.''

''No—''

''Now I see he left you living, madam, and wed you—and would not tell the archbishop, or his king, that you still lived.'' He placed the cup upon the board with surprising gentleness. ''An odd omission in one accused of your death. Did he seek to protect you, madam, from our questions?''

Johanna felt a sudden cold confusion. Adam Mauleon moved back to her side and placed a hand upon her shoulder.

''He protected me and brought me home. I—''

''Did you conspire with Payen of Rochmarin to kill your husband and wed him?''

Johanna put trembling hands to her temples. ''No, your grace. He never knew my husband. Walter Malebis and six men-at-arms died in Nantes, killed by brigands.''

Hubert Walter stepped forward. ''Your grace, the woman is distraught. At a later time she may—''

The king's fist fell upon the high carved side of the chair. ''I have a city to occupy and a pack of English lords to tax and have little time for this matter. If Payen of Rochmarin were any other man, I'd send him in chains to the lord of Dinan to be judged, but I will hear him, for he has given his skill to my cause when others gave me up for lost.''

Mauleon's hand tightened upon Johanna's shoulder.

The chamber was silent following the king's words. Upon the faces of his councilors, Richard Plantagenet's words had cast doubts and no little fear. Only Hubert Walter, secure in the knowledge that none could have done more to bring his king to freedom, stood unconcerned in the silence.

The king made a small gesture. "The woman wanted an early judgment, did she not? Well, she has it. I have sent for Payen of Rochmarin; we'll end this matter now, once and for all time, when he appears."

Richard Plantagenet turned to a grizzled warrior who stood, still in his mail, beside the chair. "William, send twenty men south to find my mother's party. She should have reached Nottingham by now. And tell them—" The king's voice lowered to a murmur as he began to address the details of the council he had called to the conquered city.

Adam Mauleon drew Johanna to a bench against the wall. "Sit," he said. "Sit and do not speak until questioned. As you have seen, the king has a short temper, and his trials have not improved it. Do not speak out of turn."

Johanna took her arm from his grasp. "Who has accused Payen of Walter's death?"

Mauleon gestured to the bench. "Sit," he said, "and I will tell you."

She sank to the bench and waited, afraid to breathe.

"Two men from your garrison at Rochmarin were with me when I sailed for England to join King Richard. A day past Sandwich, as we were marched out of Canterbury, the man called Payen joined the king's forces. The Rochmarin men-at-arms recognized him. They had seen him, Johanna, in the brothel at Nantes as he and his companion attacked your husband."

"His companion?"

"A man who fought at his side."

"Two men, against six—seven from Rochmarin?"

Mauleon frowned. "Not a difficult feat if the larger group was taken unawares, and—" He turned from her to look to the chamber door.

Johanna would not have recognized Payen had he not been standing between two guards. He was clean-shaven, revealing for the first time since Brittany the strong line of his jaw, which had been covered by heavy beard when he had left her at Gunndale. And his eyes held a terrible coldness she had not seen since that night of Samhain when he had looked upon her in the moonlight and spoken of death and gold and flight.

Upon the face of the stranger whom she had wed, Johanna saw recognition replaced by horror. Cold, visceral horror that he saw her here.

She rose and walked to him, heedless of Mauleon's growled order to stop.

Something in Payen's eyes warned her not to touch him.

He looked past her to the king, then turned his opaque gaze back to her and said one word. "Go."

"Payen—"

"I saw Rolf's sons below, in the hall."

"They brought me here and—"

"Take them and ride out of here. Leave me, and don't come back."

"Too late." Mauleon had followed her and stood staring at Payen. "Whatever you may have done against Walter Malebis, your—wife—must answer as well."

"Damn your black soul to hell. My wife had nothing to do—"

"Walter Malebis died in a brothel. Payen had nothing to do—"

Mauleon turned back to the king. "The two Rochmarin men are waiting below. They will identify—"

Richard Plantagenet rose to his feet. Mauleon stopped in midspeech and waited, as silent as the rest.

The wolf's eyes turned their glittering gaze upon Payen. "Payen of Rochmarin, approach."

Johanna let her hand fall from Payen's arm. Alone, he walked to the hearth to stand before his king. Unbowed, he looked into those bitter Plantagenet eyes and waited for King Richard to speak.

The royal hand, abraded and bruised in the fighting, held the hilt of his sword before Payen's eyes. "Swear," said Richard Plantagenet, "swear that you will speak the truth, Payen of Rochmarin."

"I so swear."

"Did you kill Walter Malebis?"

Payen did not hesitate. "I did," he answered.

Johanna's small cry was lost in the rising murmurs among the knights.

He would not look at her. Payen drew an unsteady breath. "It was not murder, not planned. And my—and Johanna Mercat knew nothing of it."

Richard Plantagenet raised his sword higher. "Not murder?" he asked. "Was it not done to gain back your lands through Malebis's death?"

"No."

The councilors exhaled as one.

"Not murder," Payen said again, "but a fight in a brothel." He looked back over his shoulder at Johanna. "It was an ambush, not of my making, waiting for me when I came to Nantes. Had I not slain Walter Malebis, he would have killed me." He turned back to the king. "Malebis made the first move," Payen said. "I swear it, upon your sword, and upon my hope of salvation. It was his life or mine, in a fight not of my choosing."

King Richard looked about the chamber. "Does any man here," he called, "believe that Payen of Rochmarin has spoken falsely?"

At Johanna's side, Adam Mauleon stirred. "Sire," he said. "Can this man say why he and Malebis were to meet?"

The king growled the order.

"We were to meet," Payen said, "to speak of Rochmarin, and my wish to return my brother to his lands. The gold I had brought was but the first payment of what I had offered to Malebis. If he had accepted, he was to have agreed to give up Rochmarin and take the lands which you, sire, wished to offer him when you returned to your kingdom. He was to have had my gold for his good faith, and new lands in Devon."

Richard Plantagenet nodded. "I had offered you that, before we sailed from Palestine, to reward you. And Hubert Walter has told me that I owe you still more for deeds done in secret to speed my return to my kingdom." He raised his sword once again. "Will you swear, Payen of Rochmarin, that you kept faith with my demands and intended no bloodshed in your efforts to recover your lands?"

Payen bowed his head. "I swear it is true."

"Yet it ended, despite my wishes, in bloodshed." The king's gaze sought Johanna. "And your wife, Payen—"

"—knew nothing of Nantes, until this day. There was a price put on her head—I never discovered why—and I warned her. Later—Later she was—" Payen's voice lowered to a whispered growl. "I wed her, sire. But not for the lands."

Not for the lands. Not for the lands—but for love. And still he had not given her the truth—had not told her why he, of all men, might one day bring her new grief in the death of her first husband. Johanna tried to see, in Payen's features, some hint of a reason for his secrecy. He might have trusted her to understand. Might have warned her—

But that stranger's face—that shaven jaw, the dark, haunted eyes and hollowed cheeks—gave her no sign.

The king turned from Payen. "Well, Mauleon? Will you bring your two witnesses to say he lies?"

"No, sire. The man has sworn before you, and I'll not take his word amiss."

"And the woman?"

"Must be without blame. Of course."

"Then the accusation shall be forgotten." The king inclined his head to Payen. "Your sword is here, in Hubert Walter's care. Take it back and wear it in honor, as you have done to this day." He sat down and threw his head back against the carved lions upon the crest of the chair. "And stay, if you would, and lend your voice to ours in planning how best to loosen the purse strings of the English lords who will attend my council two days hence."

Richard Plantagenet moved his fierce gaze to the silent lords beyond the hearth. "We could begin by forcing my Nottingham subjects to yield up chairs for the Great Council to sit upon. They've hidden them with their gold, in the caves below—" He broke off and beckoned Payen. "Here is your sword."

The bishop offered, upon the flats of his palms, the sword that had driven through Walter Malebis's body and had cut the life from him. In the light of the fire the iron shone crimson, as if the blood were still upon it. Just as the blood had glittered upon that other sword upon the Rochmarin garrison ground, beside her dying brother. Just as—

Payen took the weapon, looked to Johanna, and turned from what he saw in her eyes.

Mauleon took her arm. "I have sworn an oath before Hubert Walter," he said, "to keep your lady safe. Will you accept my word, as I have honored yours?"

"Johanna?" There was more than one question in Payen's eyes.

"I'll go with Mauleon," she said. And through a haze of unshed tears and cold anger, followed Adam Mauleon from the chamber.

Chapter Twenty-seven

"Will you wait for Agnes here?"

"It doesn't matter."

"Your men are in the great hall, waiting."

Johanna saw, with dull recognition, that Rolf and Edwin were below them in the common hall. She had forgotten they were there. She had forgotten—

Mauleon looked to the noisy confusion below them. "Do you want to go down to them?"

"Not yet," Johanna said. "I'll stay here for a moment. Payen will be coming soon—"

"You didn't know?"

"No. And in all our—in all the months since Rochmarin, I never suspected."

He drew a long breath. "I believed him when he said he had not intended that Malebis die."

"I—" With difficulty Johanna drew a breath. "I believe him. But in all our time together, he never told me."

"For your sake?"

"It might have been."

"He must have feared you would turn away from him."

Johanna shook her head. "I'd not have— If he had told me, I'd have stayed, for I—" She began to weep. Great, wrenching sobs came from her, and she could not cease. Could not breathe for the force of them.

Mauleon held her to his side and drew her to the shadows at the top of the stair. Johanna wept against his shoulder and cried into his tunic all the rage she had felt when Payen had spoken the single word that changed everything. Nothing would ever be the same.

At last her weeping ceased. Mauleon growled something low and dark beside her cheek.

Johanna raised her face.

"For that man, Johanna, you spurned me. I would have wed you had you not turned from me that day of Samhain. If you had but told me—"

The scent of roses came to Johanna. Roses, and a hint of spices.

"What? Told her what, Adam?" Agnes Malebis mounted the last stair to reach the darkness of the passageway.

"Agnes—"

Adam Mauleon's wife went to his arms and kissed him with all the young fervor of a girl well and newly wed. She turned from him at last and looked to Johanna.

She opened her arms and received a delicate, cool kiss upon her cheek from Agnes. Hand in hand they descended the stair to the light of the great hall. With a quick pressure to Johanna's fingers, Agnes stopped and drew her to an alcove in the thick northern wall. There, in the light of the tapers and cresset lamps set the length of the great chamber, Agnes touched Johanna's face and made a small sound of dismay.

"You are weeping. We have found you at last, dear sister, but you are weeping. You must have been terrified, far from your family—both your families. You know, of course, that your uncle—''

''Yes, I heard before Yuletide.''

Agnes tilted her face and touched Johanna's cheek. ''You wintered in Whitby? Dear Johanna, we thought you dead, and when your uncle died, and there were none to—to take his place, we collected what we could and brought the ships south, as we thought you would have wanted us to do. There was no reason to leave them, or—''

Johanna covered Agnes's hand with her own. ''No matter. You did what was right. You thought I was—gone.''

''And Adam was frantic, and spoke of nothing but revenge all last winter. It was only by luck that the Rochmarin men saw Walter's murderer among the king's warriors—'' Agnes hesitated and wiped a tear from her eye. ''And when I came just now and heard that you were here, seeking a husband's release from the king's justice, I understood. Oh, Johanna. How you must be suffering.''

If Agnes started to weep, Johanna would be helpless to stop her tears or her own. She placed her hands upon Agnes's shoulders and set her at arm's length. ''Agnes, tell me quickly. How goes it with you, wed to Mauleon? Are you—''

Agnes smiled and began to smooth the small creases in her fine silken surcoat. ''He is everything I had imagined, Johanna. Years ago, when I was not yet a woman, I loved him, and I knew that he must be mine. And I was right, Johanna. I was right.''

She looked up and made a small sound of dismay. ''How can I speak so when you were tricked into wedding a murderer. My brother's murderer—'' She looked beyond the alcove and saw Mauleon waiting. ''Do you see, Johanna? Adam is here to take us to lodgings in the town.'' She looked with distaste at the crowd of armed men in the great hall. ''We'll be safe there.''

Johanna looked across to the broad stair that led to the king's private chamber. None of the knights had descended to the hall. "I will wait," she said. "My husband is there, and we have much to say to each other."

Agnes touched Johanna's cheek. "Is he condemned?"

"No. He swore before King Richard that he killed Walter when outnumbered in an ambush, in a fight he never intended to happen. The king let him go free."

"Walter would never—"

Johanna closed her eyes. "Of course not. It was a mistake. Some confusion in the night. Payen was given his freedom."

"And you have left him behind?"

Johanna shook her head. "He stayed with the king and his advisers to speak of the rebellions in Normandy."

Agnes's mouth pursed, then formed into a slow smile. "Then he will go to fight for the king, and you will come home with me, to wait. Mauleon won't mind. He holds you in high regard, Johanna. I think he might have wed you had you not fled when you did."

"Agnes—"

"Hush," she said. "I don't mind. I love him as he is, and understand that I will never be the only—" She broke off and attempted a smile. "I am his wife, and one day may bear his children. He's mine in every way that matters. And I will keep him so in every way I can."

"Agnes, I—"

She placed her fingers upon Johanna's lips. "Not a word. Please?" And once again she enfolded Johanna in an embrace of rustling silk and the essence of roses. "Mauleon is waiting. Come with me now, and we'll send later to tell your husband where he may seek you. But consider, Johanna, that if you wish, you have a place with us. Always—"

It was as if they were at Rochmarin and she had never left on that long-ago Samhain night. Agnes was there, shy before

Mauleon, watchful and solicitous of Johanna, forceful only when the talk touched the matter of her brother's death. And Mauleon was as he had been, careful of his words, and kind to young Agnes, and thoughtful when he looked upon Johanna.

Of Mauleon's failure to maintain distance between them, of his suggestion, in the passageway outside the king's chamber, that they might have wed, Johanna heard no further hints. He was, if anything, more distant than Johanna had seen him before, and more careful of his wife's every gesture.

And Agnes seemed determined not to speak of the words she had overheard—words that would hurt a young wife as no others could. It would be possible, in the long evening Johanna would pass with Agnes, to turn their words once again to the subject of Mauleon, and reassure his wife that she alone held his devotion.

Agnes insisted that she come to lodge with them in the house of a wine merchant who had fled the town at the return of King Richard. Below the house, in the cave cellar that connected, beyond its wooden door, with the other storage and hiding places below the cave-pocked town of Nottingham, there was wine enough to provide decent drink for Mauleon and his men.

When they reached the lodging, Agnes had disappeared into the cellar and had emerged with a bottle for Mauleon. She and Johanna, Agnes announced, would drink from the jug of well-spiced mead she had discovered in the buttery.

Johanna waited in the modest solar, glad of the solitude after the wrenching pain she had suffered under the eyes of King Richard himself. This night, in the solitary bed Agnes had promised her, she would allow herself to weep. Until then, silence was the only luxury she craved.

Mauleon did not expect her to speak. He came into the solar and sat staring at the small heap of clothing and saddlebags Agnes had left, in her haste to the cellar, in disarray beside the door. Then he rose and stood over the small table beside the hearth, toying with the half-filled cups Agnes had set there to warm.

He spoke over his shoulder, without turning from the table. "Where did you go," he asked, "when you reached Whitby to find your uncle dead?"

"I was at Gunndale," Johanna said. At Gunndale, where she had known passion, and peace with the man who had killed her husband.

Mauleon turned from the table, moved back to his chair, and set his boots upon the small travel chest, exactly as they had been.

"And the Breton? Was he there all the winter past?"

Johanna nodded. All the winter past. The memory of his touch, of the warmth that kept the winter from her bed, set tears to forming below her eyes. She attempted to shrug. "I wed him willingly—he never harmed me or threatened me."

"He didn't need to do either," said Mauleon. "He wanted you, and won you through patience. The Breton could not have been ignorant of your wealth."

"He had no interest in living as a sheep farmer, nor as a wool seller, and had no need of gold. Rochmarin—the land itself—was what he wanted, and he wanted it for his brother." Johanna said. "No matter what he did before he came to Rochmarin, he treated me well and helped me reach home. Without him I might have died—at Rochmarin or on the journey north."

"Then you believe that if you have an enemy, it is not your Breton. Though he killed Malebis, you do not suspect him of using you for his own purposes?"

"Only to prove, once I was safe, that his family had not harmed me. I was no use to him, save for that."

He looked at her with an intensity that frightened Johanna. Mauleon would have had a reason to see her dead, in that first month of her widowhood, when it had still been possible that she might have carried an heir. And when she had refused him—

He had wed Agnes. Adam Mauleon was rich—much richer than Malebis had ever been, and in no need of Rochmarin's lands or Johanna's Mercat gold to fill his coffers. His name was filled with honor, and his forefathers the stuff of legends. Would such a man pay an assassin to kill a woman who might, if she had carried Walter Malebis's child, have stood between him and the small treasures of Rochmarin?

Agnes returned with a flask of wine. "Do not stare so," she said. "You will frighten Johanna, my lord."

"Johanna does not frighten so easily, my love." Mauleon waited until she had poured his wine into the horn cup she had taken from the merchant's shelf and rose to his feet to take the goblet nearest Johanna. "Mead?" he asked.

Agnes frowned and took the goblet from his hand. "It's a posset of sweet herbs," she said, "mixed with mead."

"I have had a pain in the head since the first day of the siege. This might cure it."

Agnes gave the cup to Johanna. "These are herbs chosen to bring health to women. Believe me, husband, it is not for you."

Johanna offered it back to Mauleon. "If you would like to have it—"

Mauleon frowned. "Agnes will find something else for me." He reached to take up his brandywine and raise it before him. "May you have a safe journey, Johanna. I'll send your ships back to Whitby, and your uncle's wealth from the London goldsmiths."

Johanna rose and managed to smile. Gunndale and the stone house upon the Whitby harbor would be her life henceforth. And every corner of those rooms would hold some memory of Payen.

She raised her cup to Mauleon and smiled at Agnes. "And may you prosper and have many sons. Will you come to me when next you travel north? You must come to me at the Whitby house beside the river.''

Agnes raised her cup and smiled back. ''I promise, Johanna. We will come to your house, and our sons with us.'' She drank from her cup and nodded to Johanna. ''Your health—''

Johanna drank of the sweet mead and set the cup aside.

''Drink again,'' Agnes said. ''And I will bring you to your bed. There's a fire in the hearth and the fine coverlet we brought away from your uncle's house.'' She smiled over the brim of her cup and tilted it to her lips.

Johanna smiled back and drank the sweet honey wine down to the swirl of violet petals that had sunk to the bottom of the cup.

Mauleon set his cup aside and took the empty goblet from his wife. ''Will you come to bed, my lady?''

A blush came bright to Agnes's face. ''Soon, Adam.''

He turned to Johanna. ''I'll see to the guards,'' he said. ''You will be safe in this house, for my men will sleep below and post sentries outside the door. We'll have no drunken men-at-arms storming the house—be they rebels or the king's men.''

''If—''

He turned back with a question in his gaze.

''If Payen—if my husband should come here—''

''He does not know where we lodge,'' Mauleon said. ''He will not trouble you this night, and in the morning we will speak of what you want to do.''

''Promise you will not let him be harmed,'' she said.

''I will not raise my sword to him, nor will my men,'' Mauleon said. ''But I will not allow him near you until dawn.''

Agnes stepped before her husband and took his arm. ''When you come back from setting the sentries,'' she said, ''I'll be here, at the hearth''—her smile deepened—''waiting for you.''

He looked down at his wife's adoring face. ''I will come to you here,'' he said. And turned to leave.

* * *

They would not let him leave until he had spoken once again with the king. And when they had agreed upon the terms and length of Payen's future service to Richard Lion Heart, it took some time for Hubert Walter's men to find Payen's saddlebag and to return his money pouch to him.

Mathieu had lost sight of Mauleon when he had taken his two kinswomen from the audience room, and had faced Payen's anger in the street that skirted the great, steep rock upon which the castle stood.

"There were ten men-at-arms with them," he said. "And there was no reason to risk my neck following them. Especially when I already knew where they were going."

"What's this?"

Mathieu smiled. "Johanna saw me and spoke to me. The lady Agnes came back to tell me where they lodge. Said she had never believed you meant the lady Johanna harm. Not," he went on, "that it would take much wit to realize that, not when you brought the lady safe home, across half of Richard Plantagenet's empire. But Mauleon came to fetch the lady Agnes away and told me he'd slay the man who touched Johanna's sleeve."

Payen held up his hand. "Just tell me, Mathieu, where to find my wife."

"The lady Agnes told me that they have taken a wine merchant's house near the river. They will be here for the days of the Great Council, then go north to Clipstone, in King Richard's train, to the meeting with the Scots king."

"And Johanna with them?"

"She didn't say. My guess is they'll send her on north, with an escort—" He broke off and hurried after Payen. "I crossed the cold sea to follow you and the lady," Mathieu raged. "Will you not stop and listen to me? Mauleon looked with lust upon your lady. I saw him. But he deserves no bloodshed for that.

He treats his wife with courtesy and would not seduce your lady under the same roof as young Agnes."

Payen did not stop. "Agnes told you where they lodged in order to save Johanna from Mauleon's bed—and possibly from his knife. She did it because she wants the scoundrel and wishes Johanna removed from their presence tonight. Well, she is right to have summoned us, and she shall have her wish. I'll not let Johanna spend even one night under Mauleon's roof."

"What will you do? Mauleon is not guilty—"

Payen turned upon him and shouted a denial. "Have you forgotten how we began? Johanna would be dead now had we not been in Mercadier's camp that night when the trouvère came. Mauleon may wish Johanna well now, since she bore no child to Walter Malebis. But at Samhain, in the fortnight after Malebis's death, Adam Mauleon wanted Johanna's death. Who else could it have been? Who else?"

Mathieu coughed and raised his brows. "What of Agnes Malebis? She's a cold young bitch if I ever saw—"

With a sound of disgust Payen turned away and begun to cover, with long, violent strides, the distance to the north gate, to the wine merchant's house.

Mathieu caught up and attempted to match his strides. "Leave your lady to her marriage kin this night and find her in the morning, when she has had time to think. By God's eyeteeth, Payen, she has just learned that we killed her first husband. How could she share your bed—if you had one—this night? Mauleon's wife will keep him occupied. That Agnes is a fierce young bitch for all her smiles—"

"You turn from the obvious villain and accuse his young wife? Your mind has turned to—" Payen broke off with a hurried oath and sent his doubled fist against a timber corner post as he turned away from the wandering street that encircled the castle rock. "Do not plague me with your talk. If you don't want to help, then go back to the keep. You owe me nothing more."

Mathieu puffed behind, losing the battle to keep up when

Payen reached a deserted, moonlit street and began to run. "I owe you no more, it's true. But by all your Breton demons, Payen, I can't let you ruin yourself over a lady who wants nothing more than to see the last of you. We killed her husband, Payen. We killed Malebis. Now that she knows, it might be ended between you."

"That doesn't mean she must die at the hands of Mauleon."

They settled into a desperate search, seizing those they found to ask for the wine merchant's house, sending some running silent into the darkness, bribing others, with silver flung from Payen's hand, to tell them whether a knight and two fair ladies had passed, making their way by torchlight to the vintner's shop.

When they found the river and began to look for the wine seller's sign, they were running like madmen. Right into the swords of Mauleon's guards. Right into the trap.

Payen had fought like the madman he had become, but there were too many of Mauleon's men and they had fallen upon him in the darkness, closing about him before he could reach his sword to draw it from the scabbard.

They brought him down and piled three deep upon him, stifling his enraged words. When they took him by the hair and raised his head, he knew the hour of his death had come and expected the bite of a knife across his throat, then straight into the flesh, as he would have done to one he wished to kill in haste and silence. But it was a gag they brought to him, and he was helpless, pinned under the weight of three burly men, to keep them from using it.

Since they were not to kill him immediately, he looked beyond the blur of scuffling feet and cloak hems to where Mathieu lay upon the cobbled walk, gagged as Payen, only now losing the use of his flailing arms as the weight of his attackers shifted, and strong cord tied his hands together.

Payen heaved himself to his feet and took a blow to the knee when he attempted to kick a guard aside.

They could have killed him by then, and few of the sleeping houses about them would have wakened. And none would have dared come to his aid, stranger as he was, beset as he was by a score of heavily armed men in a city newly conquered. Why had they not killed him?

Firelight appeared behind him and cast a shadow as tall as his own. There were torches burning near enough that Payen felt their heat. He began to gauge the distance he must cover if he turned to charge into them, to cause confusion when these new men fell. If the torches dropped and flamed beneath the feet of his pursuers—

Mauleon's voice came from behind him. "Why have I not killed you?"

Payen's captors allowed him to turn and to face Adam Mauleon. He was there, with four men behind him, blocking the merchants' street. If Payen managed to break free, he would not get past Mauleon's men.

"I would like you to think," repeated Mauleon, "and imagine why I have not killed you and your man."

If Mauleon was here, with these many guards to act for him, the house where he lodged must be near. There might be a way, before the guards moved against him again, to warn Johanna. Behind him he heard Mathieu stumble forward.

"If I remove your gag," Mauleon said, "will you give me your oath you will not cry out and wake the town?"

Payen looked past Mauleon's men. There were houses beyond the torches. Johanna might be near—

Mauleon sighed. "Of course you will not swear. I will have to speak to you without your answers. The lady Johanna is abed in the house of a wine merchant, not fifty paces behind me, down this lane. In the house are none but some men-at-arms and my wife. Agnes—"

Mauleon hesitated. "You look as if you would kill me with

your hands still bound. Listen to me. The lady Johanna is well in body, if something poor in spirits, shaken by what she heard today. She will, in time, overcome her grief that you had slit Walter Malebis's gut before you came to her.''

Payen's gaze darted to the men behind Mauleon. If the man continued to babble thus, there might be a chance to break away past them; though he was gagged, he could throw his shoulder against a door or a shuttered window to rouse the house. But which house?

Mauleon made a small gesture; the guards beside Payen pushed him down once again upon the foulness of the lane. ''I fear,'' said Mauleon, ''that you listened with but half an ear, and your eyes looking upon my lodging. But listen you will, and with understanding, or I will begin to regret that I troubled myself to come speak to you, to tell you a thing you do not know. The thing that these men cannot hear.'' In a curt gesture Mauleon sent the guards from them.

With one last blow to Payen's shoulders, Mauleon's men left him upon the cobblestones and dragged Mathieu back with them up the lane, away from the house Mauleon had taken when the city had fallen.

In the light that streamed from the far torches, Payen saw that Mauleon had drawn his dagger, a weapon of mercy to kill a downed enemy. ''Listen well, and do not think of striking me. If you move against me, your life may end right here, right now, and when your shade reaches the gates of hell, its keepers will tell you a thing that will torment your soul for all eternity, as it will mine.''

Mauleon shifted slightly and brought the point of the dagger to Payen's throat. Payen closed his eyes and sent a desperate plea to any saint or demon who would heed him. Do not let this madman live to touch Johanna. Do not let him—

''My shade would count it just if this dawn found me in hell. But you, Payen of Rochmarin, have a longer journey to damnation. Now, listen, or you'll begin that journey this night.''

When Mauleon moved closer, when he raised the dagger for a killing strike, it might be possible to survive the blow. Payen tensed. If he turned his head at the last instant, if he took the first slash of the knife across his skull, where it could not go deep— If he could get to his feet and run closer to the house, if the guards before it could be provoked to shout as they felled him, it would be a warning to Johanna—

Mauleon shifted the dagger. "Your lady, as I said, is fifty paces from here, in a bedchamber in the wine seller's house. She came with us willingly and sat at board with us, and my lady—my wife—brought her mead to send her to sleep."

Mauleon's voice lowered still softer. "Agnes is solicitous of the afflicted, and she prepared just such a posset for old Hugo Mercat to help him in his grief over Johanna's disappearance." The dagger trembled against Payen's throat. "The old man died later that night."

Payen's body convulsed in a desperate attempt to rise and run, though he might have Mauleon's dagger in his throat, to that house of death, batter the door, and bring Johanna from her last sleep.

Mauleon dropped upon Payen's back and held him down with a cruel knee upon the backbone. The dagger came once again to the enraged pulse in Payen's neck.

"Doubt it if you will, but I knew nothing of the old man's death save what his neighbors observed—that he was old and frail and like to die from grief. But tonight—"

The dagger moved against Payen's throat; Mauleon would not finish his words before the end came.

"Tonight," Mauleon continued, his voice thick with emotion, "tonight Agnes brought out the flask of mead she had taken in her saddlebag and proposed that Johanna drink with her. And I—I changed their cups, one for the other, when she did not see."

A sound came down the lane and moved past them in delicate hesitation. Then came again. It was a harp. It was a slow, careful progression from one soft-plucked sound to the next, forming in long, agonizing precision a pattern that had hung in a crowded, ale-foul hall in a Breton inn. It had been sung, not played, by a young trouvère too drunk to hold his harp upon his knee.

The sound that came from Payen's throat was not human. Mauleon's dagger moved again, and the cold bite was no longer at Payen's throat. "If I cut the gag, you will whisper. If you speak loud enough to fright her, I will kill you. Quickly. Without regret."

There was a small motion, then release. Payen spat the gag from his mouth. There was no move to free his hands. "The song," he croaked. "That is the song he sang."

"Who?"

In Mauleon's voice was all the pain Payen had felt but moments before. "The harper," he whispered. "The one who brought gold to Mercadier to buy Johanna Mercat's death. That was his song. I heard him sing it at Aleth but knew only later that he had been the messenger."

Mauleon stood up and began to examine the knife in his hand. For a moment Payen believed he would use it upon himself.

"Agnes?" he asked.

"Agnes," Mauleon answered.

Payen stumbled to his feet. "You cannot allow—"

"It came to me," whispered Mauleon. "The possibility came to me when I saw her gaze upon Johanna Mercat and saw the flask of mead she had offered the old man at Whitby."

Payen began to run toward the house. The guards came forward to stop him, gathered together in a crowd of torch flames and arms. Mauleon caught his arm and threw him back to the ground. "I changed the cups, one for the other," he whispered. "Listen, you fool. I changed the cups. One for the other." He looked to the house. "I wait now. And so will you. If my darkest thoughts are true, and Agnes meant to send your lady into—that sleep, then my wife will be the one to find that long sleep this night. I will not have you fright her."

"If Johanna drank—"

"She did not. The cups were set out in their places, and I changed them. Agnes never saw. And if she is to die, she will do so without fear. If I need to kill you to stop you from raising the alarm, I will."

Never before had Payen felt his own blood as ice in his veins. "If you have lied to me," he whispered, "I will find you and hack the life from your body inch by inch."

Mauleon turned his terrible gaze upon Payen. "It would be no greater pain than I have found in my soul this night." He looked back to a square of firelight high above the street.

Payen looked up to the window and saw the figure of a young woman holding a harp. "Is it she?"

Mauleon turned from the sight. "She is my wife."

Her voice came again, sweet as it continued the harper's song. Brisk as it reached the final words. Slow to move, with lingering skill, to the next of her songs.

"The harp?" Payen asked.

"Bought, she said, from a serving maid at an inn near Aleth."

Payen began to believe the impossible truth. "If she drank poison— You would have her die unshriven?"

Adam Mauleon shook his head. "It must be the juice of the poppy she used, for old Hugo Mercat slipped into sleep and never made a sound, and we found him dead in his bed at morning. An easy death, if there be such." His voice thickened in grief. "I will have time, before she sleeps, to bring a priest to ask her for her sins. When this sleep is near upon her, she will feel no fear, for both spirit and body will be drunk from the poppy." Mauleon turned his gaze from the light at the window. "She is young, and I would not have her suffer the common justice."

Payen reeled back from the sound of the thin, slowing voice. "This cannot be true. Why would such a woman kill?"

"She must have discovered," Mauleon said, "that I had offered to wed Johanna Mercat in the first days of her widowhood. And from that—choice of mine, the evil began. When Johanna disappeared, and we thought her murdered in the forest, Agnes came to me and spoke of the betrothal her brother had proposed for us in the weeks before he died. And she told me that she would inherit Johanna's wealth to bring to the marriage. I wed her then. Not for the Mercat wealth, but because I had been at the point of wedding her when Malebis died. She was—" Mauleon's voice failed.

The song slowed. "There was nothing else," Payen whispered. "I see there can be nothing else for her."

Mauleon cut through Payen's bonds. "Go, then. And come back at dawn to find your lady. Take her away so that she won't know that Agnes—"

Payen shook his head. "Johanna must know—not now, but before I leave her for Normandy. If she wants me back after Normandy, I'll come to her with no secrets between us." He gave a final glance to the light at the upper window. "I'll bring a priest to your door and wait here until dawn."

Behind them the guards approached with Mathieu, still bound and silenced. He stood as if stupefied, staring from Mauleon's anguished features to Payen's streaming eyes.

"At dawn, then," Mauleon said, "take your lady and her two lads away from this place. I'll tell the king that you will be back to fight for him when he sails for Normandy."

Payen nodded. "And you?" he asked.

Mauleon sheathed his dagger. "If I live past the fighting in Normandy," he said, "I will think of the future."

And he walked to the wine seller's house and stood gazing at his young wife in the window above. When she finished her song, he opened the door and went up to her.

Chapter Twenty-eight

Johanna had not wished to leave the wine seller's house before dawn, before Agnes could wake to bid her farewell, but she rose and dressed in the late, dimming moonlight and crept down the stair when summoned. Edwin and young Rolf had been eager to be gone from the crowded lower chamber in which they, and twenty of Mauleon's men, had passed a noisome, uncomfortable night. Mauleon, too, had seemed sleepless and abrupt when Johanna had followed him to the solar; he had greeted her in silence and had directed her, with a curt gesture, to look down into the narrow lane before the house.

"Your husband is there," said Mauleon, "and his comrade Mathieu. They expect to take you back to Whitby and want to start at dawn."

"Agnes will—"

Mauleon placed a warm cloak upon her shoulders. "There is no time," he said.

Payen was in the street below, his face dark in the shadows of early dawn; he saw her the moment she appeared. If he had made a gesture to summon her, or had looked away from her regard, Johanna might have returned to her chamber. But seeing Payen's silent, intense gaze, Johanna knew that her husband was weary beyond speech and determined to bring her away from King Richard's newly conquered town.

She looked back to Mauleon and saw the siege had been as difficult for him as for Payen. He, too, was weary; his eyes were narrowed and bloodshot, as if he had not slept for many nights. "Will you tell Agnes—"

He had looked up as if struck. "She knows." Mauleon picked up Agnes's harp and considered it for a moment, as if he had forgotten Johanna's presence. At last, he looked up and managed a thin smile. "Send a message to her when you are safe home in Whitby." He went to the shutters and made a sign to Payen.

"I'll go, then," Johanna said.

Mauleon nodded. "Before I sail to Normandy, I'll send your ships back. And the gold, as we agreed."

"Keep enough of it to make a fair dowry for Agnes," Johanna said. "She was to have a part of my own dowry to take to you when she wed. Walter spent it though, and Agnes was upset that there would be nothing for you. Tell her that—"

"It does not matter." Mauleon's tone was not as easy as his words. "It never did." He lowered the harp to the small bench before the window. "Go now. You'll have your ships back, and the gold, as I have said."

"If you need the ships to take your men to Normandy, use them," Johanna said. "Send them to me later, in June, when there will be new wool to sell."

Mauleon bowed his head but did not thank her. With a soft word of farewell Johanna moved quietly past the chamber in which Agnes slept and descended the narrow stair.

Payen was waiting at the door, his eyes shadowed by sleeplessness and his features sharp in the new light, as grim as Mauleon had seemed.

Until Nottingham, Johanna had never looked upon the faces of men after battle. In the haggard faces of Payen, Mathieu, and Mauleon, she saw that they must have passed the night after the surrender in an uneasy wakefulness Johanna would have expected in the vanquished, but not in King Richard's victorious knights.

She walked to Payen and looked into the darkness of his eyes. "I'd be content to wait, to leave tomorrow. You haven't slept, have you?"

"We're ready," he said, "and want to see the last of Nottingham, if you're willing." His tone demanded nothing but invited no dissent.

It was not a time to speak of the past or to decide the future beyond the journey back to Whitby. As they walked from the wine merchant's house, Payen spoke of the packhorse he had recovered from the Normans and the difficulty with which he had bargained for Johanna's palfrey and saddle to be restored to her. Mathieu walked before Rolf and Edwin, told them where they might find their own mounts, and suggested the number of deniers that might constitute a reasonable bribe to the guards at the garrison stable.

They set off for the keep, and to the gap in the city wall that had once been a gate closed against Richard Plantagenet. The smoke at the ruined gates still rose above the walls, curling through the cold gray light, drifting black across the low sun.

Edwin and young Rolf followed Mathieu to the stables. The sound of their dealings with the stable guards rose and fell; there was torchlight then, and the ring of silver coins falling from one palm to the next. Payen and Johanna waited outside the loom of the light, watching the sun rise.

"I should have told you," Payen said.

"If you had, there would have been nothing between us."

He placed his hands upon her shoulders and turned her to face him. There were bruised shadows below his eyes, darker than they had seemed yesterday, when he had bargained for his life. ''Of all my sins,'' he said, ''that secret was the blackest.''

''I understand that you had no choice but to kill him once the fighting had begun.''

''Killing Malebis was not a sin,'' Payen said, ''though you may hate me for it. My sin was to keep you ignorant of my deed—to allow you to love me for a time—'' He lowered his hands and stood back from her. ''We thought our time together was to be brief when we first loved. When I leave for Normandy, you must tell me, Johanna, whether we were right.''

To hear the gentle resignation in his voice, to feel the sweet weight of his hands leave her body, was a torment she could not bear. Johanna stepped forward. ''You never lied to me, Payen. I asked you in the forest at Rochmarin whether you had slain Walter Malebis; you said you had not been paid to kill him.''

''I twisted the words to keep you from fleeing alone. And later, when the danger was past, I did not tell you. It was as good as a lie.''

''And for that falsehood, however you made it, I should be grateful. For I—''

She broke off and turned to face the sudden assault of voices and hoofbeats that announced Mathieu's success in bargaining for the return of their Gunndale mounts. ''One of your lads turned back,'' Mathieu called. ''Said something about silver buried in the mud. Did you hide a cache back there, Payen? In the bailey, right under Richard Plantagenet's nose? Marriage has made you clod-witted, Payen. Next, you'll be hiding your gold in Count John's shoes.''

Payen checked the girth strap of Johanna's mare and lifted her onto the saddle. ''That was a foolish thing to do,'' he said. In the faint light of the coming dawn he smiled at his wife. ''I was trying to learn better ways from my wise lady. I'll have to ask her to begin again.''

Johanna reached to touch his hair. "The first lesson is not to squander the time we have been given." Her hand moved to the stubble upon her husband's jaw. "And the second," she said, "is to consult your wife in all decisions concerning your beard."

They rode past the great field in which King Richard's army had camped before the surrender of Nottingham, and once they had passed the sentries, moved faster to leave that place of death. Twice, when they stopped to rest the horses, they heard the sounds of the royal hunt in the wilderness beyond the track; each time, the small party increased their pace and left Richard Plantagenet and his lords far behind them.

At noon they halted upon the crest of a long hill and saw a small manor hall nestled in the dale below them. The north wind had come up, driving a bank of dense clouds south to hide the sun.

A smile curved Payen's lips and grew into a wide grin. "There's no help for it," he told Mathieu. "It's a good storm coming, and we'll have to find shelter now, before the rain comes."

Mathieu shrugged. "When did you become so dainty of riding through a little rain?"

"Since I discovered there are better ways to pass an afternoon." He turned to Johanna and pointed to the settlement in the dale. "Do you think those folk would give us their sleeping loft if we offered them a muddy silver coin?"

"I'd give them half the bag if they gave us a bedchamber."

Mathieu snorted and glanced back to see Edwin and Rolf coaxing the packhorse up the track. "Go ahead, then. I'll bring the lads and bargain to bed down in the barn; we'll come to wake you at dawn tomorrow." He turned back and saw that he would get no answer. "Or the next day," he muttered.

* * *

Of all their nights together, it was the first that had begun without words, without the slow courtesy that had graced the nights at the Templar fortress, and the long winter's pleasures at Gunndale.

They had scarce reached the sleeping loft and taken the ladder up behind them, when Johanna stopped Payen's unspoken question with a hunger and passion that left no space for doubts, no possibility of regret. There, in the far, shadowed corner of their haven, there was fire between them, a single flame that held them both within its blaze and brought them to rouse and quicken as one.

They did not hear the manor folk return from the stables, nor did they listen for the voices of Mathieu and Rolf's sons. It was only when the sweet madness receded that they knew, or cared, that they had not reached the comfort of the wide straw pallet beneath the sweet herbs drying in the rafters.

Payen lifted his head and smiled. "If we had waited another moment, we might have found the bed beneath us."

Johanna opened her eyes. "Would you have noticed?"

He laughed. "No. And will you notice, at dawn, that your kirtle is covered in straw and your mantle torn on the ladder?"

"At dawn," Johanna said, "I'll be in a temper, and you will promise me anything to stop my fretting." She smiled then and began to stroke the line of his jaw.

"You'll have me promise to shave my chin," he said.

"I'll have you promise never to leave me."

Payen sighed and gathered her to his chest. "Only once more. I'll leave you once more, at Whitby, and keep my vow to fight for the king in Normandy. And then I'll come home to you and never leave again."

"Must you go?"

He began to smooth her hair back from her temples. "Once

more. Then never again.'' His hand stilled. ''You will be safe, you know. At Gunndale, or in Whitby, you should be safe.''

She nodded. ''I know. It wasn't Mauleon, was it?''

''No. Not Mauleon.''

''I believed him,'' Johanna said. ''He swore upon Hubert Walter's ring that he had never sought my death, and I believed him.''

Johanna heard a deeper sigh, then felt Payen's arm move beneath her shoulders. ''I believed him as well,'' he said.

''He treated Agnes well. She adores him.''

Payen's arm tensed. ''She seemed to love him.''

Johanna shifted closer to Payen and felt the warmth of his body beneath her own. ''He was her greatest desire, and she spoke of little else from the time I first came to Rochmarin. Even the kitchen maids knew better than to look upon Mauleon when Agnes was present. But now—''

''Go on.''

''But at Nottingham, though they were wed, Agnes seemed more jealous of Mauleon than before. As if—''

''As if she feared that Mauleon would turn to you and give you his love.'' Payen closed his eyes. ''And if you had died, your wealth would have given her a dowry that even a man as rich as Mauleon might have wanted.''

''Is it possible—''

He kissed her brow. ''It might be possible. If Agnes thought that you stood between her and Mauleon, in the matter of her dowry, or in Mauleon's affections, she might have been tempted to end your life.''

Johanna sat up. ''Agnes was a maid in love. Young, and in love—''

''And content once she was wed to Mauleon?''

She shook her head. ''She seemed as devoted as before but not content. She said an odd thing—''

Payen began to take the narrow ties from her braids. ''What did she say?''

Johanna frowned. ''She spoke of Mauleon's loyalty—praising him, then claiming she was indifferent to his desires for other women. She seemed cold one moment, and angry the next, as if her mind wandered.''

Payen's hands stilled. ''She may have been ill. A fever brings nonsense to the mind.''

''Yes,'' Johanna said. ''It must have been a fever coming.''

''When your ships go back to Whitby, Mauleon may send word.''

Silence filled the loft. Johanna began to trace the rough, stubbled line of Payen's jaw. He caught her fingers and raised them to his lips. ''Tell me your will, Johanna. Shall I be bearded or not when I return from Normandy?''

Johanna heard the voices of Mathieu and Rolf in the hall below the loft. Soon she must leave this haven, and within the fortnight Payen would be gone, and there would be no more nights together until—

''Swear to me—'' Johanna said.

''Anything,'' Payen whispered.

She smiled into his deep azure gaze. ''Swear that you will not make me a widow again.''

Chapter Twenty-nine

Whitby, England
August 1194

From the stable-yard gates she could look down to the river and watch the longships come in from the sea.

Only one of her two ships had come back to her in the early summer. Mauleon had sent it north with gold and a message that the other had foundered at its mooring in Portsmouth harbor during the storms that had kept King Richard's army ashore in the early days of May. In the hard passage from Portsmouth to Barfleur, King Richard's English fleet had labored against the worst the sea could give them, turned back once to Portsmouth, and had then succeeded, at the second attempt, in taking the king's army to Normandy.

There had been a second message, written by Hamo the Templar, to say that Payen had landed at Barfleur with the king but had not tarried to witness the celebrations of that royal homecoming. Payen had disappeared, as he so often had done, to further the king's interests in matters requiring discretion and skill with a sword; he had charged Hamo with sending word to Johanna that he hoped for an early truce in Normandy and would make his way home to her as soon as it was accomplished.

Six weeks had passed since the rumors of peace had begun to reach Whitby, but still there was no sign of Payen. In the ship that had come back to her, Johanna had sent Gunndale's wool to Flanders. When it had returned, she sent the next load to Dinan, in the hope that the merchant Guy would have news of Payen. But the ship had returned with only gold—a good sum of coins Johanna would have traded for a single word to tell her that Payen had survived.

Some wool sellers in the north had prospered, and many had recovered, in the fragile new peace, the ships King Richard had seized for his use in the war. Now, in the good summer weather, each day brought a ship into the mouth of the Esk; some came into the quays along the riverbank, and others continued up the coast without landing. To all of them Johanna had sent messengers to ask how the wars had gone, and whether there had been word of a man called Payen who might have rejoined Mercadier's band of mercenaries to fight for King Richard. From each of those ships Johanna's messengers had returned with no news to comfort her.

In this warm August morning Johanna looked down to the riverbank to watch a longship turn a fine, carved prow to the south bank and drop its anchor stone just beyond the quays, in the busy, sparkling waters of the shallows.

"You haven't eaten," Hadwen said.

Johanna turned from the river and smiled at her friend. "I'll come soon. Would you please—"

"I already sent Edwin down to the river to speak to the crew of that new ship. Now will you come and eat?"

"Look, Hadwen. This one has horses in the deck shelter. There might be knights aboard with news from Normandy."

Hadwen placed a gentle hand upon Johanna's arm. "Edwin will ask all the questions you gave him. The lad must know the list well by now."

"I don't see him."

"Edwin's on his way down to the quays, Johanna. Now, come with me, and give that poor babe some bread and cheese."

Johanna's hand smoothed her surcoat over the new bulge of her belly and smiled at Hadwen. "We dined well yesterday, thanks to your fine hand at the cauldron."

"And you must stop staring at the river long enough to eat a morning meal as well, or I'll take you all the way back to Gunndale and put you to bed." Hadwen's voice softened. "Come, you know he'll return to you as soon as he's able."

"I know. But this ship may be the one—"

"And standing out here, hungry and fretful, does no good."

Johanna nodded and turned to walk with Hadwen to the house. "They were leading the horses from their shelter on the deck," she said. "The ship's master may intend to sell them."

"You have no need of a horse, Johanna. Not now. If you'd stay here in Whitby until Yuletide, the birth will go easier."

She smiled at Hadwen. "With you nearby, this babe wouldn't dare be slow in birthing, or troublesome. But I'll stay in Whitby until it's born."

Hadwen snorted as they went into the kitchen. "You'll stay in Whitby so you can torment every shipmaster and sailor you can find, shooting questions as thick and fast as the king's archers rained arrows upon Nottingham. If you continue in this way, the ships will begin to avoid our port."

They sat at a small trestle board beside the kitchen hearth. Johanna turned her face to the breeze coming from the long hall. "The far door must be open," she said.

"May be Edwin."

"If it's Edwin, tell him to go back and tell the ship's master I'd like to buy the finest horse on his deck."

"It's not for sale."

It was not Edwin's voice. Johanna turned to the door and saw a tall figure in the open frame.

"The ship's master knows better than to sell a single strand of wool without consulting the ship's new owner," said Payen of Rochmarin. "She's a fierce lady who drives a hard bargain—unless there's a gaudy saddle to trade."

Johanna was across the room and in her husband's arms before Hadwen thought to caution him. "You're here," she said. "You came back to me."

"Back to stay," he said. "I've done my last fighting for the king, and said my farewells to Mercadier. I'm a wool seller now, if my wife will have me."

"She'll have you," whispered Johanna. "And she has decided, in all her lonely nights, that she loves you so well that she'd live at Rochmarin if it pleased you."

He smiled and shook his head. "Alain is now lord of Rochmarin, and Mauleon has vowed to keep peace with him. When the vows were done, I left half my gold with Alain and took the rest to the coast and bought Hamo's new ship. It's your wedding gift, Johanna."

Behind them there was an indignant cry. "Set her down," Hadwen said. "Set her down, or your son will be dizzy from that foolishness."

Payen slowed the spin and set Johanna on her feet with trembling hands. "It's true? You're with child?"

Johanna touched his cheek. "We'll have a child by Yuletide."

Hadwen scraped a bench across the floor. "Sit," she said.

"I'm fine," Johanna said. She raised her arms and brought Payen's face down to her lips. "I'm just fine."

"Not you," Hadwen muttered. "Your husband, Johanna, looks like to faint."

* * *

They lay in the splendid new bed in Johanna's chamber, watching the river through the open shutters. Below the Mercat house, moonlight caught small ripples upon the river, and waterfowl moved across the silver tide.

"This is all I need," Payen said for the third time. "To live here with you and learn to help with the trade."

"And to keep your sword sharp lest thieves come to take all the gold that new ship will bring us?"

Payen smiled in the moonlight. "Of course."

Johanna nestled closer to her husband. "I had thought that if I could build a second ship to replace the one that sank at Portsmouth, I'd like to sail to Brittany and see whether Rochmarin is flourishing with its true lords come back. That is what I'd like to do with my wedding gift, Payen."

"After all the trouble I took to bring you north?" Payen began to tease Johanna's cheek with the end of a silken tress. "I'll need a good long time to recover."

"Until Yuletide," she said, and smiled as Payen moved his hand to cover the fine swell of his child within her belly.

"Not before next summer," he said, "when the seas are calm."

Johanna touched Payen's cheek and raised her face for his kiss. "We have months," she said, "to argue about it."

He kissed her into silence and smiled at her in the moonlight. "We have a lifetime, my love."